Praise for William S. Cohen and *Dragon Fire*

"The best espionage and political intrigue novels are written by insiders. *Dragon Fire* by former Secretary of Defense William S. Cohen is among the best of the best. William Cohen opens the doors to the halls of power and gives us a peek into how the world really operates. Great writing, great insight, and the ring of authenticity combine for a hell of a read."

—Nelson DeMille, *New York Times*
bestselling author of *Night Fall*

"Rich details . . . A smart, fast-paced book. His characters are interesting and believable. Cohen splices much of his experience and beliefs about foreign policy and his views of power-seeking men in this fictitious account." —*The Tampa Tribune*

"Thrilling and inspired. Though fiction, *Dragon Fire* is an electrifying tale packed with insights about everything from White House infighting to the Pentagon, the CIA, and on to the world stage and the potential threats from Russia and China. All from a former senator and secretary of defense who has been there and seen it all." —Bob Woodward, bestselling author of *Plan of Attack*

"A chilling story told by one who knows about national security, espionage, political intrigue, and the Washington halls of power. Cohen's timely novel is written as only could be by someone with firsthand knowledge of conflicts between international politics and geopolitical world powers. . . . Cohen's fast-paced story, packed with suspense, makes for great entertainment." —*The Oklahoman*

"Chilling—told as only one who knows could tell it."

—W. E. B. Griffin, *New York Times*
bestselling author of *The Hostage*

DRAGON FIRE

WILLIAM S. COHEN

A TOM DOHERTY ASSOCIATES BOOK
NEW YORK

This novel is a work of fiction. Any references to real public figures, events, establishments, organizations, or locales are intended only to give the fiction a sense of reality and authentication; the depiction of events and actions involving the CIA, FBI, DNI, Mossad, members of the Chinese military, and any real public figures is the product of the author's imagination and should not be construed as being factual. Other names and characters are either the product of the author's imagination or are used fictitiously.

DRAGON FIRE

Copyright © 2006 by Thomas Schühly Filmproduktion GmbH

A Forge Book
Published by Tom Doherty Associates, LLC
175 Fifth Avenue
New York, NY 10010

www.tor-forge.com

Forge® is a registered trademark of Tom Doherty Associates, LLC.

ISBN-13: 978-0-7653-5528-7
ISBN-10: 0-7653-5528-0

First Edition: August 2006
First Mass Market Edition: November 2007

Printed in the United States of America

0 9 8 7 6 5 4 3 2 1

To Janet,
whose spirit can be found in these pages and beyond

ACKNOWLEDGMENTS

I'm indebted to many people who helped me tell this story. First, I thank my close friend, Munich Attorney Wolfgang Seybold, for introducing me to the brilliant film producer Thomas Schühly. Thomas not only provided the financing for this project, but also the creative spark by suggesting the Rapallo Treaty of 1922 between Russia and Germany as the basis for a novel. The force of his intellect, grasp of history, and sense of drama were instrumental in the shaping of *Dragon Fire*.

Second, my sincere thanks to a mentor, friend, and frequent collaborator, Thomas B. Allen. Tom helped me understand the customs of the Uighurs, the machinations of the Russian Mafia, and more. He has been a continuous source of inspiration and help.

When I asked my colleague, Gen. Joe Ralston (ret.), the former Vice-Chairman of the Joint Chiefs of Staff and Supreme Allied Commander Europe, how I might travel to China in world-record time, he directed me to the Blackbird and Col. Buz Carpenter, a retired Air Force officer. Buz was one of our finest SR-71 Blackbird pilots, who took me on a virtual tour of the cockpit of one of these technical wonders. I enjoyed the entire flight to Beijing, Buz. Many thanks!

I'm indebted to editor Bob Gleason for his many suggestions in adding to and refining the novel's story. My thanks also to Tor's Eric Raab for slogging through the multiple drafts of the novel, catching the most minute errors and omissions.

My thanks to trial lawyer and bestselling novelist Richard North Patterson for his persistence in taking me to the court of creativity where he presides.

I remain grateful to my colleagues at The Cohen Group:

H.K. Park for tips on where I might find a pair of spies or an-thrax spores; Frank Miller and Koma Gandy, who have the eyes of jewelers and examined every facet of the novel to detect its imperfections; and Ambassador Marc Grossman, whose suggestions both softened and strengthened several crucial elements in the story.

Wunderkind Jared Caplan rescued my words countless times from cyberspace and returned flawless manuscripts to me. He is an exceptionally talented young man who has turned his gifts to the service of his country as a Foreign Service Officer in the State Department.

My thanks to literary agent Susan Danziger for her indefatigable efforts in overseeing the entire project.

Finally, I'm eternally grateful to my wife, Janet Langhart Cohen—author, television personality, and true patriot—for enduring the many hours of loneliness while I was laminated to my laptop.

DRAGON
FIRE

PART 1

The ground on which I do battle with
   him cannot be known;
Then the enemy's preparations are many;
When his preparations are many,
I battle the few!

—SUN-TZU, *THE ART OF WAR*

PRELUDE

Jason Andrews could not believe what a day this had been. He was just thirty-two years old. He had already served a stint in military intelligence before opting out after three years to join the reserves. Because he was tagged as a brilliant analyst, the Defense Intelligence Agency had quickly brought him into the DIA as one of its most promising stars. He was a little quirky, according to his psychological testing, but not so unhinged as someone with his IQ might be. Because of his photographic memory, analytical abilities, and communication skills, the Director of the DIA, Lieutenant General Frank Mikowski, assigned him to give the morning brief to Thomas H. Koestler, the hard-driving Secretary of Defense in the Bradford Jefferson Administration.

What a career move! A schoolboy from Boise, Idaho, sitting in the most powerful military office in the world each day, briefing the Secretary of Defense on the DIA's assessment of what was happening in all the hot spots around the world. And now, on this day, Jason had been brazen enough to offer Koestler a theory that was keeping him awake at night.

Liza Jackson—shift leader in the real-time monitoring station at the National Reconnaissance Office—started it. She switched the China satellite to the wall screen, looked at the image for a few moments, and hit the *URGENT SAVE* button.

That was the fourth such save in the past hour. Every *URGENT SAVE* was instantaneously copied to the top tier of analysts, the high priests of the NRO, the huge bureaucracy that operated U.S. spy satellites. The headquarters was a one-million-square-foot office complex in Virginia, not far from Dulles International Airport.

Liza came home early that morning, and Jason was fascinated by her description of what happened next. Jason and Liza had been living together for about three months and were planning to get married as soon as his next promotion came along.

"So I get called on the carpet by this senior analyst," Liza said in closing. "And he tells me to stop obsessing over China. He practically ordered me to not save anything about Lop Nur. Said there already was enough obsessing about China."

"Well," said Jason, "tell me again." He did not need to take any notes. He had what his teachers always called a perfect memory.

Next day, Jason did a search of DIA files on Lop Nur, a forsaken wasteland in far western China. There was a great deal of information on Lop Nur because it was the nation's major nuclear testing site.

Jason, shielding Liza, decided to tell Koestler that a satellite had seen construction activity near the conventional test site. This was clearly a sign that the Chinese were preparing for some kind of nuclear test, one that would probably be subcritical and seismically undetectable. But what convinced Andrews, even though he had only that single source named Liza, was one more nugget. During a tour of duty in Germany, he had made contact with German intelligence people whom he continued to cultivate. Now, he had the chance to make a back-channel request for any intel they had on activities around Lop Nur.

Andrews took the chance of passing on a vague note about construction work near Lop Nur. And back had come his reward: The Germans had reports that people in that area were dying horrible deaths. He told all this to Koestler.

"My gut tells me that the Chinese have been up to something near Lop Nur," Andrews blurted out.

Koestler encouraged him to come back after a week to authenticate what his gut had told him. Koestler was not one to put any stock in hunches. He was a strictly by-the-books man. "I want facts," he would bark, instilling fear in virtually anyone who had to deal with him.

Jason picked up a little more and, a week later, passed it on to Koestler: National Security Agency intercepts had detected a surge of cell phone use southwest of the Lop Nur testing area. From what the eavesdroppers could make out, some local people had been speaking a Turkic language. Some of the words were *death* and *bomb*. The NSA intercepts also included encrypted Chinese military communication indicating that a high-ranking general and his entourage had visited the area. A week after the satellite picked up the construction activity, Liza analyzed another set of images, which she described as indicating a great deal of funeral activity among the monuments in the walled graveyards outside three villages near Lop Nur.

"Here's how I figure it, Mr. Secretary," Andrews said, concluding his off-the-record twenty minutes with Koestler. "I figure that there was a test—small-scale, maybe a test of their version of the small W-88 warhead they stole from us. Maybe something went wrong—you know, like that anthrax accident at the Soviet bioweapon plant at Sverdlovsk in 1979. I looked it up. When Western nations asked the Soviets about the deaths, they blamed the deaths—estimated at about seventy— on tainted meat. Well, sir, if we package all this and slap it down in front of the Chinese, I wonder if they're going to say anything like tainted meat."

Koestler gave Andrews the green light to pursue his instincts off line and not report it through channels. Running it through the bevy of analysts at the DIA was always the kiss of death. There were so many graybeards that would demand evidence, something far more tangible than "my gut tells me" that the Chinese are cheating or pulling a fast one on us. "Facts, Andrews," the Secretary had said. "I want facts."

Once he had facts in hand, he could persuade Secretary Koestler that we had caught them with their hands in the nuclear cookie jar. And that would convince their apologists at the

United Nations that it was time to impose sanctions on them.

Well, the facts said that something was not right. Jason had managed to get a peek at a highly classified report showing that at least one CIA analyst suspected that a secret underground test may have been conducted. The report said that several hundred people from a Uighur village near Lop Nur had been killed or hospitalized with radiation poisoning. He then looked up what the DIA had on the Uighurs. They spoke a Turkik language and were Muslims. They lived in the Xinjiang Uighur Autonomous Region, which was nearly as big as Alaska. The United States had declared the Uighurs terrorists, which, in China's view, they certainly were. A Uighur movement, which would make Xinjiang an independent nation named Eastern Turkistan, had inspired many clashes between Chinese security forces and Uighurs.

The victims of whatever happened seem to have been Uighurs. He added that to his briefing of Koestler. Sure. The report about the possible nuclear test was single-sourced—a source he could not cite. But to get more, Koestler had to push buttons.

The Navy's "sniffer" aircraft could not get near Xinjiang. They had been pushed offshore even farther into international waters by the Chinese MiG aircraft. There had to be a way to contact German intelligence to send an agent—maybe a missionary or archaeologist under cover—to Lop Nur, gather some soil samples, and possibly interview some of the Uighurs to confirm what was happening.

He glanced at his watch. 5:30 A.M. here, 11:30 there. He decided to fire off an encrypted e-mail to his German contact, Christoph Stiller, before going off for a jog.

Jason liked to jog with Liza along the Mount Vernon Trail that paralleled the Potomac River and the George Washington Parkway. A side trail took him to the Pentagon, so he could jog at 5:30 A.M. on his way to his DIA office. Liza would split off and return to the apartment to pick up her car and head out to the NRO headquarters in Chantilly, Virginia.

It was two days before another jogger found Jason's and

Liza's bodies. A soft-nosed .22-caliber bullet had entered his right temple and exploded in his skull. A similar caliber bullet had shredded Liza's heart. The National Park Service Police, which doesn't investigate many murders, announced that they'd been shot by a sniper hidden on the pathway, or, less likely, from a passing boat. There was no apparent motive. So the National Park Service concluded that a deranged shooter had picked a target at random. Much like the two snipers who had terrorized the Washington area several years earlier. People who used the path were urged to be cautious.

CHAPTER 1

WASHINGTON

For Secretary of Defense Thomas H. Koestler and other major Washington news sources, Sunday mornings meant either being on one of the talk shows or watching them. On this Sunday, Koestler was in the kitchen of his manorial home in a Virginia suburb of Washington. Perched on a high stool at the marble island that curved through the room, he nibbled on half a bagel, lathered with cream cheese, and watched *Meet the Press* on a small television set placed under the garland of hanging pots and pans. Tim Russert had managed to snag Joseph Praeger, President Jefferson's National Security Adviser. Well, not snagged exactly. Praeger, Koestler knew, was on *Meet the Press* because he wanted to handle "the Taiwan thing," as he called the issue that he and Koestler had been wrestling with.

And so when the assistant producer of *Meet the Press* asked for the Secretary of Defense, the White House communications handlers had deftly intercepted the invitation and offered Praeger as a real catch. Praeger rarely appeared on television, and Koestler, looking at this diminished version of him, was surprised at how ill at ease he appeared to be as Russert went into his ritual: a tough question, then an incriminating or enlightening news clip scrolling down the screen.

"Well, Mr. Praeger," Russert said, "let's start with Taiwan. Is the United States planning to rattle China's cage by giving Patriot anti-missile weapons to Taiwan?"

As Praeger opened his mouth to speak, Russert said, "Let's look at this," and an excerpt from a *Washington Times* news story appeared on the screen:

The Taiwan Defense Minister went on to say that his country would establish what he called the "Taiwan Missile Defense System," which seems to be a version of the U.S.-developed theater missile defense system. His reference to the system appeared to be an attempt to raise a hot-button issue: Taiwan's intention to join the U.S.-initiated theater missile defense project.

The Defense Minister said that Taiwan would purchase foreign equipment while at the same time developing systems on its own. As part of the program, he said that Taiwan would install an early-warning radar system and purchase the U.S. Patriot III anti-missile system.

As the clipping faded, the screen was filled with the image of a Patriot anti-missile streaking skyward.

"There you are, Mr. Praeger," Russert said, swinging his gaze toward the adviser. "Patriot anti-missiles, special delivery to Taiwan?"

"Let me make one important point, Tim," Praeger began. "The Patriot III is not on the table—yet."

"Yet," Koestler repeated, smiling and shaking his head. Pure Praeger, he thought. Tantalizing the truth.

Koestler picked up his coffee cup. Suddenly, his hand began shaking. He had never felt so tired, not even at the end of the Marine Marathon. The cup fell to the white-tile floor and shattered. He heard a long, yowling cry and looked across the kitchen to see Sheba, the old black cat, stagger in. Her shrieks were echoed by her old mate, Grayfur, making banshee yowls somewhere in the house.

Koestler started coughing—a wet, hacking cough that ripped through his body. He coughed so hard that he could hardly breathe. His throat burned with a greater pain than he had ever known. He stood and turned toward the sink. He needed water. But he could not make his feet move. He leaned his big, broad-shouldered body against the island, gripping the smooth edge to keep from falling. Now he was shaking all over, and a hot, vile-tasting fluid rose from his stomach. He was gagging. Blood was running from his mouth and nose. His body began heaving as he threw up, strands of blood glistening in his vomit. His bowels opened, and a warm, stinking mess ran down his right leg.

His beefy hands opened, as if on their own, for he knew that he could no longer control his body. He coughed one more time, spewing blood. Then he fell, the left side of his face slamming down on the shards of porcelain. He summoned enough strength to scream. Another echo of the cats, he thought. But they were no longer screeching.

He screamed again. He could hear Gertrude calling his name again and again—"Tom, Tom . . ." Doc Gert, he remembered, for his brain still worked. Gertrude Koestler, M.D., who so loved to bring babies into this world. Then she was there, kneeling at his side, pressing her hands on his chest, then pressing her lips on his mouth, giving him breath, giving him breath. . . .

As she tried to bring back his flickering life, she knew what was happening inside the body of the man she had loved for thirty years. She recognized the symptoms immediately. Two recent anthrax poisonings had been plastered all over the front pages and the evening news. Anthrax! Spores of *Bacillus anthracis* were smashing against the membranes of cells throughout his body, opening cell after cell. The spores were maturing into deadly bacteria, multiplying so fast that his immune system could not develop antibodies. Crippled, the immune system still tried to function, seemingly killing the bacteria and bearing them to the lymph nodes for disposal. But the insidious bacteria was resurrecting now, she knew, multiplying, producing toxins, and spreading into the bloodstream.

Dr. Koestler stood and reached for the phone on the wall. When she dialed 911, the numbers appeared on the screen of a console in the gatehouse, where members of Koestler's security detail stayed when he was home. Two men wielding MP-5s burst out of the building and ran up the half circle of the driveway. One pressed a button on a remote device that opened the front door. He entered the house while the other crouched and covered him, swinging the MP-5 from right to left.

"In here," Gertrude Koestler shouted. "Help me move him."

They came in, their eyes and guns scanning the room.

"For God's sake, put down the guns and help me get him on the couch," she said, pointing toward the hall that led to Koestler's study.

One of the men put his gun on the marble island and squatted at Koestler's shoulders. The other man, still holding his gun, said, "What happened? You're both bleeding."

Gertrude Koestler realized that her face had been bloodied by the wounds on Koestler's face. "Never mind the blood," she said, moving to help the squatting man. The other man put down his gun and slipped his arms under Koestler's twitching legs. Koestler, eyes closed, struggled against death. He was gasping for breath, blood now streaming from his gaping mouth.

"Don't worry, Sam," Gertrude Koestler said, looking into the fearful eyes of the man at her side. Half-carrying, half-dragging, they had reached the study and had placed Koestler on the couch. "We're all inoculated. But Tom wasn't."

CHAPTER 2

WASHINGTON

Michael Patrick Santini, squeezed between a network anchor-man and an aerospace lobbyist in the fifth row of pews, lis-tened to the noble words of eulogies rolling through the great nave of the National Cathedral. "An outstanding public ser-vant" (the Vice President). "A champion of freedom" (the Di-rector of Homeland Security). "A natural born leader" (the Chairman of the Joint Chiefs of Staff). "A man for all sea-sons" (Chairman of the Armed Services Committee). "A man taken in the prime of his life" (his brother, a prominent Wash-ington lawyer).

The subject of the eulogies, Thomas H. Koestler, had been Secretary of Defense for a little over two years. Odd, Santini thought now, all these words of tribute pouring out. No one spoke of "murder" or "evil" because none of the speakers wanted to tell the truth, if any of them knew it. Bloggers had spread the false report: Koestler had caught anthrax from sick cattle on his Montana ranch. That report had been picked up by the conventional media, who pointed out that the death-by-anthrax was accidental, not a terrorist act. That's what the White House wanted. It would buy the Administration some time until someone from the Pentagon or the FBI leaked word to friends in the media.

When anthrax vaccinations had been given to thousands of federal workers and their relatives in Washington—beginning with the President and continuing down to the cleaning crews in government buildings—Koestler had joined the relatively few people who had refused to be vaccinated. He explained to his physician at the Pentagon the reason for his refusal: "I've always depended on God to keep me healthy." Three weeks later he was dead, a victim of pulmonary anthrax poisoning.

Santini, at the President's request, had been briefed by a Secret Service agent. The FBI found heavy traces of anthrax in Koestler's home in suburban Virginia. The source seemed to be Koestler's two cats, apparently dusted while they napped on a window seat overlooking his patio.

The tape of an exterior security camera showed a man using a blower to pile up leaves in the yard that spread out from Koestler's patio. The man, Julio Alvarez, who drove a truck belonging to a company cleared to work on Koestler's yard, wore what looked like the normal noise-muffling headgear and respirator mask used by landscape workers. As he neared the patio, the security tape showed him switching off the blower and walking to the French doors. He turned his back to the security camera, blocking the view of what he was doing. In a moment he was back in the yard with the blower. Apparently he had blown the anthrax through the keyhole.

Two days later, Alvarez's body was discovered in a Suitland, Maryland, cemetery. His brains had been blown out. Investigators suspected he may have been murdered by the Mara Salvatrucha (MS-13), the Washington area's most violent Latino gang.

The time span between inhalation and Koestler's death coincided with the date of Alvarez's visit. His wife, Gertrude, a physician who had been vaccinated, was not harmed. The cats died. The FBI had another anthrax case with no suspects. The media banged at the doors of the Pentagon, the FBI, the CIA—and got nothing except vague assurances that the anthrax mystery was being pursued with great diligence.

They'll never solve this one, Santini thought, his mind roaming as, half-listening to the eulogies, he wondered how he would go out and what someday they would say about him.

Santini was not a handsome man in any classic sense. His

nose was not quite straight, having been broken twice. Once in the boxing ring and a second time during one of his torture sessions at the hands of the North Vietnamese. He was nearly six feet tall, but the thickness of his neck gave him the appearance of being shorter. It was his presence that made him stand out. He was a man who filled any room he entered, and commanded the attention of all who were present.

He had a temper that he struggled to keep under tight control, but he could use its display to good advantage when the occasion called for it. For the most part, however, after what he had endured as a prisoner of war, most people tended to overlook any imperfections he might have. Besides, he just was not someone you wanted to make mad.

Now, a roulette wheel was turning in his mind. How much of his life had been pure luck, good and bad? Should he have bet red or black? Gone high or low? Just how much was in the hands of Providence?

Churches always took him back to the first he had ever known, St. Dominic's in Boston's North End. An Italian church, which he attended because of his last name. But not his first name. He lived on a double track. The Italian kids didn't like him because, blond and blue-eyed, he wore the map of Ireland on his face. And the Irish didn't like anyone whose name ended in a vowel other than *a*. He took just so many "Mick" and "Wop" taunts before he started swinging his fists.

He was back for an instant to a moment in Boston when he had Frank Murphy on the ground and was about to slug him in the jaw. A cop came by, grabbed Santini by the back of the neck, and said, "If you're going to punch him, go to it, toe-to-toe. Let him up." The desire to pummel Murphy passed and, prodded by the cop, they shook hands. A week later they were teammates on a Boys Club basketball team.

Santini would go on to win letters in football, basketball, and baseball in high school while managing to stay on the honor roll—an accomplishment greatly inspired by the browbeating of his Irish mother and Italian father. He got a full academic scholarship to Harvard, and by the end of his junior year he was named captain of the football team. In the off-season, he would stay in shape by battering opponents in amateur boxing contests. In New England, he ranked in the top ten of the light heavyweight division.

After graduating with high honors and preparing to enter law school, Santini impetuously decided to join the Army. Even though Richard Nixon was President, it was John F. Kennedy and his call to "ask what you can do for your country" that fired Santini's imagination. "Yes, the war in Vietnam is going badly," he conceded to his classmates, "but maybe that's because people like us aren't doing our share."

Or so he rationalized.

Six months after receiving his diploma and listening to some vacuous commencement speech, he was leading a squadron on a search and destroy mission in the jungles northwest of Danang. He and his unit found themselves trapped in a savage cross fire with regular forces of the North.

Santini was the only survivor. Badly wounded, he was transported north to Hanoi, where he took up residence for the next three years in a grim torture chamber known as the "Hanoi Hilton." He was not a model prisoner. Nursing broken bones, he spent most of his days and nights in solitary confinement in a hellhole.

Finally, in 1973, after Richard Nixon decided it was time to bail out of what the press called an "unpopular war," Santini was released with all of his American brethren. Thin, nearly emaciated, he arrived in Washington and, after receiving extensive treatment at Walter Reed Hospital, was presented with a host of medals for his undaunted courage and leadership in inspiring his fellow prisoners of war.

Santini wasn't satisfied to bask in the glow of a light that he knew was sure to fade. He returned to Harvard, entered law school, and graduated near the top of his class. Determined to pursue a life of public service, he began to build a political base almost as soon as he passed the Massachusetts Bar.

Joining the prosecutorial team of the U.S. Attorney's office located in Boston, he quickly drew the attention of the electorate for his vigorous action against organized crime figures.

He broke up the drug ring of Tony "the Neck" Labonti and sent Tony's competitors scrambling to safer climes in New Orleans and Las Vegas.

But Santini wanted to do more than just put crime lords behind bars. He wanted to influence events on a much larger scale. He fixed his eyes on a seat in the United States Senate. Name recognition—the sine qua non of politics—was a nonfactor for him. Capitalizing on his status as a war hero turned crime-buster, he sailed into office on a tidal wave of popular support.

Immediately, Santini was hailed as a new politician, a man of toughness, independence, and integrity. Somehow the American people remained undiscouraged by the persistent scandals and shortcomings of those they had previously elected. Like Diogenes with his battered lamp, they were still convinced that someone could measure up to their expectations.

Selected to serve on both the Senate's Intelligence and Armed Services Committees, Santini immersed himself in the study of terrorism. He saw how the Bader-Meinhof gang of Germany, the Red Brigades in Italy, the ETA—the Basque Separatists of Spain—had used terror as a weapon against innocent civilians. He knew that it was not a matter of whether America would ever see wholesale slaughter on its streets; it was only a question of when.

He worried that the FBI continued to treat incidents of terror as a legal issue, and argued that America needed to reform our slow-moving judicial system to cope with the gathering of a violent storm. Indictments, preliminary hearings, jury trials, appeals—the process took years. Meanwhile, those who plotted our destruction wrapped themselves in our flag and stuffed our constitutionally guaranteed rights down our throats.

"Terrorism isn't a crime," he would fulminate during debates in the Senate. "It is war."

Predictably, his comments generated controversy. Civil liberty advocates trashed his views as un-American, while editorialists opined that evidence to support his proposals was insufficient to justify a radical departure from existing legal requirements.

In the end nothing happened.

Lots of sound. Little fury. No action.

Once hopeful that he could help prevent America from squandering her future, Santini slowly grew disenchanted with life in the Senate. After twelve years, he had grown weary of the trivia that consumed so much of the Senate's time. After serving just two six-year terms, he announced his retirement.

He was fed up with what had seemed a descent into the time sink of partisan posturing and finger-pointing. Too many hours were devoted to endless motion without movement and interminable debate without decision.

And he wasn't alone. A dozen other senators had bailed out, too. Sure, they offered all the right reasons: health, family, financial needs. But at the core they all knew that "the world's most deliberative body" had become dysfunctional, sclerotic. Rather than spend their remaining years trying to swim in molasses, they opted out.

All but Santini delivered brilliant swan songs from their desks in the Senate chamber. Who he was and what he had done spoke for itself. He saw no reason to hurl mud at those who wanted to stay in the parade. More power to them. And he meant it. He had been coasting on six cylinders instead of running on eight. The people of Massachusetts deserved better.

Thanks to a combination of good luck and good instincts, he had found a new life in the trenches of Wall Street. A chance offer by a friend had led to an executive post in a small investment bank that was on the verge of expansion. Although untested in business, Santini was trusted, and he managed to handle the details of a key merger without creating any enemies. After he made his first million, the next few millions came easily. He weathered the stock market collapse after the September 11 attacks, along with the end of a short, unhappy marriage.

He was still absorbing the news of Koestler's death when he got the call from the former governor of Florida who was now the President of the United States. The country, Bradford Jefferson had said, needed a man to take over the Pentagon to show instant continuity, and he desperately needed a replacement who would sail through the Senate confirmation process.

When Santini left the Senate more than ten years ago, he had promised himself that he was through with public service.

So why would he even consider letting Jefferson pull him off his Wall Street moneymaking machine? Real simple. America was under attack. The shadow of terror continued to spread across the country. Planes bombed out of the skies, trains carrying hazardous chemicals derailed, anthrax in the mail—or, in Tom Koestler's case, on the backs of cats. There was no end to the creative evil that was the enemy of the modern world.

There was simply no way that Santini could walk away from the call to duty. The chance to serve as the second in command of the finest military in the world was not something that was offered to many.

But Santini knew that his name would not go down well with the other players on Jefferson's team. They regarded senators—even former ones—as preening prima donnas. But Santini was even worse. Too independent, too immune to pressure because of his war hero status.

"Never hire a man you can't fire" was the advice Joseph Praeger, Jefferson's National Security Adviser, had given to Jefferson. Santini had been to hell and back at the hands of his jailers in the Hanoi Hilton. That experience would give Santini leverage with the President when there was a major internal or political policy dispute. He'd have too many back doors to his former buddies on the Hill.

The President had weighed all of that and concluded that he had little choice. At this time, Santini was the most qualified person to handle the job. And time was something of which the President had very little to waste.

Now the organ was booming "The Battle Hymn of the Republic" and the military pallbearers were escorting the flag-draped coffin down the aisle. One by one, the pews emptied and the aisle filled with murmurings as people sighted one another, nodded, and passed Washington whispers.

"Got to hurry. Briefing at State."

"Yes, I saw the column. Damn pack of lies."

"It's been ages. Absolutely will call you for lunch."

As Santini moved toward the exit, he noticed a woman in the distance moving away from him. She was tall and moved with the fluid grace of an athlete. Dressed in an appropriate black dress, she shielded her face with a subtly fashionable hat.

He had only caught a glimpse of her. She was no more than a shadow, really, but there was something familiar in her movements.

He stopped, turned around, and was about to call after her; the surge of the crowd behind him carried him in its momentum toward the cathedral's east exit. By the time he was able to extract himself from the crowd, she was gone.

It was Elena, he told himself. It had to be. The very thought of her name stirred memories that he thought he had buried long ago.

But what was she doing in Washington? And why here? Today? Did she know Koestler? Was he a friend? Or, he could not suppress the thought, foe?

Elena was capable of killing anyone if called upon to do so. She was a killing machine. Beautiful. Intoxicating. Deadly. But poison was not her specialty. Hollow-point .22-caliber bullets to the brain were.

Maybe it was just his imagination, he reasoned. A ghost that never quite went away.

At the top of the broad cathedral stairs, a number of Koestler's friends gathered, speaking in normal voices now, but mostly saying the same things. Santini—nodding, smiling, but emitting few words—broke out of a cluster and started down the stairs.

As he reached the bottom of the stairs, Santini spotted Randall Hartley, the famous *Washington Post* investigative reporter. Hartley was pretty much out of the business of daily reporting. Mostly he spent his days researching and writing blockbuster bestsellers on just about anything or anyone he chose as a victim. Santini had read somewhere that he was writing about President Jefferson's foreign policy team that some snipe had dubbed as "Darth's Vaders."

"Didn't expect to see you here today," Hartley said in his slow, familiar way that was a trap for the unwary.

"Hello, Randall," Santini said, nodding, not offering to shake hands. "Funerals aren't my favorite events, but Tom Koestler was pretty special."

"Didn't realize that you were that close, Senator. . . . Can I still call you that?" He waited a beat but continued once he saw that Santini was not going to take the bait. "Rumor has it that you've already accepted Jefferson's offer to be his new Secretary of Defense. Any comment?"

"I have met with the President," Santini said. "I can't say more than that."

Well, I could say a lot more, he thought on the way to his car, lined up in the driveway with the other idling chauffeured cars. *I could have said that I took the job and that the White House will announce it tomorrow. I could have said that the nomination will zip through the Senate the next day. And I could have said that I'm on my way to Walter Reed Hospital for an anthrax shot.*

CHAPTER 3

As Santini opened his apartment door, the camera buried in the hallway ceiling alerted his security detail that "Road Runner" (his assigned code name) was on the move. Other than having to contend with the inevitable bureaucratic in-fighting and the blusters of Joe Praeger, the NSC Adviser, there were not many things Santini disliked about the job that had been his for the past eight months now.

But being surrounded by four bodyguards any time he moved to any place but the bathroom was one of them. Occasionally, he would run down the corridor hall, duck into the elevator, zip down to the underground garage, and hop into his car before they could get their pants on. He would race out into the street, cross Pennsylvania Avenue, roar across the 14th Street Bridge, and disappear along the George Washington Parkway. After extracting every possible second of solitude, he would turn on his cell phone and take an embarrassed call from the security detail that was floundering around in the chase car: "Okay. Game's up. Meet me at the office in fifteen minutes."

The problem with his little caper was that the detail had to report that he was missing and they had screwed up their assignment. Sure, it was unfair to them, but so be it. They needed to tighten up their procedures. If he could beat them to his car, so could the terrorists against whom they were trying to protect him.

No games today. He gave himself over to the system and

entered the armored limousine parked directly outside the long canopy that marked the entrance to his apartment building, a handsome new place that rightfully advertised itself as luxurious.

As soon as he entered the car, Curtis Preston—a lean, muscular black man who served as his armed driver—handed him his copy of the President's Daily Brief (PDB). This was the same intelligence briefing book that was presented to President Jefferson and his national security team each morning. It was a ringed notebook that contained more than a dozen pages marked: *Top Secret*. As was his custom, Santini scanned the notebook and made a few notes in the margins requesting further information on several items of interest.

A few minutes later, the limousine pulled up to the Pentagon's River Entrance. Santini handed the PDB to Curtis and then got out. Curtis would hand carry the document and see that it was delivered to the appropriate intelligence community personnel.

At the top of the broad, steep steps, Santini paused to take in what had virtually been his home since the day he took this job. The building, constructed just sixteen months after the ground-breaking ceremony in 1941, had been controversial from its conception to its completion: site, size, design, costs. It covered twenty-nine acres of land and more than six and a half million square feet of space. Complaints came from congressmen, architects, labor unions, and local county officials. And now, well, now it was part shrine. The hole, that heart-breaking gaping, blackened hole, was gone. The walls were back; the people were back. And there was only a trace of scars on the outside. There were other scars, though. And they would never go away.

Over the years, the Pentagon had been allowed to deteriorate through sheer neglect and underfunded maintenance budgets. Finally, in 1991, a decision was made to renovate it. It wouldn't be cheap. Billions of dollars and more than a dozen years to complete the job.

The renovation project was well underway when al Qaeda fanatics plowed a 757 Boeing jet into the building. Ironically, they had hit the only wedge on the western side of the building that had been completed. The renovation, which included inserting steel beams and sheets of Kevlar webbing, had saved scores of lives that would have been lost had the aircraft slammed into any other part of the Pentagon.

One hundred and eighty-four people were killed, including those aboard the aircraft. It was a small number compared to those who were lost in the attack upon the Trade Center in New York, but just as important symbolically. The al Qaeda terrorists had struck the very nerve center of America's defense.

The heartache and rage that Santini had felt that day was partly assuaged a few days later by the rush of adrenaline and pride when he saw a group of Marines, wearing hard hats, climb to the top of the Pentagon and unfurl a huge American flag over the debris. That gesture said it all: "Fuck you, al Qaeda. We're still here. And soon we'll be over there."

Shorn of all exterior adornment, the Pentagon was an architectural marvel, even now, with its faint scars. If you discounted the columned facades and the porticos on the Mall and River entrances, the five-storied, five-sided, five-ringed nucleus of America's military might achieved, in fact, a functional simplicity unmatched anywhere in the world.

The Pentagon was a city unto itself, vibrant and teeming with some of the most highly educated, brilliant, and dedicated citizens in America, citizens who had proved themselves in a test of death and fire. They had a daily mission: help keep the nation secure.

For Santini, the Pentagon signified solidity. Simple. Interconnected. Enduring. Like America itself.

To most of the twenty-three thousand men and women who worked there, for a long time it was simply "the Building." Now, because *Pentagon* had become an emblem, they called it, always, the Pentagon. Ornamentation or extravagance would have diminished the gravity of its business. Here decisions were made every minute that involved someone's life, another someone's death.

Like today maybe, Santini thought. Each day would bring

a couple of minor emergencies and dozens of decisions, most of them bureaucratic, designed to be shuffled into the great and endless Pentagon archives. But on any day, anywhere, there could be a major crisis. And the chances were great, as a British general once said, that that crisis would happen at night at a point exactly between the borders of two outdated maps.

A sudden memory flicked through Santini's mind. He was remembering a war-game session that he had attended as a senator. Here, in the basement war-gaming center. Some scenario about invading Iran. It was full of what-ifs and derring-do, a chance to wield make-believe power and get a thrill out of making decisions that would change history. You could order the Pentagon to "send in the Marines!" And now he could do just that. And it was not a game.

Santini turned to be greeted by his senior non-commissioned officer, Sergeant Major Clarence Walker, who was wearing his inevitable smile, which was just short of laughter. "Did you get in that eight-mile run this morning?" Santini asked Walker, knowing the answer.

"Yes sir, Secretary Santini," Walker replied. "No problem at all, sir." Santini knew that Walker had been up since 3:30 A.M. and he would not leave the Pentagon until eight o'clock that night. He had a wife and two children, three master's degrees, and was working on his doctorate in his spare time. Santini envied the sergeant his stamina, wanted to bottle it. But he knew that there were many others in the Pentagon who already had the formula.

Surrounded by his security detail, Santini walked up the broad steps of the River Entrance, and moved through the protocol entrance. He bypassed the security checkpoint and magnometer off to the right, and bounded up one flight to the Eisenhower Corridor, located on the E-Ring, which housed the nation's civilian and military leadership. Santini stepped quickly past the armed security guard stationed at the rear door of his office and into a room the size of a football field.

In the center of the room sat General Jack Pershing's magnificent solid mahogany desk. It was deep brown in color, trimmed with gold piping on the paneled drawers, and so imposing that Santini suspected it would take ten men to lift it.

He tried valiantly to keep the surface of the desk clear of the countless classified documents that were presented to him during the course of a day. This was more than a desk. This was a piece of history that needed to remain uncluttered by contemporary exigencies. In the center of the desk was a folder with the red-and-white diagonal stripes that indicated the folder contained Top Secret information.

He grabbed it angrily. *Who in hell left this here?* Santini was a stickler for following security procedures. This was flagrant. You just don't leave Top Secret folders lying around—then he opened the folder and saw a single piece of paper with large letters written in the center of the page by his personal secretary, Margie Reynolds: *Happy Birthday!*

God, he thought. *Had another year passed? The sands just keep running through that hourglass.*

Clipped to the paper was a three-by-five card in a clear-plastic pocket-size container that measured out Santini's life for the day in segments as small as five minutes. The schedule began with *06:00: Depart residence;* continued through *06:30–07:00: Intelligence briefings; 07:30–08:00: Top 4.; 08:00–08:30: Staff; 8:30: Dpt Pentagon en route WH,* . . . ending with *19:00: Recept. iho Adm. & Mrs. Conner, 3E869/3E912.*

Santini set his briefcase down and stepped to one of the tall windows that looked directly onto the parade ground. So much had happened since that day he took his oath of office in the Oval Office.

At first, Santini experienced pure exhilaration. No more delays or obfuscation in the Senate, no more wondering about the ups and downs of Wall Street. His every order was carried out without hesitation or complaint. A new man can do that. But then those who live and breathe somewhere deep within the bureaucracy start to resist and fight back. Never directly challenging the Secretary, of course, but thwarting him by slowing the machinery down, wrapping up the decision-making process in regulations, or running to the backdoor and ever-complaisant congressional staffers.

And then there were the staffers in the White House and State Department to contend with, along with the people on the National Security Council tied to the White House and competing for turf with State and Defense and the Intelligence Community. The freedom to run the Department of Defense was just as elusive and illusory as the opportunities to be an effective, independent voice in the Senate.

"Mr. Secretary?"

Santini turned to see his secretary, Margie, in the doorway. Next to her stood a tall, slim man wearing black-rimmed glasses. He looked Chinese, and for a moment Santini wondered if he was an unexpected visitor from the Chinese Embassy. Then Santini noticed the identification badge around his neck and knew from the colors that he worked for the Defense Intelligence Agency. So this was his new man.

Santini's memory lingered for a moment, savoring his first fight with Creighton Ford, the National Intelligence Director, or U.S. Spy Czar, as newspaper headlines labeled him, when they weren't giving him the initials *DNI*. (Ford preferred *Czar*.) Taking advantage of Koestler's death (and not noticing the death of the DIA briefer Jason Andrews), Ford ordered that all DIA reports and analyses must simultaneously go to the DNI and the Secretary of Defense.

Santini made a few calls to old pals in the Senate, and Czar Creighton Ford received a secret memorandum from the Senate Intelligence Committee, which told Ford to keep his paws off the Pentagon. "It is our strong and unanimous belief," the memo had said, "that all aspects of military intelligence should be within the immediate purview of the Secretary of Defense. We also believe that any deviation from this policy could result in a committee hearing devoted to the powers and funding of the Director of National Intelligence."

Santini knew about the memo because he had helped to draft it.

Santini was still musing about his fight with Ford when Margie said, "Mr. Secretary?" slightly raising her voice to call him back to the moment. "This is Arthur Wu, your new DIA briefer."

"Thank you, Ms. Reynolds," Santini said. As she closed the door, Santini took a step toward Wu, who closed the space in two strides and stuck out his right hand, then drew it back, sensing the protocol. Santini responded to Wu's hesitation by smiling and bestowing a Senate-style handshake: right hand pumps; left hand grasps the other's upper right arm and gives a friendly squeeze.

"Sit down, Captain Wu," Santini said, motioning to two chairs at a small round table to the right of the desk.

Wu sat stiffly at attention, as if his gray suit, white button-down shirt, and blue-and-red-striped tie were a uniform. Until a few weeks ago, Santini knew, Wu had been an Army captain assigned to the Army War College in Carlisle, Pennsylvania, as an instructor teaching a required course in the history of U.S.-China policy. One of Santini's Pentagon talent scouts, seeking a Chinese specialist, had trolled the faculty of the War College. Future generals and admirals got their promotion tickets punched there or at the Naval Postgraduate School in Monterey, California, which had a reputation for turning out men and women who had learned the value of learning more.

Every morning Santini was brought up-to-date in separate briefings by a man from the Central Intelligence Agency, who was, of course, a civilian, and an Army or Navy officer from the Defense Intelligence Agency. Secretary of Defense Robert S. McNamara had created the DIA in an attempt to coordinate intelligence estimates that had been individually produced by the Army, Navy, Marine Corps, and Air Force. Santini knew that the DIA operated within the shadow of the much larger CIA. But he liked to hear the sometimes divergent views of the two agencies, and when, bypassing Ford, he had recommended to the President that Air Force General Grace Hayes become the Director of the DIA, Santini had ordered her never to have the DIA briefer compare notes with the CIA briefer. It was Santini's desire for this knowledge that had inspired his back-alley fracas with the DNI.

Three television screens behind Santini's desk were tuned to CNN, MSNBC, and FOX News telecasts. At the moment, all were running commercials simultaneously. Ironically, Santini frequently got fast-breaking news reports affecting national security faster than he did from any intelligence agency. "Well, what did our media moguls bring us today?" Santini asked, nodding toward the muted television monitors.

"Their broadcasts are outside my area, Mr. Secretary. But, if you want—"

"Just kidding, Captain Wu. Or may I call you Arthur?"

"Yes, sir. It's Art, sir. And I'm a Reserve captain now."

"So, how do you like your new job?"

"Fine, sir, fine. And, sir, I am grateful for being selected. I want—"

"I told the War College I wanted their finest Chinese specialist detailed to DIA. And I asked General Hayes to look you over and decide about making you the briefing officer. She's the one who did the deciding. Now, what have you got?"

Wu sat at the round, ornate table that also was part of General Pershing's legacy. Sitting ramrod straight, he breezed effortlessly through the briefing, touching on overnight attacks.

"Hamas claimed responsibility for setting off a remote-controlled bomb at a crowded concert hall in Jerusalem. Twenty people were killed, more than seventy wounded. In Russia, a Chechen woman drove her car into the garage of an apartment complex and detonated what experts believed was four hundred pounds of dynamite. No figure for the number of casualties is available yet, but the number was expected to exceed two hundred.

"There was a clash between Muslim and Hindu factions in Kashmir."

In a tone that was flat and unemotional, Wu continued ticking off the checklist of violence that had become a permanent staple of the intelligence diet. The man was an automaton. He might just as well have been reciting the stock quotes of the day.

Finally, he ended with North Korea. Rattling off names, statistics, covert operations, and HUMINT (human-provided intelligence, the polite term for spies), Wu never once looked down at the briefing book open on his lap. He closed the book and said, "About China, sir. I noticed that in your copy of yesterday's President's Daily Brief you made a note that you wanted background on two China matters and one on North Korea, which, of course, is tightly tied to Chinese foreign policy."

"Art, those queries can be handled later in the DIA backgrounder. Don't worry about them right now. They weren't needed for your excellent brief," Santini said, rising from his chair.

Wu stood, thanked Santini, and started for the door. Then, turning, he tapped his forehead in a gesture of apology and said, "Mr. Secretary. I forgot to mention it, but late last night Carole Minter, the *Washington Post* reporter, opened a letter that she thought had been sent by a friend. After slicing the seal, she tried to open the envelope by blowing into it. She nearly choked on a white powder."

"Hasn't that happened to her before?"

"Same lady. Apparently somebody doesn't like her."

"Apparently, she hasn't dropped the habit of blowing into envelopes. Is she okay?"

"Looks like another hoax," Wu said. "First lab reports have tested negative for anthrax, but CDC—the Centers for Disease Control—wants to do more tests today to be sure. As you know, all the mail that goes through the postal system in the city is irradiated now. So the chances are pretty high that she'll be fine even if the substance turns out to have been the real deal."

As Wu started to leave, Santini said, "Art, can you stay for a minute?"

"Of course, Mr. Secretary. Is there something else?"

"This anthrax hoax, if that's what it is," Santini said, nudging Wu toward the small table and tapping a chair, signaling him to sit down. "Something has been bothering me about how Secretary Tom Koestler bought the farm. And how after eight months not a clue from the FBI about who did it."

Wu shook his head. "And from what I understand, it's unlikely they'll ever know. There's tons of the stuff out there. Hundreds of technicians who can slice and dice it in home labs."

"Art," Santini said, "let me ask you something. How many people knew that Koestler had refused to be vaccinated?"

For the first time, Wu was without a rapid response. "Why, I wouldn't know, Mr. Secretary. I wasn't here at the Pentagon at the time. I'd guess only a few people." He glanced away from Santini, momentarily shifting his eyes to the opposite end of the room. "I assume his wife. His deputy, Walt Wilson, had to know. Probably Doc Brewster, the Pentagon's chief physician. The folks at the clinic upstairs where Secretary Koestler's medical records were kept."

"But that's still a limited universe of people, isn't it?"

"Yes, sir," Wu responded, his voice reflecting discomfort with where Santini was going. "But there's no telling how secure those records were. As you know, the Pentagon is target-rich territory for hackers. We get hit well over a thousand times a day. Some get through the firewalls. Could be teenagers or . . ."

"Or terrorists," Santini said, completing Wu's thoughts.

"Yes, sir. It's quite possible."

Santini remained silent for a moment, reflecting on what had happened to Koestler. The pause in the conversation left Wu uncertain as to what to say.

"Is there something you want me to do? I can call Vic Sanders over at the FBI to see if they have anything more."

"No, Art. Just curious. Someone had to have had specific information of Koestler's vulnerability. Someone who had a strong motivation to kill him." Santini stood, and stretched his back muscles. "Just looking at some of the hate mail that gets sent my way, that could be a pretty big number."

His tone carried a note of jest, but the number of security personnel that were assigned to protect him was a constant reminder of the number of the dangers that went with the job. "Sorry to hold you up, Art. I'll see you tomorrow."

As Wu walked toward the door, Santini had mixed feelings about his new man. And he wasn't sure why. Wu was impressive, to be sure. Smart, confident, ambitious. His record said as much. And he was personable enough. But there was something about him that struck Santini as being out of sorts.

Santini was a man of intuition. Some thought he was too quick in judging people. He either liked you or not, trusted you or sent you packing. No one ever got a second chance to make a good first impression. Usually, however, Santini's instincts had served him well.

Wu had seemed uncomfortable, a shade defensive when discussing how many people might have known that Koestler refused to be vaccinated. He hadn't, as he said, been at the Pentagon at the time, and it wasn't really his bailiwick to know about Koestler's religious beliefs or fears. But, as an intelligence officer, shouldn't he have been just a little more curious?

Then again, Santini thought, maybe it was just his imagination at play. After all, working at the Pentagon was the equivalent of drinking water out of a fire hydrant. Events came rushing at you with a velocity that left little time for reflection. In fact, until he had been reminded about the anthrax threat just now, he hadn't given it much thought himself.

As Wu opened the door, Margie stuck her head in and announced, "The Chairman is here, Mr. Secretary. The others are on the way. Shall I show the Chairman in now?"

Santini nodded.

The "others" to whom Margie alluded were Walt Slater, Santini's deputy, and General Hector Ramirez, the Vice Chairman of the Joint Chiefs, George Whittier's second in command. Together they comprised the "Top Four" and met for precisely one half hour each day to review overnight events and items on their respective agendas. Santini never wanted to keep General George G. Whittier cooling his heels. His ambivalent feelings about Arthur Wu would have to wait.

After the ritual of shaking hands, the two men sat at the small conference table. Whittier was one of those tough, hard-bodied Texans that the Air Force spawns. He had started his career as a pilot but had shifted to the Special Forces and risen to head the Special Operations Command before being picked for Chairman of the Joint Chiefs.

"Mr. Secretary," General Whittier began, "we just received word that one of our electro-optical, low-earth-orbit satellites was out on its last two passes yesterday. It's the one that gives us coverage over North Korea."

"Was? Is it back up now?"

"Yes, sir."

"Do we know what happened?"

"Not yet. We've got everyone on the case. Boys out at NRO, Space Command, NSA. No evidence of any laser activity or other foul play. Could be just a mechanical failure of some sort. Those birds are pretty old."

"Let me ask you something, Mr. Chairman. I've thought about this before and I just don't have a solution." Santini dropped his pen on the table and linked his fingers together in a stretching motion. "What if that bird or any one of the others was permanently crippled or just died? What options would we have?" Santini suspected the answer, but he hoped he was wrong.

"No good ones. Not in the short term, at least. We could shift some of our other satellites around for coverage. But that's a zero-sum game. Robbing Peter to pay Paul, so to speak. As you know, over the years, we've slowly been going deaf and blind in space. Trying to cover more and more areas with fewer systems. We've got to do more on the procurement side."

Indeed, Santini thought. They were saying the same thing ten years ago. Nothing had changed. "Or simply live with less coverage. Run the risks. Accept the darkness."

"Afraid so, Mr. Secretary. We could move a U-2 spy plane from the Middle East to over there," Whittier said as he scratched some notes on the pad of paper that he never seemed to be without. "But we're stretched pretty thin in that category, too." Making another note on his pad, he said, "You know, if the Blackbirds were still around, we could deploy them for emergency tactical intelligence. But they're pretty much in the boneyard now."

"Don't remind me. Congress voted, over my objection, back in 1988 to kill the program. SR-71s, the fastest spy planes ever made. Faster than a speeding bullet. The Pentagon comptroller claimed they were too expensive to operate, that satellites could do a better job, and were cheaper. No one stopped to think what it cost to build today's satellites or how many we'd lose on the launch rockets that exploded on lift-off."

"As a former Air Force man, I tell you, Mr. Secretary, it broke my heart to see them laid to rest," General Whittier said.

"One other thing," Santini pressed, eager to change the subject of how he, as Chairman of the Intelligence Committee, had failed to save the Blackbird. "Couldn't we take temporary possession of some of the commercial satellites out there to give us emergency coverage?"

"We could. Yes'r. Problem is we wouldn't get the same quality resolution. If it's cloudy or we need to take a peek at nighttime, we're screwed. There's one other thing?"

"Which is?"

"We'd have a helluva time keeping secret the reasons that we're commandeering the commercial birds and their frequency spectrum allocation. Wouldn't take long for the word to spread that we're a dollar short and a day late on our intelligence takes. Then everyone who is already cheating on the margins would start taking a bigger slice."

"Damn," Santini cursed. "I guess we'd better pray that Congress fully funds the intelligence budget instead of pork barreling it again next year."

"I agree, Mr. Secretary. We're really up shit creek without a paddle."

He rushed on, speaking emotionally, in a tone that Santini had rarely heard him use.

"We've got more trouble than a blinking satellite, Mr. Secretary. I'm told that the State Department is going to recommend to the President that we send our soldiers to participate with NATO as part of a peacekeeping and stabilization force in the Middle East.

"This is really bad news for us. Our forces have been stretched to the breaking point. Especially the Army. The war in Iraq put our people and equipment through pure hell. Congress wants us to add at least two new divisions but we aren't making our quotas now. Recruitment is way down. Big enlistment bonuses aren't doing the trick. Unless the country dips into a deep recession, I don't know how we can even hold our current numbers. Too many deployments are driving people out of the service."

"I can add another one for you," Santini said. "I'm getting pressure from Homeland Security to pull almost all of the remaining Guard and Reserve forces off frontline duty in Afghanistan and Iraq to serve as the first responders against terrorists' attacks and environmental catastrophes here at home."

"Mr. Secretary, we've got the finest fighting forces in the world. The best ever. I don't like the thought of giving up on the all-volunteer force. But if we have to maintain the current pace of deployments and shoulder the burden of nation-building from here to hell and back, well, we may have to re-think our opposition to the draft."

"I agree," Santini said, shaking his head. "I don't think either we or the American people want to go back to a draft with all the problems that come with it. But there may be no alternative. Whenever I try to change the 'tooth to tail ratios' by outsourcing all nonessential military work to the private sector so I can shift our support personnel into combat roles, Congress screams, 'Hell, no.'"

Santini leaned back in his chair and tossed his writing pen into the air in a gesture of frustration.

"We're being asked to do more and more with less and less, Mr. Secretary. It's hollowing us out," Whittier said solemnly.

"Okay, let me talk to Doug Palmer when we meet at the White House later this week. Maybe if I yell loud enough, he'll back off."

A soft knock on the door broke the air of pessimism that had begun to settle over them. It was Margie. Without waiting for a response, she opened the door, cheerfully announcing that "the others are here, Mr. Secretary."

"Okay," Santini said. "Send them in so they can join the wake."

When he saw that his sarcasm produced a look of puzzled disappointment on Margie's face, he added, "It's okay, Margie. Tell them it's an Irish wake."

CHAPTER 4

MOSCOW

The Boeing 767 arrived over Moscow as the city awoke to a snowy dawn. The pilot, an American, once flew for a CIA proprietary airline in Venezuela. He still wore the big-link gold bracelet that he had never had to use to ransom himself. The copilot, a Russian, was a veteran of the war in Afghanistan. They did not talk much, but when they did, they managed to converse in a Russian-English patois, and what they talked about was how they would spend the money they made on these flights of the Money Plane. The only passenger, seated in one of the half-dozen seats at the rear of the plane, was Arthur C. Cartwright, executive vice president of New York Intercontinental Bank. Around him, strapped down on skids fixed to the cabin floor, were dozens of white canvas bags full of freshly minted, uncirculated one-hundred-dollar bills, all stacked in wrappers bearing the imprint of the U.S. Federal Reserve Bank of New York City.

Cartwright shifted in his seat and switched on the overhead light. He took deep breaths and tried to meditate, the way he had learned long ago from his first wife in California, back in those simple days. This was his last flight as babysitter of the Money Plane. He had to stick to the routine, not act nervous. But he was. When he returned to New York he would be taken again to the FBI safe house in White Plains for the debriefing and to meet with the U.S. Attorneys who would prepare him for the grand jury. He would be the star witness, the banker who could explain it all.

Cartwright unbuckled his seat belt and walked forward to speak to a pilot. He needed someone to talk to, to talk to about anything. But as he was about to turn the handle, he remembered that the door was undoubtedly safety-locked and any attempt to open it from the passenger side would set off alarms in two countries.

He walked back to his seat and took a flask out of his small black bag. He unscrewed the cap and filled it. Fine vodka, Vladimir Berzin had told him when he handed him the bottle on the last trip. Very fine vodka; a friend-to-friend vodka, he called it. Cartwright opened a pack of peanut-buttered crackers and washed them down with another capful of vodka. He always resented the fact that he never knew when Berzin would order the Money Plane. First the call from somewhere: Far Rockaway? Moscow? Smolensk? Almaty? The FBI said the National Security Agency—that eavesdropping outfit—was working on that. Then out of the office, into the armored car to the Fed, the paperwork there, then more paperwork at Kennedy, and onto the plane. Grab a candy bar or crackers and throw them into the bag. Next time he'd have emergency rations in the bag. Next time. Well, there would be no next time.

The U.S. Marshal had routinely explained the federal witness protection program. As soon as the FBI and the U.S. Attorney debriefed him, he and Svetlana and little Victor would be put up in a safe house far from the Russian Mafiya in New York. At the trial, he would testify under his real name and identity. Then, on the day the trial ended, he would become Roger Shadduck. He and Shirley Shadduck (Svetlana would love that name), with their son, George, would be living in Greenville, South Carolina, and the newly minted Mr. Shadduck would be the owner of a chain of dry cleaners that the U.S. Marshal Service had acquired from the Internal Revenue Service. Mr. Shadduck would have purchased the bankrupt business at auction. The paperwork would be perfect. And Svetlana/Shirley? He wondered how long she would stay with

him and whether she would take Victor/George with her. Mr.
Shadduck would have no way to follow her or sue for divorce.
That was not in the program. He took a last capful of vodka.
Berzin was right. It was very good.

He felt the jolt of the landing gear deploying. He drew back
the window's cloth shade and looked down just as runway
lights suddenly pierced the snow-filled gloom below. Whoever said April was the cruelest month must never have been
in Moscow in March.

In a few moments the aircraft landed at a former military
airport thirty miles southwest of Moscow. As the 767 touched
down, a red-and-white armored truck sped onto the tarmac,
followed by two Mercedes S-280 limousines. The plane taxied to the truck and two Russians in black leather jackets got
out. The driver shut off the engine, turned off the headlights,
and stayed in the car. The two men carried Spetsnaz AK-47s,
adapted for close-quarters firefights.

Cartwright, in a hooded black parka, appeared at the rear
cabin door. One of the Russians on the ground aimed his gun
at Cartwright; the other turned toward the Mercedes limousines and leveled his gun at the first vehicle. The driver
flashed his lights on and off three times, but the gunman did
not lower his gun. The two limousines, their headlights off,
stopped about thirty feet from the aircraft.

"The goods are delivered," Cartwright called down in fal-
tering Russian. He ignored the gun; it was part of the routine.
He stepped back into the shadow of the cabin. The pilot
pressed a button. A set of steps unfolded and clanged onto the
tarmac. It was the only sound in the darkness.

At that instant, doors of each limousine opened. Two men,
garbed and armed like the other Russians at the foot of the
steps, emerged from the second car and walked slowly toward
the steps. When they had placed themselves opposite the men
from the truck, all four lowered their guns but kept their fingers on the triggers and their gaze fixed straight ahead. The
FBI special agent who was Cartwright's handler had told him
that Berzin's thugs were mostly ex-Spetsnaz, the Russian spe-

cial forces. "They're trained assassins," the agent had said. "And very good at it." Very good. Like the vodka.

A large man with a full black beard swiftly stepped from the front passenger seat of the car nearer the plane. The man wore a long black overcoat over a gray business suit. His right hand was wedged in the overcoat pocket. He spoke to a transmitter strapped onto his left wrist. As he spoke, the second car silently moved forward. Two limousines now flanked the truck. Simultaneously, their headlights stabbed the darkness, silhouetting the four gunmen in such a way that the men from the truck were momentarily blinded. They did not look away.

The man with the transmitter on his wrist inserted three fingers into an opening under the handle of the right back door of the Mercedes, clicked the hidden lock, and opened the door. A tall, slim man stepped from the car. He wore a black raincoat over a dark blue, faintly striped suit. He must have been freezing under his pearl-gray homburg, but he looked as if, to him, there was no snow.

A whitened sepulcher. Cartwright was startled by the biblical phrase that passed through his mind. *Inspired by coming redemption,* he thought, looking down upon Vladimir Pavlovich Berzin. A gangster in a bad, expensive suit. But, gangster or not, Berzin was the best customer the New York Intercontinental Bank had ever had, and Cartwright, as always, kept his thoughts to himself. Bankers who crossed Berzin did not live to cash their pension checks. It was in his eyes, those dark eyes that never blinked. Cartwright and Berzin had never met, except like this, the banker in the shadows, the Russian stepping out of the shadows and into the headlights. The routine. It was always like this. Gangster choreography.

Tonight, however, had a surprise. Another man got out of the car, sliding across the passenger seat to follow Berzin. He was as tall as Berzin, and nearly as slim, but with blond hair that was slicked back. He wore a black cashmere topcoat. The blond man looked around furtively, and even from that distance Cartwright could see that the man was nervous, anxious to get this over with.

The man stayed two paces behind the swiftly striding Berzin, and the banker got a better look. Cartwright was good at faces, but this man he did not recognize. He stepped nearer, poised by the top of the steps so that he could pick up some details for the debriefing. The man was fashionably dressed, obviously fond of fine clothes.

Berzin began speaking rapidly in German. Another surprise. The banker, who had worked for several years in Intercontinental's Berlin branch, listened and made mental notes. The FBI had wanted to wire him. He had refused, telling them that he wouldn't last five minutes. Not five minutes.

Berzin turned to the man at his side. "I am so glad you could come, Wolfgang," Berzin said. Wolfgang Wagner did not reply. He concentrated on not looking nervous, on holding back the anxiety that seized him when he felt he was in a place where he should not be. And he was freezing.

"None of my business associates have ever seen this," Berzin said, ignoring Wagner's lack of response. "It is my flying bank. I call it the Money Plane." He nodded to the man in the black raincoat. "Tell them they may unload, Tago."

Tago barked an order in Russian. The men from the truck slung their weapons over their shoulders and mounted the steps. The driver got out. He wore the uniform of a Moscow armored-car-service employee. The butt of a 9mm Beretta jutted from a holster on his hip. He spun the combination on a rear door, which opened to a shelved, well-lit interior. As he entered the compartment, the first man off the steps arrived at the rear door and dumped a white canvas bag from his shoulder to the grilled steel floor.

"Excuse me for a moment, Wolfgang," Berzin said, motioning to Tago to precede him up the steps. Cartwright tried to get a better look at the man called Tago. But his face was deep in shadow and was buried in a full beard.

"And so we meet again," Berzin said to Cartwright in heavily accented English, stretching out his right hand and bowing slightly. He nodded toward Tago. "Please help Mr. Cartwright to the car, Tago," Berzin said in Russian. Then, looking over his shoulder, he said in German, "Just wait right there, Wolf-gang. We're not going to be very long."

"But I'm . . . I'm not leaving the . . . ," Cartwright stammered. Tago, who towered over Cartwright, stepped behind him, pinned his arms against his sides, and marched him down the steps. When he reached the ground, Cartwright shot a terrified glance at the man called Wolfgang and started to speak. Tago reached his left arm around Cartwright's throat in a hammerlock, muffling him and keeping him moving toward one of the limousines. The two men who had arrived in that Mercedes waited for Berzin, fell in step on either side, and all three followed Tago and Cartwright. Wagner slipped into the shadows behind Berzin.

The two men held Cartwright while Tago tore off Cartwright's parka and tossed it to the ground. Tago grabbed Cartwright's black attaché case out of his hand and gave it to Berzin.

"What are you doing?" Cartwright stammered. "Why—?"

Tago ripped open Cartwright's white shirt and roughly patted him down. "No wire," he said in Russian.

"So it is true," Berzin said. "You refused the FBI wire. Very wise."

"I . . . I don't know what you are talking about."

"I am quite sure you do, Mr. Cartwright," Berzin said. "Open the trunk," Berzin said in Russian. The man unlocked the trunk and the lid swung smoothly upward. The trunk was lined with black plastic. Tago reached in and picked up a neatly folded white towel.

At the edge of his vision Berzin could see Wagner staring at the Mercedes trunk. Berzin motioned for Tago to drag Cartwright forward, where the headlight beams sliced into the darkness. Tago pushed Cartwright to his knees and grabbed his chin to bare his throat. Cartwright tried to utter a cry but made only a mewing sound. Berzin, in one swift move, reached under the back of his suit coat, pulled a knife from a sheath, and held its serrated edge against Cartwright's flesh.

The knife, Wagner thought, his eyes fixed on the gleaming

blade. *The girl in Berlin.* His memory raced back to a dark moment like this, when his friend Vladimir had held his knife against the throat of a prostitute kneeling before him. Drunk and furious over her demand for extra marks, he had carved a mark along her jawline, leaving a long, jagged red line that disfigured her beauty. Her prices would not be so high to future customers.

But this time Vladimir's knife bit deep, severing an artery. Cartwright's blood pulsed in spurts that arched onto the tarmac. Cartwright fell forward into a widening red puddle. Tago and another man lifted Cartwright's body into the trunk, careful to place it so that the blood poured into the folds of the black plastic. Then Tago wiped up most of the blood with the towel, tossed it into the trunk, and began wrapping the body tightly in the plastic.

The suddenness of Berzin's action startled Wagner, but he knew that his friend was capable of such violence. This, however, was different. Now he was a witness to murder and that made him uncomfortable. That made him an accomplice.

"So, my friend, you disapprove?" It was not really a question.

"Was this necessary? To involve me in this . . . this mess?"

"Ah, Wolfgang, your German sensitivities are showing again." Berzin laughed at the thought. "The man was a traitor. He had to die. He had been cooperating with the FBI."

"But why involve me?"

"You can't keep your hands clean all the time. You think you can just take the money and run? All profit, no risk? You've been a limited partner, Wolfgang. Now you are a full one."

Wagner shrugged, unhappy with his sudden predicament. He was wary, however, about expressing his regrets too openly. Even friends—perhaps *especially* friends—had to be careful around Berzin. He was capable of turning on Wagner just as well. Berzin draped a muscular arm around Wagner's shoulders, walking him toward the Mercedes. "Come, partner, let's go discuss business."

Tago and the other men got into the car. The doors slammed shut and the car sped off, its headlights stabbing the night as it passed through an open gate and onto the road, heading away from Moscow.

Berzin, carrying Cartwright's black attaché case in his right hand, wrapped his arm around Wagner's back and gripped his shoulder, holding him up, half-dragging him toward the men who were still unloading the white canvas bags. "Well, Wolfgang. I will now continue my tour. The plane left New York—"

"But Vladimir Pavlovich—that man," Wagner said. "What was that about?"

Berzin turned to look Wolfgang Wagner straight in the eye. Berzin's face was as hard and unemotional as a skull. "We are not in your beloved Berlin with all your nice aristocrats, Wolfgang. This is Russia. We make up the rules as we go along."

By now, all the canvas bags were neatly stacked in the armored truck. The men entered the truck and headed toward the open gate. Suddenly, the gate rolled along a track and snapped shut. A yellow-and-black spike-studded steel barrier swung up in front of it. From the gatehouse, pointing a pistol at the driver, stepped an elderly man wearing jeans and a Red Army tunic arrayed with medals. The driver grimaced and cursed, then handed a one-hundred-dollar bill to the gatekeeper.

Berzin, watching the transaction from his limousine, laughed and turned to Wagner. "Dues, Wolf. Everyone must pay his dues."

CHAPTER 5

BEIJING

It was not unusual for the general to be in his office on a Sunday morning. His responsibilities demanded great dedication. It was up to him to handle all of the details involved in the running of a large bureaucracy. But for him, work was no burden. Rather, it was more of an aphrodisiac, a stimulant that drove him to spend days and nights weaving the pieces of his plan together as a shield, one that would save his country from the snares and treacheries of others.

He glanced out through the dusty slats of the venetian blinds on his office window. The slats were stained with age. The blinds should have been replaced long ago, but he considered that an extravagance, an unnecessary waste of money. His high rank entitled him to a much larger office and grander appointments, but he had always spurned every form of luxury. This was not to say that he was beyond reproach or corruption. Indeed, he had indulged in creative financial bookkeeping, maintained secret Swiss bank accounts, and transferred significant amounts of cash to foreign nationals. But he had never sought personal gain from these illicit activities. He had always acted in the service of his country.

Outside, the sky was gray. People were gathering their fur hats and bulky coats about themselves while dipping their heads against the wind. *Always trust the people,* he thought. They knew that a storm was not far away.

He reached behind his desk to the shelf that served as a credenza. Picking up a book whose pages were tabbed and underlined, he silently repeated the words found there as if he were reading from a catechism.

Come like the wind, strike like the hawk and move like a ghost in the starlight. Ancient words, timeless wisdom.

He had struck once before, not on the wing, but on cat's paws. The thought caused him to grin smugly. America had too many arrogant leaders who made rash, provocative promises. Thanks to him, they had one less. And his messenger, the subordinate and his girlfriend, who liked to run along the river, they, too, were gone. *Strike like the hawk.*

But much more had to be done if he was to shatter the grand schemes of those puffed up with missionary zeal, so eager to wage a moral crusade the world over. Things had not gone so well for them and their British friends in Iraq. After declaring victory, they had been forced to hide behind concrete barricades, terrified of the next wave of suicide bombers, and then beg the United Nations for help. But the world had turned against them. What America breaks, America must pay to fix. This was the answer the imperialists received from their so-called friends.

A strong rap on the door snapped his brief reverie. "Enter," he said.

The door was opened by a young officer who had been assigned to serve as his aide. He saluted and stood at attention before his superior motioned him to sit in a faded cane-backed chair in front of the desk.

"General, I have a message that was received earlier this morning. It had to be translated and transcribed."

"And who performed these services, Colonel?" he asked, a hint of something more than curiosity in his voice.

"Sir, I did. I'm aware of the need for total secrecy. The communication has not been seen by anyone else. The only written record is in the notes that I have here." The colonel held up a single sheet of lined paper. "Nothing else is in writing."

"Excellent, Colonel. Excellent. Please proceed."

"I'm not sure of the meaning, General. It appears to be some kind of code. It said: 'The cake will be delivered soon, my friend. Everything is on schedule. The bakers are checking to be sure they have the best ingredients. They take great pride in producing a quality product. Don't worry. There are no delays. The shipment will arrive precisely as I have promised.' "

"Thank you, Colonel, well done," the general said, extending his hand to retrieve the sheet of paper. Walking his aide to the door, he said, "That is an important message. Highly classified. Our national security demands that it not go beyond us."

"Yes, sir. I understand."

Slipping his arm through that of the colonel as he escorted him out of the room, the general added, somewhat menacingly, "Any breach of security could lead to extremely serious consequences."

He felt the colonel's arm go taut. He was certain that the colonel understood. Returning to the window that looked out onto the paved plaza below, he saw that it had started to snow.

Everything was unfolding as he had planned. He hoped that his Russian friend had done his homework, that he had the right people for the job.

CHAPTER 6

HOLLOMAN, NEW MEXICO

Visitors to New Mexico often said that the immense sun-drenched land looked desolate. But they did not know New Mexico the way Hal Prentice did. He knew his homeland was full of life, full of danger, full of secrets. "It really is the Land of Enchantment," he told first-time tourists. "Just like it says on our license plates."

He had walked these deserts and scrublands and mountains all of his life. As a young man he had walked into the mountains along the Jornada del Muerto, the Journey of Death, as the Spaniards who came here called the dry, snake-ridden trail. He had walked across the desert northwest of Alamogordo and had looked into the pit created by the first atomic blast in 1945. The test weapon had exploded in the desert dawn, created the pit, and fused the sand into strange green pieces of glass. Prentice had a piece of that glass on a shelf in his mobile home, back at the trailer park near Tularosa.

Prentice had explored the old pueblos, where Indians had lived long before the Spaniards came. On many nights he had slept in pueblos built on sites where people had lived twenty-two thousand years before. Some historians said that those long-lost people were the original Americans, the oldest indigenous tribes found anywhere in North America. Hal Prentice liked that. He liked the idea of living where America really began. He thought of those original people as people like his own kind: white men.

The original people had to be white people. He knew that. A matter of faith. He parked his pickup under some stubby pine trees off a dirt road that did not show on any maps. He took his M-16 rifle off the rack behind the seat, slung a small knapsack over his shoulder, and headed up a trail along the foothills of the Sacramento Mountains. After a few minutes, as the trail zigzagged and became steep, he was puffing. Every twenty feet or so he had to stop, get his breath back, and wipe his brow.

He was fat and stubby, no longer the slim young man who had climbed this trail years before with a thirty-pound pack on his back. Now Prentice carried a thirteen-pound beer belly. He wore a black Stetson with a rattlesnake band and a camouflage uniform that looked as if it were camouflaging a large pear. The black beard that covered his cheeks and chin was flecked with gray. His feet hurt, and he wished he had on his slippers instead of these black military-style boots. But he walked on, for he was the commanding officer of the Scorpion Militia, and he was on a mission.

The trail climbed into a box canyon, slipped through a narrow fissure, then faded as it crossed the floor of the canyon. Smoke rose from the chimney of a low building about a quarter of a mile ahead. When Prentice had walked about five hundred feet, a man's voice called out, "Don't move." Prentice stopped. The canyon walls were about seventy-five feet high. He looked up to his left, where the voice came from, and saw the glint of a rifle behind rocks about halfway up the canyon.

"Your goddamn weapon shines like a headlight, Frank," Prentice shouted up to the wall. His booming voice echoed down the canyon.

A man wearing a cowboy hat and a camouflage uniform stepped out from behind a rock pile and for a moment peered down at Prentice through binoculars. "Thought it was you, Colonel," he said, waving. "Just had to make sure."

Prentice did not respond. He kept on walking, stopping at the gate of a high wire-mesh fence topped by razor wire. The fence ran the length of the canyon floor and disappeared into the shadows of the rocks.

A paunchy man, who was clad like Prentice and carried a rifle with a telescopic sight, walked over to the gate. "Password, Colonel?" he asked.

Prentice paused for a moment, unable to recall the word. "Liberty," he finally said.

The guard nodded and opened the gate. A path lined with whitewashed stones led to an old ranch house, badly in need of repair. An American flag, hung upside down as a sign of distress, was nailed to the wall next to the front door.

Behind the ranch house was a barn. Cottonwoods, their leaves a moist, bright green, grew along a stream that trickled through a cleft in the canyon wall. Nestled under the trees were the small cabins that Prentice called "the Freedom Academy," a boarding school for the children of Scorpion members. A woman and several children were gathered outside one of the cabins. The woman looked up as Prentice approached and waved. He hesitated a moment on the path to the ranch house, then cut across to her.

"Hello, Martha," he said. "How's the learnin' goin'?"

"Just fine, Colonel," the woman replied. She pointed to a boy about seven years old. "Sam? Tell the colonel where you live."

Sam stood up, looked unblinking at Prentice, and said, "I live in the in-*dee*-pendent *re*-public of the *true* America."

"So, Sam, do you live in the United States of America?"

"*Negative!*" Sam said. "I live in the *true* America!"

"And what are you going to do when you get to be sixteen years old?"

"I'm going to enlist in the Scorpion Militia," Sam said, "just like my dad and Uncle Fred."

Prentice nodded to the woman and the other children. He made a quick salute and turned back to the ranch house. As Prentice mounted the worn stairs, a man standing next to the front door saluted and opened the door.

Prentice stepped into a hall that led to a kitchen and, beyond that, to a dormitory. Large rooms opened to the left and right of the hall. Prentice entered the room on the right. Two men were sitting at a long table, stuffing pamphlets into envelopes. He spoke to them for a moment, then turned to the door on the right. He knocked at the door, which was locked, and said, "Colonel Prentice."

An inside lock slid and the door opened. In the doorway stood a tall, slim man wearing jeans and a blue work shirt with the sleeves rolled up. Sticking out of the waistband of the jeans was the butt of a U.S. Army .45. "Howdy, Hal," he said. "All's well?"

"Greetin's, Charles," Prentice said, frowning at Charles' failure to address him as "Colonel." "Yes," he replied curtly. "All is well. Do we know the time?"

The man called Charles smiled. He was a handsome man, clean-shaven, with crew-cut blond hair. He moved his head slightly, indicating a corner of the room where a teenage boy sat in a folding chair and was working intently on a Toshiba laptop computer set on a table before him. A cable connected the computer to a portable printer on the back of the table. Another computer cable snaked across the floor and out a half-open window. Through the dust-smeared window a satellite dish about the size of a pizza pan could be seen. It had, in fact, once been a pizza pan.

Prentice followed Charles to the boy, who seemed not to notice their approach.

"Show Hal what you've got, Bobby," Charles said. He touched the boy on the back of the neck and ran his hand around Bobby's long sun-bleached hair. Bobby turned, looked impassively at the two men, and stroked two keys.

On the screen appeared the home page of the Scorpions, with *The Scorpion Militia* in bold letters along the top. In one corner, Prentice was glad to see, Old Glory was waving—just as if there were wind blowing it—waving over the words *God Bless America*. And running along the bottom of the page were the words that had been there since the beginning, words that Prentice had first written long ago:

Take Away Hate from Brave Men and You Have Men
Without Faith

Prentice opened his knapsack and placed two new power-pack computer batteries on the table. The boy turned back to the computer and struck a few keys. A series of images rapidly came and went on the screen as he spoke. "It's mighty tough, you know, Colonel, working on batteries, no place to plug in the recharger, no electricity, except for that old generator you've got rigged up, and hooking up to the Internet through a pizza-plate satellite link, using the stuff that Charles gave me, and—well, here it is."

On the monitor came a screen showing words in white against a sky-blue background.

U.S. Air Force Base, Holloman, New Mexico
WARNING

This is a secured node on a classified U.S. Government computer-telecommunication network. *It is not part of the Internet.* If you are an accidental user, CUT OFF NOW!!! If you are an authorized user and proceed beyond this point, you are subject to Federal prosecution. This network contains classified information affecting the national security of the United States within the meaning of the espionage laws, US Code, Title 18, Section 793, 794, and 798. The law prohibits its transmission or the revelation of its contents in any manner to an unauthorized person.

Bobby scrolled down the page to a menu offering several choices. He chose MAINTENANCE SCHEDULE, opened up that sub-directory, and found ROSTER. He searched through the roster for the name of Staff Sergeant William Johnson, found the name and Johnson's identification number. He moved to a file labeled *Personnel* and, using Johnson's identification number, opened up the sergeant's personnel record, complete with photo.

"You're right, sir," Bobby said to Charles. "He does look a lot like you."

"Good boy," the man called Charles said, putting an arm

around Bobby's shoulder. "Now go back to the Maintenance Schedule. When will he be working in the German Tornado area?"

Bobby made several keystrokes, came up with an image that looked like a large calendar, and clicked his computer mouse through the calendar, day by day. When he reached the box labeled *20 March,* information popped out of the box and spread across the screen. "Right," Bobby said. "Johnson's assigned to the Tornado fighters section for 'routine maintenance.'"

"Now go to the next day," Prentice sharply ordered. He did not like being dependent upon anyone or anything, especially a boy.

The March 21 box was labeled: *Air show: Maintenance stand-down except for flight line.*

Prentice and Charles exchanged glances. Prentice smiled.

Prentice spent most of the rest of the time talking to small groups of men under the cottonwoods. He had a vague idea that the FBI had somehow infiltrated the militia. He had no proof, but he and some other militia leaders had met in a motel in Phoenix the week before, and he had been stunned to hear that some of them had actually *talked* to FBI agents! It seemed that the FBI was trying to sort out the "peaceful" militias from the ones that had terrorists in them.

"Bullshit! The FBI is trying to bust us up. Like the Klan," Prentice was saying under the cottonwoods. He had the confident, inflated air he always had. Something was pecking away in his mind, but he never let on. "Terrorists? We're patriots. And don't you forget it!"

In the ranch house, Charles watched Bobby for a while, then went into a small, closetlike compartment that had been built in a corner of the large room. He locked the door behind him and turned on the light over a workbench. The light, powered by a generator, flickered as he began to assemble the items on the workbench circuit boards—AA batteries, a small black box, and coils of puttylike plastic.

Toward the end of the day, Prentice walked out of the ranch house and headed toward the trail out of the canyon. Charles sprinted after him, shouting for him to stop. "I want to get down to the truck while there's a little light, Charles," he said irritably. "What's the problem?"

"No problem," Charles said calmly. "Bobby just down-loaded and printed a photo I thought you'd like to see. In case you have any doubts about what's happening at Holloman."

For years now, Holloman Air Force Base had served as a training site for German fighter jets.

Charles handed Prentice a printout of an American flag and a German flag flying on staffs side by side. "Look what's on the cover of the program they'll be giving away for the air show," Charles said.

The German flag was about a meter higher than the American flag. "Whose damn country is this anyway?" Prentice said, crumpling the photo and throwing it to the ground. "God damn, God damn, God damn," he said, as if he was chanting an oath.

"Be patient, my friend. Be patient," Charles said.

CHAPTER 7

MOSCOW

The Mercedes pulled up to a warehouse at the edge of the airfield. Tago, who had been sitting next to the driver, got out of the car and opened the right passenger door. Berzin stepped out, followed by Wagner. They had barely spoken on the ride from Moscow to the field. Now, emerging from the car, Wagner could not keep his gaze from turning toward the trunk. Cartwright's face flashed through Wagner's memory. Berzin noticed the glance, caught Wagner's eye, and shrugged. Tago unlocked the padlock on a side door, flicked on the lights, and stood back for Berzin and Wagner to enter. Bathed in the flickering batteries of overhead lights were crates neatly stacked in racks along three walls. Wagner could read some of the stenciled labels: *Panasonic TV, JVC Video Cassette Player, Sony X512 Video Cassette Player, Godfather DVD Collection, Samsung DVD Player.*

"This is Tago's little sideline," Berzin said in German, gesturing toward the shelves. "Petty smuggling and thieving. It keeps him happy, gets him his women. I let him keep the profits, as long as he doesn't get greedy."

Berzin preceded Wagner up a spiraling metal staircase that led to a platform built into the girders of the warehouse. From the platform they walked across a catwalk. Three spotlights, switched on by a motion-sensor, shone down on them. Wagner felt that there was at least one sentinel in the dark behind the lights. At the other end of the catwalk was a door that Berzin unlocked with a key on a gold chain strung across his vest.

Wagner stepped into one of the largest rooms he had ever seen, a great bright box at least twenty feet on a side. The light dazzled him for a moment. There seemed to be light everywhere—recessed in the ceiling like a flattened sun, pouring from fixtures on the wall, beamed toward the few articles of furniture in the immense room: a black metal table with a gleaming stainless-steel chess set on it and two high-backed chrome and leather chairs drawn up to it; a black leather sofa, a long glass table flanked by other chrome and leather chairs. Sitting exactly in the middle of the table, with a spotlight of its own, was a tall black vase, containing six white lilies. On the wall before the sofa was a bank of screens, each showing a different, muted image: a grim-faced commentator on CNN, the Bolshoi Ballet on Moscow One, two naked women and a man with a whip, a black-and-white American Western. And surrounding the room, wafting from hidden speakers, was the sound of the Moscow Symphony playing what Wagner recognized as Tchaikovsky's *Romeo and Juliet Fantasy.*

Berzin motioned Wagner to the black metal table. The two men sat opposite each other. Berzin pressed a button on the wall near the table. A white dome lowered from the high ceiling and stopped a few inches over their heads. They were engulfed in silence, except for a faint hum emanating from the dome. "Built by the same engineers who build them for the American CIA," Berzin said. "We can talk here in a kind of privacy provided by few places on this nosy earth."

He ducked out of the dome of silence, opened a cabinet built into the wall, and swung around a shelf that had on it a silver tray bearing an open bottle of chilled vodka, two glasses, and a silver container of caviar, with slices of dark bread and wedges of lemon arrayed around it. He ducked into the dome, pushed the chessboard aside, arranged the tray, poured the vodka, and sat down.

"There is more here in this room than meets the eye," Wagner said.

Berzin threw back his head and laughed. "Privacy and protection, Wolf," he said. "I get them both here. And I try to get them everywhere."

The dome so muted the laugh that it sounded spectral. Wagner felt as if he had entered a ghostly world where Berzin controlled the sound and light, a world that existed unseen beside the world that Wagner had known before he stepped into this room.

Vladimir Pavlovich Berzin was enough of a businessman to know that small talk must precede large talk. He began reminiscing about their past, and Wagner, rushing toward the sanctuary of history, joined in, trading story for story, matching glass for glass. Wagner and Berzin had met when they were boys in East Berlin. Wagner's father was a lawyer; Berzin's father was a Red Army military intelligence officer attached to the Soviet liaison office.

They talked in German, which Berzin spoke like a native. Wagner remembered teaching him some of the more colorful German curses. Wolfgang's father, with the tacit approval of the East German authorities, had set up exchanges of West and East German spies. He had also made a fortune arranging for the migration of East Germans to West Germany in deals paid for by the West German government. As a wily but trusted communist, he added to his fortune by helping to manage the KoKo (Area of Commercial Coordination, or *Bereich kommerzieller Koordinierung*), a secret East German hard-currency operation run, through dummy corporations, for the MfS (Ministerium für Staatssicherheit), the East German Ministry of State Security, the secret police agency better known as the Stasi.

Berzin's father was an "interrogation specialist" for the Glavnoye Razvedyvatelnoye Upravlenie (GRU—Soviet military intelligence). Berzin attended German schools, where he met Wagner.

In those growing-up days, Wagner always felt a Russian shadow over his nationality as a German. His father's work put him in contact with many Soviet officials and he preached (but did not believe) that the future of Germany was in the fraternal hands of the Soviet Union. Wagner sensed his father's cynicism, and knowledge of it grew alongside his own growth into manhood.

Encouraged by his father, Wagner took the awkward Vladimir Pavlovich Berzin under his wing and made him a German kid, and especially a Berlin kid, a boy who knew his way around the alleys and the storm sewers of the city. Berzin became so fluent in Berlin German that his young Soviet comrades often accused Berzin of being more German than Russian. Reports of these accusations went into his father's personnel folder.

His father did not worry. He had enough information on enough GRU officers to keep them in line, he told his son. When Berzin was nine years old, he asked his father if he had ever killed anyone. His father laughed and said that GRU officers do not talk about their work. And then he told a story. He told Berzin that the GRU once ordered a scientist to enter a foreign country illegally, become a naturalized citizen, and gather scientific-technical information for the GRU. "Well," said Berzin's father, "the scientist agreed to the assignment. But he said that he did not know the language of the country he was supposed to go to."

"And the GRU officer assigned to the scientist said, 'Don't worry. Act like a mute.'

" 'And what if I suddenly talk in my sleep?' the scientist asked.

" 'It won't happen,' a GRU official assured him. 'We'll cut your tongue out.' "

Berzin's father was grinning. It was a grin that spread across his face when he told certain kinds of jokes, the kind that Berzin did not know whether to believe. He never asked his father about his work again.

Like many other GRU brats, as the sons of GRU officers called themselves, Berzin had been slated to follow in his father's footsteps. Put on a GRU career path, he graduated from the Military-Diplomatic Academy in Moscow and was completing Spetsnaz training at the Ryazan Higher Airborne School when the breakup of the Soviet Union began. As a

Spetsnaz officer, Berzin had been qualified as a parachutist and scuba diver. He had learned the fine points of bomb making, sabotage, and assassination. One of his instructors at Ryazan had been the leader of the unit assigned by the KGB to assassinate the President of Afghanistan in December 1979, prior to the Soviet invasion.

Berzin and Wagner had parted when Berzin had gone off to Moscow to begin what was to have been an espionage career. They had kept in touch only vaguely, the way boys who grow up together often do when their paths separate in early manhood. They would not hear from each other for months, even years. And then would come a phone call, a meeting at a bar—and they would take up where they had left off.

Soon after the Berlin Wall came down in November 1989, Wagner's father adroitly slipped his family into West Berlin. The elder Wagner's complicity with the East Germans was well known to the West German government, but no legal or political action was taken against him because he had an immense and embarrassing knowledge of clandestine East-West deals. He and his family easily melded into the ranks of the new Germany's rising middle class.

Through his father's connections, Wolfgang Wagner became deeply involved in plans for the reunification of communications between what had been East Germany and West Germany. With the aid of his father's secret private fortune, Wagner quickly rose to become a dominant force in telecommunications in the reunified Germany. He had just been named in the financial press as heir apparent to Baron Frederick von Heltsinger, Germany's most influential financier. Soon after the rumors floated, Berzin reappeared in Wagner's life.

At first, that was what Wagner had expected when, after not hearing from his old friend for some time, Wagner got a call from Berzin, who asked to meet with him to discuss a joint venture. But Wagner always remembered his father's adage that "every coincidence can be tracked back to an inevitability."

An out-of-the-blue "joint venture" and Wagner's imminent relationship with Baron Frederick von Heltsinger had the air of inevitability. When Wagner discreetly checked on his friend in financial circles, he had been amused to learn that his old comrade in communism had, in the new Russia, become a capitalist. But, Wagner's research revealed, Berzin was not merely a capitalist. He controlled financial and industrial firms that employed nearly half a million people. He was a shadowy operator with access to the highest government officials. He was the kind of businessman known as an oligarch in polite society and a leader of the Russian Mafiya among people who had felt the bloody reality of the oligarchs' power.

In a Russia where money meant survival, Berzin had sold his Spetsnaz skills to the highest bidder. He began as a bodyguard for a Mafiya mob in Moscow, vanished into the underworld, and became a legend: the man who could arrange disappearances. It was said that many toughs in the Mafiya would *offer* to sell their mothers, but Berzin would actually do it.

In the new Russia it became more and more difficult to distinguish the Mafiya from the legitimate ruling class. Berzin emerged from the underground and into that fog of crime and capitalism where police looked the other way as merchants paid protection money to "the Roof," as the Mafiya gangs were known. Where politicians financed campaigns with Mafiya money. Where the cunning and the ruthless became the rich and famous. Where the $5,000 Berzin paid for a mistress's designer gown equaled two years' pay for an honest laborer in Moscow.

Berzin, arms flailing, laughing uproariously, had done most of the reminiscing. Wagner smiled and nodded. During a rare lull, Berzin stifled a yawn and tapped a finger on his watch. "I'm not used to such late hours, Wolf," he said. "I have to get some sleep."

"You're tired? Too much playing around with your new girlfriend?" Wagner asked in a mocking tone.

"Girlfriend? I have many," Berzin chortled.

"Yes, but not many like Miya," Wagner teased approvingly. "Miya . . . Takala, isn't that her name? The one you met at the Chancellor's dinner for President Gruchkov last January. Lovely Finnish girl."

Berzin looked surprised. In an instant his expression changed, stern jaw tightening, red spots appearing on his cheeks. "You've been having me followed? Your old friend?"

"No, no. Just something I heard. A rumor."

The explanation rang hollow. Wagner did not traffic in gossip. "Don't bullshit me, Wolfgang," Berzin said menacingly.

"Okay. Okay," Wagner quickly assured him. "You *are* being followed. My information is that your shadows are from the BND," Wagner said, using the German abbreviation for the Bundesnachrichtendienst, Germany's Federal Intelligence Service.

"The BND—but they're just interested in spies and terrorists."

"There's more to the BND than that, my friend. They have struck some kind of deal with some of the anti-hoodlum officers in the FSK, your Russian security service. They're cooperating on combating organized crime. Someone in the BND made an inquiry about you . . . about our long friendship."

"The FSK. I'll put their fucking heads in a basket!" Berzin scoffed. After taking two or three paces away from Wagner, Berzin spun around and moved to within inches of his friend. "I have two assumptions. Either the Bundesnachrichtendienst"— for emphasis, he spoke the name instead of the BND initials— "is making the Vlad–Wolf connection on its own. Or you have been talking to the BND about me."

"That is absurd, Vlad. I have no dealings with the BND."

"No. But your old baron friend does. Frederick von Heltsinger. He's been a contact for the BND ever since Gehlen turned his spy organization over to West Germany after the war. And you *do* know about the BND. Your father worked for Gehlen during the war."

"Gehlen was a traitor," Wagner said, surprised at his loud voice. His East German patriotism flared up from his schoolboy memory. He had been taught that General Reinhardt Gehlen, head of German military intelligence for the Eastern Front during World War II, had fled with all his files to the West as Soviet liberation forces surged into what would become East Germany. Gehlen became the first director of the BND.

"Of course I know about the BND, like Americans know about the CIA or FBI. What I mean is—"

"What you mean," Berzin continued, "is that you are not a BND informant. Yes, I am satisfied that the BND did work out the Vlad–Wolf idea on its own."

"You trust no one," Wagner said. "You never have."

"Not true, Wolf. Not true. I trust you, because I now *know* that I can trust you."

"And now I am to trust a man I saw murder in cold blood." He waited a beat for a response. There was none. "In cold blood," he repeated.

"And?" Berzin asked.

"It has always been this way, Vlad. Distrust. Casual crime. It is in your blood. You have your father's blood."

"To our fathers," Berzin said, raising his glass.

"To our fathers," Wagner repeated, touching his glass to Berzin's. They both drained their glasses.

Berzin quickly refilled the glasses. "And to our past, our days gone by," he said, raising his glass again.

"To the past," Wagner said, draining his glass. "But enough of the past, Vlad. We need to talk about *now*. I'd like to start with the Money Plane. And . . . and about what happened . . . what I saw."

Berzin erupted in another laugh. "I see your old schoolboy conscience is still there," he said. "You are very, very *German*." He dragged out the last word and extended it into the Russian word for German. "*Nothing* happened tonight, old friend. Please do me the honor to remember that: *Nothing* happened."

Tago had entered through an unseen door, replaced the empty bottle of vodka with a full one, and disappeared. Wagner, who tended to become a careful drinker as a night waned, was falling behind in the glass-for-glass contest and curiously feeling more and more sober by the minute.

"*Nothing?* How can murder be nothing?"

"That was not murder, my friend. That was the execution of a traitor."

"I will try to forget what I saw—what you forced me to

see," Wagner said, putting his hand over his glass as Berzin attempted to refill it.

"Tell me about the Money Plane," Wagner said. "All phenomenally legal, I am sure," he said sarcastically.

"Very, very legal," Berzin said. "But probably not known in your high-finance circles."

Berzin then explained, with cool precision, how the Money Plane worked. The cycle begins, he said, when he sells oil on the spot market in Rotterdam. The proceeds from the oil sale are then wired to a bank in Zurich. "When I need, say, one hundred million or so dollars in U.S. currency," Berzin continued, "I have my Moscow bank—and it is *my* bank, though not on the record—I have my bank wire the New York Intercontinental Bank and place an order for one hundred million dollars in U.S. currency. Intercontinental then buys the currency, in new one-hundred-dollar bills, still in the wrappers, from the New York Federal Reserve. At the same time, Intercontinental gets a wire transfer from the Zurich bank. Intercontinental gets a commission on the purchase and on transfer of the currency and makes the arrangements for the currency to be loaded on an aircraft and flown to Moscow. Simple as that."

"But the U.S. Government must—"

"The U.S. Government loves the deal. Wolf, I'm surprised at you. Is finance so musty in Germany that you don't know modern tricks of the trade? Is it the euro that confused you?" He slurred an occasional word but continued, sounding as if he were making a presentation to a bright college freshman.

"It costs the U.S. Treasury about four U.S. pennies to print a one-hundred-dollar bill. Each new one-hundred-dollar bill that flies into Russia is worth ninety-nine dollars and ninety-six cents to the U.S. Treasury because it circulates entirely in Russia. It is essentially a piece of *Russian* currency—and, as you must well know, the only kind of currency that means anything in Russia. I can show you official reports from the U.S. Treasury, from the U.S. State Department, from the Federal Reserve. They all say the same thing: The sale and transfer of U.S. currency to Russia is good for market forces and for relations between the two countries. You know, the usual Washington bullshit. And the U.S. Treasury earns about fifteen *billion* dollars a year selling the dollar abroad. Every dollar that I buy is an interest-free loan to the United States. I *love* the United States."

As Berzin spoke, Tago made another round-trip from the unseen kitchen, this time removing the vodka and glasses and bringing a carafe of coffee, black for both of them. Wagner wondered how Tago managed to be so psychic, and decided there was another button somewhere.

Wagner took a sip of coffee and tried to look Berzin in the eye. The lights had softened around them and Berzin's face was in shadow.

"Thank you, Herr Professor, for the lecture. I knew of such things only theoretically. I feel privileged to have met a master."

Berzin moved the chessboard toward the center of the table and began to fiddle with the chess pieces, moving them randomly.

"Tell me, Wolf, where do you see Germany fifty years from now?" Berzin asked.

"Fifty years?" Wagner started to laugh. "I have no idea where Germany will be in *five* years. You ask me to prognosticate. For a company, yes, but for a country, *my* country? Well, I am no fortune-teller."

Berzin would not be put off. He picked up a black knight from the chessboard and knocked over a white pawn. "No. I am serious. You must think about it," he said. "Where does the future lie? And with whom? Look around the world. What do you see?" He paused for a moment, grasping for an example. "No, look only at America. You have been there many times. So have I. Not as many times as you probably. But I see an America you may not see. And the America I see is a nation in advanced stages of decay, an America that is running around swatting at terrorists and losing its way.

"The moral fiber of the country has rotted. They are consumed with drugs, sex, pleasure, comfort." He used the knight like a little club to knock over a rook. He removed the piece from the board. Using a long match, Berzin went through the ritual of lighting up a Davidoff, a brand of cigar he regularly imported from Cuba, and offered one to Wagner.

"People without vision perish," Berzin said. "The Bible says so, eh? You need to think beyond your next business venture, Wolf. Rewards go to those who dream. I'm talking about big rewards."

"What are you talking about, Berzin? What kind of reward? How big?"

"Right now, Germany and Russia are both too dependent on the United States for our futures. And the United States is too tied to the Israelis. Think about it. This little tail wagging the biggest dog. And we can only sit and watch and complain.

"There is never going to be peace in the Middle East, Wolf. You know that. The Jews and Arabs have been fighting for centuries. They will always be fighting. So many people, so little land, so much hatred. So much for the terrorists to foster. There will always be terrorists bred in those godforsaken countries. And there will be another war in the region, and the Americans will insist that the Germans carry some of the load then, not as you refused to do in Iraq. But Iran and others— they will be better armed and better prepared. The flow of oil will be cut off, and where will the West be then, Wolf?"

Berzin laughed and moved the black king laterally, disdaining the rules of chess as if he were above all rules, moving black and white pieces as if he and his thoughts were the chess game. "You see my queen, Wolf? Think of her as China. See how she is protected?" He placed his black knights and the two white knights on the squares around the black queen. "See how my knights surround her? She could become the power of the new century. Not the United States, and not Japan. America has become too soft, too satisfied with its comforts.

"You see, Wolf, the Americans are not real warriors. Take away their fancy computers, laser toys, satellites, and they are no longer giants."

"They seemed pretty impressive in Afghanistan and Iraq," Wagner shot back.

"Really?" Berzin scoffed. "Impressive because you know

nothing about warfare. Oh, the fireworks may have impressed you. But their technology couldn't protect them against suicide bombers or simple RPGs. Their Black Hawk and Chinook helicopters dropped from the skies like crippled flies.

"What happened then? Their vaunted discipline and morale started to crack. Their political leaders began to beg others to provide assistance, to share their pain," Berzin spat.

"Russia helped them in Afghanistan."

"Afghanistan. The Taliban. A bunch of warlords hiding out in caves!" Berzin exclaimed. "Wolfgang, do you think Afghanistan was a big victory for the United States? A few of Bin Laden's men blow up America's phallic symbols. The stock market plunges. Thousands of companies fold. Congress empties everything but the gold in Fort Knox and wants to give every family an anthrax shot and a gas mask when a few spores showed up in the mail!

"Of course, Russia offered help. A few scraps of intelligence and the consent to operate out of shitholes like Uzbekistan and Tajikistan. But at a price. Everything has a price, eh, Wolfgang? Cover for what we do in Chechnya. Reductions in America's nuclear weapons so they can build their stupid missile-defense shield. We have weapons that no shield can stop."

Berzin smiled tightly. "And what happened when they lost a few thousand of their precious soldiers in their holy war against terrorism? A mere fraction of those killed on American highways each year. The world saw the cracks in the feet of the great colossus. Superman didn't even have enough bulletproof vests in his closets. They couldn't wait to hand the whole mess over to the Iraqis. And now the Shiites are running a theocracy backed up by the Mullahs in Iran. G.I. Joe is on his way out while the blood continues to flow in Baghdad."

Berzin waved his hand dismissively. Then he began tossing the black king up in the air and catching it. "Let me ask you something. Do you see China squandering its time and political capital on the Middle East? Do you think they give a shit whether they lose ten men or ten thousand? Or what the world says when they want to set off another nuclear bomb test?"

"So the future belongs to China?" Wagner pressed.

"Only if we let it."

"Meaning?"

"Germany and Russia. Don't you see? America has given us the opportunity to became great again."

Berzin had been tossing the black king from one hand to the other. Wagner caught it in mid-air and said, "An arrangement interesting in theory." He put the king back in its place. "But it would be impossible to carry out. I know the Chancellor quite well. He is a besieged man. Look at the problems that he's had to cope with. Nationalists on the right, Greens on the left. The American doghouse in the center. People are talking about a breakup of parties so disastrous that German politics could be balkanized."

"This Chancellor would never risk alienating the United States again. Germany needs all the help it can get. And he would be afraid of raising old fears about a powerful Germany. Haven't you noticed? He's even afraid to use the word *Macht*—power is a word England and France don't like to hear because Hitler used it so often."

Berzin sat down, finished his coffee, and shook his head, his thick black hair shimmering in the shadows. "What makes you think that we need the Chancellor or anyone else to agree to anything?" he asked. "It is *business* that drives the politicians today. We are the ones taking the risks, creating the wealth, not bureaucrats in Bonn or the Kremlin—or Beijing or Washington, for that matter. We make the policies and they have to follow. We initiate and they just respond. . . ."

"It is fun to think about such an arrangement, Vlad. But it could never become a reality."

"Never say never."

Berzin moved deftly across the chessboard, picking off the white rooks and knights with surprising speed. As if he were playing a real chess game all this while, he moved two rooks near the white king and shouted, "Checkmate!"

Wagner looked down at the board, startled. Berzin had been playing a game only he understood. Wagner looked up. Berzin was staring directly into his friend's eyes.

"I am going to change myself, Wolf," he said. "That was

my last trip to the Money Plane. I took my last bonus from the Russian bank system. I am going to become a new man. I'm going to be the President of Russia. And you are going to become one of the most powerful men in Germany."

Wagner stared at his old friend as if he was indeed seeing a new man in the making. "You are crazy, Vlad. You talk and perhaps now and then you act—sometimes even with a knife. But this is the real world. It contains, among other obstacles, the United States. You may rave all you want, change yourself all you want. But we could be no match for America."

Berzin stood. Tago silently entered. "You are in for a surprise, Wolfgang." Berzin ostentatiously looked at his watch, a gold-banded Rolex. "I remember what my father once said during a particularly bitter interlude of the Cold War. He said, 'If you want to fuck with eagles, you'd better know how to fly.' Soon, Wolfgang, we will see if America knows how to fly."

CHAPTER 8

HOLLOMAN, NEW MEXICO

"Politicians! They're all whores," Konrad Stiller laughed as he tipped a bottle of Coca-Cola to his lips. Whatever differences existed between Berlin and Washington, they were not shared by members of the military.

Ordinarily, Stiller would have slugged down a cold Heineken with his fellow pilots. But tomorrow he would be putting on a show for all of the VIPs in the audience, and he couldn't afford any nasty hangover to dull his senses. Their aircraft would be traveling at the speed of sound, only inches apart from one another, doing steep climbs and even deeper dives. There would be no margin for error.

"You're right," shouted Captain Ken Dugan. "Maybe one day they'll let you into the real deal. Nothing like havin' a hot sidewinder trying to crawl up your ass."

"And miss!" Stiller parried back. He laughed again, this time more coarsely, trying to camouflage the sting he felt at never having been in real combat. He wanted desperately to engage the enemy, any enemy. Germany had no war heroes. He hoped that one day he might become one.

Well, at least tomorrow those politicians would see that he and his team could hold their own with the best of America's best.

But tonight was a time for him to relax, to watch a movie and enjoy the camaraderie. The film was R-rated. Skin. Action. Violence. A winning combination for hot-blooded jet jocks.

Charles Burkhart shuffled slowly, almost painfully, about the hangars that sheltered the three German aircraft. He wore a gray shirt and gray trousers, the uniform of the local cleaning service that for several years had had the janitorial contract at Holloman.

Charles was a recent hire, but he had quickly gained the trust of the military community. After all, he had served in the Army and, according to his service records, during Operation Desert Storm had suffered serious wounds that earned him a Purple Heart and an honorable discharge. To those who had proudly worn the uniform, he was one of them.

Had anyone been interested, they would have discovered that he had extensive training in demolitions, along with several racially motivated brawls with black soldiers at Fort Bragg.

His routine for cleaning the lavatories and sweeping the floors in the hangars never varied. Arriving at 11 P.M. for the night shift, Charles would move with obvious discomfort through his menial chores, departing at 7 A.M. the next morning. He didn't talk much and never complained. Anyone who knew anything about him attributed his remoteness to his war experience and left him alone.

Tonight was different. Tonight he moved with a swiftness that belied his disability. Knowing that the armed sentries with their leashed German shepherds would be focused on perimeter security, he counted on free access inside the hangar. In the lavatory he changed into coveralls with *JOHNSON* stenciled over the upper left pocket. He clipped on a photo ID tag that would pass casual inspection and headed toward the Tornadoes and moved quickly to the undercarriage of one of them. Stepping onto a small flatbed cart, he reached up with a battery-powered screwdriver and within seconds unscrewed a panel that gave him access to the aircraft's powerful engine. Staff Sergeant William Johnson had left him everything he needed.

It was so simple. A piece of cake. Using a pair of pliers, he crimped the line that ran to the fuel tanks. Next, he wrapped a small amount of a puttylike substance just before the crimp, shaping it so that it was virtually indistinguishable from the line itself. The putty was Czech-made Semtex, the demolitionist's favorite explosive.

Then, he took one of the thin wires and attached it to the filaments protruding from the small flash lightbulb whose glass he had broken. This would serve as his initiator. He implanted the second wire that ran from a cylindrically shaped timing device into the explosive. He set the alarm to go off at precisely 9:15 A.M. the next day. He had witnessed the pilots' dress rehearsal. The Germans were going to be flying in a formation tighter than a gnat's ass. Precision was key to their mission. And to his.

It was going to be quite a show.

Glancing around to be certain that no one had seen him, Charles quickly descended the ladder. He returned to the lavatory, changed back to his work uniform, and resumed his regular tasks, his limp now more exaggerated. By noon tomorrow, he planned to be in Mexico.

Outside, two armed sentries, restraining their German shepherds, roamed the perimeter of the base. The desert air was cool; the moon hung suspended like a dazzling jewel against the vast, velvet breast of the universe. They could hear the raucous banter of the fighter jocks wafting from the clubhouse in the distance.

"Sure sounds like they're having a good time," one of the sentries said.

"Yeah," the other responded wistfully. "Lucky bastards."

"Turn on your TV, folks, and see with your own eyes what I've been telling you," said the gravelly voice on the car radio. "It's on CNN right now: the beginning of Project Global, the plan of the Faustian financial fraternity to turn the U.S. of A. into a United Nations protectorate."

"There he goes again," Major Sally Jackson said, half to herself. "Turn it off, Jeff," she told the driver.

"No, please, Major. Leave it on," Senator Clarence Granon-ski said. "And enlighten me. I've heard a little about this anti-German campaign. But here I am, and I can get it straight from the horse's—from, that is, the public affairs officer of Holloman."

The radio voice continued: "Go ahead. Turn on the TV, and see the German flag flying higher—like I said, higher than Old Glory. And see those Germans goose-stepping around. Well, more on that in a moment. Now hear about the best re-tirement resort these old eyes have ever seen. . . ."

As a commercial came on, the blue Air Force car stopped about fifty feet from the main gate of Holloman Air Force Base. Granonski, Chairman of the Senate Armed Services Committee, turned toward the window. Six sheriffs' deputies in Stetsons and crisp khaki uniforms stood along each side of the road, facing a crowd of about one hundred people, mostly men, also in Stetsons. Here and there was a woman clutching the hand of a child. Some teenagers sat on the hoods of their cars, laughing, talking, and listening to rap radio. Lined up closest to the edges of the road were men and women waving American flags and jiggling their signs in the deputies' faces: *Out Krauts! U.S. Forever. Stop the New World Order!* Through the closed windows and over the whir of air-conditioning came muted shouts and the rhythmic sounds of unfathomable chants.

A CNN cameraman jumped out of the stopped van ahead and filmed the crowd. Granonski, a large man, twisted around to view the image on the small television set on the seat be-tween him and Jackson. For a few moments, the image on the screen mirrored, in black-and-white, the full-color tumult out-side the window. Then the scene switched to the main gate just ahead. In front of the gate was a shoulder-to-shoulder line of Air Force military police, each wearing a white helmet with a transparent riot shield.

Jackson, conscious of Granonski's gaze, tugged at the skirt of her dress uniform. She was glad that her little television set was between her and the VIP guest she was escorting. "The man on the radio," she said, "is the most popular talk-show host in the area. He has been hammering for two solid weeks now. This is his hobbyhorse, and he rides it every day. He says the Germans are here as part of a conspiracy involving the United Nations, the World Bank, and the White House. He's telling his followers—including a lot of armed militia groups—that the conspirators are planning a coup that will put the United Nations in control of the United States. It will start here, with the ceding of New Mexico to the UN."

"Oh, sure. We get that kind of talk from some nuts in New Jersey, too," Granonski said, smiling. "Black helicopters. Tranquilizers in our reservoirs. Anthrax in the cereal. The wonderful world of my New Jersey nuts."

"Around here, Senator, we don't just *hear* the nuts. We have to live with them. The added wrinkle is that the Germans *are* here, and the true believers say that the White House brought in the Germans for the time when UN storm troops round up protesting U.S. citizens and put them in concentration camps. The idea is that American troops might mutiny if they get orders to fire on fellow countrymen. But the Germans will obey the UN orders."

"You know, I've heard that there are people who believe that. But somehow I never believed that those people actually existed."

"Well, they certainly do, Senator; at least around here they do. And not just on the radio. The militias have been overwhelming our Web site, jamming our phone and fax lines, even threatening the German dependents who live off-base. And they've resurrected that snip of tape showing the flags. CNN and MSNBC have both used it two or three times already today, and the ceremonies haven't even started."

"Then it's true what he was saying about the flags—that the German flag flies higher than the American flag?"

"Not true, Senator. If there is anything that a U.S. base knows, it is how to fly the American flag. It is perfectly correct to have the American flag and another nation's flag fly at the same height from side-by-side staffs. But if you photograph the flags from a certain angle, you can make either one look as if it's higher. And, when we had the opening ceremony, that's what happened.

"The flag inspired the local patriots to claim that the Germans were occupying U.S. territory. We started a pretty effective counter–PR campaign, explaining that the deal—providing a sunny-every-day training base to about nine hundred German pilots—would bring about two thousand dependents here and add millions to the local economy. We even adjusted base commissary prices to keep them in line with local stores to undermine claims that the German families were getting cheaper prices than 'real Americans' were paying.

"But, nearly five years later—just when we thought things were calm—the flag image appeared on a local-access cable show and people started talking about it again. They put the image on the Internet, made copies and sent them out by e-mail, and even plastered posters around town. It all seems to have come out of nowhere, just in time for today's event."

"Well," Granonski said, with a theatrical laugh, "you can't blame the commies anymore. Have any suspects?"

"The militias, especially one that calls itself the Scorpions. But the local authorities don't want to touch them."

"And don't expect a Senate investigation, either, Major. Senators have to get elected, just like sheriffs."

The car moved forward. At the gate, the line of MPs opened. A sergeant saluted and waved the vehicle through after Jackson routinely showed her photo ID tag. The car stopped in front of a grandstand under a white canopy. Granonski and Jackson emerged, with Granonski casting an appreciative gaze at Jackson's legs. Brigadier General Paul Desmond stepped forward, heartily shook the senator's hand, and escorted him to a bar set up in back of the grandstand.

At a nod from Granonski, an Air Force mess attendant behind the bar poured a German beer into a stein and presented it to the senator. The airman then poured a Coke for Desmond. On cue, Desmond's chief of staff, a lieutenant colonel, appeared with several German officers, led by Desmond's German counterpart, General Major Erich Königsberg. It was precisely 8:30. Desmond liked to run his base on a strict schedule, to the admiration of his German tenants. Desmond, who spoke passable German, had been given command of the base just before the German Luftwaffe unit was assigned to Holloman.

Desmond was privately celebrating a milestone in that program. Sure, there were public relations problems with the idiots waving signs about the Germans. But Major Jackson had that under control; she had even got Desmond and Königsberg on the *Today Show* early this morning to talk about the first U.S. Air Force–German Luftwaffe Air Show. And she had arranged for all the dignitaries to be here for the show—the German military attaché and his staff, the U.S. Air Force Vice Chief of Staff, the lieutenant governor of New Mexico, a sprinkling of local politicians, and, of course, Granonski, of whom it was often said he had never seen an Air Force appropriation he did not like. The rest of the grandstand was filled with local residents, all carefully selected by Jackson, who made sure that the beneficiaries of the Germans—the store owners, the bankers, the realtors, the restaurateurs—got the best seats.

Desmond had no need to introduce Königsberg to Granonski; the senator had met the German general twice before, when congressional delegations had visited Holloman to observe the U.S.-German operation. Neither Königsberg nor anyone else in uniform was drinking beer. When Granonski joshed him about this, Königsberg frowned briefly. He did not have a firm grasp of American humor, especially the humor of members of Congress. Smiling wanly, he introduced Granonski to the three German pilots who would open the show with three American pilots in a close-formation demonstration.

Granonski mumbled acknowledgment of the introduction as he shook the hands of two of the pilots. When he heard the name of the third pilot, Konrad Stiller, he asked whether Stiller was related to Christoph Stiller, Assistant Director of the BND.

"Your brother has been very helpful on several important matters," Granonski said. "I hope he is well."

"Extremely well, Senator," Stiller said in crisp English. "He never tells me what he does. I am glad to hear that his work is important. When we were boys, all that seemed to be important to him were girls."

Königsberg frowned again, aiming his steely blue eyes at Stiller. No wonder these eternally adolescent fighter pilots never became general officers. "You will be so good as to check your aircraft," Königsberg said in German. Stiller saluted and ambled off.

"Good man," Granonski said. "I like the way he handles himself. I'd bet he'll be a general himself someday."

"Perhaps," Königsberg said.

At 9:10, precisely on time, three silvery German Tornadoes, each carrying a pilot and observer and each bearing the Luftwaffe cross on its wings and fuselage, screeched in swift succession down a runway, their jet blasts becoming shimmering heat waves behind them. An instant later, from another runway, three U.S. Air Force F-117 Nighthawks rose in another tight line. The black, bat-winged Nighthawks flew directly over the Tornadoes, and the six planes closed on one another so that from the grandstand it looked as if one great roaring monster were filling the sky.

In the press section of the grandstand, a CNN cameraman swung his camera around. Jackson, two rows behind the camera, could see the action on the small television set on the seat next to her. She had given CNN an exclusive on live coverage, to the outrage of the local network affiliates. They had boycotted the show. As part of the deal, CNN would make four minutes of the shoot available to the locals, with CNN credit. She knew that they would not be able to resist these great shots of the wild blue yonder.

"There was a time when the Luftwaffe cross would rekindle harsh—even savage—personal memories in U.S. Air Force officers who had fought the Luftwaffe over the skies of Germany," the CNN reporter was saying. "Today, however, World War II is long forgotten. And Germany, which fought side by side with the U.S. in the air over Bosnia, is a staunch NATO ally."

The three Tornadoes pulled away from the Nighthawks and formed a V, drawing together until there were only thin streaks of blue between the planes. The Nighthawks, just as closely spaced in their own V, now nosed into the German V so that, from the ground, the six aircraft again seemed as one. Then, as the double-V climbed, the three German planes zoomed out of the V and, still tightly together, began an inside loop. A sudden hush fell upon the grandstand as every head turned to follow the rapidly curving V. The maneuver left even the CNN reporter speechless. Jackson glanced down at the television set. She was looking at the screen rather than the sky at that moment. So, instead of the reality, she would see an image that would appear on every news show in the world for days to come.

A sudden red cloud burst out of the sky where the lead Tornado had been. A hundredth of a second later, the red cloud bloomed larger, enveloping the other two Tornadoes.

Jackson looked up as the sound and shock wave of the explosion struck the grandstand, rattling the wooden seats and fluttering the flags. The cloud, now black and sending off tendrils of oily smoke, filled an immense patch of sky. Out of the top of the cloud soared two Nighthawks. The third emerged trailing smoke. A Tornado with one wing tumbled out of the blackness, along with bits of aircraft. Another Tornado, its fuselage ripped and blackened, fell straight down. It hit the ground first, sending up a geyser of boiling red and orange. Next came the Tornado that, for a long moment, had seemed to be pulling out of its dive. Its left wingtip struck the sere earth like a blunt knife.

As the Tornado began to cartwheel, the wing crumbled and the fuselage smashed down upon it. The desert suddenly was still. Then the pile of metal exploded, shooting up flames that transformed the wreckage into a pyre.

CHAPTER 9

WASHINGTON

Beginning another day, Santini wasn't sure why he didn't feel right. He had slept well enough. Four and a half hours wasn't long, but it was a deeper sleep than usual. No call had come through from the Pentagon, alerting him to another overnight tragedy. He had hit the gym in his condo for an hour, cruising through his routine of weight lifting and aerobic exercises. Showered, dressed, coffeed, and on his way to the car. But he was just out of sorts. A small shadow was hanging on the edge of his mind, and it wouldn't go away.

The world had grown far more complicated and dangerous since Santini had left the Senate. Once during an interview with a reporter from *The Washington Post,* he mused that Americans might one day come to rue the breakup of the Soviet Union. The reporter did not share Santini's foreboding. The article began: "Senate Intelligence Chairman Nostalgic for the Cold War." It went downhill from there. But, of course, that's precisely where the world seemed to be heading.

Not entirely, to be sure. The United States still held on to the title of Superpower, with an annual military budget climbing toward $500 billion. Economically and culturally, it was unmatched in the global marketplace. NATO membership was spreading like ink on tissue paper. And the seeds of democracy had taken root in Ukraine, Georgia, South America, and parts of central Asia, shallow as those roots were. But the

roots of ethnic and religious-inspired hatreds were far deeper
and more dangerous. Iraq, Bosnia, Kosovo, Chechnya, Afghanistan, India, Pakistan, the Philippines, Indonesia. And
now it was a race against the clock to prevent the haters from
getting their hands on a ball of plutonium or a vial of smallpox or Ebola. Sooner or later, the fanatics would score again,
and the only question would be: How big? There were tons of
highly enriched uranium and plutonium stored in the former
Soviet Union. Most of it secured only by a chain-link fence
and possibly a padlock. Nuclear terrorism was only a bolt-
cutter away. Or maybe some cleaning outfit hired to sweep
Washington's underground Metro stops would release a
deadly gas or virus from an aerosol can that would inflict
thousands of casualties in a matter of a few hours.

The Department of Homeland Security was issuing cover-
its-ass warnings with the frequency of weather reports.
Doomsday was coming! There was a time when the butterfly
nets would come out for street-corner prophets and toss them
in loony bins for screaming that the end was near. Now, it was
the government telling the American people that catastrophe
was imminent, but they should pucker up and be sure to take
their MasterCards and Visas to the mega shopping malls. The
world had gone mad.

At his desk, Santini had to push back the dark clouds that
seemed to envelop him when he least expected it. His soul always seemed half-full of Irish gloom. Or was it Italian fatal-
ism? He could never be sure. The mood was always
momentary, lingering just long enough until his instinct for
survival would fight back, refusing to give ground to the grav-
itational pull of the negative.

He focused on his job, began methodically going through
the pile of papers. Not a damn day could pass without something going down. A collision at sea. A supersonic fighter
nearly ramming a commercial jumbo jet. An alleged rape of a
sixteen-year-old in Okinawa. A senator on the line about a
black Marine punching out some rednecks in a North Carolina bar. The Inspector General at the Transportation Secu-

rity Administration had found that TSA's background checks were sloppy. The policy of allowing foreign nationals, particularly those of Arab descent, to operate screening and detection equipment at airports and seaports is a vulnerability that could be exploited by al Qaeda and other terrorist groups. . . .

The door to his office flew open and Scott O'Neill, a three-star admiral who served as Santini's senior military adviser, burst in. "Turn on the television," he said, without his usual *sir.*

Santini spun around and aimed the remote at one of the monitors behind his desk. O'Neill stood next to it, watching the screen as he spoke.

"Three German jets just exploded in mid-air out at Holloman Air Force Base."

"What do you mean, 'exploded'?"

On-screen, as if in answer, Santini saw the red bursts that had been aircraft and men.

"We don't know exactly what happened," O'Neill replied. "Might be some malfunction with wiring and fuel systems."

"With *three* aircraft at the same time? Bullshit, Scott. What 'or else' have you got?"

"Or else, sir, it is more likely a case of deliberate sabotage."

"Terrorism?"

"Yes, sir."

"How in hell could terrorists get into Holloman?"

"Don't know, Mr. Secretary."

"Well, *find out,*" Santini said, his gaze fixed on the screen.

An hour later, O'Neill entered again, this time preceded by an intercom warning. Santini motioned him to a chair, but O'Neill hesitated, as if he had to remain standing to give his message.

"It's about Holloman, sir. We have learned about something I wanted to tell you personally." O'Neill paused a beat, as if it might soften the impact of what he was about to pass on. "Your friend Christoph Stiller at the German BND?"

"Yes?" Santini's tone made it clear he was not asking a question but telling O'Neill to get on with it.

"Stiller's younger brother, Konrad, was one of the pilots killed."

Santini's shoulders tensed, then shrank, as if the weight of what O'Neill had just said had forced all of the air out of his lungs.

"Has Christoph been notified yet?"

O'Neill nodded. "As soon as investigators verified that there were no survivors."

"Okay, Scott. Make sure that I get a call placed to him as soon as I get back from the White House."

"Got it, sir," O'Neill said, his voice snapping a smart salute.

As soon as O'Neill left, Santini buzzed for Margie. "One question, Margie."

"And what is that, Mr. Secretary?"

"What do you know about this meeting in the Situation Room? It wasn't on the regular meeting agenda."

"My understanding is that Mr. Praeger called it and it has to do with Russian money laundering."

"Money laundering? What the hell does DOD have to do with that? That's Justice and FBI business."

"As they say, Mr. Secretary, that's above my pay grade."

CHAPTER 10

BERLIN

Chancellor Klaus Kiepler was more agitated than usual today. Ordinarily, the tall, lean former mayor of Berlin maintained an air of absolute confidence. That had been his most compelling feature. Yes, all the women loved his long, salt-and-pepper gray hair that he let curl rakishly over his shirt collar, and rumors of his past amorous adventures only heightened his allure. But it was his gift at oratory, the ability to reach deep down into his soul and stir the passions of his people, that gave them hope that life was going to get better for them and their children.

But that, of course, was the face he wore for the public. Visionary. Man in charge. The one who would finally release the German people from the chains of guilt that they had been forced to wear for so long and allow them to assume their rightful place in the new century. But words were not deeds. The rhetoric had helped vault him into office; the reality was pulling him down.

While serving as the leader of Germany's most dynamic city, he had watched a disaster unfold as Eva von Merz and Manfred Breuer tried to cobble together a "grand coalition" to hold on to power. To him it was utter nonsense. A racehorse designed in the back rooms of the Bundestag by a committee predictably had produced a three-legged camel. A right-of-center chancellor chained to a left-of-center cabinet trying to pull a social welfare wagon out of a ditch! He knew it was doomed to fail from the beginning.

When new elections were called, Kiepler had seized the moment. He made thunderous speeches pointing to the folly of what the German people had done to themselves, calling for sacrifice and discipline. He wanted Germany to ride a tiger into the future. But he was handed the reins to the deformed camel.

Kiepler looked at the bust of Bismarck that sat on the credenza behind his desk. He stifled an ironic laugh. Bismarck, the Iron Chancellor, had been his inspiration. A man of strategic genius and absolute ruthlessness. How vain and foolish to think that he could hope to emulate Bismarck's manipulative skills! He stood up and shoved his chair away from the desk, a massive mahogany structure whose front bore seven niches in which stood the carved figures of seven Teutonic Knights, each wearing the white habit with a black cross granted the Teutonic Knights by Pope Innocent III in 1205. The white coverlet over the armor of each carved knight was made of ivory and ebony. The desk was built in 1834, to mark the Emperor's decree reestablishing the Order of Teutonic Knights. The cabinetmakers who had built the desk traced back to the Middle Ages and to the origins of Kiepler's own family. When the Habsburg Empire collapsed in 1918, the desk passed from its noble owner to Kiepler's grandfather, a grandson of one of the cabinetmakers. Kiepler often told the story of the desk to instill in the listener how deep were the German roots of the cabinetmaker's great-great-grandson, now the Chancellor of the Republic of Germany.

He paced back and forth in front of the gas fire that hissed behind the curtain of lacelike metal that was supposed to protect him from imaginary sparks. Fake logs. *How appropriate,* he mused.

His poll numbers were blasted all over *Der Spiegel,* the magazine with the largest circulation in Germany. Leaks had been springing out of the Bundestag like water out of a perforated paper cup. Military spending had been down so far and for so long that even Luxembourg had a greater percentage of

GDP committed to defense. Luxembourg! Christ, they barely had a police force! But the comparison was beginning to stick and even the Greens were finally coming to realize that Germany was rapidly becoming a laughingstock throughout Europe. His political enemies were growing bolder each day, inspired by the caustic editorial cartoons and late-night television comedians.

His campaign promises were turning to ashes. But what was he to do? He was a captive of past mistakes. The legendary German discipline had evaporated in the European Union's grand schemes. Exports were starting to pick up, but the economy was still sputtering along. Unemployment stuck at levels that were once unimaginable.

A soft knock on his door interrupted the cascade of problems that had come to preoccupy him these days. Elke, a slim and attractive woman who had been his personal secretary since his days as mayor, entered the room. She carried a large sheaf of papers that were dressed in a handsome gold-leafed leather case, a gift from Morocco's King Mohammed VI. "These need to be signed today," she said, placing them on the right corner of his desk. "And Minister Joffe has arrived. Shall I send him in?"

Kiepler nodded, relieved to be rescued from his brooding thoughts. As Gunter Joffe entered the room, Kiepler stood up to greet his Minister of Defense. The two men had served together in the German Army and later in the Bundestag. Both were committed to revitalizing the German military and both suffered the same frustration and disappointment that public opinion still favored more spending for health and social welfare programs instead. These priorities, along with the full integration of all of the European countries, left little for military modernization on the scale Kiepler envisaged.

Kiepler motioned Joffe to the leather chair and couch away from the desk. "Come, Gunter," he said, draping his arm around Joffe's shoulder. "Let's sit over here so we can be more comfortable." As the two men arranged themselves around an ornately carved coffee table, the office door opened and a waiter dressed in dark slacks and white jacket entered.

He placed a coffee decanter, cups, and a tray of small cakes on the table, and silently exited the room.

"One sugar or two?" Kiepler asked Joffe. "After all these years, Gunter, I can never seem to remember."

"You have much more important things to remember, Klaus." In private the two men dropped all formalities of their titles. "One will do," Joffe said, picking up one of the hard, sugared crumpets, and holding it aloft. "I don't want to over-dose so early in the morning."

"Ah," Kiepler said, limiting himself to the same. "Tell me, Gunter, any more news on what happened at Holloman?"

"Very little and none of it good. One body—Oberleutnant Stiller's body—is destroyed beyond recognition. So was his crewman. They did not eject. There is nothing left to them. Two other bodies—those of Leutnant Frauwirth and his crew-man, Hans Gerhardt—were found some distance away. Their parachutes opened, but apparently not in time. The bodies from the third aircraft have not yet been found. The search has been extended and the Air Force officers believe it is only a matter of time. Still, even if the bodies are found they cannot be returned immediately."

"Why is that?"

"It is a technical—a legal problem," Joffe said. "There is a New Mexico officer of the law, a coroner. The bodies were found beyond the boundaries of the base, technically taking the case out of the hands of Federal authorities. The coroner will not release the bodies pending autopsies. This may be difficult. I'm told it may take a couple of weeks or more but have been assured that ultimately the Federal officials will be in charge."

"I will speak to our ambassador or, better yet, to President Jefferson again. Surely he can speed things up," Kiepler said. He set his coffee cup on the table and paused as if to indicate that the conversation was over. But Kiepler suddenly spoke again. "Can this be some attempt at a cover-up? Are the Americans playing games with us?"

"It's possible, Klaus. But I remember reading that some-thing like this happened after the assassination of President

Kennedy. A minor functionary in Texas held up the moving of the body to Washington."

"But, Gunter, these are Germans, not Americans. The families want what remains of their sons back now, not next month!"

Kiepler reached up with both hands to massage his temples. "I called the White House yesterday and talked directly with President Jefferson. You know, he still insists on calling it an 'accident.' What do you think, Gunter? What intelligence do we have?"

"Our people are convinced it was no *accident*. Those were our very best fighter pilots. Our Top Guns, as the Americans say. There was absolutely no way they could have collided with each other. The American press has reported that the lead aircraft exploded and sent flames and fragments into the two that were flying in tight formation."

"Is it possible that an engine exploded, a fuel line snapped? These were our newest aircraft."

"Anything is possible, Klaus. Even with those coming right off the assembly line." Joffe paused to sip his coffee. "We just don't know at this point, but my gut tells me it was sabotage. An act of terror directed at us."

"Why against us?" Kiepler asked. "We did not bomb Afghanistan or Iraq. We are not acting like some Schwarzenegger Terminator out to hunt down and kill every radical Islamist in the world. Why us?"

"We have done virtually everything the Americans have asked of us. Intelligence sharing. Peacekeeping, troops in Afghanistan. . . . Perhaps we are too accommodating, Klaus. Perhaps we are seen by America's enemies as conspiring with them. Or, worse, that we, like the British, are simply their lapdogs." Joffe caught himself, shutting down a tirade that was starting to spill out.

"It's all right, Gunter. I'm not offended," Kiepler said, patting Joffe on the knee. "I've seen the polls, too. Anti-American sentiment is spreading everywhere, and Germany is no exception."

"I'm sorry, Klaus, it's just that it's getting harder and harder to deal with them. You know how little I think of our French friends. But they've been telling us for years about the dangers of a 'hyperpower' straddling the world and the need to form coalitions to constrain it. I hate to concede they may be right. The Americans have declared us to be irrelevant to their holy war against terrorism. They are the true warriors and we are the peacekeepers. We are the ones they want to clean up the mess they leave after they have unleashed all of their exotic weapons, killing innocent civilians they consider of no more value than dogs! As if we are street sweepers following a parade of elephants. Germany deserves better." Joffe's voice dropped off, his frustration finally dissipated.

For a long moment, Chancellor Kiepler said nothing. He did not mention to Gunter that part of his conversation with Jefferson where he complained that the United States had undermined his attempt to have Germany become a permanent member of the United Nations Security Council. America, for what Jefferson had described as the need for "geographical balance," had decided to support India's effort over Germany's. Was it just more payback for Germany's position against preemptive wars? Just how much more did those in the White House think he could swallow?

Finally, he stood up, signaling that the meeting had come to an end. "You're right, Gunter," he said. "We need to get off their lap. I will call Jefferson again. We need to know what happened. They will never admit that their homeland security apparatus failed again. They will call it pilot error. We don't have to take it anymore."

CHAPTER 11

WASHINGTON

When his limousine stopped at the lower level of the West Wing entrance, Santini got out and, accompanied by a security man, walked under a canopy to the entrance.

Santini stepped into a small vestibule and through another set of doors, where a uniformed Secret Service guard nodded. By the rules and traditions of White House security, Cabinet members were not required to show their photo identification badges. Santini walked past the guard down a short corridor whose walls were lined with official White House photos showing the most recent activities of President Bradford Jefferson. On Santini's left was an elevator. He walked a few steps farther and went down a short staircase to a door into the Situation Room. A Navy lieutenant commander whose gold shoulder cords of the aiguillette marked him as an aide stood, saluted, and motioned to the Marine guard, who opened the door and stood aside for Santini to enter.

The Situation Room. Presumed to be as large as an auditorium, filled with ten-foot-high plasma screens that could zoom in on a worm's ass through the lens of ten-mile-high satellites. A fiction. It was just large enough to accommodate a small, rectangular conference table, around which ten people could find low black-leather seats. More befitting an upstart boutique law firm than the most powerful nation in the world.

Joseph Praeger, the President's National Security Adviser, sat at the head of the table, the power seat, telling all involved that although he was an unconfirmed adviser to the President and not a Cabinet officer, this was his room and they were mere subordinates here.

This wasn't the way it was supposed to work. Praeger was a coordinator, not a decision or policy maker. His role was to reconcile the positions and recommendations of the Cabinet members. Discuss them at length to develop a solid consensus on any given issue so that the President wouldn't have to be a daily referee between State, Defense, Treasury, and Justice. The President was free to accept, reject, or change their recommendations. But he rarely questioned or rejected a unanimous Cabinet position.

When Praeger could not get agreement, then he was duty bound to arrange for the Cabinet members to meet with the President so that they could try to persuade him of the merits of their case. Creighton Ford, as Director of National Intelligence, had presented Praeger with a new problem in the algebra of White House power. Ford, the ultimate editor of the President's Daily Brief, wielded enormous influence. His intelligence, served up red-hot, often overshadowed or even contradicted the more measured information coming from Santini or Secretary of State Douglas Palmer. And Ford met with the President one-on-one more than any other Cabinet member.

Praeger had realized Ford's unique status, of course, and had made him a special ally. Prager and Ford, like members of the same secret fraternity, recognized each other's thirst for power-through-knowledge. Rather than sparring for dominance, they allied, Praeger showing no resentment for Ford's access to the President and Ford showing generosity toward Praeger by bestowing on him tidbits of intelligence that bolstered Prager's policy recommendations.

Santini did his best to be a team player. But loyalty had its limits. Today Santini wasn't going to sign off on the State Department's determination to send American soldiers into Israel as peacekeepers.

"Let the Europeans pick up the load just once," Santini demanded, pounding the table to tell his NSC nemesis that he was going to take this to the President.

Praeger, his thin forehead and receding hairline giving him a hard, hatchet-faced appearance, cautioned Santini to ease off. "Let's not let emotion cloud judgment here, gentlemen. We're all supposed to be adults. So let's put away the temper tantrums and get down to the business that we were all hired to conduct." It was a condescending and phony ploy on his part. He almost always went off like a Roman candle when he didn't get his way. Now, he was trying to come off as a source of pure reason.

"I got more than a little excited," said Santini, "when President Jefferson told the American people during the campaign that a new team was coming to the rescue. That our troops were being squandered on wasteful peacekeeping missions. How many times did we hear him on the campaign trail tell the American people, 'Our soldiers are not trained to be cops. They're trained to kill those who are trying to kill us.' You are going to drive them out of the service. Recruitment is down. Retention is down. For Christ's sake, when do they get a break?"

"Don't pull that sanctimonious stuff with us, Santini!" Praeger's bubble had just been popped. "You don't make the decisions around here. Last time I checked, only the President gets to do that. Maybe you failed your course in Constitutional law. Maybe you just think you can continue to play Lone Ranger for your wussies back at the Pentagon. This is supposed to be a team you signed onto. No one forced you to take the job—"

"Those wussies you're talking about put it on the line twenty-four and seven so you can sit here sucking your thumb, trying to convince everyone you're some kind of strategic genius."

"Gentlemen." The baritone voice of the Secretary of State cut off the verbal brawl that was starting to get out of hand. Douglas Palmer, ever the elegantly appointed patrician with his hand-tailored English suits and Turnbull & Asser monogrammed shirts, rose from his chair, moved to a small table near the entrance to the room, and reached for a coffee cup. "Joe is right, Michael; we have serious issues that have to be discussed seriously."

"Very noble of you, Douglas," Santini shot back. "Since State is trying to get us committed to becoming fodder for the Hamas and Hezbolla jihad bombers."

"I don't like the prospect of putting GIs over there any more than you do. I once wore the same proud uniform that you did, Michael."

"As I recall, you wore the same proud uniform sitting behind a typewriter in Hawaii. What was your MOS? Journalist? Propagandist?"

Palmer ignored Santini's attempt to bait him. "I'm truly sorry about what happened to you in Vietnam, Michael," he said, not sounding very sorry.

While the word game was going on, DNI Creighton Ford, Director of the CIA Jack Pelky, and Attorney General Gregory Fairbanks entered the room. Next to General Whittier, Chairman of the Joint Chiefs, sat Treasury Secretary Daniel Gleason.

Santini noticed that there were FBI blue folders in front of every place. Pelky took the seat next to Santini. He leaned toward Pelky and whispered, "What the hell is this about?"

"Some money-laundering deal, from what I got from McConnell."

"Well, maybe your shop is looking at that kind of stuff, but I've got a lot of different issues on my plate. Like a few Special Forces in Iran," Santini said, his voice loud enough to produce an inquiring look from Fairbanks across the table. "What the hell am *I* doing here?"

"Michael!" Fairbanks called in his high-pitched, faintly British accent, a product of his lengthy sojourn at Oxford on a Fulbright. "Good morning. Looking grouchy as usual. Smile! We have a visitor."

Just then, Frank McConnell, the voluble FBI Director, swept into the Situation Room escorting a young woman, his hand gently nestled into the small of her back.

When Santini saw the woman he flinched.

"Gentlemen," McConnell said. "Let me introduce to you Inspector Leslie Knowles. She will be presenting a brief which represents the Bureau's year-long investigation into the money-laundering activities of Russian criminal groups operating out of New York and Moscow."

Everyone in the room responded with silent nods of welcome to Knowles as she slipped into the remaining chair at the conference table, quickly unzipping a leather briefcase and spreading out a sheaf of papers on the table.

Today Leslie Knowles looked all prim and proper, upright and professional, the classic agent that the Bureau loved to advertise during their recruitment drives. But that's not how Santini remembered her the first and only time they were together, more than a year ago.

They had met at an event hosted by the Council on Foreign Relations. At the time, she was a member of an FBI counternarcotics task force. The Council's Director, Richard Nash, had asked her to deliver a lecture on criminal organizations operating in the greater New York area.

Santini was immediately attracted to her. Leslie, he judged, was cut from a different mold than most FBI agents. Slim, athletic-looking, she dressed in the type of casually elegant outfit that was the hallmark of Ralph Lauren. The gold Cartier Panther watch that graced her left wrist told Santini something else. Either she had means beyond her government salary or she was living beyond her means. He doubted the latter possibility. She would have been waving a bright red cape in front of the Bureau's counterintelligence bulls. Then again, how many times had they whistled past the obvious?

Whatever the case, the package she presented, along with her obvious intelligence, was magnetic.

Following her extended question and answer session with Wall Street bankers and media elite from *Time* magazine and *The New York Times,* Santini managed to engage her in small talk.

After ten minutes or more of polite conversation, Santini

detected that she might be interested in something more than talk and invited her to join him for dinner at Nobu, one of New York's fashionable restaurants that attracted and catered to celebrities. Ordinarily, Nobu required reservations at least a week in advance. But Santini was a friend of Robert De Niro, one of the restaurant's owners. And if you knew De Niro, well, you didn't need reservations.

What Santini had planned to be a quick dinner turned out to be a long night over tall drinks at his apartment at the River House. Leslie, contrary to her reserved appearance, was surprisingly uninhibited. There was no lovemaking that night, but there was the hint that future encounters could be very rewarding. But nothing came of it. No follow-up attempts by him. No calls or letters from her. Nothing.

Which suited Santini just fine. After a bad marriage and a nasty divorce, he had no appetite for long-term companionship or commitments. Besides, there was only one woman in the world that totally consumed his thoughts: Elena. And she would always remain a ghost, a mirage, a vision that taunted him during sleepless nights. A love lost before it was ever gained.

He parted company with Leslie that night on friendly enough terms. If she bore him any ill will, she failed to reveal any hint of it as he sat across from her today. She looked at him with cool professionalism, as if she were seeing him for the first time. Santini decided that it would be wise for him to make as little eye contact with her as possible.

Still, he found it curious that Leslie had made no effort to contact him again. Maybe his charm was slipping. Or, the thought occurred to him, that she might have been on a mission for the Bureau, that he was being tested. But that didn't make any sense. He no longer had access to classified information. And none of his business activities could possibly be of interest to Justice or the FBI. Maybe it wasn't anything so nefarious. Just a case that she was waiting for Santini to call her. A matter of protocol or pride.

"Let's get started," Praeger growled, glancing at his watch. "I've taken your word that what you've got is worthy of presenting"—he looked at Knowles for an instant—"at this level. I have exactly eighteen minutes." He waited a moment, frowned, and continued. "Well, Greg?"

Fairbanks nodded. "You all have in front of you Mac's excellent report on what's going on with the bad guys in Russia."

Santini glanced down at the report at his place. It was standard FBI: blue cover, FBI seal, the *TOP SECRET* stamp, and title: *Rogue State Crime*. He flipped it open and skimmed through pages. Some words and phrases caught his eye . . . *Chinese missiles* . . . *Russian helicopters* . . . A map of the United States showing FBI investigations of the Russian Mafiya in Boston, New York, Newark, Philadelphia, Los Angeles, Miami, and several other U.S. cities.

Fairbanks droned on, using some of the words that Santini had been glancing at. He hated to agree with Praeger, but this was not Cabinet-level material. "So, without further ado, I'd like to turn to FBI Director McConnell," Fairbanks said, and sat down. He patted Leslie Knowles on the arm, and Santini could detect a quick frown crossing her unfurrowed, honey-brown brow.

McConnell, who had been chief of police in Boston before becoming FBI Director, stood to speak. Fairbanks once told Santini there was only one thing you had to know about McConnell: The gift he was given at his Boston farewell dinner was a black sweatshirt that said *FBI* on the back and *Ready, Fire, Aim* on the front.

McConnell turned his square jaw toward Praeger and said, "The Attorney General was giving you his word on the basis of my word, Joe. So if you wind up thinking this is a waste of time, blame me." He looked across the table at Santini. "And you'll soon see why you're invited, Michael."

McConnell motioned toward Leslie Knowles. "Inspector Knowles will do the talking for the Bureau. She's worked all the major divisions, done some nice undercover work that only a few people know about. She's one of our very, very best. One of her previous assignments was FBI legal attaché in Moscow, where she was nearly assassinated—but she shot a couple of the bad guys with forehead bull's-eyes. It was all jointly hushed up by the State Department and the Russian Foreign Ministry, which politely asked that she be shipped home. Now she's running what the people at headquarters like to call the X Files Office because it's so secret that even its name is classified. It's the Office of Rogue State Crime, and one reason we have to keep it secret is so people won't think we're straying onto Doug Palmer's turf." The note-taker behind the Secretary of State started scribbling frantically.

McConnell resumed his formal briefing-the-Cabinet voice, saying, "I have asked Inspector Knowles to deliver this at a Cabinet level because I believe that the activities of Russian organized crime, particularly the group known as 'the Orchard,' represent a multi-faceted threat to U.S. national security, even at a time when our principal focus is on al Qaeda and international terrorism. The Orchard operates in a country that on the surface is friendly to the United States, but one in which there is a vast criminal element—the Mafiya, if you will—that controls virtually every aspect of Russian life.

"The Orchard lives up to its name. It comes from a line in Chekhov's play *The Cherry Orchard*: 'All Russia is our orchard.' Its tentacles reach across the country and across the world. The Orchard is involved in alien smuggling, bank fraud, drug trafficking, extortion, the manufacturing of fraudulent documents, prostitution. And now, Michael, we get to the reason you are here. We believe that the Orchard is increasingly getting involved in acting as a supplier for terrorists by trafficking in materials for nuclear weapons, including triggering devices and heavy water." McConnell turned toward Knowles. "Okay, Leslie. Let's hear it."

Leslie Knowles did not stand. She picked up a remote control device and clicked it. A map of the world appeared on the large monitor. Santini already admired her. He had seen four-star generals cuss and turn florid trying to make that gadget work. "Rogue State Crime centers cover the globe," she said. Her voice was firm, with the faintest touch of South Carolina tideland, Santini guessed. Red dots on the map showed Moscow, St. Petersburg, Kabul, Hong Kong, Taipei, Bangkok,

Yunnan, Caracas, Bogotá. *No surprise there,* Santini thought. *But Frankfurt, London, Vancouver, Toronto, New York City, Miami, Los Angeles?*

Knowles noticed Santini's frown. "We're not saying Germany, Canada, and America are rogue states. Rogue states export crime and criminals just the way legitimate states export legitimate products," she said. "Russian and Chinese rogue state criminals build up connections in the large Chinese populations in Vancouver, Toronto, and New York. You'll see that developed in the report we distributed here.

"And now, Secretary Santini, as Director McConnell said, we get to the reason you are here. The Rogue Office—in conversations at the Bureau we just call it 'the Office'—got its start through the Bureau's legal attaché program. As you know, the FBI has agents stationed at many U.S. embassies. The idea was that we would work with the host nation's investigative organizations on cases that involved both the host country and the United States. But I soon learned—as Director McConnell mentioned, I had a tour in Moscow—that many times there was no way to tell a law-enforcement officer from a member of the Russian Mafiya. Sometimes, in fact, they were both.

"When I got back to Washington, after the incident that Director McConnell referred to, I suggested that the U.S. Government find a way to deal with this plague. Through the efforts of National Security Adviser Praeger, a classified Presidential Directive was issued, creating the Office, which is staffed by representatives from State, Justice, and the CIA, with the FBI acting as the lead agency. The Office operates independently of, but cooperates fully with, the DNI's National Counterintelligence Executive."

Santini stared at Knowles with a look of surprise. Doug Palmer had sent a directive around saying that State would no longer refer to certain countries as "rogue states." Now, according to Palmer, they were supposed to be "nations of interest." So now Praeger and McConnell were sticking with "rogue." Another Praeger dart into Palmer.

"More than seven billion dollars has left Russia illegally in the past twelve months alone," Knowles continued, "flowing primarily through front-company accounts at the Intercontinental Bank of New York. The money is being washed to mask criminal enterprises and to evade Russian taxes and customs duties. The bank even handled the transmission of a five-hundred-thousand-dollar ransom payment to Russian Mafiya gangsters who had kidnapped a Moscow banker. They killed him after they got the money—in freshly minted one-hundred-dollar U.S. bills, by the way. That money came through a transaction that one of our snitches in Moscow helped us track."

"Your *what*?" Pelky asked. Before Knowles could answer, Pelky continued. "As I understand the FBI–CIA agreement on legal attachés, we do the spying and you do the lawyering. Why the hell don't I know about this?"

"I am sure, Director Pelky," Knowles calmly replied, "that you will find a reference to this case, code-named Grapple, in one of your Moscow station chief's recent cables. I'm afraid he doesn't think much of this case, and so it's probably buried too deep for you to notice. The snitch, or, if you prefer, informant, was killed by a car bomb a week after giving us the name of the New York contact."

She turned from Pelky and went on with her briefing. "As I was saying, we tracked the transaction to Intercontinental and found that the Mafiya's money handler was Arthur C. Cartwright, an executive vice president of Intercontinental. Mr. Cartwright looked at the case we had against him and the bank—charges included aiding terrorists, aiding criminal activity, operating an illegal money-transmission business, and tax evasion—and he agreed to cooperate with us. In exchange for a guarantee of entry into the federal witness protection program, Mr. Cartwright agreed to testify at a trial of New York's Mafiya boss, and also to tell us what he knew about the money-laundering operations in Russia.

"While I was in Moscow, I became aware that the Mafiya— the Russians have rather proudly appropriated the name, with a Russian pronunciation—had close ties to a banking and oil empire controlled by Vladimir Pavlovich Berzin, a prominent

Russian financier and close friend of President Yuri
Gruchkov, who was recently killed in a helicopter crash.
Berzin was one of the few oligarchs that Gruchkov had not ar-
rested and placed in prison. Perhaps because he feared
Berzin's ties to the FSK, Russia's Foreign Intelligence Service. Berzin, we believe, is the hidden director of the Orchard.
The visible head, or street boss, is a Chechen named Tago, a
survivor of the gang wars of the 1990s. In the distributed report, only Tago's name is listed.

"We've connected Berzin with a few attempts in the past to
get nuclear substances out of Russia. Nothing happened,
thank God, and so not too many people know about it. A radioactive container with strontium 90 in Kiev, a pound of low-
enriched uranium 235 fuel pellets in Georgia, some
radioactive material that a Russian Army officer stole from
the Baikonur space center in Kazakhstan. Small-time stuff by
the small fry. We have an idea that Berzin was just warming
up. His guys—many of them ex-officers or deserters—have
been spotted in Petropavlosk, trolling for uranium and maybe
missiles from those Pacific Fleet nuclear submarines that are
rusting at the dock."

Santini noticed Pelky and Praeger shift simultaneously
from being bored and visibly detached to being abruptly
aware of what Knowles was saying.

Knowles clicked the remote and a man's face flashed on the
screen. High cheekbones and thin lips made the face seem
long. The eyes were dark and half-lidded. The hair was dark
brown and combed back without a part. The man was seated
at what looked like a restaurant table. There was an empty
gold-rimmed dinner plate and silverware arrayed before him
on a creamy white tablecloth. At his right, her face turned
away from the camera and her long blond hair caught
swirling, was a woman whose silvery dress framed perfect
breasts, neck, and shoulders. A wine bottle and a cut-crystal
glass stood to his left, at the edge of the image, which had the
furtive, slightly blurred look of a surveillance photo.

"Vladimir Pavlovich Berzin," Knowles said. "From this
photo, Mr. Cartwright identified Berzin as the man who met

what they called the New York-to-Moscow Money Plane."
She briefly described the way Cartwright and Berzin used the
Money Plane. "Cartwright was on a flight that arrived in
Moscow on March 19. He did not return. Questioning of the
pilot indicated that Mr. Cartwright did leave the aircraft vol-
untarily. The pilot said that a man he identified as Tago entered the plane after unloading was accomplished and told the
pilot to refuel and take off. Usually, it was Mr. Cartwright
who gave the order to take off. When questioned by the pilot,
Tago would not say where Mr. Cartwright was. Tago became
agitated and told the pilot not to ask any more questions. The
pilot obeyed. The plane took off after refueling. We believe
that Mr. Cartwright was assassinated—a typical fate for recal-
citrant bankers in Russia—at the orders of Berzin. More than
forty Russian bankers have been assassinated in the past year
alone.

"We estimate that Berzin's Orchard can reach out to more
than five thousand organized crime groups of varying size and
structures, with a total of about one hundred thousand members. At least two dozen of these groups are conducting activities in the United States. Russian crime groups are about ten
times larger than our own Mafia. I will pass over some of the
schemes of the Russian criminals in the United States—such
as control of about fifty million gallons of gasoline a month,
evading, each month, about seven million dollars in federal
excise tax. Or the health-care frauds aimed at putting
Medicare funds in criminals' pockets.

"We are dealing with Berzin's *vory v zakone* or 'thieves-in-
law' organization, which is recognized by the Russian underground as the elite. Under the thieves-in-law code, its
members accept only Berzin as the absolute ruler of the organization. Criminals in prison remain under the *vory v zakone*
code. Members of the organization are like the American
Mafia's 'made men.'

"We have seen the sale of plutonium and uranium in quan-
tities and at enrichment levels well below weapons-grade. But
we now believe that these sales are masking the grave possibility that nuclear weapons and highly enriched weapons-

grade nuclear material are being sold to criminal elements in China for possible re-export to Middle East terror groups. The Russian Interior Ministry recently investigated a death due to exposure to extremely high levels of radiation.

"Through the same Moscow snitch who was killed, we learned that Berzin has become very active in providing highly sophisticated weapons to China." Knowles paused, as if deliberately giving Santini a chance to interrupt.

"A lot of this, Inspector, is just updated news," Santini said. "I'm aware, from CIA and DIA briefings, of those Mafiya Russian–Chinese weapons deals. But I must admit I never heard about the Orchard or this man Berzin."

"I have found by bitter experience, Secretary Santini, that so-called low-level intelligence, especially HUMINT, often doesn't find its way to the upper reaches of government," Knowles said. "I am quite sure that information on the Orchard is in the files of both the CIA and DIA."

Before she could go on, Pelky shot a glance at Santini; she obviously saw the glance as well as Santini's slight nod to acknowledge Pelky.

"If you wish, Secretary Santini, I can put together a supplement to the report distributed here today by Director McConnell."

"Thank you, Inspector Knowles. If I need any more information after reading the report, I will take you up on that. Please go on."

Knowles continued, telling about the way Berzin had arranged for the acquisition of an American infrared thermal imaging camera for the Chinese government. The camera, used on Chinese missile and reconnaissance systems, went into immediate production in China. A prototype of the camera was stolen from a Baltimore manufacturing firm by a Russian émigré working for the Orchard. She also said that Berzin had been involved in a complex deal that smuggled U.S. Stinger missiles from Afghanistan to China, which used them as models for upgrading their missile designs.

In another Berzin operation, he was believed to have personally handled a deal in which he sold three Beriev A-50E early-warning aircraft, similar to the American AWACS system, to China. He also arranged the transfer of Chinese anti-aircraft missiles to North Korea. "These should have been straightforward government-to-government transactions," she said. "But Berzin has developed such high-level contacts in China that he was allowed to handle the deals. He has connections at the highest level of the Russian government."

When she shifted to narcotic deals, Santini began to lose interest—until she again linked Berzin and China, a country of prime interest to Santini. She told about Berzin's role in the development of a heroin highway from Myanmar into China, then, sometimes using the old Silk Road, into Kyrgyzstan and Kazakhstan, and finally into Russia for distribution throughout Europe.

"Berzin," she continued, "is also financing a state-of-the-art heroin refinery in Tajikistan and is building up opium production in Tajikistan, Kyrgyzstan, Turkmenistan, and Uzbekistan. His goal seems to be the creation of a heroin industry in these former Soviet states, an industry that will compete with the traditional, Chinese-dominated heroin trade from Myanmar through Yunnan to Hong Kong. Berzin's next logical step would be a transaction to take over the heroin highway that delivers heroin to New York via Vancouver and Toronto, both with large Chinese populations. His criminal alliances with China recently expanded to set up another transaction, a drug-running operation through Panama, with Chinese-controlled front groups at both ends. The front groups are run by the Chinese military, the People's Liberation Army. At the same time, Berzin appears to be using his crime connections and the media outlets he owns or controls to crack down on heroin trafficking in Russia itself."

Knowles briskly concluded her presentation by projecting on the screen a spidery diagram showing Berzin's crime network. Santini looked down at the report before him and turned to the color representation of the image on the screen. The live performance by Knowles now coincided with the canned facts and figures in the report. When that convergence occurred, it was the definitive sign that a Washington briefing was over. Even before Knowles made her "thank you for the opportunity . . ." ending, everyone else in the room began getting up from their chairs, with Praeger in the lead. *A man in a hurry,* Santini thought as he picked up the report and put it in his scuffed brown briefcase. He was turning toward the door when Pelky caught his eye, signaling with a cock of his head to follow him.

Outside the Situation Room, Pelky motioned for Santini to move to a small empty office belonging to the Navy captain in charge of the Situation Room. Dropping his voice to a mere whisper, Pelky said, "We've got a small problem, Michael."

Santini smiled. He had heard that sentence many times. It meant *we've got big problems.* When Santini was in his final term in the Senate, he was the Chairman of the Senate Intelligence Committee. Pelky, a tall, athletically trim African-American, was serving as the head of the corresponding committee in the House. They had spent many long hours on the fourth floor of the U.S. Capitol in the dark caverns where the committees met and discussed the nation's innermost secrets. It was there that Santini and Pelky had forged a friendship beyond the usual backslapping Capitol Hill cliché. When the Director of Central Intelligence resigned after being accused of violating CIA security standards by allowing his wife to be present during a classified briefing, Pelky's name had appeared on a long list of possible successors. Santini used his influence to get Pelky's name onto the President's short list and lobbied the White House for him.

Pelky had survived as DCI when Jefferson was elected. No mean feat. But then Congress created the position of National Intelligence Director and removed Pelky's hat as DCI. Now he was just the CIA Director. And rumors were floating that Jefferson was tiring of him and was about to give him a President's Medal of Freedom and put him on the lecture circuit as a private citizen. Pelky had the wary look of someone who didn't know whether he should jump or wait to be pushed.

But Santini had a lot of confidence in Pelky, and after Santini became Secretary of Defense he and Pelky often got together to talk over issues, sometimes settling them without the knowledge of their respective staffs and without writing any memos for the record. Santini knew that this would be one of those get-togethers.

"Is the problem about turf, Jack?"

"That's only a small part of it, Michael. The FBI's been muscling in on intelligence ever since J. Edgar's day. Nothing new there. But this 'legal attaché' stuff is getting out of hand. Praeger is working out a special relationship with McConnell, making the FBI a kind of private intelligence collection service for the National Security Council. I'm still confused about what in hell Creighton Ford does as the DNI. So are my folks out at the Agency. No matter what the Intelligence Community's table of organization says, I'm still the guy who's in charge.

"Well, I can handle what I'm supposed to do—making sure that intelligence gets to the right people, who will probably ignore it, anyway. Leslie Knowles is sure right about that. No, this is more serious than turf. It's something beyond top secret or code word, Michael. It's something that isn't even in my office safe. I've got to tell you so you can help me figure out what to do with it, with him."

"Who is *him*?"

"I don't even like to say his name out loud. It's that certain gentleman that Leslie Knowles mentioned many, many times. She told us a lot about him, but there are some other things she didn't tell. I still—" Pelky was looking over Santini's shoulder.

Santini turned just as Gregory Fairbanks opened the door, hoping to make a quick phone call. "Oops! Sorry," he said apologetically. Then, breaking into a smile, he teased, "Now what are you two cooking up? Will I need to appoint a special prosecutor?"

Santini looked upon Fairbanks as a genial apparatchik who ran the Department of Justice with the same kind of casual, golf-on-Wednesday style that he had used to run Washington's most prestigious law firm. He was always vague and amiable on the outside while being wary and smart on the inside.

"Just a coup, Greg," Santini said. "Nothing to worry about.

Jack wants to use the 101st Airborne and I'm selling it to him. Rogue stuff."

"Well, let me know if you need a good rogue lawyer," Fairbanks said, continuing on toward the elevator.

"We're conspicuous here, Jack," Santini said. "Quick, what's on your mind?"

"Berzin. We just picked up information that he's planning to run for top dog in the special presidential election that's been set for the end of April."

"But he's got less than two months," Santini said.

"He'll pour millions into the race to buy it."

"Jesus! A crime lord openly running Russia. It would be like Dapper Don Gotti being President of the United States. But you said there were other things she didn't tell us."

"We can't prove it, but we're convinced that Berzin arranged for President Yuri Gruchkov's death. As you know, Gruchkov had been ailing for months. Not alcohol. Believe it or not, he was not a drinker. There are some indications that he was being poisoned. The kind of thing that happened to Yushchenko in Ukraine. Well, now we think it was Berzin. And then he got impatient with the poison and set up the rocket attack that took down the helicopter while he was touring military units in Chechnya. Berzin's Orchard has a lot of trees in Chechnya."

"A presidential assassin as President!"

Pelky nodded, drew closer to Santini, and said, "There's more."

"There's *more*?"

"One more. He's been working for us for years. He's the best asset we've had since the breakup of the Soviet Union."

"*Had?*"

"He's no longer on the payroll. He had a meet in Vienna with his case officer about a year ago and said he was through. And he told the case officer he'd have him killed if the CIA didn't immediately assign him to Langley and made him keep his mouth shut. I reined in the case officer immediately. We really feared that guy's power, especially for killing people. At the time I didn't know about his political plans. Now I see an incredible scenario: We can make him work for us again—as President! He knows we could blackmail him, threatening to expose him about working for us."

"Who knows about this?"

"On his side, I would think nobody who is still alive. On our side, myself and fewer than five people in the Agency, all in clandestine. And I would bet my life that none of them would ever go public about him under any circumstances."

"Creighton Ford?

"Nada."

"What about the Hill?"

"Nothing. You know that we always try to keep them in the dark as much as possible on the covert side."

"We've got to find a time to talk about this, at the usual place. Let me think for a while and call you. As the Chinese say, we are cursed to live in interesting times."

"Yeah. And, speaking of the Chinese, McConnell and Knowles got it wrong about some mafioso stealing the infrared thermal imaging camera. That was an inside job, an espionage job. There's a Chinese spy in the system, pretty high up. We'll talk about that, too."

Once Santini entered his armored limousine and Curtis flicked on the flashing red and blue "emergency" lights and began the race back to the Pentagon, he thought about his conversation with Pelky. Pelky had revealed only half the equation. Maybe he knew that he didn't have to lay it out for the former chairman of the Senate Intelligence Committee. Sure, the prospects of having the man who might become President of Russia on the hook as a former asset offered intriguing possibilities. The Agency would be in a position to urge him to follow certain "suggestions" from his old friends or risk having his past exposed.

But this was a very sharp, double-edged sword they were holding. It could just as easily cut off the hand that was wielding it. Particularly when they were dealing with someone as brutal and treacherous as Berzin.

If the CIA overplayed its hand, Berzin might preempt any

exposé and declare to the Russian people that he had played Uncle Sam for a fat sucker. They had paid him handsomely to betray Mother Russia. He, in fact, had betrayed only the United States. He had been a double agent, a man loyal to his country and contemptuous of the arrogant buffoons who had thought they could purchase his patriotism with gold. No, now their stupidity would be disclosed to the world. Every secret he purported to give them had been reviewed and vetted by Russia's Foreign Intelligence Service (which most Russians still called the KGB). Every scrap of intelligence was designed to take the Americans down blind alleys where their famed operatives could be mugged. Berzin's name would now have to be emblazoned on America's wall of shame along with Walker, Ames, and Hanssen.

And, Santini mused, Berzin, just to thrust the sword in deeper, would claim that it was the CIA that had engineered the murder of Berzin's predecessor because he was trying to make Russia great again. Now it had fallen to Berzin to pick up Gruchkov's mantle, his vision.

The CIA had a time bomb on its hands. And, no doubt, that's why Pelky wanted to share some of the exquisite agony of it all.

CHAPTER 12

WASHINGTON

All the days now began with Vice Admiral Scott O'Neill meeting Santini at the limousine's open door. This, Santini knew, was always a tip-off to bad news. He said his usual, "Good morning, Curtis," to the driver, then slipped past O'Neill to enter the car. Santini decided to sit down before he said good morning to O'Neill.

"Well, Scott," Santini said, "I want to say good morning. But from the look on your face, it's not going to be one, is it?"

O'Neill handed him a Top Secret folder, saying, "This is just a preliminary report from Holloman. The FBI is the lead agency. McConnell arranged for you to get a copy of what went to him. Nice gesture."

Santini picked up the folder, opened it, and glanced at the first page. "Sabotage? Are they sure?" He closed the folder, knowing that O'Neill had all but committed it to memory, and also knowing that no one in the Pentagon could boil down papers better than O'Neill.

"Not a hundred percent. But the debris scatter is consistent with a powerful explosive, not aviation fuel," O'Neill said, glancing out the window as the limousine crossed the 14th Street Bridge over the Potomac. "Neither the Tornadoes nor the Nighthawks were armed. So the explosives had to be *in* the Tornado that exploded."

"Maybe someone goofed and loaded the Tornado with ordnance," Santini said.

"Negative. A rocket or a shell would not have gone off like that. It's sabotage, all right. And not the kind we're always talking about."

"Meaning?"

"Meaning that this isn't an embassy going up. Or the World Trade Center. This isn't that kind of a terrorist job. It was aimed at *that* Tornado for *that* air show. It's a message, some kind of message, about the Germans at Holloman. The Bureau boys so far figure it's a militia nut. But that's not entirely satisfactory."

Santini waited expectantly. O'Neill's "not entirely satisfactory" always preceded a crisp series of sentences that analyzed a problem. The Pentagon was full of people who called themselves analysts. But they all churned out long reports speckled with colored graphs or long lectures that for some reason were called Power Points, though they always lacked powerful ideas and seemed always to be pointless. O'Neill's idea of an analysis was a series of declarative sentences in plain English, either written or spoken.

"Usually, the Germans do their own maintenance. But two months ago the base commander decided that Air Force maintenance men should get a look at Tornadoes. The idea was to advance their education." Santini caught in "education" just a hint of the condescension that crept into the admiral's voice when he had to discuss anything pertaining to the U.S. Air Force.

"That means that an American would be able to enter the German maintenance area. He presumably knew the maintenance schedule and had a thorough knowledge of base security. He—or, more likely, a hacker accomplice—expertly attacked the Holloman computer system. He got right through the firewalls. It looks like someone put in a kind of trapdoor—that's what the hackers call it—and could enter and leave almost at will. And they could find out all they needed to know about mechanical access to the Tornadoes. The FBI has a Computer Security Go Team at Holloman looking into that. So it's an inside job. Someone on the base, who knew about the change in procedure, either did the job himself or managed to get the saboteur in to do his job."

"Okay. We have opportunity. Now means and motive," Santini said, reverting to his years as a federal prosecutor.

"I'm straying from the report here, sir. But you don't have to be an FBI agent to see that this is too sophisticated for a solo loony, even someone as talented as, say, the Unabomber was. There's a lot of thinking, a lot of planning. My first thought was an al Qaeda–type group. Then I thought of a well-endowed militia, or even a couple of domestic terrorists. But this is no fertilizer-in-a-rented-truck, as in Oklahoma City, and it's not something aimed at the heart, like the World Trade Towers. I'm betting on a rogue state. Or are we supposed to call it a nation of interest?"

" 'Rogue state' is back in fashion. Even at the State Department."

"Thank you, Mr. Secretary," O'Neill said, smiling. "So it's rogue state in the E-Ring. But with a twist. I think we should get the intelligence boys working in that direction."

"Okay. Set up a secure conference call with McConnell and Pelky," Santini said. "And we don't need to get Czar Ford into this." Looking up, he saw that the limousine was approaching the Pentagon's River Road checkpoint. "And now on to another day."

"Yes, sir. And perhaps this would be a good time to call the German Minister of Defense."

"Yep. Set that up, too."

The moment that Santini reached his office, Margie notified him that the White House, which had tracked his movements, was coming on the line. Santini punched the first button in the first row of sixteen buttons on the console. The President was on the line in a few moments.

"Just spoke to Chancellor Kiepler for the second time this week," the President said. "He's steaming. Not only about the incident. He's in a rage because of a delay in returning the pilots' remains to Germany and because he can't get any information on exactly what happened. He thinks that we're dragging our feet and maybe engaged in a cover-up. Can't any of you guys break this thing loose? I need something to tell Kiepler. Please, Michael, help me out on this."

Santini hung up the phone. Another light flashed on the console. It was O'Neill. "The German Defense Minister is, quote, unable to speak at the moment. Unquote."

"Right," Santini said. "He's probably in with Kiepler. The President says he's furious because he can't get the pilots' bodies back and thinks we're stonewalling."

O'Neill, as usual, had an answer. "I've got a friend. In my class at the Academy. Retired as a rear admiral. Now he's a commissioner of the New Mexican State Police. Let me call him and see what he can do about completing the autopsies and getting the bodies on a Hercules to Germany."

"That'll help."

"As far as more information about the investigation, we need to be careful. We can't tell Kiepler that we think it's sabotage. Christ, that will hit the German press in ten seconds and we'll be on our ass with our guys over here. Give me a few minutes," O'Neill said. "I'll think of some way to deal with it."

"Get back to me on that ASAP. The White House needs it."

"Yes, sir," O'Neill replied, looking at his watch. "Ready for the Top Four?"

"After the intel briefings. And ask the Chairman to keep it short. I need some time to get ready for the MOD."

"No problem, sir," O'Neill said. "I'll tell the Top Three to double-time."

Through all this, Arthur Wu had been waiting patiently in the anteroom outside Santini's office. As soon as Wu came in, Santini began rushing him through his briefing. Just as Wu concluded his briefing, he said, "Mr. Secretary, you are meeting today with Xu Ling, the Chinese Minister of Defense."

"I am aware of that, Art, believe me," Santini said.

"Yes, sir. But I was wondering, sir, if I could in any way be present."

Santini rarely showed annoyance. He believed such a display was a pointless waste of energy. There were times, however, when his controls slipped. "Back off, Art," he said.

"You're new on the job. Don't get pushy. You're here to give me briefs. Period. The State Department takes care of providing interpreters. I don't want a DIA guy in here trying to pick up some tidbits while I am conducting some very important business. Stick to your knitting, Art."

"Knitting, sir?"

"Oh, for Christ's sake, Art! It's a goddamn saying, a cliché. The briefing is over. Thanks."

Wu, showing no embarrassment or any other emotion, nodded and withdrew, leaving Santini to wonder whether the *Knitting, sir?* was subtle impertinence.

Robert Sommers of the CIA entered and, quickly sensing Santini's impatience, shaved back his briefing to six minutes and left.

Next came the Top Four meeting. O'Neill was true to his word. The Top Three, sensing that the Top One was unusually impatient this morning, moved swiftly through their discussion items. The Chairman, Whittier, put on his glasses, extracted a single sheet of paper from a red-and-white-striped folder, and began the litany.

"Hold on," Santini said, interrupting Whittier's recital. "In the wake of Holloman, what about alerts, especially at bases in the United States?"

Whittier glanced at the Vice Chairman, who nodded. "All bases worldwide on heightened alert within an hour after the incident."

"Good. We'll need to keep it there until this gets sorted out," Santini said. "I'll be talking to Director McConnell shortly about the incident. I'll prepare a précis on the progress of the investigation for the President. And I'll ask the White House to send a copy to you. I want you fully informed."

"Yes, sir. Thank you, sir."

"Okay. Now, what's next on your agenda?"

"The Lashkar-e-Toiba, militants out of Pakistan, attacked the Presidential House in New Delhi. Nine of them killed. Six presidential guards killed. India's threatening to end the cease-fire with Pakistan."

"Sounds more like something for Secretary Palmer's department. But maybe you should brush up on embassy evacuation plans in case something really goes off there."

"Pretty big embassy, sir. We'll need a lot of assets."

"I realize that, Mr. Chairman. But make it an action item."

"Yes, sir."

"Next," Santini pushed.

"Twenty-seven North Korean soldiers crossed the Demilitarized Zone and defected as a group. They would only talk to a ranking American officer." He looked up.

"Let General Craig handle it for now. The South Koreans will probably demand we hand them over."

"Yes, sir. But they always think defectors are spies."

"Well, whatever the hell they are, let's squeeze them hard and fast before the State Department gets involved in this. Kim Song Jo has been playing rough lately and we need to know what the Great Leader is up to. Okay. Any other big ones?"

Whittier and the other two men all said, "No, sir," almost in unison. They rose, again almost in unison, and filed out of the room.

Santini moved to the large judge's chair that was a match for the Pershing desk in size and pomp. He rifled quickly but methodically through the voluminous briefing book that had been prepared for his session with Xu Ling.

The top sheet gave him a five-paragraph biography of Minister of Defense Xu Ling. Birthplace: Shenyang, Liaoning Province. Son of a colonel in the People's Liberation Army (PLA). Then came a list of military assignments, including military attaché in Paris. "This was considered a plum and confirmed his inner-circle status in the PLA. He began his Ministry of Defense career as a regional ministry representative in Shenyang. He has a solid interest in modern Chinese literature. He has used his influence to protect Shenyang's Spring Breeze Literary Press, whose books are considered somewhat anti-establishment, especially a series called *Cloth Tiger*, a daring pun on 'Paper Tiger.' "

An excerpt from one of the *Cloth Tiger* books was listed as Attachment B. Santini turned to it. Apparently it was from a short story about a provincial party bureaucrat who had been directed to set up in a bicycle factory in a rural area. The bureaucrat, seeking talent among the peasants in the village, finds a bright young woman from Beijing. She got in trouble with the authorities there, and the bureaucrat knows he should have nothing to do with her. But he falls in love with her. And—

Much as he would like to keep reading the story, Santini broke away. He knew he should be reading about the MOD's attitude toward the United States sharing its missile-defense plans with some of its Asian friends. "Xu is one of the new-breed officers. He heads up the wait-and-see bloc," the briefing paper said. "This makes him, at least in Chinese terms, somewhat pro-U.S. The dominant bloc in the Ministry of Defense—and in the civilian leadership—believes that an effective anti-missile defense is an absolute threat to China's security. If that bloc ultimately prevails, China will begin a costly arms race. If Xu and his bloc continue on their present path, there would be a more nuanced dialogue with the United States—though the present buildup of strategic nuclear weapons would continue. Xu is no dove. Rather, his inclinations seem to take him into a simultaneous association with the United States and Russia. He has twice visited Russia within the last 18 months, and he was warmly received. (See Russia Arms Sales to China, Appendix D.)"

Santini scanned down to "suggested talking points," produced by the combined effort of many in the Pentagon and Intelligence Community, with a minor contribution from State.

The talking points began with a phrase Santini detested—"As you know." *A Janus phrase,* he thought. It simultaneously said you were smart but still needed to be told. There was nothing he could do about it except, perhaps, mention it to Scott O'Neill. But maybe that was too small-fry to use up O'Neill's talents on. Well, on to the talking points.

• As you know, Xu is a member of the Central Military Commission, which controls China's nuclear weapons. (Latest estimates put the number at 400, with about 20 deployed in Dong Feng-5 [DF-5] liquid-fueled missiles, which have a

range of 13,000 km. Another 230 nuclear weapons are deployed, or ready to be deployed, on aircraft, Xia Type 092
nuclear-powered submarines, and regional-range missiles.
The other 150 are apparently seen as tactical weapons.) You
may want to feel him out on the size and condition of
China's nuclear arsenal. Whatever he says will be of value
for analysis.

• He will certainly bring up Taiwan. If you want to throw him
off-stride, you might casually ask about the construction of
an advanced long-range missile base in Zhangzhou, Fujian
Province, opposite Taiwan. Although he has a poker face
(and is, in fact, an inveterate gambler), he may show surprise.
The Intelligence Community requests this so that he will
know, if he does not know already, that the building of missile bases in the satellite era cannot be a secret.

• Should seek Xu's support for preventing Iran from producing
nuclear weapons.

• Suggest that mil to mil ties need to be improved. Although
China has agreed in the past to allow visits to the Second Artillery Corps Command, they refuse to allow us to visit their
equivalent of the Pentagon, which is a command center located in the Western Hills near Beijing. Make it clear that if
the relationship is to improve they will have to display
greater transparency into their defense establishment and
budgeting process, and greater reciprocity in giving our military professionals the same access that we extend to their
people.

• We need to raise issue once again of the need for a "hot line"
to their MOD. Suggest you do this privately if the situation
permits as he's unlikely to agree in the plenary session.

Santini was skimming through the lesser talking points
when Margie knocked on, then opened, the door and ushered
in Colonel Rick Patterson, who commanded the Pentagon's
military honors unit. "Minister Xu is in hold, Mr. Secretary,"
Patterson said in a voice that filled the room. Santini motioned
Patterson to come in and go through the briefing for a ceremony that was both routine and impressive. Both Santini and

Patterson knew its choreography by heart. But it was well worth a minute or two to go over it again.

From a window in his office Santini looked down on the parade ground. The honor guard had already assembled, their uniforms pressed crisply and their rifles' bayonets gleaming in the unusually warm and sun-filled morning. Several members of the band had started to loosen up their fingers and run scales on their instruments. The colors fluttered in the brisk wind that had started to pick up. He stood motionless for a moment, his thoughts transfixed by the sight of the gathering of the troops.

Then he saw the black limousines carrying Minister Xu and his party waiting to move toward the parade ground. "It's time," Patterson said, and Santini briskly followed him out of the office, into the corridor, and down the flight of stairs that led to the lobby of the Pentagon's River Entrance.

The honor guard and the Army band were in place, flanking the rectangular greensward of the parade ground. Santini walked down the broad outdoor steps and felt a spring wind brush him. The wind ruffled the flags before him, as Xu stepped out of his limousine. Santini greeted him and introduced him to Colonel Patterson, who repeated, through the Chinese interpreter, the ceremony's protocol. Then both men strode toward a small platform set up at the edge of the parade ground. The two men—Santini tall and erect in a blue suit, Xu shorter, but in good shape, wearing a well-tailored olive drab uniform—reached the platform at the same moment. Santini stopped while Xu climbed the two steps to the top of the platform.

As the two men stood at attention facing the parade ground, unseen howitzers began firing a nineteen-gun salute. At the first blast of the guns, a startled flock of gulls rose from the nearby Potomac marina, where they had been dining on scraps.

Lined up to the right of the platform and shepherded by Pentagon protocol officers were four female and nineteen PLA officers, their plain tunics of Chinese uniforms in contrast with the beribboned chests of U.S. officers. Several of the Chinese officers clutched or had at their feet shopping bags whose labels—*Gap, CVS, Hecht's, Macy's, Bloomingdale's*—not only reflected their shopping trips but also revealed their distrust of the PLA baggage handlers who would be loading the aircraft that would take them home.

The band struck up "The Star-Spangled Banner." Santini placed his right hand over his heart; Xu snapped to attention and saluted. The band paused for an instant and played the Chinese national anthem, a musical accomplishment that seemed to impress Xu. The band stopped playing as a fife and drum corps, playing "Yankee Doodle" and wearing Revolutionary War uniforms, passed in review. Xu looked puzzled. A Pentagon interpreter materialized at the platform and translated Santini's remark to Xu: "They're wearing the uniform of our PLA in 1776." Xu nodded and smiled broadly.

Sure is one of the new breed, Santini thought. *Those look like caps on his teeth. No more gold teeth, at least for generals.* But capped or not, they bore the unmistakable evidence of Xu's addiction to tobacco. The intelligence profile didn't miss much.

The band switched to a Sousa march. Santini and Xu stepped down from the platform and began walking down the rows of the honor guard, trooping the line of Army, Navy, Marine, and Air Force men and women while Pentagon photographers filmed the scene. Everything, as usual, went off like clockwork, Santini noted. No one missed a beat. Colonel Patterson had done it again.

"Thank you. Thank you very much," Xu said to Santini as they walked back toward the steps of the Pentagon. "It was very well done." The comment surprised Santini, remembering the briefing paper: Xu had learned English on his own, from an old set of long-playing records that had belonged to his father. But he preferred to use an interpreter when in the company of his colleagues. He personally had escaped the punishments inflicted on his father during the Cultural Revolution. But he did not like to remind present-day hard-liners about his knowledge of English. Santini wondered whether

Xu's speaking English just now was a signal of trust. Maybe he would run that by Wu, get the DIA's view of the incident.

In front of the flags in the dining room of Santini's office suite, the obligatory handshake photographs were taken, first of Santini and Xu, then of Santini and Xu flanked by Chinese officers and American officers, including O'Neill and Whittier, who towered over their guests. Santini was quickly introduced to Xu's aides, in the order of their importance, beginning with Li Kangsheng, Deputy Minister of Defense. All the officers but Li saluted and shook hands; Li only saluted. Santini, marking Li as a hard-liner, needed to find out more about him.

A few Pentagon correspondents crowded into the room, hoping that the photo opportunity would turn into a full-fledged press conference. A reporter asked, "Where does China stand on the American missile shield?" Xu's own interpreter, a pretty woman officer in an ill-fitting uniform, translated the question. Before Xu could answer, Santini held up a hand and said, "It's not a press conference. Maybe later. We have work to do."

With a gentle hand on Xu's right elbow, Santini ushered Xu into his private office. An American security man in a dark blue suit closed the door behind Santini. A protocol officer then led the rest of Xu's party to a nearby conference room. There General Whittier would speak a few pleasantries, turn over the meeting to the Army Chief of Staff, and leave. Gathered around a long, gleaming table in what was known as the plenary session, high-ranking officers of the two countries would discuss points on an agenda developed weeks before by their staffs. The results of the one-hour meeting would be substantively meaningless, but a rite called "military-to-military contact" had been established. And possibly in some future crisis this contact would enable officers on both sides to put faces to the crisis. That was not meaningless.

In Santini's office, Xu and Santini sat at the table near Santini's desk. An orderly entered and placed before Santini his favorite coffee mug and a small thermos of coffee. Before Xu the orderly placed a white porcelain teapot and a porcelain cup and saucer. Xu sipped tentatively and smiled. "Yangtze green tea," he said. "My favorite. Your CIA is very thorough." His speech was tinged with an accent more British than American. The LP language records, Santini thought, must have been made in England.

"Actually," Santini said, smiling back, "that information came from the Defense Intelligence Agency."

"Your military attaché in Beijing—Brigadier General Waters, I believe—is very observant." Xu took out a silver cigarette case, opened it, and proffered it to Santini.

"I'm sorry, General," Santini said. "There is no smoking in the Pentagon."

Xu was startled. He swung the hand holding the case around, as if to take in the enormous office. "But here—?"

"There are some things that even I cannot order," Santini said. "I am sorry."

Xu frowned and pocketed the cigarette case.

"Minister Xu," Santini said, deciding to change the subject. "Ordinarily, I give to my important guests a replica of the sword that one of our Civil War heroes carried into battle. That's a painting of Colonel Joshua Lawrence Chamberlain on the wall over there," Santini said, pointing to the striking portrait of the man he regarded as one of the greatest citizen-soldiers in American history. "But the sword represents the past."

Santini reached into the top drawer of his desk, took out a palmtop computer, and handed it to Xu with a slight ceremonial flare. "This, I thought, would be more forward looking," he said. "This little computer has a video-streaming capability that will allow us to see and talk to each other directly. And it has an encryption feature that enables us to send confidential e-mails. This can serve as our own personal hot line. We won't have to go through our ministries to contact each other. This will be direct. Just you and me. Please accept it as a remembrance—and an opportunity." This little beauty wasn't what DOD's bureaucrats had in mind in their "talking points" memo, Santini thought. But screw it! The Chinese military wasn't going to sign up to a formal hot line, not without months of delay. Xu just might be willing to buy the idea. And if not, no harm done.

"I believe that my associates will be very interested in this," Xu said, examining the device.

"And your intelligence people," Santini said. "Looking for bugs."

Xu acted as if he did not understand.

"This is a gift from one friend to another," Santini said. "Not from one national official to another. I hope that you'll treat it as personal and confidential."

"Yes, thank you. I hope that we will continue to be friends . . . and not merely officials. But we are merely figures—or actors playing roles for our countries. We are men of duty, and we must not forget that our duty is above even friendship. And so, Mr. Secretary, I must remind you that Taiwan is the most sensitive issue at the center of the relationship between our countries. If the question of Taiwan is handled well, all is well with our relationship. If it is handled badly, there will be problems."

"I, too, hope that no issue between us is handled badly," Santini said. "As for problems, we see a potential one in Zhangzhou."

"That is a lovely city, and very prosperous. Have you been there, Mr. Secretary?"

"Not personally. But I have seen photos of it, and they show that China is building an advanced missile base there. We feel that is a direct threat to Taiwan."

"Photos can lie, Mr. Secretary. There is a great deal of construction going on in Zhangzhou. Luxury hotels. Factories. Housing for workers. Thousands of hectares of construction."

"These photos do not lie. In fact, I wish that I could show them to you. You can count the bicycles in the streets. And you can count the missiles. I can give you the exact geographic coordinates, if you wish."

"Mr. Secretary, let us not play this game. As you well know, there is continued reckless talk in Taiwan about taking a vote to declare independence. We cannot accept this. Taiwan is also increasing its purchase of offensive air weapons from you. If there is a Chinese response, it is a self-defense response, not an offensive move. China is investing its energy in peace and prosperity, not war. But, as your own Mr. Roosevelt said, it is prudent to speak softly and carry a big stick."

"And Mr. Roosevelt won a Nobel Peace Prize," Santini said. "Perhaps that should be our goal: winning at peace, not war."

There was a soft rap on the door. Then Margie opened it and said, "The plenary session beckons, gentlemen. There are schedules to keep and papers to sign."

"Be there in a minute, Margie," Santini said.

Turning to Xu, he said, "Mr. Minister, I'll raise this in the plenary session, but I just want you to know how important I think it is for us to break through the barriers that keep us from having a truly cooperative relationship. We need to have a clearer picture of your military in terms of growth and strategic goals. And the complaint my military officers give me upon their return from your country is that they get the 'Potemkin village' treatment. . . ."

"Meaning?" Xu interrupted.

"I'm sorry. It's an expression that means we get to see just the surface of things. That there's nothing behind the structures. Just empty space. A phony village, in other words. A waste of time. And they want to give you and your people the same treatment when you come here. Reciprocity is what we want. Equal treatment."

"I understand, Secretary Santini. It's been a slow process. There is still great suspicion among many in the PLA about America's intentions. But I believe we are making progress. I'll try to encourage more, as you say, reciprocity."

"There is one final thing," Santini said. "We need your help with Iran. It will be very dangerous for all of us should Iran develop nuclear weapons. This falls more appropriately with your Foreign Ministry, but any assistance you can provide would be very well received by our government."

"I understand," Xu said, nodding his head. "But as you suggest, this matter is beyond my responsibilities."

* * *

At the plenary session, Santini and Xu examined the drafts of agreements, negotiated weeks before, on a program of ongoing military-to-military contacts, on ways to coordinate disaster relief aid and training for mutual search and rescue missions in the future. Much of the Chinese work on the agreements had been done by Li Kangsheng, the Deputy Minister of Defense.

Santini extended his hand, thanking Li for his hard work in negotiating the new rules. He bowed stiffly but again did not take Santini's hand. Li, a stocky and powerfully built man, mumbled something to the Chinese interpreter.

"Minister Li would like to know where he can smoke in America," she said, bowing her head and looking a bit embarrassed.

Santini's American interpreter, who had been standing a few feet away, reached his right hand across his forehead, a standard prearranged signal that the translation had not been accurate. Santini's interpreter then shrugged slightly, signaling that the inaccuracy was not worth pursuing at the moment. Santini beckoned to him and said, "Please tell Minister Li that the plenary session will end in a few moments. Then he and any other Chinese guests who wish to smoke can go where American smokers go—to the Pentagon courtyard. One of the escorts will show them the way."

The interpreter relayed the words. Xu and the other Chinese laughed. But Li maintained what Santini perceived as a permanent frown. There was something about Li that mystified Santini. He made a mental note to get more about Li from the DIA. But like many mental notes, this one lay forgotten for a while.

CHAPTER 13

As the President's National Security Adviser, Joe Praeger had bestowed upon himself the power to call meetings in the Situation Room. This one, which Praeger had set for six o'clock, was to be private and held in Praeger's corner office in the West Wing. That meant Santini had to juggle his evening schedule, which included a reception and dinner for Xu and his party. As usual, Praeger did not give a reason for the meeting. But Santini suspected that Praeger would play at being Secretary of State and use the occasion to lecture Santini on Chinese–American relations.

Praeger sat in the President's chair at the table. He perfunctorily greeted Santini to his right and then began a rapid tour of the world as he saw it. The tour reflected what Santini had heard in his morning briefings, with added rhetoric ("In Israel, we must remain in an aggressive, but watch-and-wait, facilitator role") that mixed the jargons of policy wonk and social worker. Praeger did not mention the Holloman incident.

When the Praeger tour reached China, Santini began to pay attention. In the Administration's continual debate over China, Praeger inevitably preached a hard line. And Praeger's hard line was becoming the President's hard line. He often echoed Praeger's pronouncements on China, politely rebuffing the advice of Santini and Secretary of State Palmer.

Santini had pretty much figured out Praeger's agenda. He was trying to position himself to be the Secretary of State when Jefferson won a second term. Praeger was virulently anti-Chinese. But publicly he had to hide his real sentiments under a phony statesmanlike moderate cloak until after the next presidential election. He was convinced, however, that the American people shared his view that China was the enemy of the twenty-first century, the new Soviet Union that had to be beaten back from their dreams of dominating the world stage at the expense of the United States.

Santini held no illusion about Chinese aspirations. Their human capital was extraordinary. They had more than a billion people. The Chinese had been around for more than five thousand years and were the proud possessors of a cultural heritage second to none. And they were determined to occupy a major seat at the table of geopolitical power. Santini thought that those who believed that the Chinese could somehow be contained or deterred from their goals were either hopelessly naive or ideological zealots who were playing a dangerous game of "Chinese roulette" with the lives of 275 million Americans.

Santini was no apologist concerning Chinese objectives. But he was convinced that the best way to deal with them was to find common ground whenever the opportunity presented itself, but be willing to muscle them when it was clearly in America's interests to do so. Diplomacy first, power second was a safer road to success, not the other way around.

The problem was that Praeger had proximity, just feet away from the Oval Office. And proximity meant power, giving him the ability to see and talk to the President almost at will. And Santini, well, he was not the President's first choice to head the Defense Department, only the most recent. He was outside the power circle, and Praeger was not going to let him inside.

And so every meeting in the Situation Room at the White House gave Praeger an opportunity to taunt Santini subtly, to push him into an untenable defense of Chinese misconduct or to agree to join in the consensus that China had to be rebuked.

It came as no surprise to Santini when Praeger would not pass on the opportunity to suggest that the ceremonies at the Pentagon planned for Defense Minister Xu, including the nineteen-gun salute, amounted to decidedly inappropriate kowtowing.

"Why the hell are we bowing and scraping to a country that's helping Iran get nuclear weapons?" Praeger blurted next.

"You've got something new on that one?" Santini asked.

"Maybe I do, but I'm certainly going to hold my cards close. Give it to you and you'll have your DIA guys running around and messing up the intel."

"My DIA guys don't *tailor* intel," Santini said.

"I'll let that pass," Praeger responded. "You might ask your Chinese friend about some intel reporting I saw that said with China's help, Iran is going to cross the threshold at their nuclear plants at Natanz and Arak and start producing nuclear weapons. Estimates are as many as twenty or more nukes a year."

"The source?"

"The NCR."

"The National Council of Resistance of Iran? You've got to be kidding! Christ, Joe, that's the group the State Department put on the list of terrorists back in 1997. Is that the best we can do? Haven't we learned anything from past mistakes?"

"Knock 'em all you want. Just remember they were the ones who blew the whistle on Iran's secret nuclear program and gave the IAEA the leverage to demand inspections of the suspect areas."

"Yeah. And Ahmed Chalabi was the one who claimed to have solid intelligence about Iraq's weapons of mass destruction."

"Come on, Michael. The Iranians have been lying to the world for years. They've been building power plants with a total capacity of 6000 megawatts. Why? They give us the same bullshit line that they intend to use the power for domestic use and sell their oil and gas on the international market to generate foreign currency. Everyone sees through this. Even the fucking Europeans."

"So what do you want to do, Joe? Launch a preemptive strike against all of Iran's nuclear sites? You want us to risk releasing radioactive clouds over the entire Middle East? You want a kill tally from DOD?"

"I've talked with a number of Israeli generals and they maintain that they will never allow Iran to go nuclear."

"Did they tell you how they plan to stop them? Pull off a surprise air strike like they did against Saddam back in 1981? I don't think so. Too many targets, too far away."

"And so," Praeger said, "your answer is to do nothing. Or go to the UN Security Council where the Russians and the Chinese will stick a veto up our ass or make us swallow some watered-down compromise?"

"No, Joe. If we really have the goods, I'd recommend to the President that we go to the few friends we still have in Europe and persuade them to boycott Iran's exports. Japan would join us because they know that if Iran is allowed to go nuclear, North Korea will take it as a green light to do exactly the same. And then, it's Katie bar the door. That's the way I'd handle it."

"How diplomatic. Why does this not surprise me? Maybe you should try a little of that diplomacy tonight and tell Minister Xu to help us out instead of trying to bring on Armageddon."

When Santini did not respond, Praeger changed his tone and tried to sound less argumentative. "Michael, I'm serious about this. It's not only Iran. China is playing with fire with us over Taiwan. The latest satellite imagery clearly shows a continuing buildup of ballistic missiles." He shifted to his professorial symposium style. "To quantify the current situation, I'm tempted to measure the current Chinese provocation against the Soviet decision to place nuclear missiles in Cuba."

"That's a helluva stretch, Joe," Santini said. "The Soviet Union was a powerful nation and Cuba was its puppet. China is—"

"China is going in the same direction as the Soviet Union," Praeger interrupted. "Intelligence estimates put the number of Chinese nuclear warheads at about four hundred, with an estimated one hundred and fifty reserved for what Chinese military strategists call 'tactical' use. This could mean anything, including a preemptive nuclear strike on Taiwan."

"Joe. You can't be serious. China knows damn well that a strike, even a non-nuclear strike, on Taiwan would mean—"

"Would mean what? A lecture from Palmer? Withdrawal of our ambassador? Or"— Praeger stood and leaned forward on his fists—"a military response?"

"Maybe. It depends on what the President orders."

"Don't give me that, Michael. You should have contingency plans. A phone call from the White House—and then what? Do you have a contingency plan that could be carried out in a New York minute? Or would it be a Washington minute that would go on and on?"

"What the hell brought this on, Joe? What makes you so paranoid about China?"

"Paranoid? Damn right I'm paranoid. When I see China building a blue-water navy, I get paranoid. When I see them scooping up IBM's computer business . . . trying to buy Maytag . . . and for Christ's sake, the move to snatch one of our oil companies and tell Congress to butt out! What balls! And on top of that, remember how one of the PLA's generals said if we ever moved to help Taiwan from an attack, they'd drop nuclear bombs on us from Maine to California?" Praeger jumped up from his chair and started to pace back and forth. "Yeah, Michael. I'm paranoid. And it would be a whole lot better if you stopped playing the statesman role and all the bullshit about 'engaging' them and getting with the program. These bastards are not our friends."

"Well, I'm not paranoid," Santini said. "Certainly we need to keep an eye on China. And we have to be prepared to respond to any move she makes on Taiwan. But she has no facilities for an amphibious assault. And if she started gearing up her missiles, we'd see it."

"Don't be so sure of our satellites. They can be knocked out. Blinded." Santini knew that Praeger had to have been briefed by the CIA on the temporary loss of satellite coverage over North Korea that General Whittier had alerted him to.

"That would be a warning in itself. We'd have recon aircraft in the air—in that New York minute."

"Yeah. If you had the Seventh Fleet in the Taiwan Strait. But is that where the Seventh Fleet is right now?"

"As you well know, we're keeping the Seventh Fleet out of

the strait expressly so we *can* send it there to show the flag if China acts up."

"I'm not satisfied with that, Michael. I'm recommending to the President that we put the fleet there permanently."

"What? Just like that? I'll believe it when I get that directly from the President. It would be a provocative act, Joe, and you know it."

Praeger, now back in his seat and looking studiedly relaxed, said, "Not provocative. *Protective.* We're protecting our friends in Taiwan. All I want to do is react to those missiles going up in Zhangzhou."

"Exactly. I brought up Zhangzhou today with Xu."

"And he said, 'So what.' Right? Michael, the Chinese don't understand anything but power. I'd like you to say something about the Seventh Fleet tonight when you dine with your Minister Xu. Tell him the President is contemplating the placement of the fleet in the strait permanently."

"No soap, Joe. There's a big difference between your saying you've got something to recommend to the President and my saying that the President is 'contemplating' it."

Praeger looked at his watch. "I have a seven-thirty appointment with the President. I may show up at your dinner to have dessert and coffee. Then I'll do the talking about the Seventh Fleet."

"I'm going to be late, Joe. Unless you show up yourself to give Xu—and me—a letter from the President, I'll stick with the program."

"And what is that, Michael? Some jawing about military-to-military bullshit?"

"You'll get a memo from me tomorrow morning, detailing what I say and what he says. The way I see it, Joe, is we can rattle a saber, but we can't pull out a sword. Chinese nuclear weapons are under the control of the Central Military Commission. Xu is a member of the commission. The Deputy Minister of Defense, a guy named Li Kangsheng, is also on the commission. So we have two members of that commission in Washington tonight, and maybe there will be some talk about nuclear weapons. Xu seems accessible. He spoke in English to me privately, but not in public. Li, though, is a guy to watch. He seems to be hard-line."

"I've heard of Li," Praeger said. "He's after Xu's job, that's for sure."

"When I told them that they couldn't smoke in the Pentagon, Li made some kind of crack. The Chinese interpreter covered him. My interpreter told me what Li really said."

"Which was?"

" 'Fuck America's rules. China makes the rules.' We had a DOD cameraman recording the meeting. I had it played back. Xu was visibly shocked by Li's crack. I think Xu is a guy we should support as much as possible."

"I don't trust any of them, Michael," Praeger said, standing. "By the way, heard you've got a new DIA briefer."

"See your spies are working overtime. His name is Wu, Arthur Wu."

"Chinese, isn't he?"

"American-Chinese. Reserve captain in the Army."

"A hyphenated American," Praeger said, contempt curling into a smile. "I don't give a damn if he's got stars or stripes carved into his ass. Like I said, I don't trust any of them." He folded his briefing book and stood up.

Heading for the door, he turned and said, "Be sure to count the silverware. And save an extra fortune cookie just in case I decide to show up."

CHAPTER 14

Back in his office, Santini composed a memo to the President, tapping it out on his own secure laptop. O'Neill would get it to the President by the usual back channel. As Santini well knew, Praeger had his own back channels, and an undeclared, unacknowledged memo war had been going on between them on the subject of China. When the Administration wanted opinions on China, the President turned to Praeger and Secretary of State Palmer, not Santini. But Xu's visit would give Praeger an opportunity to score points for his hard-line approach to China. His threat to burst into the dinner was probably a bluff; sudden confrontations were not in the Praeger style. Still, Santini felt it was a good idea to slip a memo in fast.

"Mr. President," Santini began, "my preliminary talks with Minister Xu convince me that he represents a reasonable China. But I feel that he, like other moderates, is being pressed by hard-liners who would rather ally themselves with Russia and Iran than the United States. There is no immediate problem with China. It is not a superpower. The Chinese don't have the money or the technology base to compete with us, especially in the development of the weapons of the future, such as satellite-controlled weapons. As to Taiwan, Xu presses the usual party line. But I foresee no aggressive action against Taiwan. I am meeting informally with Xu tonight. I will report on anything that develops from that conversation." He signed the memo: "Santini."

* * *

Minutes later, Santini was in the limousine for the trip across the Potomac. Curtis turned on the red and blue flashing lights and the security chase van closed in behind. Santini hardly had time to look at the notes on his three-by-five cards before the limousine pulled up to the concrete barriers that marked the checkpoint for the C Street entrance to the State Department.

Soldiers, sailors, and Marines, stationed precisely nine feet apart, lined the entranceway and foyer to the security checkpoint there. While other latecomers filed slowly through the metal detectors, Santini and a security man hurried to a waiting elevator that whisked them to the top floor. The elevator opened onto a hallway that led to the State Department's ornate reception rooms, which were decorated in the eighteenth-century style and contained rare pieces of art and furniture that reflected America's early years as a nation.

Corinthian columns lined the walls. Gilded decorative plaster filled the seam between walls and ceiling. Cut-glass chandeliers hung from coffered ceilings. The Great Seal of the United States, in plaster and gilt, looked down from the center of the ceiling. On one wall hung a portrait of the man for whom the room was named, Benjamin Franklin. On another was a painting that had become known as *The Spirit of '76.*

The reception had spilled through the French doors to the balcony. In the softening light, Washington was a panorama of blue sky, greening Mall, white monuments, and a gray Potomac. Santini, seeking out Xu, spotted a network anchorman, a newspaper publisher, two senators, three members of Congress, a former Secretary of State, and an actress who happened to be in town and had wrangled an invitation through a White House protocol contact. She had cornered Xu, whose interpreter looked stunned. Santini heard her saying something about Tibet as he hurried to Xu's side.

Grabbing two club sodas from a passing waiter's tray, Santini handed one to Xu, and said to the actress, "I am sure that General Xu appreciates your comments and is also looking forward to seeing your next movie."

O'Neill was approaching, looking every inch the naval officer in braid and rows of medals. Santini quickly introduced him to the actress and, taking Xu by the elbow, hustled him to the balcony. Several Chinese officers, who had been approaching from another direction, quickly filled the void around the actress.

"I am sorry to be late," Santini said. "I had to make an unexpected stop at the White House. Sorry."

"No emergency, it is to be hoped," the interpreter replied, her monotone surprising Santini, who had expected to hear Xu's voice. He had forgotten that Xu was careful about where and when he spoke English.

"No. Only the usual bureaucratic matters," Santini said.

When the interpreter finished translating that, Xu took a step toward the balcony rail, pointed toward the Washington Monument, and said softly, in English, "In case anyone happens to be watching, Lieutenant Hua, I am asking Secretary Santini the height of the Washington Monument." He turned to Santini as Lieutenant Hua duly repeated what Xu had said.

"Lieutenant Hua is aware of my . . . my hesitation to speak English in public and acts out the charade of translating to amuse herself and me," Xu continued. Hua smiled and lowered her head as, again, she translated her boss's words.

"The reception will soon end and we will be going into the formal dinner," Santini said. "I suggest that we try to have a few minutes of private time."

Lieutenant Hua provided the needless translation. Santini nodded toward a woman in a crimson dress, part of the security detail. She stood by the door of a lounge that reflected the decor of a room in Mount Vernon designed by Martha Washington. As the door shut behind them, Xu suggested that Lieutenant Hua examine the painting—Edward Hicks' *William Penn's Treaty with the Indians*—at the end of the room.

Santini and Xu walked to a gleaming table on which sat one of the reception rooms' treasures, an eighteenth-century porcelain punch bowl that commemorated Western trade with China. A painting on it depicted the port of Canton, where traders bustled along the shore of the Pearl River.

"Very appropriate," Xu said, pointing to the clusters of

traders in front of their warehouses, from which flew flags proclaiming their nationalities. "Trade, not warfare."

"This bowl is not ordinarily in this room," Santini said. "I had it moved here so that you would have an ostensible reason for our tête-à-tête. Something to tell General Li."

Xu frowned at the mention of Li's name but did not respond immediately. With a sweeping gesture, he encompassed the room. "This is the place of the State Department—trading, keeping diplomacy and markets open. Why do we have the reception here and not in the Pentagon?"

"The Pentagon does not have any facility like this. The State Department loans it to us."

"And, occasionally, do you loan helicopters to the State Department?"

"Only when there is trouble and people must be moved quickly away from the trouble."

"Yes. Moving away from trouble. We very much want you to move away from trouble by not sending air-defense systems to Taiwan. And by repudiating the Taiwan Relations Act."

Santini was prepared for an anti-Taiwan remark, but not one that was quite so blunt.

"That is more a matter for Secretary Palmer," Santini sparred.

"When Americans destroyed the Chinese Embassy in Belgrade," Xu said, "one of Secretary Palmer's predecessors came to Beijing and explained the incident. And it was I who accepted the bombing as a tragic accident."

U.S. intelligence assessments had put Xu high on the short list of Chinese officials who believed that the bombing was accidental, thanks mainly to the State Department's detailed review of events. But several other high Chinese officials still did not believe the U.S. explanation.

"I've personally reviewed the reports on that tragic accident, General," Santini said. "You have my word that it was an accident. You are right. Others who still doubt are wrong."

Xu nodded. "I closed the matter long ago. New subject: The military-to-military agreement is vague. There is little that is concrete."

Santini was relieved to hear a shift away from the bombing incident. "We hope that we can have a tabletop exercise for humanitarian relief and perhaps eventually a joint military exercise. We can go to work on that immediately."

"That is in the future," Xu said, his stagecraft frown reappearing. "China wants something specific now. China wants a guarantee that U.S. Navy warships will not transit the Taiwan Strait."

"The United States would also like to have some guarantees. As I mentioned at our meeting earlier today, the United States wants something from your government—particularly with Iran. We've received reports that China has been helping supply Iran with nuclear technology and that Iran may be about to declare itself a nuclear power . . ."

"Secretary Santini," Xu said, staring directly into Santini's eyes. "I can assure you that your intelligence is a fabrication. We have done nothing of the sort. While we may not support your efforts to punish Iran through any UN Security Council action, we will do all in our power to discourage Iran from developing weapons of mass destruction, including nuclear weapons . . ."

"I appreciate your directness, Minister Xu, and will report your assurances personally to President Jefferson. But enough of our respective desires. They are too important for a casual conversation in a beautiful room."

The door opened. The notes of a Strauss waltz wafted in as the Army's Strolling Strings walked past, heading for the state dining room.

"I will report this conversation personally to the President," Santini said. The patient Lieutenant Hua was still at the end of the room, her back turned to them. Santini reached into the inside pocket of his suit coat and took out an envelope. "In the event you can't reach me with the device I gave you, call me directly at this number," Santini said. "If you need to contact me, night or day, your message will reach me."

Xu responded by giving Santini a sheet of paper on which a telephone number was written. "I believe you call this back-channel communication," he said, smiling. "This number is to a phone in Switzerland. But it reaches me and only me."

"Thank you, General. And now we must go to the banquet," Santini said. "I believe that lotus-seed soup and goose with apricots are on the menu."

Xu smiled. "Your military attaché Brigadier General Waters should receive an additional star," he said. He called to the lieutenant in Chinese and the three filed out of the room.

CHAPTER 15

BEIJING

Chi Zhiqiang, the President of China, was in a light mood this morning. Gathered around a large burled-walnut conference table were six of his most trusted advisers. They sat in black, glove-leather chairs that easily accommodated the soft girth of some and the taut angularity of others. At the far end of the low-ceilinged, richly paneled room were three separate projection screens, each bearing the colorful symbol of the Military Intelligence Service.

Only in his early sixties, Chi was fit and mentally sharp. He was a man who exhibited in his every word and gesture the serene confidence of one who has been tossed on life's most turbulent waves and survived, neither bent nor broken. He was young for a head of state by Chinese standards, and he planned to remain in power for at least a decade longer. All at the table but Peng Fong, an old party functionary ever ready to talk about Mao, were comfortable with Chi's leadership and his steady helmsmanship.

Chi, as usual, had allowed several minutes to pass in silence as he fussed with his teacup, lit a cigarette, and scribbled a few lines of calligraphy on a pad before him. He prided himself on his calligraphy, an obsession that had much to do with his being sent as a young boy to a prison farm during the Cultural Revolution.

Protocol dictated that Chi spoke first at these leadership meetings. He turned to Xu, the Minister of Defense, and said,

"Tell us, Minister Xu, how you were received in Washington? We are eager to learn about your impressions of Secretary Santini and whether you think he is someone you can make progress with on issues of importance to us."

Xu did not answer the President's question directly. A consummate bureaucrat and a very cautious man, he stuck to the report that he had prepared.

"I went," he began, "to the U.S. Military Academy along the Hudson River above New York City, had lunch with the cadets, and attended a very boring game—a baseball game—between the soldier cadets there and sailor cadets from the American Navy's officer school in Maryland, near Washington. I believe that the soldier cadets won. Apparently believing that the Great Chinese Revolution was somehow a civil war, my American hosts also took me to a famous battlefield of their civil war. I politely listened while my hosts tried to make me understand that what happened in America in the nineteenth century somehow had something to do with China in the twentieth and twenty-first centuries. By then I was exhausted, but I continued on in a kind of flying Long March.

"My next stop, in the middle of America, was the most interesting one. It was the headquarters of America's Strategic Command. I was amused by the proverb—the slogan, they call it—that I saw everywhere. It said: 'Peace is our Profession.'

"I spent some time in the command center, which is underground. I have already sent a report on the center to the appropriate intelligence officers. It was a rather enticing tour, not unlike the dance of a seductive woman: I am shown many attractions, but I cannot touch them. And I cannot take the attractions home."

Chi laughed, and the others instantly joined in. The President stopped laughing abruptly, and so did the others.

"In time of war," Xu continued, "the underground installation would be sealed off, and American officers could run the war from there rather than from Washington. I was particularly interested in the miniaturization of electronic facilities. They only need a few square feet for command and control equipment that in China would fill a large building. We need to take into account—"

"Please, General Xu," Chi said with exaggerated weariness, "do not use this occasion for a speech about your budget needs." He looked toward Li Kangsheng. "Tell us what you learned on your American travels."

"I was taken to the Joint Forces Command, what used to be called the Atlantic Command, in Virginia, a place south of Washington, and—"

"Norfolk," Xu interrupted irritably. "The base was at Norfolk."

"Yes, my general, Norfolk. Many ships. Nuclear submarines—I entered one tied to the dock and had hamburgers and ice cream with the crew members. Many were black men. I then was taken, in a large aircraft similar to the President's Air Force One, to an Air Force base in New Mexico and an Army base in Texas, where I was given a very amusing briefing on what the briefing officer called Operations Security, a program aimed at preserving secrets, particularly about computer and signals security."

"Amusing in what respect?" Chi asked.

"In telling me what they were protecting," Li responded, "they were telling me what was the most valuable and perhaps most accessible intelligence," Li said. "I, too, have presented my observations to the proper intelligence officers. I also visited the nuclear weapons design facility at the Sandia National Laboratory, also in New Mexico. I saw many Chinese there. Some of them were American and some were countrymen, visiting scholars from China. As you know, it is in that laboratory that—"

"We will not go into other matters at this time," Chi said. "Now, Minister Xu, tell me about Defense Secretary Santini."

"Santini was open and receptive," Xu said, speaking quietly and slowly, a trait that annoyed Chi, for he sensed that Xu was being condescending. But Xu had another reason for speaking slowly; his mind was entwined around questions raised by Li's report. It was incomplete and did not coincide with Xu's knowledge of Li's itinerary. There were omissions. Li was, more and more, straying off, developing his own agenda.

Xu kept working on these thoughts while continuing his report . . . "It is obvious," he continued, "that Santini had his marching orders"—Chi frowned at Xu's use of the American idiom, which sounded odd in Chinese—"from the White House. I heard the same script everywhere I went in Washington—at a meeting with members of the National Security Council and at a meeting with Chinese specialists at the State Department." Xu paused and sipped from the hot tea that had been placed on the table by soft-footed servants, who moved like sylphs as he spoke.

"There was, of course, an unspoken agenda. The officials I talked to were quite frank about the anti-Chinese atmosphere that has arisen since the American media began pounding the drums about what they see as Chinese villainy."

Chi again showed surprise. *"Villainy?"* he inquired.

Xu sighed. "I have been accused of being outspoken in my discussions with you, President Chi," he began. "Allow me to be outspoken again. You are shielded from the Western media. Your advisers do not tell you what journalists are saying on FOX Television, what *The Washington Times* or the *New York Post* is reporting about China."

Chi leaned forward for a sip of tea. Three of the other officials made identical gestures. A cone of silence enveloped the moves. Xu well knew that the silence signaled displeasure with his words. He also knew that hidden microphones were recording these words. The words would be entered in his dossier and someday, perhaps, they would be used to cast him away from the leadership cadre or raise him higher. Either could happen at any time. Xu remembered one of his father's many proverbs: "There are many paths to the top of the mountain, but the view is always the same."

He plunged on. "For well over three years the American media have been building up China into the successor of the Soviet Union as the next 'evil empire.' The so-called war on terrorism changed the focus for a short time. But China is still being viewed as a potential enemy. There are some who say that the Cold War has not really ended but is beginning again, with China as the new enemy. We acted unwisely with our surreptitious donations to the American politicians. Frequently we have brought down big trouble for small, silly acts. Now we have a chance to act more intelligently, more responsibly. And the man we should be cultivating is Secretary Santini.

"I sensed that he was genuine in his hospitality, especially in his remarks at the banquet in my honor—in China's honor. He was doing more than going through the motions, as the Americans like to say." Chi frowned again at Xu's translation of what seemed to be an Americanism. "There was something else, though," Xu continued, the tone of his voice rising, signaling for more attention from his listeners. "Santini seemed preoccupied when he received me for the honor guard reception. His mind was focused on other matters." Xu glanced over to where Li was seated.

"I noticed that he seemed to focus on Deputy Minister Li with deep curiosity." Xu kept his eyes on Li as he said, "It was as if he somehow knew him from somewhere." If Li read anything into Xu's comments, he did not show it.

"Any discussion about our concerns over Taiwan and Japan?" President Chi interjected.

"Yes, of course," Xu replied. Xu decided that he first needed to mention his private exchange with Santini at the State Department.

"President Chi, at one point Secretary Santini said the United States had received reports that China was helping Iran with its nuclear program."

"He said that?" Chi asked, a tone of disbelief in his voice.

"Yes, but he did not seem to be serious. He said this in response to my request that the United States agree not to send any of its warships through the Taiwan Strait. I took that as little more than a tactic to see how I might respond."

"And you said?" Chi pressed.

"Of course, I denied it as preposterous. He seemed satisfied. It was all a part of the parrying that took place. Santini reassured me that Washington was not trying to undermine its one-China policy, that they were not supporting any independence move by Taiwan, and that it was hardly in its interest to encourage Japan to play either a larger or a more aggressive role in Asian affairs."

Chi seemed unimpressed with what he had just heard about Santini's assurances. "Yes, of course," he said in an acerbic tone. "That explains why they continue to sell what they call defensive weapons to Taiwan, push the Japanese to acquire missile-defense systems, and quietly urge them to provide the Americans with greater assistance should a conflict erupt on the Korean Peninsula."

Chi's sarcasm provided Li with the opportunity to intervene. "Precisely, President Chi," Li said. "I have a number of reports on American activities. Their deeds speak much louder than the platitudes they continue to serve us." Li turned to the large screens at the end of the room. "Lights, please."

Xu frowned. Li was not even pretending to be a subordinate. Boldness in a military officer was appropriate, Xu thought, but not in a conference room.

As the room darkened, Li stepped toward the screens and, using a laser beam for his pointer, began his weekly intelligence trip around the world. The screen to the far left displayed a digitized map of Europe, with geographical boundaries being erased by a dark wave that washed up against the borders of Russia.

"The Americans are using Iraq as a launching pad for their greater ambition to control the oil wealth of the Gulf. They continue to use NATO's so-called Partnership for Peace program as a ruse to prepare more nations to enter NATO. Soon, Russia will find its back up against a firing wall. The United States' alignment with Russia in the so-called war on terrorism was only a ploy."

"Nonsense!" Chi cut in, interrupting Li before he could even get started. It was a favored technique of Chi's to keep his officials on their toes and remind them that he did not swallow any precooked bromides. "Iraq sticks like a bone in America's throat. And NATO is far weaker than it appears. By spreading its arms to embrace more nations, it has weakened its heart. Look at what the American Congress is saying to its European friends: 'Why have you not matched your pledges with your money?' And what do the Europeans say? Nothing. They just continue to cut back on their military budgets and declare that more money is unnecessary, that the United States is simply trying to create a market for its defense industry where none is necessary. Russia's problem is not NATO. Russia's problem is Russia."

Xu smiled. Russia was Chi's particular specialty, and Xu knew that the subject had now definitely changed from America to Russia.

"The Russian Army is still in a state of disarray," Chi continued. "It will take years to build a conventional capability, and now they must rely on nuclear weapons in a false claim to power." Dismissing Russia as a threat to China, Chi remarked that they were using Russia as a supplier of major weapons systems at bargain prices. He mentioned Vladimir Pavlovich Berzin, somewhat to the surprise of Xu; the Minister of Defense had not realized how much detailed defense information was at the President's fingertips. *It comes from Li,* Xu thought. *Of course.*

Berzin was China's principal supplier of sophisticated electronic equipment. And, Xu knew, Berzin had opened a grisly but lucrative sideline: human organs. Every time a Chinese prisoner was executed, every time a young and vigorous man died in a hospital accident ward, the victim's organs were removed and given to a secret organ-selling enterprise. Xu knew that the People's Liberation Army was involved in the organ selling—and that Li controlled the PLA trafficking. Intelligence Bureau operatives loyal to Xu had given him transcripts of telephone calls between Li and Berzin.

Xu had been warned by a loyalist in the headquarters of the PLA General Staff to stay away from the organ-selling enterprise, which was viewed as a private activity involving Li and Berzin. Over the years, the PLA had marched down the capitalist road, setting up more than twenty thousand profit-making enterprises and creating one of the world's largest business empires. The PLA operated factories making everything from tourist trinkets to aircraft. The PLA also had seized land for luxurious golf courses (golf was a new pastime for ranking PLA officers), started a tourist cruise line on the Yangtze River, bought professional basketball teams, and was running a chain of disco bars where drinks, karaoke, and women were all available. The PLA had also joined forces with the People's Armed Police, China's major uniformed security force, in large-scale smuggling. One of Xu's loyal agents had leaked information about the smuggling to a correspondent of *The Washington Post*. The report estimated that the PLA-PAP smuggling ring was costing the government $12 billion a year.

When Xu had shown the report to President Chi, who had warned Xu to be careful about what he called "the People's Capitalistic Army," Chi had cautioned Xu to turn his eyes away from the excesses of the PLA. Such selective blindness, Xu believed, was the price that Chi had to pay to maintain PLA support of the civilian leadership.

Soon after showing the *Post* report to Chi, however, Xu had been given secret orders to purge the PLA of its business ventures. Chi had seen to it that the secret order became known to the Western media, which produced numerous stories about Xu's crusade. Xu had seen the publicity as a form of protection and a guarantee that he would not be purged while he himself was purging the PLA.

At the same time, Xu had worked to transform the PLA into a Western-style army, the kind he had seen in the United States. But again and again, he had been confronted by obstacles that Li threw in the way. Soon after Xu had been told to get the PLA out of its business role, for example, the civilian leadership had handed down another secret order: All enterprises owned directly by the headquarters of the General Staff would be exempt from the purge. These enterprises included a huge weapons-selling company, a real estate firm, and the chain of discos.

Xu had wanted to get rid of Li. But Li was too well entrenched—a good word for the way the military protected him. And there were other trenches, too: secret graves for officers who challenged Li and then vanished.

Now, here was Li, still onstage, still going on about Berzin. "He is a very resourceful man," Li was saying. "Without entering Russian government channels he has managed to sell us technology that cannot be legally exported. With this technology we are rapidly improving our air-defense systems.

"Yes, he's a good man, or should I say an unprincipled one? He has acquired a considerable following in the political world and has a chance to become the next President of Russia. We should support him financially. Although he is in no need of money, he will appreciate the gesture. Russia's election laws—unlike those of our American friends—are written in sand. We will not have any embarrassments in giving our money to a *Russian* candidate." While Li laughed, President Chi did not share his sense of humor. He motioned for Li to continue.

Li had all the confidence of an ideologue, for whom zealotry was a mark of honor. As the next large wall monitor flickered on, he presented a series of satellite images showing U.S. Navy warships in the Philippines, in ports in Japan and Okinawa. Another image showed a huge new dock in Singapore.

"This is of particular interest to us," Li said, "for its dimensions are such that it is perfectly designed to accommodate a U.S. aircraft carrier—a warship armed with nuclear weapons."

Xu interrupted. "With all due respect, Deputy Minister Li. As you may have forgotten, U.S. aircraft carriers and other surface ships do not carry nuclear weapons."

"And with all due respect to you, Defense Minister," Li said, his tone shading toward disrespect, "how do we know that this is true?"

Xu, looking toward President Chi, shrugged, hoping that his shrug answered Li's question. Xu had only recently privately assured the President that Chinese military intelligence in America had proved amazingly accurate. On his recent visit to Washington, Xu had visited a private estate in Virginia and personally decorated a high-ranking U.S. security official who had been spying for China. The Defense Minister maintained firm and direct control over military intelligence, taking extraordinary precautions to keep Li and his allies from knowing the identities of Xu's American operatives.

"I do not share Minister Xu's trust of the Americans," Li said. "They are continually pushing, pushing, trying to surround us, contain us."

Li felt himself losing control and took a breath. But it was too late. Words came tumbling out of him. "We should have bombed Taiwan. We showed weakness. We could have tested them—and they would have buckled. We waited and the Americans used the delay to urge Taiwan to be bolder. This strengthened the ties between the United States and other Asian countries. Look at how they outflank us. Their aircraft carriers are docking in Singapore; Japan is a Pentagon colony; American companies that front for the Pentagon and the CIA are setting up operations in central Asia."

He calmed himself and moved on to the next image. "And there are indications of U.S. Navy activity at Cam Ranh Bay in Vietnam. A port visit, they say. As you know, I was opposed to the resumption of port visits so quickly after the *deliberate* American attack on our embassy in Belgrade."

Xu looked as if he was about to say something, but he did not speak.

Turning to the center screen, Li directed his laser beam to the Persian Gulf. "The Middle East, as the Americans and British call it, remains the same. There will never be peace between Jews and Arabs. Thanks to us, Iran is more powerful now and could shut down the flow of oil for days, and the United States would find the Iranian Navy more than a match for it in close quarters."

Xu wanted to note that this was not an unqualified bonanza, for China was importing millions of barrels a day to fuel its own industrial growth. And could China outbid the West for oil? He did not speak. He looked at the President and judged that if there were to be any more interruptions, the President would make them.

"The United States," Li continued, "is unlikely to strike Iran. But Iran will strike at American targets all over the world, especially in America itself. It will be a worldwide war. One for which the American people are not prepared."

Li seemed to find particular delight in this notion.

As Xu and Li were leaving, President Chi nodded for his assistant to stay behind. He pointed to a tapestry-covered couch. "Can you stay a moment, Zhao?" It really wasn't a question. "I need to discuss something with you."

"Of course, sir," Zhao said, closing the door behind Li and Xu before he slipped onto the couch.

"I continue to hear rumors, whispers about General Li," Chi said in a voice that was little more than a whisper itself. He was never sure whether the recording system was ever turned off, even if he had ordered it turned off.

Zhao said nothing. He waited for China's leader to continue.

"I know about his illicit activities," Chi continued. "The deals that he strikes with his Russian friends. I have enough to fire him for corruption and self-dealing and send him to prison." Chi reached for a cloisonné box resting on the long coffee table in front of the couch. He extracted a cigarette and lit it with a snap of an ornate butane lighter that lay next to the box.

He drew the smoke deep into his lungs, closed his eyes for a moment before exhaling. "I realize that his self-dealing is not unique. There are others—many others—who should go to prison."

Zhao nodded. This was not news. Chi had had this conversation with him before.

"President Chi, I think there will be time enough for that. Li has the support of many in the PLA. It is too soon for you to provoke a confrontation with the military." Zhao's voice was barely audible. "Wait until you have consolidated power. . . ."

"I understand this, of course. I can't consider moving against him yet. Not on these charges. But I'm worried that he is engaged in something far more dangerous. That nuclear test that was set off in Lop Nur was a mistake. I was not told about the test until after it had been conducted. Many died, and many are dying still, of radiation poisoning. The Uighurs do not need any more reasons to hate us. They have been handed a new grievance. Li deliberately concealed the test from me so that I would not be able to stop it. Then I would have no choice but to pretend that I authorized it. He is bent on showing that, when it comes to national security matters, his power is superior to mine."

"I disagree, sir," Zhao said deferentially. "Li is headstrong. But he's not so foolish as to engage in such a brazen act of defiance. The PLA, whatever its faults, would not condone open insubordination. There has been talk that the United States has decided to proceed with what they called nuclear-tipped 'bunker-busting' earth penetrators. General Li no doubt wanted to build morale in the PLA and assure them that two can play the same game."

"But it is not acceptable for him to make a decision like this without my consent!"

"I agree, President Chi. But be patient. In a few more months you will be in a position to remove him."

CHAPTER 16

Li Kangsheng emerged from a black Mercedes staff car, followed by an officer who had sat along the wall during the meeting with President Chi. They shouldered their way through a milling mob of young people and entered a disco. That was what they called it. Disco. There was no Chinese name for this place, this small item in the bulging investment portfolio of the People's Liberation Army. *This building,* Li thought, *had been a hatchery, a place where we hatched the young chicks who would become the falcons of China. And now this—*

Conscience was a bourgeois idea, his teachers had told him in the school for promising sons of party members. Conscience was a Christian capitalist invention designed to put an individual's thoughts and wants into a channel created and maintained by the ruling class. And yet . . .

Li experienced the mental spasm of an unacceptable doubt. He felt that the PLA takeover of the cadet auditorium was somehow wrong. Li was at what he called the balance point, the place where the firm old ideals of the party confronted the ever-changing new practices of the party. Thousands of prospective officers had marched into the auditorium and had heard lectures on the conduct expected of an officer.

Now officers like Li were expected to enjoy the fruits of the double economy: old-line communism that controlled the masses and state-sponsored capitalism for the elite. Frequently, the two economies collided—as had happened only days before in a dismally poor little village in the south. The teachers in a grammar school had forced their pupils to make firecrackers for an export company controlled by the PLA. The teachers sold the firecrackers at a profit, enhanced by the fact that the pupils received no wages. When the school exploded, killing dozens of children, the local party leader had threatened the grieving parents with jail if they breathed a word of the incident to the outside world. Li and others in the ranks of the elite had learned of the incident through a secret party report that said the local leader had been officially reprimanded and sent to another province.

To Li, the incident was additional evidence that the double-economy doctrine was weakening China and would ultimately destroy communism, returning the nation to the warlords of old. The peasants would rebel, and the PLA would be called out to quell the revolt. It would be as if the PLA were to be like the running dogs of Chiang Kai-shek. *And yet . . . and yet . . . In revolution, worst was sometimes best.*

Li led the other officer through the crowded entranceway, past a coat-check girl in a filmy red dress, and to the edge of the crowded dance floor. Li, stocky and fit, carried himself well, knowing how to convey the air of command. He stood a handsbreadth taller than the officer behind him, Major General Zhou Xi. A bald and portly man without a trace of an officer's grace, Zhou had the smiling mien of a Buddhist monk. His appearance as well as his vague, absentminded ways had made him the butt of jokes, especially among younger officers. They called him the Monk and mocked the singsong voice he used when he quoted ancient poetry to make a point.

Zhou served as Li's principal aide, providing him with insights into the world beyond China. Zhou spoke English well, Russian fluently, and French passably—languages that he had acquired in private study and then enhanced during his tours in the military attaché offices in London, Moscow, and Paris. Zhou was so cosmopolitan that many ranking PLA officers distrusted him. But Li saw him as an asset, at least for now.

Later, when times were no longer soft and when blood flecked the wind, perhaps Zhou would no longer be as useful.

Throbbing white lights pierced the smoky darkness, bounced off the silvery walls, and bathed the dancers' ghostly faces. Rock 'n' roll music of the 1970s bombarded the room from two dozen powerful speakers. The disco's sound and light systems, Li knew, had come from Taiwan, as had the engineers who had transformed the auditorium. They and their goods had been smuggled into Beijing by PLA officers, aided by the officers and crew of a patrol ship operating in the Taiwan Strait. A general on the personal staff of the party chairman had authorized the sale of the PLA auditorium to a dummy corporation that consisted of the general, his mistress, and his eldest son, Shen Quintau, a PLA colonel on Xu's staff. Shen, a slim, grinning man too young to be the colonel he was, bowed and welcomed the two generals.

Li, Shen, and Zhou stopped before a tall, unsmiling man in a tuxedo loose fitting enough to fit over a shoulder holster for a Glock 34 and a bulletproof vest. He stood in front of a door near a bar on the edge of the dance floor. Li tugged at the man's bow tie, pulled it forward on its black elastic band, and then let go. It snapped back askew. "All is well, Sergeant?" Li asked.

"All is well, General," the man replied, a quick, tight smile crossing his face. "You have one visitor." He reached his right hand behind him and pressed a button. The door slid open, Li, Shen, and Zhou passed through, and the door closed behind them. They walked down a short, dimly lit hall to another door. Li pressed six numbers on the electronic lock, turned the knob, and led the other two officers down a stairway that spiraled into the center of a large room.

At one end of the room was a maroon leather couch and two matching chairs. Antimacassars covered the arms of the couch and chairs. On a low teak table were set three blue-and-white cups and a blue-and-white teapot. A man rose from one of the chairs and bowed at the approaching Li and Shen.

"Congratulations, Wang Gui," Zhou said. "I learned today that you have become the youngest general in the Chinese

Army." Zhou approached Wang Gui and limply shook his outstretched hand.

Wang Gui was taller than Li and darker skinned, with a hint of Mongolian blood in his angular face. His uniform was well tailored, its fabric a light worsted, slightly padded in the shoulders, pinched at the waist. It was tailored in Hong Kong and contrasted sharply with the uniforms worn by Zhou and General Li, the PLA's standard shapeless tunics and trousers of polished cotton dyed a drab olive green, a humbling reminder of the days when PLA officers wore no badge of rank or decoration. Brigadier General Wang Gui, Li thought, was as far from peasantry as those stockbrokers walking down Beijing streets with their cell phones stuck to their ears.

General Li sat in the middle of the couch. Wang Gui and Shen flanked him in the chairs. Zhou took a chair against the wall. Li poured himself a cup of tea and reached over to fill Shen's cup. He put the teapot in front of Wang Gui, who would have to refill his own. Li did not offer any tea to Zhou.

Li placed his black briefcase on the table, unlocked it with a small brass key he took from his pocket, then retrieved a thin blue file folder. He opened the file and took out a paper.

"We have just attended a meeting with President Chi Zhiqiang," Li said, turning toward Wang Gui, who looked up from pouring his tea. "It was, as usual, pitifully boring. President Chi goes through the motions of running a meeting. I believe that his drifting mind lives more in the past than in the present. And my so-called superior, Minister Xu, is little better. He was reporting on our journey to America." He turned to address Zhou. "A journey you were fortunate to miss, General Zhou."

Li leaned back and sipped his tea. He held the piece of paper before his eyes as if he were reading it. But this was all pantomime. The paper was in English and Li could read no English. After waiting a judicious moment, giving the impression that he had satisfied himself of the paper's contents, he reached over and handed it to Zhou, saying, "Read this."

"Aloud?" Zhou asked.

"Yes. Aloud. So that we can all enjoy it."

"It is what Americans call a short message," Zhou said, adding, in English, " 'memorandum.' It appears to have come from the office of the American Defense Secretary, Santini, and it is addressed to"—he looked up, confusion and astonishment playing across his usually bland face—"addressed to the President of the United States."

"Very good translation so far," Li said, laughing. "Please continue."

" 'Mr. President,' " Zhou read, " 'my preliminary talks with MOD Xu' "—Zhou stated the English letters, then, continuing in Chinese, added, "Minister of Defense." He paused again for a moment, then resumed reading and translating: " 'Convinced me that he represents a reasonable China. But I feel that he, like other moderates, is being pressed by hard—' "

"That is enough," Li said, reaching for the paper and replacing it in his briefcase.

"But how . . . ?" Wang Gui asked, springing forward. "How . . . ?"

"I have my own channels," Li said. "You are perhaps too young to remember that China once had a spy in the CIA, a patriot named Larry Wu-Tai Chin. He was unmasked by the traitor Yu Zhensan, who had been Director of the Foreign Affairs Bureau of the Ministry of State Security. Yu Zhensan defected to the West. It was a very long time before the Ministry of State Security developed another spy. As you know, I do not trust the Ministry of State Security. So I have found my own spies. Such intelligence is needed for my plans."

Wang Gui stood and placed his hands together. "It is as General Sun-tzu wrote many centuries ago," he said. " 'If you know the enemy and know yourself, you need not fear a hundred battles. If you know yourself and not the enemy, for every victory you will suffer a defeat.' "

"Yes," Li replied. "General Sun-tzu. We learn from the past. We also learn from the present. We learn that Minister of Defense Xu became very close to Santini. We learn that Xu may be on a traitor's path. He is giving away"—Li waved the paper—"giving away Taiwan. And to give away Taiwan is to give away China."

Li took a breath and leaned forward, as if drawing them all into a closer group. "President Chi," he said quietly, "is a great fool. He refuses to see what the Americans are doing to us. Bases in Pakistan—our former ally—and in Kyrgyzstan, Tajikistan. They have set up operations again in the Philippines. More weapons to Taiwan. Port visits to Cam Ranh Bay.

"We sit and watch them spread their imperial arms—all in the name of fighting global terrorism. And Chi tells us to be patient! No, I tell you. It's absurd what we are doing. We make so much out of the fact that the Americans turn a blind eye to what we do with the Falun Gong or in Tibet.

"Our fearless leader preaches to us that our goal must be a 'quiet imperialism.' Build our economy. Avoid stoking fears over our increasing presence in Panama, Southeast Asia, and Saudi Arabia. The Americans did not detect our test in Lop Nur. They continue to underestimate us. One day they will get a taste of our power."

"And the death of the Uighurs?" Zhou asked. "Do the Americans . . . know of the deaths?"

"Koestler, Santini's predecessor, started down that path," Li answered. "But he did not live long on that path."

Li leaned back on the couch and allowed a long silence to settle upon the room. "We—we few now, we many very soon—we must isolate America, make the Superpower impotent. A sharp sword, as Sun-tzu would say, is the best way to the heart. To weaken America, we must weaken the Pentagon. And we have already begun. I direct your attention to the destruction of German warplanes in America, at an American Air Force base."

Wang Gui and Zhou exchanged glances. "Do you mean that you somehow caused that collision?" Zhou asked. Shen wanted to ask the same question.

"I believe that the Americans often call the Chinese inscrutable," Li said, laughing again. "I shall remain inscrutable even from you, my friends. But allow me to become a seer."

He picked up his teacup, swirled the last few drops of tea about, and peered at the tea leaves arrayed on the bottom of the cup. "I see even greater accidents coming—tragedies for many people."

CHAPTER 17

SHANGHAI

The New Shanghai, as the Chinese liked to call the city, appealed to Vladimir Berzin far more than Moscow did, especially now, when Moscow was so drab and dull and full of homeless drunks. "Whore of the East" and "Paris of the Orient" had been the names for Shanghai in its wild, lawless past. And that past still hovered in the shadows of what was now China's largest and most prosperous city, a city that made Beijing seem like a smoky backwater still groping its way out of the twentieth century. Berzin had stashed a small fortune in Shanghai, pouring dollars into both legitimate real estate investments and some murky but profitable arrangements with the Chinese gangs that ran prostitution and the drug trade in the city.

Shanghai was a center for child prostitution in China. Berzin avoided that business, not from a sense of morality but because that was not where the real money was. The new millionaires in Shanghai wanted style in their pleasure. The money was in escort services and $1,000-a-night courtesans. Only two years before, Berzin had bought shares in the three biggest escort services in Shanghai. Now he owned a controlling interest in one of them, and soon he would control all three.

He stood on the balcony of his suite in the Grand Hyatt Hotel, a white terry-cloth robe wrapped around him, and watched the swirl of traffic along the Bund, Old Shanghai's riverfront district. Behind him he heard the door open and close as Hsu Lin departed, as usual without a good-bye. She would be back in a few hours, wearing, he imagined, the sea-green gown he had selected for her during yesterday's shopping spree. They would dine in a quiet upstairs corner of the Dragon-Phoenix Restaurant, listen perhaps to very tame jazz in the bar downstairs, and then he would enjoy another glorious night with the talented Hsu Lin. He turned, entered the bedroom, and began dressing for his appointment.

Li arrived precisely on time, accompanied by a slight, stoop-shouldered young man in an ill-fitting brown suit, green shirt, white tie, and yellow sandals without socks. "My interpreter," Li said by way of greeting. Berzin nodded, smiling at Li's absolute lack of cordiality. To him, Berzin thought, courtesy—even mere civility—was a sign of weakness, a veering toward bourgeois values. Berzin knew the type. He had met many as a child and adult, in East Berlin as well as in Moscow.

Li and Berzin had met several years before, when Li was working for a PLA general who had studied missile technology in Russia and then gone to work for the China Trade Company (CTC), a firm in which the PLA had a large secret stake. CTC's mission was the development of telecommunications technology for military use. Li had been sent to Moscow to look up former KGB officers who could help him get that technology the easy way—by stealing it from the United States. Not much happened in Moscow without Berzin's knowing about it. He heard what Li was looking for and showed up unexpectedly in Li's hotel room with a Chinese-speaking interpreter at his side. Berzin became a commission agent for CTC and, after extracting a large fee, arranged for Mafiya confederates in the United States to set up a legal-looking U.S.-Chinese joint venture company. The company delivered U.S. telecommunications equipment, encryption software, and thousands of miles of fiber-optic cable to the Chinese.

What Li did not know was that Berzin was also a CIA asset.

So he passed all the information (including solutions of the encryption) to his case officer in Moscow. And what the CIA did not know was that Berzin subsequently made a deal to get versions of the equipment to Iraq for the Iraqi air-defense network. In one last twist, Berzin created a nonexistent agent, whose identity was not known to the CIA case officer. And this counterfeit agent, for a fair amount of cash, gave details of the Iraqi system to the CIA, thus making it easier for U.S. warplanes to attack Iraqi missiles. Eventually, the CIA got a whiff of Berzin's deals. As the CIA was about to drop him with a vague explanation and a large exit bonus, Berzin made his own exit with the demand that his case officer be immediately removed from Moscow.

The CTC success had led to Berzin's rise as a fixer for PLA ventures. Li could openly and legitimately deal with him. So the comings and goings of Li to Russia raised no suspicion in Beijing. Li's Revolution, as Berzin called it, was steadily increasing Berzin's wealth and steadily providing him with insights into the ways and plans of China's leadership.

Berzin's involvement in Li's Revolution began when Berzin learned that Secretary of Defense Koestler was going to recommend to President Jefferson the secret deployment of Patriot III missile batteries to Taiwan, as defenses against Chinese missiles. Koestler had discussed the proposal with Praeger and with arms dealers who would handle the arrangements. After Berzin learned this through his own arms-dealing connections, he passed the information along to Li, who was outraged. As a demonstration of his resources, Berzin told Li he would eliminate Koestler. The deed, as Li called it, bonded Berzin and Li.

When Li learned that he would be in the official party visiting the United States, he contacted Berzin, telling him that more deeds were needed. As Li saw it, a lessening of U.S. power and prestige was vital to his plans. He felt frustrated, he had told Berzin, because he had no way to reach beyond the shores of China. But the assassination of Koestler had convinced Li that Russian operatives in the United States and Europe were far more able to gather intelligence and commit acts of sabotage than Chinese agents. "A Chinese just can't get away with much," Berzin had said, and Li had reluctantly agreed.

Li empowered Berzin to find ways to split America off from Germany as the first step in a plan to limit U.S. power throughout the world. Out of a discussion like the one they were having now had emerged Berzin's plan to use American militia members as dupes for carrying out what Li and Berzin called "the New Mexico incident."

They were meeting on Li's territory today, but Berzin was the host and decided that he would show a sliver of authority by moving the site of their conversation slightly.

"Shall we begin on the balcony?" Berzin asked, pointing to the open double doors. The sheer white curtains billowed into the room.

The interpreter translated so softly that Berzin could barely hear the Chinese sounds. Li, Berzin knew, was uncomfortable with interpreters. He never used the same one twice, and Berzin wondered whether Li had an inexhaustible supply.

Li acknowledged the suggestion by turning on his heel, parting the curtains, and striding onto the balcony. Berzin and the interpreter followed, the latter taking from his jacket pocket a small device that looked like a tape recorder. "I am checking for electronic devices," he said directly to Berzin in perfect Russian.

Berzin motioned Li to a chair at a round, glass-topped table, sat down opposite, and indicated a chair near the railing for the interpreter. In the center of the table was a bottle of Stolichnaya, a siphon, an ice bucket, two glasses bearing Berzin's initials in Cyrillic characters, and a bowl of pistachio nuts. Li looked approvingly at the tabletop, smiled for the first time, and reached for a glass. He poured a generous measure of vodka, snatched up a handful of nuts, and began splitting the shells with his prominent front teeth, spitting out the shells and swallowing the tiny treasures. He set up a rhythm with the nuts and sips from the glass.

Berzin knew that five minutes of this ritual must precede

any talk. He picked up a glass, added a long squirt from the siphon to a splash of vodka, and dropped in three ice cubes. He took a sip and looked over to the interpreter, who sat iron-bar straight, his ballpoint pen, Chinese-Russian dictionary, and notebook at the ready.

The Chinese tradition, Berzin knew, was to treat interpreters, drivers, and other attendants as non-persons. In the presence of their superiors they could not eat or drink or converse or in any way indicate an independent existence. Berzin decided to take some control of the situation. He stood up without a word, put his glass on the table, went inside to the sumptuous bathroom, and came back with a glass of water. He dropped three ice cubes into the glass. "It is hot here on the balcony," he said in English, smiling as he handed the glass to the interpreter.

The interpreter gulped down most of the water. Li glared at him and said something rapidly. Berzin needed no translation. He knew that Li was demanding to know what Berzin had just said.

The interpreter repeated Berzin's comment on the weather.

Li spoke again, calmly. The interpreter turned to Berzin and said, "Before beginning the discussion"—the interpreter lowered his head—"General Li wishes to tell you that the . . . the woman who was here . . . Hsu Lin . . . will not be coming back."

Before Berzin could respond, Li spoke swiftly to the interpreter, who riffled through the dictionary, scribbled something in his notebook, and looked up at Berzin. "The woman, Hsu Lin, does not have a current health certificate. A woman who does have a current health certificate will come to this apartment this evening." The interpreter looked at Li, who nodded. "We will now go on with the discussion."

"Tell General Li that I appreciate his concern for my health," Berzin said, smiling. He assumed that Hsu Lin would be thoroughly questioned by one of Li's officers. Berzin had routinely debugged his suite. So Li wanted to know if Berzin said anything interesting to Hsu Lin. There could be nothing interesting because Berzin did not speak Chinese and Hsu Lin did not speak Russian. But that was exactly the kind of reality that Chinese intelligence officers usually ignored.

Li said something, and the interpreter interpreted: "Look upon the east side of the Huangpu River, the Pudong. Once it was barren. Now, because of the foresight of the Chinese government, the Pudong has many tall buildings, the Shanghai Stock Exchange, and the Oriental Pearl Television Tower. Shanghai has the greatest population of any city in the world."

Berzin smiled again. *Perhaps,* he thought, *Li believes the interpreter is carrying a recorder and felt the need to spout some propaganda.* "A very beautiful and prosperous city," Berzin said. "And a place, I am sure, where businessmen do not waste each other's time."

Li seemed momentarily distracted, his eyes fixed on Shanghai's dramatic skyline. He struggled to suppress his contempt for all that he saw around him. Yes, the Grand Hyatt Hotel in Shanghai was a marvel to behold. The world's tallest hotel, soaring high into the skyline in the Pudong, which seemed to have more steel and glass arrayed in exotic, architecturally breathtaking structures than any other place in the universe. From here on the eighty-eighth floor of the Hyatt, Li could see the ninety-five-story Shanghai World Financial Center, one of the tallest buildings in the world.

Did Deng Xiaoping's vision of the Four Modernizations contemplate such extravagance, such decadence? Li wondered. Oh, the reclamation projects and sky-bending and impressive buildings were testament to Chinese genius and imagination. But at what cost? Discos, McDonald's, Kentucky Fried Chickens, all had sprung up like mushrooms in the dark. They were everywhere and soon Starbucks would spread like a cancer on people who would have to demand higher and higher wages to pay for coffee. Not tea but Colombian coffee was to become the beverage of choice for the newly rich in their Japanese and German cars. And sexual promiscuity had delivered onto them its voracious penalty—AIDS, courtesy of the same people who imported their cars and junk-food operations.

And what did this new go-go generation care about those

who had to live on a penny a day? Or did they know what was happening to the people in Xinjiang, and other remote provinces? In Aksu, the Islamic extremists were assassinating local officials, blowing up buildings, and poisoning livestock. They were trying to destroy the Communist Party there and replace it with a state of their own, called East Turkestan. This was pure terrorism against civilians. Even the hypocrites in Washington had put a Uighur group on the terrorist list—as a sop to China. But Washington was not stopping Pakistan from sending weapons to the Uighur terrorists. In the meantime, China was forced to suffer Islamic slaughter of her people impotently and in silence. *Well, not entirely in silence,* Li thought. *The explosion in Lop Nur was not silent.*

Li could feel his pulse race. The hate that filled his veins was bad for his health, he had been told. But all around him was the constant reminder that Chinese leaders were selling out their souls for this bubble of prosperity that would one day burst. It was inevitable.

Li cared deeply about Chinese history and culture. But above all, he was a military man who had devoted his life to protecting his country. And what he saw unfolding both frightened and enraged him. American-designed air-defense systems and Aegis technology going to Taiwan. American interceptor missiles to Japan. American bases in the Philippines. And the talk of American naval forces returning to Cam Ranh Bay in Vietnam was more than a rumor! They were being surrounded, while America justified its presence in the name of its war on terrorism. Everyone had to be either with them or against them. *Well, count me in as against the bastards. . . .*

"I said," Berzin repeated, "a place where businessmen do not waste each other's time."

The interpreter moved slightly to attract the attention of Li.

Li nodded, snapped out of his reverie, reached into the small leather case he carried, and extracted several sheets of paper. He was about to speak when Berzin said, "General Li, I must confess that I have difficulty separating our two lines of business."

When the interpreter translated, Li looked uncomfortable.

"You are," Berzin continued, "the supervising procurement officer for the PLA. You also are a member of the board of directors of the China International Trust and Investment Company, sometimes called CITIC, to use the Western letters for it. And, to my understanding, that firm is owned in large part by the PLA. So, my question is this: Am I now dealing with General Li, the supervising procurement officer, or *Mister* Li, the board member of CITIC?"

It was a bold move. But Berzin was used to dealing boldly with partners far more menacing than Li. He had not only revealed that he knew of Li's connection with CITIC. He had also told anyone the interpreter cared to inform. The interpreter looked wide-eyed at Li, who spoke sharply to him and poured another glass of vodka.

"You speak too frankly, Mr. Berzin," the interpreter translated. "You are not fully aware of the situation."

"Nor do I believe that you are fully aware of the situation, General Li."

Li motioned for the interpreter to move his chair to the table and poured a generous slug of Stolichnaya into the interpreter's water glass. Berzin sensed a change in Li's tone and demeanor, from gruffly authoritative to conspiratorially friendly.

Li introduced the interpreter as Captain Chang K. Y. Yew, an officer of the Ministry of State Security, the principal Chinese intelligence agency, and said that he had Li's full trust. "So your indiscreet remarks about CITIC"—the acronym remained in English letters during the translation—"will go no further."

As the interpreter translated this, he laughed and shook his head vigorously. "Perhaps we should review the past briefly and then look at the future."

The translations continued more rapidly as the interpreter fell into a more relaxed rhythm. Li and Berzin both picked it up. Berzin assumed that none of the previous interpreters had been from the Ministry of State Security. For a moment he locked eyes with Captain Chang, who now somehow looked less like an interpreter and more like an intelligence officer who had a dossier on Berzin.

An authentic business mission had brought Berzin to Shanghai. He had flown in to supervise the conveying of a shipload of weapons purchased openly from Russian manufacturers by the PLA, under Li's supervision. The weapons included SA-15 short-range surface-to-air missiles, SS-N-22 Sunburn supersonic anti-ship missiles, and S-300 MPU SAMs for the advanced long-range missile base in Zhangzhou on the Chinese mainland opposite Taiwan. During the official Chinese Defense Ministry trip to America, Li remarked, Defense Secretary Santini had mentioned the Zhangzhou base.

"Good intelligence," Berzin said.

"Mine is better," Li replied through the smiling Chang. He could not resist reaching into his case and pulling out a copy of Santini's memo to the President. Attached to it was a Russian translation.

Berzin tried not to look astonished. "How much did you pay my intelligence friends in Moscow for this?" Berzin asked, handing the papers back to Li.

"That is my business, my friend. And I have my own sources. China long ago ceased its dependence upon the Big Brother," Li replied. He used the favored 1960s phrase for the Soviet Union.

"But Big Brother no longer exists," Berzin said. "The Soviet Union is no more. Russia is weak and troubled. And so you must deal with me, a champion of capitalism, not communism. And I expect you, too, wish to be a capitalist—as do so many officers in the People's Liberation Army."

"That is what I mean about not understanding the situation," Li said. "I am a patriot and a revolutionary. I fervently believe that China must cleanse itself and then find its true destiny—the destiny foreseen by the Great Navigator, Mao Zedong."

"But you are like so many high-ranking officers. You want riches. You deal with me as a board member of a profit-making enterprise."

"We live in a complex time, Comrade Berzin. What we see is not always what is happening. You, for example. You are so many things. Part capitalist, part criminal. And, I believe, patriot. I am well aware that you will do anything—*anything*—to become President of Russia."

"And you, General Li? What are you?"

"I am tolerating what is going on today for what I will cause to happen tomorrow. I oppose the whoring of the People's Liberation Army. I oppose the use of the Army as a capitalistic organization. I want China to return to its revolutionary roots. But, for now, I must make it appear that I am part of the whoring."

"Whore or not, you managed to escape Major Case 4-20," Berzin said. "I've heard a great deal about 4-20. But I'm curious to know more."

At mention of Major Case 4-20, Li and Chang looked at each other, puzzled. Then Li began speaking in what to Berzin sounded like jagged phrases that the interpreter had to string into understandable Russian sentences.

"Major Case 4-20 was an investigation that almost achieved what I had hoped for. Had that case been made known to the Chinese people, I would have launched my new revolution openly. I am as much an admirer of Fidel Castro as of Mao. I have pictured myself leading a revolutionary army into Beijing, throwing out the old and ushering in the new. I fervently believed that the case would bring down the regime, and my people and I would be able to strike. But that was not to be.

"I was secretly given the special assignment of ferreting out corruption, especially in the People's Liberation Army. I set Major Case 4-20 in motion by finding investigators brave enough to stamp out corruption at the highest level. I focused the investigation on one notorious city—the smugglers' port of Xiamen, on the Taiwan Strait. Since the time of the Ming Dynasty, Xiamen has been a pirates' roost. You, Comrade Berzin, undoubtedly know it well.

"I was able to learn—to prove—that leaders of the party and high-ranking officers in the People's Liberation Army had grown rich on billions of American dollars paid for by the oil and cars and computer equipment smuggled into Xiamen from Taiwan. All of these imports evaded taxes, bringing huge profits to the traitors when they sold the contraband to their customers, the second tier of the corruption.

"I had my trusted agents secretly take over a huge new hotel in Xiamen, built with smugglers' dollars. My agents then began bringing the traitors into the hotel on various ploys. One by one, they were retained—a member of the Politburo, three senior generals, bankers, and many local officials who had aided the higher-ups. Some escaped, fleeing to Taiwan. But most remained captive: more than one hundred and fifty criminals, held incommunicado for interrogation. On each one of them we had compiled a large dossier for state prosecutors.

"And then, suddenly, the word came from the absolute highest level: Stop. Release the traitors. Close down Major Case 4-20. Forget that it ever happened.

"And so here we are, Comrade Berzin, planning my revolution. That is the result of Major Case 4-20. I have joined them to destroy them. I am using their greed to finance my revolution. I have access to unlimited funds because they think I stopped the case. I am now the major hero of the major criminals."

"Very well done!" Berzin exclaimed, clutching Li's right arm. "I could not have done that bit of deception better myself. And now to business?" Berzin asked, switching to a discussion of the arms shipment.

As the officially designated procurement officer, Li legitimately accepted the weapons after carefully going over the inventory. He signed a document acknowledging official acceptance of the weapons and signed another document authorizing a $70 million payment in U.S. currency from an account of the People's Liberation Army in a Beijing bank to Berzin's bank in Moscow. Berzin assumed, but did not know, that Li was acting in an official government capacity. His only concern was that the check cleared. It always had before.

Li, in turn, did not particularly care whether Berzin was selling the weapons legitimately. Nor did Li know how much of the $70 million went to the Russian treasury, to Russian arms merchants, or to Berzin himself. Arms sales from Russia had become a gray, ever-shifting area for both sides. For Li, the purchase meant a stronger PLA for his future purposes.

Next, Berzin handed Li the number of the Swiss account into which Berzin's bank would deposit $3 million. That was Li's own private commission from Berzin. That, too, would be for the revolution. Or, Berzin thought, for an escape fund if the revolution failed. Berzin had no interest in Li's fate or, for that matter, in China's fate. Anyway, at the dark heart of his master plan was the thwarting of China's and America's plans for domination.

"May we now talk of the other matter?" Berzin asked, tilting his head toward Chang.

"Captain Chang is fully aware of your activity," Li said through Chang, who bobbed his head in acknowledgment of his role as trusted aide. As Chang interpreted Li's words, Berzin noticed that Chang's voice had a decidedly firmer timbre. He was no longer speaking as an interpreter but as an intelligence officer.

Berzin and Li continued talking, always looking at each other and never at Chang, as if both knew that faces and gestures were as important as words when men had to judge each other's promises and deliveries.

"Did you make the payment to Professor A. Q. Khan?" General Li asked.

"Yes. Last week. I drew on the account in the Caymans. He promised to deliver his special dessert to the Iranians soon."

"Can we trust him?"

"Of course. He likes the money—and he likes living."

"Excellent."

"But I'm curious. Why do you want Iran to have nuclear weapons? President Chi has said that China is opposed to the spread of these weapons."

"President Chi is a fool. He's pandering to the so-called international community. It's very simple. Iran should have nuclear weapons because Israel has them. This will deter Israel from ever striking Iran. Or run the risk that Iran will destroy them in return."

"But China is doing a lot of business with the Israelis."

"For now. We gain access to their technology. Once we reverse engineer what their scientists—and those from their American friends—give us, we will build our own laboratories and industrial base."

"And then, they'll be dispensable?"

"Mr. Berzin," Li said, sounding exasperated. "The Israelis have brains but no oil. Soon, we will be in no need of their brains. Thanks to America, Iraq no longer poses a threat to Iran. Once Iran develops its nuclear weapons, it will be the dominant power in the region."

"And the PLA will receive an uninterrupted flow of oil—at a substantial discount, no doubt," Berzin laughed.

"As I said, it's all quite simple."

"Does President Musharraf know of this sweetheart deal you've got with Professor Khan?"

"I do not believe so. But even if he did, what would he do? Arrest Khan? Put him in jail and incur the wrath of the Pakistani military?"

"And President Chi?"

"You ask many questions, Mr. Berzin. Too many. We need to conclude our conversation."

As afternoon shadows fell across the balcony, they reached the end of their talk. "As you know," Berzin said, "I have a much bigger operation planned. It will be better if you do not know the details at this time. It will cost you one hundred million dollars. And it will be worth it."

"May I at least know your estimate of the size of the operation?" Li asked.

"You will know about it when it happens. I promise you," Berzin said.

After escorting Li to the door, Berzin took a moment to look into the future. Smiling in amusement at the thought, once he became President of Russia, he just might expose China's connection to Khan through his old CIA connections. And then, of course, there would be no reason why Russia should not take over Li's deal—on even better terms.

CHAPTER 18

NEAR HOLLOMAN

Hal Prentice walked across the porch, unlocked the padlock on a hasp on the front door, and entered the parlor, as he liked to call the main room of his home—an old, low-slung ranch house fourteen miles north of Holloman Air Force Base. A stone fireplace, built by Prentice's grandfather, spanned half of one wall. Over the mantle hung a flintlock rifle whose stock was made of curly maple with silver inlays. The engraved brass lock plate was signed: *S. Moore/Warranted.* A silver plate on top of the barrel was inscribed: *R. Prentice, 1817,* Hal Prentice's great-grandfather. With this rifle Hal Prentice had shot off a turkey's head at a local turkey shoot and served it last Thanksgiving to the leaders of the Scorpion Militia. By long habit, upon entering the room he reached up and touched the rifle.

R. Prentice would recognize the room's rough-hewn log walls, the big rag rug, the pine floor, the flintlock, the fireplace, and the rocker, a replica of an earlier version. The only new touches were the large television set to the left of the door, the lounge chair in front of the television, and the telephone on the table next to it. To the right of the door, next to a window, stood an old maple cabinet. On it, in a silver frame, was a black-and-white photograph of a young man in a U.S. Marine dress uniform and a lovely young woman in a bridal gown. She had died, at the age of sixty-three, four years before.

On either side of the fireplace was a doorway, one leading

to a big kitchen and the other to Prentice's bedroom. Beyond that, behind a locked door, was the small room that served as Prentice's office.

Prentice hung his sweat-stained Stetson on a deer antlers hat rack behind the door, walked into the kitchen, took a bottle of beer out of the refrigerator, twisted off the cap, took a long pull, and put the bottle on the table. A cat entered the kitchen from somewhere and rubbed against Prentice's ankles. Prentice took a can of cat food out of the cupboard over the sink, opened it, and emptied it into the cat's feeding dish under the sink. He stood up, massaging the slight twinge he felt in his back, and returned to the parlor.

He picked up the remote and turned on the television. He clicked again and the CNN logo appeared on-screen. He looked at his watch. The evening news show had begun eight minutes before. There was a report on the latest round of violence in the Middle East and then a report on what the newscaster called "the incident at Holloman." Once again, the image of the explosion filled the screen. "The FBI says it has several leads on the explosion," the newscaster said, "and progress is being made."

Prentice snorted, drained the bottle, and switched to a movie channel. As he rose to get himself a second beer, the telephone next to his chair rang. "Prentice here," he said, speaking loudly, as he usually did on the phone.

"The password is *liberty,*" the voice on the phone said.

"The password is *liberty,*" Prentice repeated, and hung up. He looked at his watch and walked through the doorway to his sparsely furnished bedroom. He switched on an overhead light, and pulled the shade on the room's only window, blocking out a twilight sky that was darkening into night.

He pulled out from a pocket in his jeans a key ring on a chain, inserted a key into a padlock on a hasp on an inner door, opened that lock, then inserted another key into the lock under the doorknob, opened the door, and stepped into a closet big enough to hold a table and chair. Prentice stepped into the darkness and snapped on a goosenecked lamp, which cast a white beam onto the table. It was bare except for a cellular phone. He looked at his watch again, turned on the phone, sat down heavily on the faded green cushion of a straight-backed chair, and waited. After ninety seconds, the phone rang. He waited for the third ring and picked it up. "Go," he said.

"Delivery at site number twelve."

Prentice turned off the phone, put it back on the table, stood up, left the room, locking the door behind him, and returned to the parlor. He turned off the television, grabbed his hat, and opened the front door.

In the sharp crack of an explosion, the porch lifted off the ground in a cloud of smoke and dirt. Prentice's hat flew out of the cloud as his body burst into fragments. Secondary explosions ripped along the foundation of the house, setting off an inferno that engulfed the log walls and all that they had enclosed. Within minutes, the flaming roof fell in, sending cascades of sparks into the sky. A window shattered and a cat, its black fur afire, leaped through the collapsing frame, ran toward a lone, blazing pine, and died as its front claws dug into the bark.

Several hours later, a yellow tape, labeled *FBI Crime Scene,* was looped around the tree and encircled the remains of the house. Men and women wearing blue FBI jackets were sifting through the smoldering ruins, placing shards of potential evidence into black plastic bags. George Miller, agent in charge of the Santa Fe Bureau of the FBI, was talking to a deputy sheriff, who had been the first law officer to respond to the sound of the blast. "The son of a bitch got what he deserved," the sheriff was saying for the second time. "Fooling around with those explosives. I guess there's no doubt he did those German planes."

"No doubt," Miller said. But he was far from convinced. He had to file an update on his Major Terrorism Incident Report, which had gone to the Inter-agency Action Group and had been read by DNI Ford, McConnell, Pelky, Santini, and the President—and he was not going to write Prentice off as a "Paddy." When Miller was in London, he had heard that label from his liaison, a British Special Branch inspector. A Paddy was an IRA chump who blew himself up with a home-made bomb.

The search had turned up a startling piece of information. In the charred remains several newspaper clippings from *The New York Times* had somehow managed to go untouched by the flames. One contained a profile of Secretary Tom Koestler. Several lines in the story had been highlighted with a yellow Magic Marker. *Koestler was the son of Jews. German-born Jews.* The rest of the sentence, *survivors of the Holocaust,* had not been highlighted. Nor had the next sentence: *Secretary Koestler had converted in college and was an Episcopalian.*

My God, Miller thought. *A twofer.* The militia could have been involved in Koestler's murder. But how? How would they get their hands on anthrax? And how in hell could they have figured out how to penetrate Koestler's security? It didn't make any sense. But then he reminded himself that they somehow had managed to get inside Holloman.

Miller began to arrange in his mind the words he would put in a memo that he was about to dictate. *Two hours before the explosion, the U.S. Federal Court in Santa Fe had issued a search warrant of his house. News of this could easily have been passed to Prentice or his accomplices via the militia group, whose members are believed to include court and law-enforcement personnel. My suspicion is strong that Prentice was killed to destroy him and evidence. It is my further belief—*

"Sir!" one of the agents shouted. "Look at this!" Her face was smudged and her eyes red-rimmed. She held up her right hand. In her palm was a crumpled piece of metal. "It looks like an MST timer," she said.

Miller gingerly made his way through the embers and plucked the fragment from her hand. "I think you're right," he said. "Nice one. Bag it for the lab."

Miller was elated. He now had something solid for the up-date. He had been on the task force for Pan Am 103. The key clue then had been a twisted piece of metal like this. A CIA tech expert identified it as a very sophisticated timer, made by a Swiss firm named Mebo and known commercially as the MST-13. A Libyan intelligence operative had one in his baggage when he had been picked up in a sweep. And that intact device was used to identify the Pan Am fragment.

Now, according to the Bureau's terrorist assessors, there were real MST-13s and knockoffs all over the world. Mossad used a variant for telephone bombs. It pointed to what Miller suspected. Somebody had decided to kill Prentice so that the investigation would dead-end with him. And whoever did the job did not mind sending an MST message. But why? Miller saw the answer unfold in his mind. In his update he would say: *I believe that the perpetrators wanted to shift the blame for the sabotage from Prentice's militia to another, higher-echelon entity. It is a message: International terrorists are targeting U.S. territory. But it is a message without a signature—yet.*

PART 2

Bread of deceit is sweet to a man; but afterwards his mouth shall be filled with gravel.

—PROVERBS 20:17

CHAPTER 19

"The committee will come to order," John Phelps, the Chairman of the Senate Foreign Relations Committee, declared as he banged his gavel hard trying to silence committee members and staff who were conversing noisily.

In order to accommodate an overflow crowd, the open session was being held in the cavernous hearing room in the Hart Senate Office Building.

Santini gathered himself at the witness table, sipping from a water glass. He had not slept well last night. His secure phone kept ringing throughout the night. It was Admiral O'Neill alerting him to a cascade of bloody violence.

A homemade bomb exploded at a posh day care center in London. Sixty people had been wounded, twenty-two critically. Thirty-eight were dead. Thirty-five children and three babies. Their heads and limbs had been ripped away by the nails, bolts, and ball bearings that had been stuffed into several school supply boxes containing more than twenty pounds of dynamite. A radical group that called itself the Brotherhood of the True Path, affiliated with the Abu Sayaf in the Philippines, had claimed credit for the carnage.

In Rome, Bob Kelner, the CIA's station chief, was cut in half by a powerful IED (improvised explosive device) as his lightly armored BMW pulled away from his house. His driver and two bodyguards were also killed in the blast. Three men wearing ski masks were seen riding away from the smoldering wreckage on high-speed motorbikes.

Brig. Gen. Scofield, serving as a defense attaché in our embassy in Amsterdam, was stabbed to death while purchasing coffee in a Starbucks coffee shop. Dutch officials said that it appeared to be a random attack.

Santini knew better. The dogs of terror were running loose in the world, and the only surprising thing was that the blood hadn't run red in America's streets last night.

But it wasn't terrorism that brought Santini to Capitol Hill this morning. Wesley Blackburn, the junior senator from Oklahoma, had introduced a bill to impose economic sanctions against China and to suspend all aspects of military cooperation with what he considered to be an implacable enemy of the United States.

Senator Phelps had tried to arrange for Santini to appear along with the Secretary of State and the National Intelligence Director, but Santini begged off, indicating that a long-scheduled trip to Colombia to explore the growing threat posed by the drug cartels prevented him from participating with the other Administration members.

This was partly true. But the real reason was that China's Minister of Defense was scheduled to visit Washington in a week and Santini didn't want to be forced to respond to questions that were likely to be provocative and inflammatory, possibly causing Xu to cancel his visit.

He had another reason for invoking a "scheduling conflict" with the Foreign Relations Committee. He didn't want to appear in the company of others. While there was some comfort to be found in a crowded foxhole, sitting at the witness table in the company of others would reduce the deference that his former colleagues were likely to pay him. In tandem, he would be treated as just another Administration witness. Alone, he would be seen by most as still one of them, a member of the world's most exclusive club.

That is, except by Wesley Blackburn, the author of the sanctions legislation, and a few of the young Turks who had joined ranks with him.

Blackburn was one of the newly arrived legislators who was anxious to make his mark in national politics. He came to the Senate after Santini had departed and so felt little fraternal kinship for Santini and had no inclination to defer to his judgment.

"We're pleased that you could join us today, Mr. Secretary," Senator Phelps intoned. Phelps possessed a deep and mellifluous voice and had a cadence and manner of speech that was mildly reminiscent of one of the Senate's revered giants, Everett Dirksen. Like Dirksen, he had a shock of white hair that always seemed to be in need of a comb, but the comparison stopped there. Phelps was not given to Dirksen's courtliness or rhetorical grandiosity. Those who challenged either his expertise or authority could expect to be on the receiving end of some very sharp verbal slaps.

"Mr. Secretary, as you know, the committee is deliberating on a very serious matter involving our relations with China. What we say or recommend will have profound consequences not only for our country but for some of our closest allies and friends. . . ." Phelps continued to stress the need for a thoughtful discussion of the proposed legislation, rarely straying from a text that he had distributed to the press moments before he opened the hearing. At the conclusion of his remarks, he recognized each of the committee members for brief opening statements.

When Phelps finally recognized Blackburn for his opening remarks, the bank of television cameras that lined the room swung, in choreographic unison, to capture and disseminate his face and words to the waiting world. Blackburn wasted little time on courtesies.

"Thank you, Mr. Chairman, and welcome, Secretary Santini. Since we have limited time and so much ground to cover, let me be as direct as I can.

"China has remained steadfast in its support for the brutal, Stalinist regime of North Korea, a regime that continues to develop nuclear weapons over the objections of the international community. As everyone including Secretary Santini knows, they are the world's biggest contributor to the proliferation of drugs, weapons, technology, and pirated materials. It is just a question of time before they send plutonium and enriched uranium onto the black market or into the waiting arms of Islam's most radical terrorists. That material will one day be used to reduce our most populous cities to radioactive cinders."

Blackburn paused, allowing the image of mushroom clouds enveloping our homeland to grab the attention of all who were watching or listening to him.

"When China had the chance to bring the North Koreans to heel, its leaders insisted that the U.S. had to be more flexible in our dealings with this brutal regime!"

Blackburn shuffled through his notes, discarding several pages, saying, "I'm not going to take the time to point out how the Chinese continue to flood our markets with cheaply produced goods, driving our industries into bankruptcy and workers onto the jobless and welfare rolls. . . ."

Someone in the hearing room jumped up and yelled, "You damn right, Senator. Me and my brothers in Local 47 saw our factory doors slammed shut and locked because of the slave labor goods we had to compete against. It ain't fair, goddammit. It ain't. . . ."

Others started to shout, their visible anger threatening to disrupt the proceedings.

Senator Phelps slammed his gavel down hard.

"Order! There will be order in here! Anyone who seeks to disrupt this hearing will be physically removed. And if we have any more outbursts, I'll shut these proceedings down!"

After casting a cold eye on those in the audience, Phelps softened his voice. "Now, I know emotions are running high, but we have to proceed in an orderly fashion, or we just won't be able to continue."

Again, Phelps scanned the room to determine if any were going to brook his authority. Seeing none, he motioned for Blackburn to continue.

"Thank you, Mr. Chairman. I'll try to be brief so we can hear from Secretary Santini. Chinese leaders persecute those who wish to practice their religion, be they Christian, Buddhist, or Falun Gong; they violate all concepts of human rights and the rule of law by imprisoning journalists and any and all who dare to speak out against their iron-fisted rule. . . ."

As Santini listened to the litany of charges leveled against China, he knew that any attempt to point out how far China had come since the time of its ruinous Cultural Revolution and the reforms advocated by Deng Xiaoping was likely to be futile.

A perfect storm was taking shape in American politics, with liberals condemning America's expanding unemployment rolls and China's violations of human rights, while conservatives pointed with alarm at China's dramatic increase in military power.

Blackburn finally concluded his comments and sat back in his chair. "I look forward to having the chance to pursue these issues with our distinguished witness who is with us today."

The opening statements offered by all the committee members had consumed nearly an hour, but Santini considered this a blessing. The longer they talked, the less time they had to badger him in front of the unblinking eyes of the cameras.

When the Chairman finally recognized him, Santini began by thanking the Chairman and committee members for the opportunity to contribute to the discussion on China and its growing influence on the world stage.

"Gentlemen, much of what you have said today has merit. China is becoming an economically powerful country and one that is likely to pose significant challenges to us in areas that we consider vital to our interest," Santini said. It was a standard debating tactic: make an early, but minor, concession before pointing out the danger or futility of the proponents' argument.

"The central question for me, however, is what is the best course of action for us to take with China? Can we adopt actions that are unilateral or unsupported by our key allies and have a realistic chance of success? Imposing sanctions that others refuse to follow has never proved a winning strategy."

Senator Phelps and several committee members nodded in agreement.

"In fact," Santini continued, "it has only succeeded in isolating us and putting us at a disadvantage with our allies, who in turn become our serious competitors. . . ."

"Mr. Secretary," Gordon Brewster, of Ohio, interrupted. "In times like this, we can't be beholden to our so-called friends. If we will lead, they'll follow."

Santini had heard that line before. "That's possible, Senator Brewster, but most of the countries in the Asia Pacific region don't want to have to choose up sides in this contest. And if push comes to shove on our part, I'm not confident we won't find ourselves waging a battle all on our own."

"So what's your solution? Ignore what the Chinese are doing to us? To our people? To our national security? Throw in the towel?"

"No, sir. Caving in to threats or intimidation is not something I've ever done in my life." Santini added a touch of anger to his words; just enough to subtly remind the members of what he had endured as a prisoner of war.

"But I'm convinced that by working with our allies, building solid coalitions that will hold and support us at the United Nations when we press the Chinese to open up their markets, to become more politically democratic, to see us as a potential partner rather than a competitor in resolving the challenges posed by globalization, transnational terrorism, and the spread of radical philosophies that seek the destruction of civilization as we know it . . ."

As Santini continued to speak, groans could be heard from the audience, causing Chairman Phelps to start tapping his gavel, a signal that he might make good on his threat to close the hearing if there were any further disruptions.

For the next two hours, Santini continued to reason, spar, and occasionally banter with those on the committee. The exchanges were for the most part quite civil under the circumstances, but not particularly satisfying to any.

Several members wanted to know whether the Defense Department had contingent plans to take military action against North Korea or Iran. Santini demurred, suggesting that any such discussions take place during a closed and classified session.

"What about our commitment to defend Taiwan?" Blackburn pressed. "Surely, the Department has contemplated the consequences of a preemptive attack against a staunch ally and friend. Do we have plans to counter and defeat any such attempt to attack a democratic country?"

You bet, Santini thought. Military planners at the Pentagon were working twenty-four and seven revising and updating plans for winning a war should one come. China had the clear advantage in terms of proximity and the potential to launch a damaging blow to Taiwan. The United States had superior military power, but a question remained whether it might arrive too late from Guam or Japan.

They were constantly examining our assumptions. Could Taiwan hold out long enough? What could the U.S. do to put some of China's strategic interests at risk without provoking an all-out war? What would it mean to the rest of the world if it should see the U.S. unable to protect a professed ally? And would the Congress vote to go to an all-out war over a tiny island in the Pacific, one that we agreed was a part of China itself in all of our public declarations since the days of Richard Nixon?

"Senator Blackburn," Santini responded, "as I indicated a moment ago, I think it is unwise to discuss matters of such gravity in the glare of cameras."

"Fair enough," Blackburn said, satisfied he had scored points just by raising the question. "But why not impose some economic restraints on their monstrous buildup in the south? Why do you want to continue military exchanges with the PLA? Isn't this going to come back and bite us?"

What Blackburn was really saying was, Aren't you providing aid and comfort to the enemy?

Santini was tempted to give his stock answer that, "It's good to keep your friends close and your enemies even closer," but he thought it might come off as too clever by half. Besides, part of his problem was that the White House had refused to take a clear position on the Blackburn legislation. President Jefferson continued to make public statements that he was committed to working with our allies in order to present a united front to the Chinese, but he refused to state flatly that if sanctions legislation passed, he would veto it.

And Santini knew that Joe Praeger had been working the phones to Blackburn and his cohorts to keep the sanctions pressure on.

That left Santini out on a limb. Advocating a policy on behalf of an Administration that might reverse course and saw the limb off without a moment's notice or second thought.

"Actually, the Department has simply been carrying out President Jefferson's decision. While there are some who might disagree, the President, our Commander in Chief, is convinced that maintaining military-to-military engagement with China is in our best interests."

Santini knew that this comment would send Praeger into one of his patented rages.

"The senator's time has expired," intoned Senator Phelps, as he tapped his gavel lightly.

Blackburn was not through. "Mr. Chairman, if you would indulge me for one last comment and question," he pleaded. "I have to attend another important committee hearing and won't be able to remain here for a second round of questioning."

"There are other members who've yet to question the Secretary and they have other commitments as well," Phelps said. He was putting Blackburn on notice not to test his patience. "But the Chair will accommodate you provided you're brief. You may proceed."

"Secretary Santini, I've read that in response to a reporter's question of what your biggest nightmare was, the thing that kept you awake at night, you said, 'the threat of nuclear terrorism.'"

Santini nodded. "A nuclear bomb detonated in a major city would kill hundreds of thousands, if not millions, of people instantly. Many more beyond the initial blast area would die of radiation burns and poisoning. Such an attack would have vast economic consequences beyond the monstrous human toll. It's everyone's nightmare, not just mine."

"I completely agree with your statement," Blackburn offered with apparent sincerity.

Santini knew that more than concurrence was coming from Blackburn.

"You've also said that we need to do more to reduce the inventories of those countries that possess nuclear weapons, with the goal of ultimately eliminating them from the face of the earth."

"I believe that I was paraphrasing the sentiments of President Ronald Reagan when I made those comments."

Blackburn ignored the invocation of Reagan's name. "I read a report that said that the Chinese have been covertly testing nuclear weapons at a site located in the northwestern part of the country. I believe it's called Lop Nur."

"I've not seen such a report."

"Actually, it was an article that appeared in the *Washington Times* by Bill Grotsky. I consider him one of the finest reporters in the country on intelligence matters."

"I heard about the article," Santini said, suggesting that he was not one of Grotsky's avid readers. "It's my understanding that much of what Mr. Grotsky wrote was based on speculation and surmise."

"Actually," Blackburn quickly countered, "it was much stronger than a surmise. According to Grotsky, the Chinese have been conducting tests in violation of their treaty commitments in order to improve the W-88 warhead design that they stole from the U.S. a number of years ago."

While Blackburn was speaking, Admiral O'Neill, who was sitting directly behind Santini, slipped him a handwritten note.

Santini glanced at the note and then repeated its contents. "We have no evidence that the Chinese conducted such tests."

"How much 'evidence' do we need, Mr. Secretary? Beyond a reasonable doubt? Can't we consider past behavior? Their pattern of cheat and retreat?"

Phelps saw that Santini's neck was starting to thicken and

go flush. It was a sign to cut off the exchange. Before he could do so, Blackburn turned to him. "Mr. Chairman, the only point I wanted to make is that while it's all well and good to express nightmare scenarios, we're not doing enough to prevent them from becoming a reality. We need to stop coddling those nations that by hook or crook are developing nuclear weapons or who are known proliferators of dangerous technology. We need action, not just words."

Blackburn had just taken a very cheap shot.

Santini was tempted to charge the dais, grab him by the throat, and beat the hell out of him right there.

Any thoughts of physical violence were interrupted by a long, piercing buzzer signaling that a roll call vote had just started in the Senate chamber. Members would have fifteen minutes to cease whatever business they were conducting and proceed to the Capitol either by underground railcar or on foot and cast their votes.

Chairman Phelps quickly seized on the interruption to ask members if they could vote and return to the hearing. Members were quick to indicate that they'd not be returning.

Santini knew that Phelps' inquiry was an idle gesture. It was Tuesday, the day set aside for policy luncheons and discussions by the Senate's leaders. The members would not be returning until early afternoon, if at all.

As soon as the hearing broke up, the senators started to make their way toward the exit door at the rear of the room. Their staffs, clasping bulky briefing books to their chests, traipsed after them as if they were tethered to them with leg irons.

Santini saw Randall Hartley shuffling toward him, blocking Santini's notion of a quick exit.

Hartley was a soft, pudgy man whose balding pate and watery blue eyes conveyed the impression of a lovable Irishman. He was Irish, all right, but *lovable* was a word only a fool would associate with him. He was a shark who liked to feed off the miscues of the high and mighty. He was reputed to have had more lines of communication into the CIA than AT&T. Some of it was hype and quite a bit of it was luck. But a reputation for being all-knowing has a way of reinforcing it-self to the point where the fiction becomes the fact.

"Senatore," Hartley said with just a hint of mockery in his voice. "The committee was pretty rough on you."

Santini knew Hartley was baiting him, hoping to provoke a response that was critical of Blackburn. "That a question, Randall? Or just a personal opinion?"

"Seriously, Mr. Secretary. Blackburn wasn't the only one. Pretty clear they're not happy with the Chinese and seemed to be taking it out on you."

"Goes with the territory. They've got some good points to make, but not many have any experience or perspective when it comes to China."

"What about their growing military power? Does it concern the Pentagon?" He stood with a copy of the *Post* rolled under his arms. Hartley never took notes while asking questions, forever conveying the notion that he was just engaged in a bit of informal conversation. Not to worry. Just between us two friends. But he had a photographic memory. Total recall. He could—and often did—quote verbatim every word ever spo-ken to him.

"Sure. And we need to challenge them when they start bending or breaking the rules. But if we overreact and just start berating them publicly, it's going to backfire on us."

"That the President's position?"

"Last time I checked."

Santini wished he had withheld the last statement. He had implied that the President was a weather vane that kept spin-ning in the wind. That touch of sarcasm would not go down well at the White House.

"Anything you want to add about the charge that China has been conducting illegal nuclear weapons tests?"

"Nothing I can add. We don't have any proof of any testing. At least that's what we know to date. As for—"

"Sorry, Mr. Secretary," Admiral O'Neill interjected, nudg-ing Santini gently toward the door. "You're scheduled to meet with the Joint Chiefs back at the Pentagon. We're behind schedule already by ten minutes."

Santini apologized to Hartley and then allowed himself to be wafted away in the protective arms of his security detail.

As he proceeded down a flight of stairs and walked toward the atrium of the Hart Building, he glanced up at the monstrous Calder sculpture that was supposed to symbolize mountains reaching up to touch clouds that came in the form of a Texas-size surfboard suspended from the ceiling of the building. Santini's intense dislike of the giant piece of art had not diminished from the days when he first saw it.

"Amazing," he said, shaking his head in obvious disgust. "Take one of the most expensive buildings ever constructed in Washington and then stick a thirty-nine-ton chunk of metal in the center of the building and then block out all the light from the skylight above—a skylight that was supposed to be one of the building's architectural delights. Well, that gives you some sense of why things are so screwed up here on the Hill."

O'Neill rather liked the sculpture, but decided Santini was in no mood for a different opinion.

"Understood, sir."

Everything is going according to plan, Mohammed bin Hashami thought to himself, as he placed his carry-on luggage on the conveyor belt that slowly pulled it under a hooded tunnel.

They are bigger fools than the press ever imagined. It's so easy. They don't even seem to give much of a damn!

Hashami then stepped through the U-shaped magnometer designed to detect potentially dangerous metal objects. He cleared it with ease. As he turned to look for his bags, he noticed that the conveyor belt transporting his bags was not moving. The fat lady wearing a too-tight Transportation Security Administration (TSA) uniform was staring intently at his luggage on the monitor. Hashami did not recognize her. She must have been a recent hire. He was counting on Steven Mersand or Catherine Sanger to be on station today.

A knot of anxiety wrapped itself around Hashami's stomach. What was she looking at? Seconds passed.

The woman reversed the conveyor belt, sending the bags back a foot or more before pulling them forward at a snail's pace. Hashami remained outwardly calm, pretending indifference.

The woman was about to call out for another agent to examine the ghostlike images projected on the screen when a man in a TSA uniform came up behind Hashami and draped an arm around his shoulder. "Hey, Mohammed! What's this, a day off? You know we're short around here."

Ron Gherhart's voice broke the woman's concentration. Gherhart was her immediate supervisor. Quickly surmising that the passenger had to be a fellow TSA employee, she sent his bags forward. No sense pissing off the boss on her first day.

Hashami flashed his million-dollar smile, the one that conveyed a joyous personality to the outside world. "Hi, Mr. Gherhart. I need to visit some folks in New York. I'll be back tomorrow night on the late shuttle."

"Okay, son, we need you back by Sunday. All those World Bank demonstrators will be heading home or wherever in hell it is they go when they're not starting trouble."

Hashami snapped up his bags, waved good-bye to his supervisor, and walked briskly to Gate 21. Slightly built, almost deliberately effeminate in his movements, he was the kind of person who appeared to pose no threat to others. But his manner concealed an anger that burned inside him hot as a solar flare.

The anger was not always there. He had come to America filled with hope and excitement. He loved his home in Mosul, but he knew that there was no future there for him. As soon as Saddam Hussein was dragged out of his spider hole, Hashami decided to live in the United States. His family had been helpful to the Americans and had befriended those who were initially in charge of reconstructing Iraq's political and physical infrastructure. They had arranged for Hashami to travel to America on a student visa and helped him to secure employment to pay for his tuition and housing.

Having friends in high places helped anywhere. In Iraq, it could save your life; in Washington, it could get you employed. The Transportation Security Administration was looking for young, low-wage employees. And to demonstrate that America was not anti-Muslim, as most Muslims believed, those in charge of TSA's Office of Human Resources actively pursued a policy of ethnic diversity. What could be better than showcasing a young Arab who could help screen passengers passing through the nation's capital?

Everything was fine at first. His studies were going well. He made many new friends in school and on the job. He met the daughter of a Moroccan diplomat during Ramadan after prayers at the mosque on Massachusetts Avenue. Their friendship was little more than platonic, but Hashami had hopes that one day they would marry.

Then his world unraveled in a matter of a few violent seconds and his plans for a blissful future vanished.

The call came at three o'clock in the morning, shattering a deep sleep. "Mohammed. I'm sorry. . . . It's hor . . . horrible." He recognized the voice immediately. It was his uncle, Ibrahim.

"What is it? What has happened?"

"Your father and sister. They are . . . dead."

Hashami had thrown off his blankets, swung his legs from the bed over to the floor, and jumped to his feet. "No! No! I spoke to Father yesterday, to—"

"They were slaughtered. Like dogs, Mohammed. Dogs." Ibrahim began to sob. Moments passed before he could collect himself. Then, between gasps, he related how Mohammed's father, Ahmed Abdul bin Hashami, was rushing Mohammed's little sister to a hospital after she inexplicably had taken ill. Driving at night in Mosul while a curfew was in effect was always a hazard. Driving very fast at night was the equivalent of playing Russian roulette.

Ahmed Abdul had no choice. Haifa, bleeding profusely, had fallen into a state of shock. Doctors did not make house calls in Mosul. He had to get her to an emergency room. His panic was intensified by his wife's cries for him to hurry. He laid on his car's horn, alerting anyone who had ventured out onto the streets to get out of the way.

He spotted a short convoy of Humvees that had slowed in front of him. He pulled out around them, slamming the palm of his hand even harder on the horn. Suddenly, bright lights flashed through the windshield of his vehicle, their intensity nearly blinding him. Momentarily losing sight of the road, he slammed on his brakes and swerved onto the dirt shoulder of the road. Once he regained his bearings, he downshifted and pressed the accelerator to the floor.

Seconds later, a volley of hot metal punctured the car's thin sheath as if it were aluminum foil and ripped most of Ahmed Abdul's face and brain away. Haifa's little body was riddled with scores of .50-caliber bullets, killing her instantly.

As Hashami listened to the story of carnage unfold, he felt his knees go weak. His emotions ranged from disbelief and horror to anger. He let out a long plaintive shriek.

"Who told you this? How do you know . . . ?" Hashami shouted. "What happened to Mother? Did she . . . ?"

"Your mother is in the hospital. She's suffered grievous wounds. The doctors say that she'll live. But she cannot walk again. Ever."

Mohammed continued to choke back more cries, as he tried to calm himself. He fell silent, fighting to project a stoicism that he did not feel. It was rage that he felt. A deep and profound hatred for those who had just destroyed his family.

He had grown increasingly disturbed with the nightly newscasts that revealed the abuses carried out by American soldiers against his people. At first, there was the Abu Ghraib scandal. Just a few bad apples, as the Pentagon was fond of saying. Torture, sexual humiliation, desecrating the Koran. This was not part of the American character, they insisted. But they had beaten and even murdered some of their prisoners.

Now this. Trigger-happy soldiers who shot first and cared less about who they killed. The Iraqis, after all, were worthless peasants. "Dogs," as Ibrahim said.

Hashami promised himself that night that he would one day avenge their deaths.

Now that day had come.

A more astute TSA agent might have observed something slightly odd about Mohammed bin Hashami as he walked toward Gate 21. He had a small duffel bag and a medium-sized suitcase on two roller wheels. But that was just the problem: The suitcase looked heavy, but Hashami was carrying it, not letting the wheels touch the ground. Not entirely strange, but not quite right, either.

Hashami had his reasons. Or at least Tago, the Chechen who gave him the suitcase, did. Tago had called him a few days after Uncle Ibrahim had called. Tago, who spoke Farsi, did not explain how he had learned Hashami's name and where he was working. Tago must have talked to people in Mosul.

After getting the call from Tago, Hashami agreed to a meeting at a café in Georgetown, a place where, Tago said, one could hide in "plain sight." They briefly exchanged pleasantries, huddling at a corner table, whispering conspiratorially. Tago began by trying to decipher whether Hashami possessed enough rage to sacrifice his life in an act of retribution. Within a few minutes, Tago was satisfied that Hashami's hatred for the Americans was deep and that he was a candidate for recruitment in the Army of Allah.

Tago set up another meeting at the café. This time, they went into the basement and entered a small room. On a table, under a shaded hanging light, was a suitcase. Tago began instructing Hashami about the mechanism that could give him a way to exact his revenge.

The suitcase had been specially constructed. The wheels on the bottom of the suitcase appeared to consist of a standard polymer. Actually, the wheels were made of a highly explosive compound known as Semtex, which had been molded into spherical shapes. Even on close inspection, the Semtex spheres looked like plastic wheels. Semtex, which was twice as powerful as TNT and virtually undetectable, was not chemically volatile. But Tago did not want to take any chances of the wheels being damaged by rolling on the hard surface of the airport's floor. So he told Hashami to carry the suitcase rather than move it on its wheels.

Connected to the wheels was a fine, almost invisible thread inserted into the metal housing that secured the two wheels to the base of the suitcase. Inside the housing, a small piece of flintlike material would strike a ridged piece of metal when the suitcase was dropped from a height of three feet or more, causing a spark to arc its way along the thread into the Semtex wheels. That, said Tago, was why such care had to be taken in the handling of the bag. Hashami must be sure that the TSA agents did not toss it around carelessly.

Tago took a small plastic bottle from the pocket of his black, sharply tailored jacket. "This," he said, "is holy water from Mecca. It was obtained by an imam who had been given the mission by Osama bin Laden. Drink this." He handed the bottle to Hashami. "When this sacred water enters your body, you will be absolved of the act of self-sacrifice, which is forbidden for ordinary men."

Hashami drained the bottle and handed it back to Tago. "There will come a certain day," Tago said. "And on that day—*and only on that day*—you will be told to board a certain shuttle carrying this suitcase. Do you agree?"

Hashami nodded. Tago said good-bye and Hashami left the café. Tago's men kept Hashami under surveillance from that moment to the chosen day.

Hashami stopped at a fast-food shop for a slice of pizza. He sat patiently at a small yellow laminated table, drinking a Pepsi, munching on the pizza, and watching the passengers beginning to gather near the gate. He wondered how many gave even the slightest thought about the danger that awaited them. What would they say or do if they knew they were about to be dispatched to a fiery hell?

The US Airways Shuttle agent at the counter called for the boarding to proceed. Hashami had been instructed to reserve aisle seat 10C, located adjacent to the left wing of the aircraft. The Semtex was powerful enough to bring down the plane. But Tago wanted him to take no chances. The wings of the Airbus 319 served as fuel tanks. Any explosion inside the aircraft was bound to cause a massive secondary explosion once the jet fuel was ignited. The plane would plummet like some giant broken-winged bird that had just touched the sun. And if Hashami correctly carried out his mission, the aircraft would fall just before it landed at New York's LaGuardia Airport.

Once again, New Yorkers will feel the sword of Islamic justice plunge into their black hearts, Hashami thought, as he placed his bags carefully into the overhead bin and took his seat.

Just before the doors of the cabin closed, a young, smartly dressed woman rushed aboard. She scanned the interior of the plane and quickly assessed that she had few, if any, choices for a seat. The plane was packed. Only one seat open, 10B, a middle seat, so dreaded by frequent shuttle users. She apologized to Hashami for disturbing him, as she signaled that it would be necessary for him to stand up and allow her to slip into the seat next to him.

"No problem, ma'am," Hashami said, nodding graciously, as he stood and allowed her to pass.

The woman carried only a soft leather briefcase and a small purse. Once the aircraft became airborne, she extracted a thin laptop computer from the leather case and turned it on. While trying not to look as if he was peeking, Hashami noticed the woman's name as she powered it on and entered her password. It flashed off quickly and she began scrolling through a screen full of e-mails.

Just minutes after the pilot announced over the intercom that the flight was on its final approach and that the flight attendants should prepare the cabin for landing, Hashami signaled one of the flight attendants that he desperately needed to visit the lavatory. Federal flight rules prohibited anyone from standing during the flight from Washington to New York, but US Airways usually tried to accommodate those in distress, particularly those they judged to have no malice in mind.

Hashami stood and indicated to the attendant that he had to extract something from his bag before visiting the lavatory. The attendant, recognizing Mohammed as one of TSA's employees who screened her bags frequently, nodded her approval. He snapped open the overheard storage compartment and pulled his suitcase out with a severe jerk. Then, glancing at the attendant and fixing a cold killer's stare at the woman who occupied seat 10B, he shouted, *"Allahu Akbar. Allahu Akbar."*

God is great! FBI Inspector Leslie Knowles instantly knew what Hashami was about to do. She unlocked her seat belt and lunged at him. Her last thought was that she was strangling him. Then, in a fiery instant, she, Hashami, and 160 others plunged to earth.

CHAPTER 21

Santini arrived back at his apartment shortly after 9 P.M., the usual time. Fifteen-hour days constituted an average workday. Sometimes, they ran longer.

After taking off his tie and suit jacket, he went into the kitchen and extracted a chilled bottle of vodka, along with a glass from the freezer compartment of his refrigerator. He poured a double shot and walked out onto his large wrap-around terrace overlooking the Navy Memorial on Pennsylvania Avenue, ten floors below. He stared down at the seven-foot bronze statue of "The Lone Sailor." Santini loved the memorial for its simplicity and symbolism.

The young sailor stood, feet spread, the collar of his unbuttoned Navy pea coat turned up against his neck, a full duffel bag at his feet. His cap was perched just right on his head, the coat catching a slight breeze. The sailor said many things in his silence. He looked as if he had just returned from a long deployment. Or was about to go off on one. He conveyed confidence and strength, but Santini sensed there was a sense of world-weariness about him as well. Even though he was an old Army man, Santini felt a part of that sailor.

Santini had missed the sunset again. And tonight, for some reason, he decided to miss the smoking of one of his coveted Cuban cigars. He left the terrace, walked into his study, and slipped into his favorite chair, an Eames lounge. It was the only piece of furniture that he had brought with him from New York.

Eight months ago, after he had received the call from the White House and the invitation to join Jefferson's team, he had little time for house hunting. The broker he had hired said she had found the perfect place for him. A luxury condominium located on Pennsylvania Avenue, exactly halfway between Capitol Hill and the White House, with a panoramic view of the city.

The owners, a gay couple who were interior designers, had decided to move their business to Palm Beach, Florida. They were asking a million dollars for the unit, fully furnished.

Perfect, Santini thought. Assured that the apartment was "top-of-the-line," he agreed to buy it, sight unseen. A standard "walk-through" prior to signing the contract might have spared him the surprise he received when he entered his new acquisition for the first time. It looked as if everything there had been purchased at a Chinese "going-out-of-business" warehouse sale. Virtually every space was filled with colorful garden seats, serene waterfall scenes that had been hand-painted on parchment scrolls, cloisonné bowls, and figurines.

It mattered little, however. He wasn't planning on doing any entertaining. His divorce had pretty much drained him of the desire to light any romantic candles. Besides, there was simply no time.

He swirled the vodka around in the glass before taking a drink. Snapping on the fifty-inch flat television screen, he flicked the remote control to tune in to the evening news. He tuned in. It would be another two hours before the Jay Leno show was scheduled to come on. He looked forward to Leno's ten-minute monologue each evening. It was the only chance that he'd have to laugh.

Santini wished that he had something other than work in his life, but, hell, he rationalized, it wasn't forever. After all, he was serving a cause higher than himself.

The loud ring on his secure telephone jarred him from what was becoming a slide into self-pity.

It was the Pentagon's call center, Cables.

"Sergeant McCloskey, Mr. Secretary. Sorry to disturb you, sir, but there's a gentleman who says his name is Randall Hartley. That he's a friend and needs to talk with you. Shall I put him through, Mr. Secretary?"

Santini hesitated momentarily. What in hell was Hartley calling him for?

Santini decided to take the call. "Put him through, Sergeant."

"Been a few hours since we talked, Randall," Santini said, trying to strike a cordial note. "To what do I owe the honor?"

Santini could practically hear Hartley break into a patented, slow smile.

"Forgot to mention it this morning. I'm in the press pool on your trip to Munich this week. But I'm sure you already know that."

Santini hadn't checked the flight manifest but didn't want Hartley to know that he was not quite as hands-on as was his reputation. He said, "The Security Conference is a little tame for you, but I'll try to make it interesting."

"I'm counting on it. But that's not why I'm calling. Just wanted to check with you on the situation out at Holloman. I'm told that the people who blew up the Germans had a nasty encounter with some explosives. My sources say they're sucking them up with a straw."

O'Neill had informed Santini earlier on what had happened. He made a mental note that Hartley had said "sources." Santini assumed that the FBI Director, Frank McConnell, or his deputy was the "Deep Throat" leaking to Hartley. "Sounds like perfect justice has been achieved." He tried to keep his tone flat and noncommittal.

"For sure. But there's more to it than what Joe Praeger has been out spinning today."

"Such as?" Santini asked, anxious to know what Praeger was pushing to the press.

" 'Dial Militia for Murder' makes a nice headline, but, according to the people I'm talking to, it's a little too neat. I never bought that phony story about Tom Koestler being killed by his cows. My sources tell me that the people who killed Koestler and sabotaged those German pilots were foreigners, not militiamen."

So Hartley was digging into the Koestler assassination. Maybe something would start to happen. "Don't suppose they've said who?"

"Not yet. Just that the anthrax and time bombs are beyond this group, no matter what the White House is saying. I'll keep you posted when I know more."

"Thanks," Santini said, wondering what Hartley was going to demand in return. He placed the phone back into its cradle and tried to think through the implications of what Hartley had just told him.

Motive. Opportunity. Capability. Someone had all three.

But who?

Santini turned to catch what remained of the evening news. He was surprised to see the network was replaying his testimony earlier that day. As he watched his exchange with Senator Blackburn, he began to brood. What really got to him was Blackburn's comment about Santini needing "evidence beyond a reasonable doubt."

Christ, wasn't he the one who more than twenty years ago demanded that we stop treating terrorism as if it was just another criminal act? He knew that the danger of nuclear weapons being supplied to Islamic jihadists was great enough to warrant something more than a criminal indictment in federal court! Blackburn was right about the need to take action.

But damn it! He needed some proof that China was cheating on tests. He had yet to be convinced that China had any interest in seeing North Korean balls of plutonium falling into the hands of Muslim extremists. There was no "actionable intelligence"—*God, how I hate that phrase*—on either score.

Suddenly, the intense voice of television journalist Wolf Blitzer jarred Santini to full alertness.

"Breaking news. This just in: CNN has just learned that a US Airways Shuttle plane has crashed near New York's La-Guardia Airport. Eyewitnesses at the scene said the plane exploded on its final approach. According to initial reports, a bright light or flame was seen streaking toward the plane seconds before the explosion. Rescue teams report that the cockpit and the front half of the aircraft disintegrated upon impact with the landing strip, while the remainder of the plane is scattered in the waters surrounding the airport. All passengers aboard the plane are presumed dead. Stay tuned for further information on this latest tragedy."

"Jesus," Santini shouted, a sense of dread coursing through him. There had to be military aircraft and ships in the area. New York remained a prime target for terrorists. The city had been under heightened alert ever since 9/11.

Maybe the pilots of the shuttle did something stupid or made a mistake as they approached LaGuardia. Maybe an overcaffeinated F-15 fighter jock flying cover corked off an AIM-9L missile. Maybe a spark flew along some frayed wires in the fuselage and ignited vapors in the fuel tanks. Maybe a goddamn terrorist fired off a Stinger missile or sneaked through the security checkpoints at National Airport with a bomb tucked up his ass.

Maybe . . .

Santini knew it was going to be TWA 800 and déjà vu all over again. Through his mind in an instant came recollections of Flight 800. The Boeing 747 left Kennedy International Airport on July 17, 1996, bound for Paris. Minutes after takeoff, the airliner exploded and plunged into the Atlantic, about ten miles off Long Island, killing all 230 aboard. As the FBI and National Transportation Safety Board began investigating, television newscasters aired rumors that the plane had been shot down, not by a terrorist but by a U.S. Navy missile. That rumor was fading when Pierre Salinger, who had been President Kennedy's press secretary, claimed that a French intelligence source had told him that the rumor was true and that the U.S. Government was engaged in a cover-up. Eventually, investigators concluded that the cause of the disaster was an electrical spark that had ignited fuel vapors in a fuel tank.

And now, Santini feared, it was going to happen again. All he knew was that he had to get on it now. Right now.

He reached for his secure phone and hit the button for a direct connection to the Chairman of the Joint Chiefs of Staff, General George Whittier. The line would ring directly into Whittier's quarters at Fort Myer, across the Potomac from Washington.

Whittier had to be sitting on the phone. He picked up the line after the first ring. "Yes, Mr. Secretary."

"Mr. Chairman. A commercial aircraft just went down at LaGuardia. There are reports that some witnesses are claiming that they saw a fiery object streaking toward the aircraft before it exploded. We need to get everyone on this immediately."

"Yes, sir. I understand. Flight Eight Hundred."

"George. We'll need to have as much information as we can get before our meeting in the morning. Run all the traps. How many of our folks were in the area tonight? Ships, planes. Any goddamn thing that moves. We'll need to account for all of our weapon systems. Every vehicle and piece of equipment in our inventories from tanks to Taser guns. Have our guys check and verify the time and place of any live firings in the last twenty-four—make that forty-eight—hours. There's bound to be a thousand crazies who'll claim they saw armored Humvees flying over Manhattan."

"Got it, Mr. Secretary."

It was another sleepless night for Santini.

After tossing in bed for over an hour, he swallowed an Ambien sleeping pill desperately hoping to get at least three hours of sleep. It didn't work. Finally, at 4:30, bone weary, he dragged himself into the condo gym. While on the treadmill, he turned on the television to *Headline News*. All major East Coast airports were in lockdown, which meant that air traffic was tied up from Boston to Beijing. The Internet was flooded with threats that bombs had been placed on at least twenty aircraft. Another report said that a meteor had struck the airplane. It was a goddamn mess.

Curtis picked him up at 5:30. After a quick scan of the PDB and truncated meetings with his CIA and DIA briefers, he called for the Top Four meeting to begin half an hour early.

General Whittier was the first to arrive.

"What have you got, Mr. Chairman?"

"Looks like we got a little lucky, sir. A portion of the fuselage was retrieved by the NTSB and the FBI." The other advisers arrived and silently took their places around the table.

"They were all over the scene up at LaGuardia almost immediately," Whittier continued. "They think they found a piece of the aircraft where the explosion occurred. It came from inside. Not an external hit."

"A bomb?"

"Looks that way, Mr. Secretary. But they can't say anything until a full investigation takes place."

"But that could take months!"

"If TWA Eight Hundred was any example, we're looking at something longer, sir. And we can't rush to judgment on this. The airlines are still locked down. If word is put out that it was a bomb and we're wrong on this, it could kill the industry. It's still possible that it was an internal vapor explosion, just like TWA Eight Hundred. The FAA just released a report that said that none of the airlines have made any of the safety upgrades that they were supposed to do years ago."

"I understand all that. But explain to me how it's possible to slip a bomb through all of that new equipment that TSA and Homeland Security have been bragging about. They practically assured everyone that they could pick up an ant's fart in a hurricane."

"I spoke with the Bureau's explosive expert. He said that it could have been Semtex that was used. That's the stuff that the Czechs developed back in 1966. It's the terrorists' choice of weapon. It's like C-4, only more malleable and has a greater temperature range than other types of plastic explosives. It was virtually undetectable. The Czechs finally caved in to international pressure and added ethylene glycol dinitrate as a taggant to give it a very distinctive vapor signature."

"So if they added the chemical, how did it get through the detection equipment out at Reagan?" Santini asked. He stood up and walked to the window overlooking the parade ground and the Potomac marina beyond. *The gulls are flying. Not the airliners.*

"Well, sir, the Czechs shipped tons of the shit to Russia long before they started adding the perfume. Could be that was where the stuff came from."

Santini turned sharply and asked, "Are you saying that the Russians are behind this?"

"No, sir. Just that it might explain where whoever did this might have gotten their supply."

Santini nodded. He remembered seeing General Alexander Lebed once during a television interview. Lebed had been lifted to iconic status by the Russian people for his heroics on the battlefield against the Chechens. Lebed became the National Security Adviser to Boris Yeltsin. At one point he was considered a leading candidate to become President of Russia, but he finished a disappointing third in the race. Lebed said that the Russian military was unable to account for nearly one hundred one-kiloton nuclear devices that were suitcase in size. A kiloton is equal in explosive power to four hundred thousand sticks of TNT! Lebed later retracted his statement after the Russian government initiated a campaign to discredit him. He went off to become governor of the remote province of Krasnoyarsk and later died in a helicopter accident.

Christ, Santini thought, *if the Russians can't monitor their nuclear bombs, what are the chances that they can keep tons of Play-Doh under lock and key?* He returned to his chair at the table and picked up his coffee cup.

"Anything else, General?"

"Yes, sir. Remember Inspector Leslie Knowles? The FBI briefer on money laundering?"

Santini nodded but said nothing. Indeed, he remembered her for more than the briefing.

"She was on the plane."

"Jesus!" Santini nearly dropped his coffee cup.

"The passenger list shows that she had to be seated next to a young man named Mohammed bin Hashami."

"A Muslim? From where?"

"Iraq," Whittier replied, referring to a paper in a folder. "From Mosul. Came here about two years ago."

"What was he doing—"

"Actually, Mr. Secretary, he was an employee of TSA. One of their screeners at Reagan."

Santini was dumbfounded. *How was this possible? What in hell were we doing!* "Let me ask everyone around this table," he said. "Do any of you think the plane was taken down to kill her?"

"Don't know, sir," the Vice Chairman said tentatively. "Could be. Apparently Knowles decided to travel to New York at the last minute. That would reduce the chances that she was a specific target."

"Anyone know why she decided to go to New York?"

Whittier scanned his notes. "According to a colleague of hers in the Bureau, she sent an e-mail just before the plane took off—"

"Saying?"

"She said that she had received a phone call from one of her sources who needed to see her ASAP. The source said he had information that would put Vladimir Berzin in a cell right next to Mikhail Khordokovsky. The source wanted to meet her in New York at seven this morning."

"Which meant that she would have to be on the last shuttle."

"Yes, sir. Her colleague said that was her work pattern. She worked at headquarters as long as she could, then went to Reagan for the last shuttle."

"A pattern. She followed a pattern. And if there were a bomb aboard the same plane she took, it would be a helluva coincidence. Would it not, gentlemen?"

Santini didn't wait for an answer.

CHAPTER 22

LOP NUR, CHINA

Hans Liebling lived two lives, and this was the one that he enjoyed. He was following the faint tracks of a mouse across a hardened stretch of sand in the Taklimakan Desert, as far from his other life as he could ever have imagined. The tracks led to the supply tent. He could imagine the mouse feasting on strange fare—the flat bread, the goat cheese, the rice. What, Liebling wondered, would the mouse do when the humans disappeared? The mouse would know. It and its ancestors had managed to live here on whatever they could find. And what would Liebling do when he left here? Would those men in Berlin really allow him to leave that second life?

He walked to the side of a big-wheeled desert truck, placed a camp chair in the narrow strip of shade, and sat down. He took a journal with a faded green cover out of his khaki jacket and began writing. The day was easing to an end, and the first hint of coolness had begun to stir the air. Liebling's thoughts drifted to the first time he had heard of Taklimakan.

He had been sitting in his room in Frankfurt, a lonely boy thumbing through an atlas. There, spread across two pages, was China. Then he looked for the place he had been reading about in a book by M. Aurel Stein, an explorer who followed Marco Polo's clues to a strange, barren place called Taklimakan. In the far western corner of China, far from Beijing and covering a wide swath of empty land, was China's largest province, the Xinjiang Uighur Autonomous Region, and there, in the basin of a vanished lake, was a blot called Taklimakan.

The lonely boy had devoured books by and about explorers. Stein had been one of his heroes and Taklimakan had been one of the places he had dreamed of exploring someday. The steps had been many, but as straight as the mouse's trail: earning scholarships, getting honors in university, signing up as a digger for a distinguished archaeologist, becoming his protégé, earning a doctorate, leading expeditions in Egypt, the Yucatán, China. Then the German economy had tightened, the grants dried up, archaeology became a stay-at-home occupation, and his life became lecturing undergraduates and trying to find a publisher for his papers.

That was his life, until about a year ago, when a faculty friend introduced him to Christoph Stiller, Assistant Director of the Bundesnachrichtendienst. Until he met Stiller, Liebling had never given more than a moment's thought to Germany's Federal Intelligence Service.

"A spy? You want me to be a spy?" he had said, in an astonished and angry voice when Stiller began talking about the agency's need for what he called "experienced eyes" in Xinjiang. "We merely want a good observer, and you will get a chance for a site you have always wanted to dig at," Stiller had said. The seduction had begun.

The agency funneled a grant to the university, supposedly from a German philanthropist, and created a discreet Shanghai bank account for a senior Chinese archaeologist as a reward for giving his support to the philanthropist's whim by signing off on the Liebling expedition. The philanthropist thus seemingly paid for what he wanted: an all-German expedition to the Taklimakan led by one of Germany's most distinguished archaeologists. The philanthropist showed his gratitude by giving a handsome donation to the Chinese archaeologist's institute. The Chinese also succeeded in bargaining for the donation of the two German-built desert trucks and all of Liebling's equipment, from his spades and tents and sleeping bags to his binoculars and handheld Global Positioning System (GPS) device.

So Liebling had got his dream, and his second life as a spy. "This is a onetime assignment," Stiller had told him. "Do this one thing for your country."

"My country!" Liebling had exclaimed. "This is for America, for American intelligence. Please do not insult my intelligence."

"Believe me, Herr Doktor Liebling, you are doing this for your country—and for the world. I am telling you far more than you need to know because I do respect your intelligence. It is as much in Germany's interest as in the interest of every NATO nation to learn as much as we can about China's nuclear capabilities. The Americans believe that the Chinese have stolen technical information that will allow them to make a copy of a miniaturized warhead that the Americans call the W-88. The Americans believe that—"

"The Americans. The Americans," Liebling had said. "Why are the Germans doing the Americans' dirty work?"

"Two reasons. First, America does not want to lose its relationship with China—at least until there is proof about the W-88. Second, they cannot send anyone into the Taklimakan because they have a very cold relationship with the Uighurs. The Americans, as you no doubt know, have declared the Uighurs terrorists, to please China."

Stiller was a very convincing man. So was the chancellor of the university, who appeared to be in on the plot. After a quiet conversation with the chancellor, who stressed the importance of patriotism and cooperation with the government, Liebling got the message that by carrying out this mission he would enhance his academic career, and he had finally agreed. Once he had accepted the assignment, he plunged into the quick course in espionage, treating his training as a new intellectual skill that he had to learn.

Liebling had, Stiller said, the perfect cover. He was an archaeologist and he would be doing genuine archaeological work. And, while doing that, he could easily do a few minor chores for Stiller and his American friends.

One day Stiller showed him a satellite photo of Taklimakan. Liebling, who had only seen Stein's stark black-and-white photos of a sand-covered lost city, was fascinated by seeing the site from space. The photo also showed, in tightly coiled ridges, the successive shrinking shorelines of a lake that was once 150 miles in diameter. Stiller ignored the archaeology and the geology, except for the irregular white scars around Lop Nur. "Bomb craters," he said, noting that Lop Nur had long been the site of China's nuclear tests. Liebling had known it only as a city on the Silk Road that had flourished for centuries and then began to vanish in the fourth century A.D.

The people of that city, known as Niya, had lived a good life. They fished in the rivers emptying into the lake, grazed their cattle on the grasslands that surrounded the lake, and hunted for game in the woodlands. Out of this city and the civilization that produced it came a people known as the Uighurs, an enduring people who still saw the vast Xinjiang region as their homeland.

The Uighurs had what were generally called Caucasian features, though in fact, they resembled modern-day Turks, with their high cheekbones, black hair, and black eyes, and spoke a Turkish dialect. They were Muslims, and their leaders believed that the Chinese were invaders. The Chinese translated the vast, desolate Taklimakan as "Go in and you won't come out." The Uighurs said that Taklimakan meant "Homeland of the Past," a lament for a lost civilization and an anthem for those Uighurs who were challenging China's present-day occupation.

So now Liebling sat and pondered the ways of a desert mouse. He wrote "Day 2" at the top of a page in his journal and started writing notes he would later transfer to his laptop. Their Taklimakan camp was near what Stein called the N-2 site—rows of reeds and poles sticking out of the sand, marking the location of what Stein had deduced to be nineteen houses of Niya.

This was the third expedition into the Taklimakan for Huang Wen, the Chinese archaeologist who had made a career out of digging in Xinjiang but had never learned to speak Uighur. A Japanese foundation had sponsored the first two trips, and Liebling wondered if some Japanese intelligence agency had also used the archaeology cover.

Day 1. Taklimakan at last! Flew to Urümqi, capital of Xinjiang, then a bumpy flight to Hotan, where expedition assembled. Then an all-day drive to Minfeng (whose old name is Niya). Final leg was a drive to an Uighur settlement at the edge of the desert: Kapak Askan, the Village of the Hanging Gourds. We picked up a guide named Ababehri, the village leader. He took me on a tour of the village—hardly more than a dusty road about a mile long—and talked about its history. He said the village was about four hundred years old and had a population of 432, including his three daughters and seven sons. The village is dark at night. Families take turns getting two hours of electricity a day from a generator. Ababehri invited Huang and me to his home, a long, wooden structure. He killed a sheep and boiled its meat in a large iron pot on a kind of hard-dirt patio in front of his home. We spent the night in his home—daubed mud over a wooden frame. His wife laid out reed mats for us; the drivers and other expedition workers slept in or around the trucks. Next morning, we set out again.

What Liebling did not write in his journal was the details of the village tour. During the night he slipped out of Ababehri's house and began rapidly typing on his laptop.

Ababehri led me to an area about two kilometers south of the village center, where several houses appeared to be deserted. Farther on, we passed through a massive wooden gate, put together with pegs, not nails. I followed Ababehri down a path into a sparse wilderness of stunted poplars, low tamarisk bushes, and stretches of barren, sandy earth. Scattered around are poles and spindly trees that rise around low stick fences. Hanging from most of the poles and trees are flapping, shapeless things that I finally recognize as weathered sheepskins. They seem to be memorials marking this place, which is an old graveyard.

"Many die," Ababehri said. I know enough Turkish to at least vaguely understand Uighur. So we were able to understand each other. I asked how many died, and he said, I believe, fourteen. He took me to humps of what I took to be fresh graves. He said something that I did not understand. He picked up the soil and shook his head. I then put on gloves and also picked up handfuls of dirt at the grave mounds and put the dirt in the pocket of my jacket. "Hotan," he said. "Hotan. Many more. Many more." Hotan, on the old Silk Road, is a large city south of here.

I heard shouts behind us. One of Huang Wen's assistants was calling and gesturing. Ababehri and I hurried back. I tried to tell him not to mention the graves to Huang Wen. He nodded and put a finger to his lips. He understood.

As Liebling typed, BND software encrypted his message. When he finished, he pressed a combination of letters that engaged a burst transmitter within the laptop. His message was reduced to a four-second burst and transmitted to a satellite owned by Germany's biggest cable television company. The BND was given use of the satellite by the company.

When they settled down in camp, Liebling realized that he had not been introduced to the drivers and the other men Huang Wen had brought with him. Apparently, Liebling thought, they, like Ababehri, were of a lower class and not worth acknowledging. He ignored them except to bark out orders. Now, smiling and holding the GPS device aloft, Huang Wen said something in Chinese. Liebling thought he heard the word "Stein."

A man named Lu, who seemed to be a security officer keeping an eye on Huang Wen and on Liebling, translated, speaking passable German: "Huang Wen has discovered that we are located at thirty-seven minutes, fifty-seven seconds North, fifteen minutes, forty-nine seconds West. He says this is one minute off from the position given by Stein."

Liebling turned to Ababehri. A short man, he wore a broad-brimmed straw hat, faded jeans, and a sheepskin vest over a black shirt. Liebling haltingly translated what Lu had said.

Ababehri showed his white teeth in a broad smile. "You forget, Herr Doktor Liebling, I speak Chinese. That is one reason why Huang Wen hires me."

Stiller had told Liebling that his contact would be Ababehri. Now, on Day 2, Liebling sensed that Ababehri was about to provide some more intelligence.

Ababehri handed Liebling a bottle of beer. It would be warm, but at least it was fairly good beer. Thanks, Liebling thought, to the Germans who taught the Han Chinese how to make beer. Liebling opened the bottle and took a long drink. Ababehri, holding his inevitable tin cup of tea, squatted down and said, in Uighur, "Come with me." It was a command.

Ababehri led Liebling to the ruins of a small Buddhist pagoda. On the last leg of the journey, Huang Wen had casually mentioned the pagoda, an archaeological puzzle. Captain Lu had translated, adding that Huang Wen had no interest in the pagoda. Liebling wondered why, but sentences beginning with *why* often did not get answered. Surprisingly, Ababehri had injected his comment, saying first in Chinese and then, to Liebling in Uighur, "Perhaps Herr Doktor Liebling would be interested. He should see it." Huang Wen had shrugged.

The pagoda was about one hundred meters from the camp. Ababehri crouched by a toppled Buddha and acted as if he were pointing out something to Liebling. "Here we will not be heard by them," Ababehri said, nodding toward the camp.

"A man will come; I do not know who he is or when he is coming. He will be an important man. You are to give him this." Ababehri reached behind the stele, turning his body so that his back was to the camp. He pulled out five small bags and handed them to Liebling, who stuffed them into the pockets of his jacket and trousers.

"I do this for the world, not for Germany or for America," Ababehri said, his dark eyes flashing. "There were tests. These are from our earth. Hotan, other places, marked in minutes and seconds." He smiled. "We, too, have GPS."

"Thank you, Ababehri. I know that you are doing this for the world. And for your cause. I know little about your cause."

"There is not time to tell all. For this I would need all day and all night. You stand on Uighur land, not Han land. The Han are taking away our imams to teach them, they say, what is wrong about the Koran. They stop our people from fasting during the holy month of Ramadan. Mosques have been closed down because the Han said they are too close to schools and have a bad influence on young Uighurs. And"— he spit on the sand—"and the Americans, to kiss the yellow asses of the Han, the Americans say we are terrorists. We are people fighting for freedom."

Shortly after dawn on the fourth day, one of the drivers stuck his head out of his tent, shouting and pointing to the sky. In minutes, everyone was out of the tents, looking up at a growing black speck. Lu lifted his binoculars, said something in Chinese to Huang Wen, who was crawling out of his tent while fumbling with his glasses. Lu turned to Liebling and said in German, "Military helicopter."

The helicopter hovered over the tents, blowing two of them down, then headed about two hundred meters away, and slowly lowered. A great golden cloud arose, grains of sand shimmering in the growing light. When the dust cloud settled and the rotor blades stilled, a man in military uniform stepped out.

Lu rushed into his tent and emerged wearing a military-style tunic over his T-shirt. He squatted to pull on dark brown, polished military-style boots. His trousers, Liebling noticed for the first time, had a military look: no pleats, a knife-edge crease. Lu ran toward the advancing figure, whom he obviously recognized as Major General Zhou, principal aide to General Li Kangsheng, the Deputy Minister of Defense.

Lu bowed slightly, then saluted the portly general, who raised his right hand to the visor of his hat and then, before touching it, gave a half wave. *The Monk doesn't even know how to salute,* Lu thought. *He doesn't even look like a general.* But Zhou was a powerful man, and Lu stood stiffly before him, awaiting orders. Zhou nodded for him to come closer. He spoke for a few moments. Lu nodded and, showing the proper deference, stepped back as Zhou walked toward the camp.

By the time Zhou and Lu reached the tents, everyone was

fully dressed and standing near the cook fire in two rows, with Liebling and Huang Wen in front and Ababehri, the drivers, and the other workers in the second row. Huang Wen, who also recognized General Zhou, reached out his hand and poured out an effusive greeting that Lu did not bother to translate for Liebling.

As Liebling reached out his hand, General Zhou did not reach out his. "Do you speak English?" he asked, startling Liebling and Huang Wen.

"Yes," Liebling stammered. "Yes, I do." He sensed that something had gone wrong. He thought immediately of his laptop burst transmitter and the bags of soil hidden in his sleeping bag and began concocting a story to explain them.

"Very well," Zhou replied. He glanced toward Lu and said something in a high-pitched, singsong Chinese. Lu saluted and, walking toward Liebling's tent, said something to the workers. One took three steps and entered Liebling's tent.

Zhou turned his round, impassive face toward Liebling. He spoke haltingly, his singsong rhythm prevailing in English: "I have ordered Captain Lu to obtain all things from your tent and place them in the helicopter and—"

"Wait!" Leibling said. "What is the meaning of this? Who are you?"

Zhou let half a minute pass before he replied. "I am Major General Zhou, from the Chinese Ministry of Defense. I am sent here by General Li Kangsheng, Deputy Minister of Defense. I am taking you and your things from the tent. I am taking you and it to a military place in Urümqi. From there we will go to Beijing."

"And why is this—this abduction taking place?"

"Ab-duc-tion?" Zhou said, speaking out each syllable. "Not abduction. Taking you from here."

As they spoke, the worker had removed everything, including two empty beer bottles, from Liebling's tent and lined up the items in front of the tent. Captain Lu kicked away the bottles and motioned to have clothing and the rolled-up sleeping bag stuffed into Liebling's two duffel bags. Liebling made an effort not to look at the sleeping bag.

He took a step toward the empty tent. Lu turned and said, in German, "Stop!" Smiling, he added, "You may go behind the tent and piss. It will be a long helicopter trip."

As Liebling headed toward the tent, he caught Ababehri's eye. Ababehri looked away, and Liebling thought, *He's one of them. I have been betrayed.*

"Hurry up, Doctor," Lu shouted. "Time is being wasted."

The worker was walking toward the helicopter, a duffel bag under each arm. Liebling looked at his tent. Arrayed in front of it were his laptop, binoculars, GPS device, CD player, and earphones and a stack of CDs. Zhou pointed to the laptop and said something in Chinese. Lu picked up the laptop and handed it to Zhou.

Lu took Liebling's right elbow in a tight grip and fell into step as they walked toward the helicopter, sometimes stumbling on the hot sand.

Zhou entered the helicopter first, leaving the door open for Liebling. He sat across from Zhou in a compartment closed off from the smaller compartment for the pilot and copilot. Zhou fastened his safety belt and motioned Liebling to do the same. Zhou reached up, pressed a button, and spoke three words in Chinese. The motor started, the blades began spinning, and the helicopter rose in a cloud of sand so thick that the compartment suddenly darkened.

Zhou reached over and touched Liebling on his left knee. They had emerged from the cloud, and sunbeams streamed in. Zhou was motioning to him again, pointing to a headset that hung next to his seat. He put on the headset and heard Zhou saying, "Sony. Very good, very clear."

Liebling nodded, then spoke. "What is this about, General? Why am I being abducted?"

"I am very good on electronics," Zhou said, ignoring Liebling's question. "Ever since I was a young person. I have checked these headsets are clean. No one can hear what we say. This is closed-circuit. You understand?"

"No. I do not understand. Why have I been taken from my work?"

"Safety, Doctor. Safety."

"What kind of safety is this?"

"Ababehri was betrayed. He must go to Pakistan tonight. That will start investigation. Your mission—"

"My mission? What are you talking about?"

"I am talking about what Ababehri gave you. But that is now not as important as what I must tell you. What you must tell Stiller."

"Who is Stiller?"

"Please, Dr. Liebling, believe me. I am not your enemy. Remember what Ababehri told you: 'I do this for the world.'"

"How do you know he said that? If he said that."

"It is what is the tie between us, between us all. I, too, do this for the world. It is part of what I believe."

"Falun Gong," Liebling said, half-whispering. "The religion."

"Yes. But we believe it is a spiritual movement, not a religion. We believe we can peacefully make happen a new China. Many, many people belong. I believe the pilot, perhaps the copilot, are members. But I cannot be sure. No one can be sure."

"I thought that China had all but wiped out Falun Gong."

Zhou smiled. "No. It grows. And it works."

"But I do not see how—"

"There is little time for talking, Doctor. I have learned that my superior, General Li Kangsheng, the Deputy Minister of Defense, is planning a coup. He is leader of group that is a bad . . . ? There is an English word. A bad group. And—"

"Rogue. A rogue group."

"Yes. Rogue. I have learned that Li—the rogue group— destroyed German aircraft in America. Stiller's brother— perhaps you heard."

"Yes, an accident, in America. I read about it in German newspapers."

"No accident. Li is the person who made this thing happen. And now comes something more, something more bad. Horrible. I do not know what, but something like the American Trade Towers. But this time in Germany. You must warn."

"Warn? Who? What to warn about?"

"Stiller. You may keep making believe you do not know him or who he is. It does not matter. Tell him about Li. Your Defense Ministry will know who Li is. Tell Stiller that Li is planning a terrible catastrophe for Germans, in Germany. This is all I know."

"I have no reason to believe you. What did you tell Lu—Captain Lu?"

"I am a general. I do not have to tell a captain anything. He has enough sense not to make anything out of this. I said I wanted to question you. I told him he and Huang Wen could keep your things—except for this." He pointed to the duffel bags and the laptop. "Evidence, I told them."

"And Ababehri?"

"He walks tonight to his village and then he will disappear into Pakistan. There are many Uighurs there. And they want to do this for the world."

"What is *this*?"

"Many words. Peace. Freedom. Good."

The helicopter landed at a military airfield in Urümqi. Zhou, carrying the laptop, and Liebling, struggling with the duffel bags, walked to a Chinese Air Force plane that flew them to the Air Force Headquarters field in Beijing. A black Mercedes staff car awaited them. Zhou spoke to the driver, and the car sped to one of the highways that encircled the city.

"You will be taken to the civilian airport. A Lufthansa flight has been delayed for technical reasons. It is the fastest way to get you to Berlin."

"But—but what of you? Surely all this"—he swung out his arms, as if to encompass the entire enterprise, from Taklimakan to Beijing—"surely all this will result in questions you will be asked."

"Questions are always being asked. It will be days. The bureaucracy." He leaned closer, whispering through his tight smile. "Then a visit to the German Embassy in Beijing. Stiller will get me out when that becomes necessary."

CHAPTER 23

General Zhou's apartment was five miles from the headquarters of the Ministry of State Security. He had never been a field man, so it would never occur to him to change his daily route from home to headquarters. He lived alone, partially by fate—his wife had been dead for five years—and partially by preference, for solitude seemed fitting for his work. He was an early riser, and he lived by a precise timetable. He inevitably started out for work at 6:45, reaching Tiananmen Square at 7. He then walked clockwise around the square at a slow, steady pace.

As he passed the steep, broad steps of the People's Museum, a man stepped out of a group of elderly people who were carrying cages containing their pet birds. Zhou recognized the man, who approached him and held up his caged finches. Zhou stopped and pretended to admire the birds. "You are betrayed," the man said, pointing to the cage and carrying out the miming of a casual conversation. "You will be received at the German Embassy. Go there immediately."

Zhou ran toward a taxi and waved it to a stop. The driver, looking angry the way all the Beijing taxi drivers look, nodded when Zhou asked him if he knew where the German Embassy was. He made a U-turn and had traveled about one mile when a black car cut in front of the taxi. The taxi driver jammed on the brakes, throwing Zhou forward, slamming his head against the plastic shield behind the driver.

Two young men stepped out of the car. One stood in front of the taxi. The other opened the right passenger door and gestured for Zhou to get out. "State Security Bureau," he said. "You will come with me."

"I wish to pay the driver," Zhou said.

The man turned and spoke rapidly to the man in front of the car. "He will take care of the driver," the man said. The second man was jotting down information from the driver. *I must not look frightened,* Zhou thought.

The two men took Zhou by his arms and shoved him into the backseat of the black car. One got up front with the driver. The other, who seemed to be in charge, sat next to Zhou. "You will not be going to the German Embassy," he said.

"There must be some mistake," Zhou said. "I was going to my office."

"You will begin telling the truth now, please," the man said, moving slightly in his seat so that he looked directly at Zhou. "Do not turn your head. You will begin telling the truth."

The black car turned down a street and stopped in front of a three-story building. Zhou knew it was not the headquarters of the State Security Bureau, but he did not speak.

The man got out of the backseat and tugged at Zhou's arm. "Hurry. Hurry," he said. "You will go inside and begin telling the truth."

The black car sped away and the two of them walked into the building. The man now was propelling Zhou before him. A plain door opened. They walked down a dimly lit corridor and entered a small room. A man, older than the man from the car, nodded to a stool that stood in front of his desk.

"You need not know my name, Comrade Zhou. You may think of me as Comrade Truth." He unfolded a paper on his desk and handed it to Zhou, who knew what it was without looking at it. The paper, with a small seal in the lower right corner, was a *ju Zhou an zheng,* a coercive summons warrant. There was no date on it. His name had been hastily written along a dotted line. There was no reason for the warrant. There never was a reason for a *ju Zhou an zheng.* Comrade

Truth said, "As you can see, we are summoning you in accordance to law." He snatched back the paper.

He nodded to a man on a bench by the door. Zhou had not noticed him before. Now he came forward. He was a tall man who wore a black T-shirt and black trousers. His shoulders were broad and Zhou could see that his arms were muscular. The search for truth was about to begin.

The final truth came at dawn the next day. The man with the birdcages was the first to see it. He did not react visibly. They would be watching, as they were always watching. He walked past the lamppost without speeding or slowing his pace. The birds continued to sing. The man wished that they would become silent. But he knew that they would always sing, no matter what they saw in Tiananmen Square.

Hanging from the lamppost was the naked body of Zhou. His throat was slashed. Stuffed in his mouth was a tract listing the virtues of Falun Gong.

CHAPTER 24

BERLIN

"Tell me again," Christoph Stiller said, speaking to the police sergeant who had found the body.

Sergeant Lars Kestenberg was on the list for promotion to detective in the Berlin Police's Criminal Investigation Department, and he prided himself on his ability to state facts succinctly and accurately. He risked a slight frown at this bureaucrat from BND who had appeared and taken command of a Berlin Police crime scene.

"At eleven thirty-five today," Kestenberg began, "a person calling from a cell phone called the Tempelhof-Schöneberg precinct and said, quote, Send an officer to 782 Griesenhaus Strasse. There is a body there. Unquote. My car was dispatched to the address, which I knew to be a vacant warehouse often used as a needle house by drug users. When my partner and I arrived, we entered by the open front door and proceeded down a hall to the first storeroom on our right. The door to it was open and we entered. It is the room in which we are now standing."

Kestenberg paused and pointed to a door across the long, narrow room. Weak sunlight streamed through the remains of four high windows, each one jagged and grimy. Most of the room lay in darkness. But two spotlights, mounted on tripods set in the floor's carpet of litter, bathed the door in harsh light, illuminating the figure of a man who had been nailed to the door.

tor. The man, tall and muscular, wore a dark turtleneck sweater and black trousers. He slipped into the backseat next to Stiller.

"What do you think, Kurt?"

"Mossad," Kurt replied. "Two in the head. Nothing like two hollow-point bullets in the head. Remember that job we heard about in Jordan? They went after some Palestinian there by trying to inject poison in his ear. Didn't work. Well, this did. Two in the head always works."

CHAPTER 25

BERLIN

A glass and steel dome soared over the Reichstag. "Think of it, Miya," Berzin said. "A throne for a king, a throne for Hitler, a target of tens of thousands of bombs, the centerpiece of a city cut in half by a murderous wall. And now . . . and now, what? A stage to play out democracy."

He spoke in gruff German, his words often sounding harsh. Berzin had ignored Wagner's warning that he was being watched. The Germans would not dare to touch him.

Miya Takala could follow his words—that was easy. But the thoughts behind them: that was the real translation problem. She had been sent to Germany several months earlier. Mossad had become concerned with the number of terrorists they believed were starting to gather and operate out of Berlin. She was the perfect agent to keep a watchful eye on things and take action if necessary.

Israeli intelligence had also picked up word that Vladimir Berzin, a Russian mob boss, had been engaged in covert sales of weapons to elements in China's military. Some of those military items were then trans-shipped to Iran. Then to Hamas and Hezbolla. One source said he had heard that small, suitcase-sized nuclear bombs had been put on one of the purchase lists. Although the source lacked confirmation, Israel could not afford to take any chances.

David Ben-Dar, Israel's intelligence chief, learned that Berzin had been invited as a member of a Russian trade delegation to attend a dinner in Berlin held by Chancellor Klaus Kiepler in honor of ailing Russian President Yuri Gruchkov. Ben-Dar arranged for Miya to attend the dinner and instructed her to make contact with Berzin.

Ben-Dar knew that Berzin would not ignore her.

Few men ever did.

Miya made it a point to focus her attention and subtle flattery on Berzin throughout the evening. As expected, she was successful in her assignment. He was intrigued by her. When he suggested that they have lunch together at the Park Plaza Hotel on Storkower Strasse, she accepted.

Contrary to everything she had read in the classified file that had been furnished to her, Miya actually found him rather charming in a rough-hewn sort of way. He was not highly polished in his social graces, but neither was he as boorish or uneducated as she had been led to expect. It seemed clear, however, that he was on his best behavior and determined to impress her.

During lunch, he had said that he found her "worldly," "sophisticated," and "delightful." She permitted herself a silent moment of immodesty, thinking, *No doubt far above the thousand-dollar-a-night whores you're known to consort with in Moscow.*

But at some point she knew he would want more than polite conversation, and Vladimir Berzin was not the type to take "no" for an answer. He was a dangerous man, but it wasn't a matter of the danger involved—danger was her constant companion in her line of work—it was more complicated.

Ben-Dar had demanded much of her in the past. She had killed on his command before and would do so again without the slightest hesitation or remorse. But sex was different. She would sacrifice her life for her country, but not her body.

"I don't understand it," Ben-Dar had claimed.

Miya didn't care. It was her way, or, as she was fond of saying, "the highway." She would walk.

In the end, Ben-Dar always yielded.

Now, Berzin was back in Berlin. He asked her to go for a walk. It was a nice day. "Why not?" she said.

Berzin pointed to a figure on a traffic signal. It was red with an egghead under a porkpie hat and had its arms stiffly extended. As he pointed, the figure turned green and walked with quick little steps. "*Ossie,* we called him in the East, the little traffic signal man. The West had a more formal figure to tell you 'Walk' and 'Do Not Walk.' See? That one over there. They are both in the new Berlin as one of those silly symbols of unity. But the wall, it is still there, the wall of the mind."

Near the opera house on Unter den Linden they walked over to a rectangular window in the paving and looked down. Shimmering under thick glass was a white room with white, empty shelves. A plaque said that this was the spot where, on May 10, 1933, Nazi students burned hundreds of books by authors cursed by Hitler. They looked down in silence. *One of ours, Micha Ullman, created that,* she thought.

"There was a German word I learned: *Schreibtischmörder,*" Berzin said, still looking down at the white room. "At first it was difficult to understand. I had to look it up."

"*Schreibtischmörder,*" she repeated. "Murderers at their desks. They were all around here, weren't they? Heydrich, Himmler, Eichmann."

A piece of the Wall, covered with fading graffiti, stood next to the Bornholmerstrasse Bridge, where the first East Germans had crossed into the West on November 9, 1989. And next to the piece of the Wall was a billboard advertising cigarettes.

Berzin cocked his head toward the east. "When I was a kid living there," he said, "I dreamed about the West. I thought it was something like what Disney would call the Magic Kingdom." He paused. "And now I find the kingdom less magical."

"Oh?" Miya said. "Disney disappoints you?"

She had grown accustomed to turning on the listening-and-memorizing part of her brain when Berzin's voice changed to a gentler, slowly modulated tone. She was listening now. She knew that he had spent part of the day with Wolfgang Wagner, and she believed intuitively that whatever he was about to say would reflect at least some of what they had talked about.

"Yes, completely. It's all fake, imaginary. It vanishes as soon as you leave the theater. I have something more *real* in

mind," he continued, motioning her toward a bench that overlooked a small park near the glittering Kudamm. When they
sat down, Berzin started to put his right arm along the back of
the bench, and she waited for his hand to fall on her shoulder.
But he pulled his hand back, probably because he had realized
he was going to need both his hands for his speechifying. He
was a man of wide gestures. She saw a young couple sit down
on a bench a short distance away. *Ours or theirs?* she wondered. Her briefing said that the BND had Berzin and Wagner
both under surveillance.

"I look at America and see only disappointment," Berzin
was saying. "Decadence. People who have lost their discipline
and grown fat. The American Century, as they called the
twentieth, is over."

"And so the future belongs to whom?" Now he had her curiosity up.

"It belongs to Germany," Berzin said, as he swept his arm
around, pointing out the massive new buildings that could be
seen everywhere. "To Germany and to Russia!" Berzin in-
voked the name of his motherland with particular pride.
"Think of how Russian and German companies now have
joint ventures throughout Europe. Think of even bigger part-
nerships. What that might do for all of Europe!"

"You leave out the French?"

"The French? You can't do business with them. They're too
difficult. And, besides, they can't be trusted. No. Russian
power and German efficiency. That's the key to success."
Berzin stopped, aware that he was becoming too boastful.
Then, putting his arm around her waist, he changed the tempo
of his speech, saying, "Enough about business and politics.
We must think of ways we might activate our own alliance."

Miya smiled warmly even as she felt a chill run down her
spine. She didn't know exactly what he had in mind when he
spoke about business and politics. But she knew it couldn't be
good news.

As she slipped gracefully away from Berzin's embrace,
Miya felt that this was going to be her toughest assignment.

CHAPTER 26

WASHINGTON

Intelligence agencies try to keep control over chaos through a disciplined process called compartmentalization. Each crisis, each disaster, gets its own compartment, its own set of keepers. Santini was trying to do this with his mind on the day after the LaGuardia crash. The tabloids were running a story saying that the explosion was a terrorist act and pilloried Homeland Security. There was another one, small and private. *Leslie. What were they like, those last moments?* A question that would haunt him and never be answered. And now there was the large, still-empty compartment labeled "today."

Santini plunged into his day. During Arthur Wu's DIA daily briefing, he mentioned a murder in Berlin of a German archaeologist working for the Bundesnachrichtendiens, pronouncing the name of the German intelligence agency smoothly. Santini could imagine Wu conscientiously referring to a German dictionary and then rehearsing the word. "The archaeologist was named Liebling," Wu said. "He had just returned from China on a joint CIA-BND operation." He paused for a moment. "DIA got nothing from the CIA on this, of course. Perhaps your CIA briefer—"

"Got it, Art. I'll ask, if I need it," Santini said, a trace of impatience in his voice.

"BND, which *does* share with us, says it has the look of a Mossad 'wet job.' "

The phrase touched off a chain of memories that raced through Santini's mind and . . . then vanished.

Next, Wu mentioned that a senior North Korean scientist who had defected to the United States was claiming that the North had developed a missile capable of carrying a nuclear warhead and that could reach North Dakota.

"So, once again, Art, it's the *man* who gives up the secrets, not the computer," Santini said, bringing up one of Wu's favorite topics, the penetration of computer networks.

Wu nodded and resumed the briefing.

Twenty minutes after Wu left, Margie buzzed to say a DIA courier was delivering a classified message from Wu.

"Bring it in, please," Santini said.

"When you think of secrets," the message said, "think of the enclosed. Computer security is not security."

The enclosure, marked *SECRET,* consisted of a lengthy, technical report on the vulnerability of computer systems to exotic viruses. Santini flipped through the pages, then marked *FYI* on its cover sheet, and had Margie hand it over to Scott O'Neill. Wu just wouldn't give up on the subject.

To get a fix on the FBI report he had been given at the White House meeting a few days earlier, Santini asked Robert Sommers, his CIA briefer, what the Agency knew about the Mafiya.

"I heard about that FBI brief, sir," Sommers said. "There are a couple of things she didn't tell you. May I tell you what I know personally? Not as a formal briefer, sir."

"Sure. I'll take personal knowledge anytime."

"Well, say you're in Geneva on some kind of financial business and you go into a bar in your nice hotel and this Russian in a three-thousand-dollar suit starts talking to you. After a couple of drinks he is talking vaguely about wanting to do business with you. You get his card and it says he is a vice president of some kind of modern-sounding company with a name in capital letters—TRIMEX, BETREX, NINEX—and you give him your card.

"Well, who are you dealing with? A legitimate business-man? A Russian intelligence officer? A crook? Or all three? What we're finding is that more and more times it's the last. They're all mixed together now, Mr. Secretary. And it looks as if one of them is going to run for President of Russia."

Santini stared at Sommers for a moment, trying to detect whether Sommers was one of those Agency guys who knew more about Berzin but was holding back.

Satisfying himself that Sommers appeared to know nothing more about the CIA's former spy, Santini dismissed him.

Precisely at 4:45, Margie reminded Santini that he was to leave for Andrews in fifteen minutes. She handed him a list of passengers—the usual security detail and communications specialists, three senators, six congressmen, a Yale political scientist whose book on the roots of Islamic terrorism had just hit the bestseller lists. And twelve journalists, including inves-tigative journalist Randall Hartley.

"Call the VIP lounge at Andrews, Margie," Santini said, "and tell them to make sure that Hartley gets a seat near my cabin. I need to have a private chat with him."

Santini had not been surprised to see the substance of what Hartley had given him over the phone printed in *The Wash-ington Post*. A few hours of advance notice was as much as he or anyone else could expect in today's environment. What had surprised him was that the *Post* had not treated it as front-page, big-headline material.

"I'll have Protocol work it out, Mr. Secretary," Margie said. "Everything will go smoothly, as usual."

The SecDef Protocol Office did make trips and other events run smoothly, but there was no guarantee that politicians would not insist on having "face time" with him. He hoped they would all fall asleep and not disturb him. He had two speeches to review—the one that everyone thought he was go-ing to give and the one that laid it on the line.

He usually looked forward to the annual Frederick von Heltsinger Conference. He met old friends and new ones there, heard old ideas and new ones, and enjoyed the status. The conference went back to the early 1960s, a jittery time for

Europe. With Germany divided and NATO forces confronting the armies of the Warsaw Pact, Baron von Heltsinger feared that war was the future. German politicians and generals were just "counting tanks and thinking about shooting," he had said at the time.

After World War II, von Heltsinger had become influential in German banking and financial circles, the èminence grise in top-level German political and economic circles. So he decided to organize a conference devoted to examining ways to keep the Cold War from turning into World War III. At first, only about twenty people came, including a young Harvard professor named Henry Kissinger and a young member of the West German Parliament, Helmut Schmidt, who later became Minister of Defense and then Chancellor.

As Heltsinger's reputation as a talent scout grew, so did the importance of his annual conference. His counsel was still sought by German leaders—especially the current Chancellor. Attendance at his conference was by invitation only, and an invitation meant that you were a member in good standing with the Western security establishment. The conference became the premier conference on NATO security issues.

This year, however, Santini would be a bearer of ill tidings. He knew that no one, especially his old friend Baron von Heltsinger, would welcome the message he would deliver.

Santini stuck his head out of his private cabin aboard his E-4 aircraft, the 747 Boeing jet that had once served as the designated command center in the event of a nuclear attack. He had the luxury of a bunk in his cabin. There were several additional bunks in the rear of the aircraft that usually were reserved for the Air Force personnel aboard, but almost everyone else crossed the Atlantic snoozing in a rigid upright seat.

He motioned to O'Neill to come forward. O'Neill rose from his seat and entered Santini's private room, closing the door behind him.

"Scott, I need you to send Randall Hartley up here with me. Try not to make a display of it in front of the rest of the pack." Briefing the traveling press corps was, for Santini, a necessary evil. He had a good enough relationship with journalists, and he couldn't complain that they didn't give him or the Department fair treatment. But they were insatiable, demanding constant feeding. And when they smelled blood, they didn't give a damn how much they liked or respected Santini. That was particularly true for the journalist known as "Big Foot."

Other than bumping into him at Tom Koestler's funeral and the Senate hearing the other day, Santini had not had any dealings with Hartley since the time Hartley had exposed a Senate Intelligence Committee stenographer who was being blackmailed by the Russians while Santini was serving as Chairman of the Committee.

Although Hartley rarely ventured from the office he maintained on the top floor of his large Gothic-style home in Georgetown, everyone in Washington knew that he continued to work overtime in cultivating his intelligence sources, and no one in this town had a better feel for what was really going on in world affairs.

"Mr. Secretary," Hartley said as he entered the cabin. "Here I am to pay you the honor!" There was always the hint of levity in Hartley's voice. It was part of his ingratiating charm. Courtesy, laughter, folksiness. It was also very dangerous to fall for it, because Hartley said nothing without a purpose. And his purpose was always to drag information out of you, while seeming to simply engage in polite, innocent conversation.

Santini stood and greeted Hartley, who was wearing a jogging outfit. He smiled broadly as he shook Santini's hand. Santini, while he was in the Senate, rarely initiated contact with Hartley, fearful that he would unwittingly surrender some crucial piece of information that Hartley was searching for. And when Hartley called him, it was the equivalent of getting a call from *60 Minutes*. You just knew that it was going to be a very bad day.

Santini motioned him to a high-backed leather chair on one side of a narrow table covered with briefing books and a yellow legal pad. He took a similar chair opposite Hartley.

"You must be slumming, Randall," Santini chided. "I

thought you gave up pounding the beat with all the heavy breathers. Senate hearings. Now Munich."

Settling into the chair, Hartley said, "Have to get out once in a while. Besides, my sources tell me there may be some fireworks in Munich this year."

"Could be," Santini said in a noncommittal tone. "Never know what the French will propose."

"Not the French, from what I hear."

"Randall, I assume you're not writing for tomorrow's papers."

Hartley nodded. "I'm doing a book on President Jefferson's first term."

"If that's the case, I'll give you a heads-up on what I intend to say." Hartley was thorough and relentless once on a story or book. And trustworthy. He once spent a month in jail for refusing to disclose the name of one of his sources.

"Okay."

"But first, I'm curious to know something from you."

"Depends," Hartley said.

"I'd like to know why your folks at the *Post* buried the story about the militia being responsible for Tom Koestler's murder and the bombing out at Holloman on page eight."

"You mean the story that Joe Praeger was peddling?"

"Right."

"Pretty simple. It was too easy. Too neat. The militia no doubt had plenty of intent. They hated the Germans and maybe had no love for Koestler. But planning and carrying out either operation was beyond them. Someone outside had to be masterminding it. Besides," Hartley added, breaking into a smile, "I had sources inside the Bureau. Couldn't piss on the White House publicly, but they threw cold water on the story."

"Any thoughts on who's pulling the strings?" Santini asked, *still* wondering if Director McConnell or his deputy might be leaking to Hartley.

"Not yet. But my sources say it's not domestic. And whoever it is, is indulging in a little mind-fucking."

"How so?"

"He or they wanted us to know that something much bigger and smarter is out there."

"That's just about as vague as the threat warnings we get every day," Santini said sarcastically. " *'We can't tell you who, where, when, or how, but someone is going to carry out an act of terror against us or our allies in the next week or two.'* Can you be a little more specific?"

Hartley smiled. He was notorious for criticizing the inability of government officials to anticipate or thwart terrorists' plans. "Not yet. I've been running the traps on this. Koestler had a long list of enemies."

"Goes with the territory."

"Yeah, motive is one thing, but the list gets smaller when you consider who had the capability and opportunity to execute the plans. The list that I'm working on doesn't include his cows! Man, those bloggers are determined to kill the profession of journalism."

"Let me know when you 'connect all the dots.' " A light dig at Hartley. On more than one occasion, he had used the phrase to suggest that official Washington's mental and motor skills were congenitally impaired.

"Touché, Mr. Secretary. I'll be sure to send you a copy of the story before it runs." Actually, the repartee between the two men was not harsh. They held a mutual respect for each other. Both recognized that their roles required them to maintain a certain level of distance in their relationship. Hartley was relentless in his search for classified information. Santini was equally determined to protect it.

Although eager to find out what Santini was going to say at von Heltsinger's conference, Hartley said, "There's one new piece of information I can reveal."

Santini took Hartley's offer as a cease-fire.

"In Mexico City, a man identified as Charles Burkhart was found dead in his hotel room. His tongue had been cut out. Apparently whoever did it wasn't satisfied that Burkhart wouldn't talk. Someone fired two hollow-point bullets into his brain."

"And?" Santini was having trouble with the relevance of Burkhart's murder.

"He had served in the Army. Discharged because of war wounds he got during Operation Desert Storm. Turns out his specialty was in demolitions."

"Interesting, but I still don't see what—"

"Also turns out he was part of a janitorial service employed at Holloman."

Now bells began to ring in Santini's head. "Jesus," he said, exhaling. "That means—"

"There's more. My sources tell me that they found documents in his room—passport, driver's license, credit cards—that identified him as Dana Treadwell."

Hartley paused, weighing how much to reveal to Santini. Deciding to continue, he said, "They ran the name through all of the airlines and found that a Mr. D. Treadwell had a prepurchased Continental Airlines ticket to the Cayman Islands."

The dots were all racing together. "Someone had decided to cancel Treadwell's—Burkhart's—retirement plans," Santini said. "The same someone who's behind Holloman and possibly Koestler's murder."

"That's my guess."

"You going to run with this?" Santini asked.

"Not yet. It doesn't quite add up. Why any hit team would leave all those documents behind in his room doesn't make sense unless they're trying to send the FBI down a dark alley. It's also possible that whoever hit Burkhart didn't have time to clean the place out. If that's not the case, then that someone either is playing games or is incredibly stupid. And I don't think they're stupid."

Santini nodded in agreement. It didn't make sense.

"One last thing," Hartley said. "He was wearing one of those belts that has a zipper concealed on the inside. They found a slip of paper with the word *Tago* written on it."

Santini shrugged his shoulders. "Meaning what? A code name? Acronym? City?"

"Don't know," Hartley said. "Just another one of those

'dots' for now. Anyway, that's what I've got. Now tell me about tomorrow."

Santini reached into his briefcase and pulled out more than a dozen typed pages that were stapled together. Handing them to Hartley, he said, "This is what's going to be distributed in advance at the conference." He then produced a sheaf of papers that contained his handwritten notes. "This is what I intend to say."

Hartley scanned the notes and said, "The Germans are not going to be pleased."

CHAPTER 27

MUNICH

Baron Frederick von Heltsinger's home on Prinzregenten-strasse, near the Bavarian National Museum, appeared to be rather modest for a man of his wealth. That, of course, was precisely the way he liked it. Inside the three-story stone structure, it was quite a different matter.

The chandelier hanging from the twelve-foot ceiling on the second level was cut from Hungarian crystal two centuries ago and had graced the homes of some of Germany's richest families. The walls were covered with exquisite hand-painted paper that had been imported from China. The Baron had insisted that the paper be applied with a special technique that would permit it to be removed should the house be sold after his death. The staircase rising from the foyer was made from Italian marble, and it curved with the grace of a swan's neck.

The Baron's favorite room was his library, paneled in dark cherrywood and lined with floor-to-ceiling bookcases. It was here that he would retreat following a light dinner prepared by two live-in servants. Brandy and a cigar would top off the evening while he perused the writings of Thucydides, Hegel, and Spengler. He was convinced that history was repetitive. That the same passions, ambitions, and follies could be found in the ruins of all empires. That philosophy, the highest form of intellectual and spiritual exercise, remained elusive except to a chosen few. And therefore, man was trapped in a vicious cycle of his own making. It was not a matter of original sin but persistent stupidity.

Von Heltsinger had little tolerance for stupidity or weakness. Back in the 1980s, the Soviets had targeted Germany with SS-20 missiles. President Ronald Reagan insisted that Pershing II missiles be deployed on German soil as a deterrent. The pacifists claimed that it was the Americans who were escalating tensions and that the deployment of Pershings would be a dangerous and provocative act.

"The Americans were quite right," the Baron once recalled to Santini with a laugh. "So finally, at one conference, we were able to generate enough support to persuade the German politicians to do the right thing. Meet strength with strength. And what happened? The Soviets backed down. Nuclear weapons disappeared."

Every major NATO proposal adopted during the last three decades, along with every one that was eventually scrapped, was hatched at one of his conferences. But the hidden agenda for the conferences had always been the American–German connection. "Politics," he told Santini, "is a matter of power. So if you are thinking in these terms you must not forget where the power is. You don't need many friends. Just the right one."

The Baron still clung to his lifeline of hope. Hope for more enlightened leadership. Hope for a more prosperous, proud, and secure Germany. One that would seek no wars but could not be defeated if they came. That hope also came in the form of his protégé, Wolfgang Wagner. He was the grandson of an old family friend, a young man who was highly educated and skilled in financial matters and who had taken a keen interest in politics as of late. He would make a worthy successor to the Baron's favorite cause—the promotion of German leadership throughout Europe. And one day, Wagner might very well become Chancellor.

Tonight, while sitting in his favorite leather chair, listening to a light sonata, and glancing through a few of Goethe's lesser-known poems, the Baron was troubled. Wolfgang had called earlier. He said it was urgent, that it involved the conference that was scheduled to begin tomorrow. Although the Baron was looking forward to an evening of calm and solid rest, he quickly agreed to a meeting. If there were to be any problems affecting the conference, he needed to know now.

When he arrived, Wagner was escorted into the library by Otto, von Heltsinger's servant. The Baron, still dressed in a business suit and starched white shirt, stood to greet him. "Welcome my friend, welcome. I am glad that we will have the chance to share a few quiet moments together before all the delegates arrive." Actually, von Heltsinger wanted nothing of the sort, but his voice conveyed only sincerity. "What brings you out tonight? You should be resting up. We've got heavy schedules for the next two days." The Baron wrapped a fatherly arm around Wagner's shoulder and guided him to a sitting area. "Would you join me in a touch of brandy?" It was not really a question.

"Yes. Yes, of course," Wagner quickly said. "Baron von Heltsinger—"

"Please, Wolfgang. It is Frederick. Please."

Wagner nodded but still could not bring himself to engage in such informality with the great man. "I have just learned through a source of mine in the German Embassy in Washington, that your old friend Michael Santini is going to drop a political bomb on us during his speech."

The Baron said nothing, and his silence was slightly unnerving.

"For some time," Wagner continued, "we have been concerned about what the Americans have been up to. Apparently, they no longer believe we have anything to contribute to either their security or their interests. This despite our military aid in Afghanistan. They have shifted their focus to the East, toward China. Santini is going to confirm this in his speech tomorrow."

"I have read my friend's speech, and I see nothing of the kind in it."

"Exactly my point, Baron. Sir, according to my source— and he is wired directly into the people around Secretary Santini—the White House has given him his marching orders.

The U.S. will proceed to cut thirty-five thousand from their forces here in Germany, with the prospect that more cuts will come in the near future. They claim it reflects sound strategic planning. But it is clear that it is really retribution for our working with the French to create a separate European military capability and our refusal to follow them in lockstep wherever they want to wage war.

"But worse," Wagner said, his voice rising sharply, "President Jefferson has decided to prevent the transfer of any high technology to members of NATO who lift their ban on weapons sales to China. And he has instructed Santini to say that European defense contractors will no longer have entrée into the U.S. market."

"You're sure that Santini will do this?" von Heltsinger asked.

The Baron said nothing for a moment, but the rising flush in his face disclosed the rage that was building inside. "You're sure?" he finally whispered. "Santini will do this?"

Wagner nodded solemnly. He knew that the Baron's friendship with Santini had been a long and deep one. Betrayal was not something von Heltsinger accepted. Not from acquaintances and surely not from friends.

Wagner decided that the time was ripe for him to discuss what he and Vladimir Berzin had in mind for a geopolitical partnership. Omitting the violent acts that Berzin had perpetrated and planned, Wagner laid out what Berzin had said to him that night in Moscow.

At first von Heltsinger was skeptical. The more he heard, however, the more plausible it seemed. Thoughts of history inspired him to say, "There is a historian who tells of sitting in a park in Moscow in the 1960s and hearing Russian youngsters singing a song about the bells of Buchenwald—*Buchenwald*—and not knowing what Buchenwald really was, not knowing about death camps and Nazis, not knowing why millions of their fellow countrymen died. History, for many, is fleeting, Wolfgang. Fleeting."

After a half hour of discussion, von Heltsinger signaled he was tired. "That's enough for now, Wolfgang. The idea is intriguing. I'm surprised—pleasantly so—that you have been thinking in big terms. I want to give the concept more thought. Perhaps once the conference is over, we can meet again."

"Thank you . . . Frederick," Wagner said, puffed up with pride at von Heltsinger's praise. Why not relate to him now as an equal?

Just before Wagner descended the grand staircase, he turned and said, parroting Berzin's words, "The Americans have given us an opportunity to become great again."

When Wagner left, the Baron sat for a long time, staring into some time and space that only he could see. History, personal and national, passed through his mind. His family had produced Kings of Prussia and the last German Emperor, Wilhelm II. The Baron thought back to the days of Hitler, how those days had cost him and his family so dearly.

If Stauffenberg had succeeded in the plot to kill Hitler, the Baron's father would have led Germany into a golden era. Perhaps it could happen again. The Baron was intrigued with Wagner's idea. This year the delegates to his conference included Vladimir Pavlovich Berzin. A man of considerable controversy.

A man who knew about power.

CHAPTER 28

MUNICH

Security was tight at the Bayerischahof. Even Santini was stopped by a young security man who demanded to see the identification that warranted Santini's red VIP badge. Santini graciously complied while members of his entourage, who had badges of lesser distinction, fumed their way through the hard-faced men in the lobby. As usual, the conference lived up to its reputation as a prized event. All NATO Defense Ministers put attendance as a must. Meetings in Brussels at NATO headquarters were all scripted, formal, and basically boring. But in the heartland of Bavaria, at the Bayerischahof Hotel, the meetings were free-flowing and more interesting. The same politicians and bureaucrats showed up to make canned speeches and give government position papers that were as dry as sawdust. But mixed in with them were business leaders, along with leading media personalities, providing spark and different perspectives. And they came from Russia, China, and Japan, not just the NATO nations. The meetings were televised internally, but local and international journalists could watch the proceedings on closed-circuit in an adjoining room and give greater color to their reports when they saw the participants in action.

This conference remained in high demand even though it no longer coincided with Fasching—a Bavarian month-long holiday that was the equivalent of Mardi Gras, when beer flowed and passions soared. All restrictions were off. Grounds for divorce were suspended. Members of Congress, particularly the unmarried ones, would look at the German women, who were ready and willing for the taking, and think they had slipped the surly bonds of moral conformity.

Images of his former colleagues dancing at the nightclubs were still fresh in Santini's mind. He repressed a smile at the memories. Baron von Heltsinger, concerned that conference attendees had become distracted by the celebratory mood, had insisted that the conference be scheduled to occur a month later this year. This pleased the German security agencies as well, because it had become almost impossible to provide protection to the conference during Fasching's carnival atmosphere.

Santini had first attended the conference years ago as a senator. Now he would attend as the Secretary of Defense. As soon as he entered the hotel, he could feel the difference immediately. He was the biggest man on the European campus now. He carried a budget bigger than all of the NATO countries combined. While the Europeans talked about a separate defense identity, none of them were really prepared to back their words up with real money.

But there was more to it than money. The Europeans no longer looked upon the United States as a country that shared their view of the world. Rather, they believed that ever since the attack on September 11 the United States had reverted to a policy of unilateralism. The United States, in turn, had come to the conclusion that the Europeans talked a good game but came to that game with little to offer. So the United States was prepared to act alone.

One scholar opined that "Americans are from Mars and Europeans from Venus." The Europeans chafed at the charge that their policies had been feminized. Rather, they were convinced that waging diplomacy rather than war in the twenty-first century was the only responsible course of action. Just because America held a hammer, they argued, it was folly to treat every problem as a nail. There was no place among civilized nations for a Robocop, who was ready to pound anyone who posed a potential threat to its interests.

London and Madrid had been attacked as America had

been. But in Europe the war on terror was not yet dominating diplomacy and domestic affairs. And therein lay the great divide. One that was about to grow wider.

After all, Santini was there to deliver a sober message. As he approached the raised dais, Santini could feel the energy and excitement in the ballroom that now served as the conference center. He glanced out into the audience, as Baron von Heltsinger began his welcoming remarks. He saw the faces of old friends who smiled warmly.

Moving to the podium, Santini thanked von Heltsinger for his introduction and began to speak. "First, let me express my sincere regret over the loss of German lives at Holloman Air Force Base. This was a great tragedy, one for which the American people share your sadness and grief. The matter is still under investigation, but I can promise you that we will work tirelessly to find those who were responsible for this heinous act and bring them to justice."

Santini used his condolences to segue to the subject of terrorism.

"My friends, as you know, I first came to this conference at a time when the Cold War threatened to grow hot and extinguish the lives of millions. Much has changed since that time. Today there is another war under way that requires a different kind of sacrifice."

Setting aside the papers he had carried to the podium, Santini focused directly on the faces of his friends. They were no longer smiling.

"You have in front of you my prepared remarks. As you can see, they contain language that reaffirms our strong commitment to trans-Atlantic solidarity and the importance of NATO for our collective security. But I need to be more direct with you about the situation that confronts my country. The United States can no longer maintain a large number of troops in Western Europe. We're stretched too thin. The threat to our security interests has moved to the Middle East, to central Asia, and beyond. We need to reconfigure our fighting units in a militarily responsible way."

Santini continued, laying out the timetable of force reductions and base closures that his plan entailed.

Murmurs and loud grumbling rippled through the audience. Delegates had expected some changes. There had been rumors, editorial speculation about reductions, but what Santini was proposing was too radical. No matter how much Santini was soft-pedaling it, this was going to hurt. It would require them to spend more money for collective defense at a time when most of their economies were flat or in decline.

Then he proceeded to give them the really bad news. "Although the United States has worked hard to maintain good relations with China, its respect for human rights has not significantly improved since the student protests in Tiananmen Square in 1989. Moreover, China continues to threaten Taiwan with military force. Under these circumstances, President Jefferson has decided to sign into law a measure that will restrict military technology transfers to any European nation that undertakes weapons sales to China."

His address finished, Santini accepted no questions. Those in attendance were stunned by the message and the manner in which he had delivered it. There was no applause, not even a perfunctory custom of showing respect by rapping on the tabletops of their assigned seats. In addition to the loss of bases, they were going to be punished for selling technology to China. Outrageous!

They had been taken by surprise, and by a man they had considered a friend, no less. They were accustomed to acts of betrayal from the poseurs of power. Deceit and duplicity were proclivities they readily attached to their European brethren. But America, once thought to be too idealistic or naive to engage in the art of diplomatic backstabbing, had arrived. Those cynics who had forewarned that the Americans were weakening their ties to Europe had been validated.

Baron von Heltsinger remained silent, refusing to look at Santini. His ruddy complexion deepened as his thick neck threatened to break out of his stiff-collared shirt. Without thanking Santini, he introduced the next speaker. "We will now hear from our friend Jacques de Montribial, the French Defense Minister."

Santini slipped off the raised dais and moved quickly toward one of the exit doors. Immediately he was surrounded by a half-dozen members of his security detail, hard-eyed men who wore formidable frowns. Wrapped in their security cocoon, he made his way past the speakers who were scheduled to address the conference following his remarks. As he emerged into the lobby of the hotel, Christoph Stiller greeted him. The two embraced warmly.

They had met at a conference held in Bonn more than twenty years earlier. The dogs of terror were out and running then. A German banker had been found stuffed into the trunk of his Mercedes. He had been shot several times in the head. The German government wanted to discuss how the international community could respond to the increasing threat to society. Santini, serving as a U.S. senator at the time, was asked to address the conference, along with a number of foreign policy experts. Stiller was there as a university student representative. The academics were concerned that the German authorities would use the threat as an excuse to limit the civil liberties of the German people. No particular policy changes were recommended by the panel of experts who attended.

Santini had been struck by the level of security that the German government had provided the participants. Armored personnel carriers lined the streets surrounding the conference center. All the police were armed with automatic weapons. Santini thought that such a scene would never be possible in America. Of course, that was before Mohammed Atta and his men brought their brand of terror to America.

Santini and Stiller sliced quickly through the throng of conferees who were knotted in the lobby of the hotel. Two security details now surrounded the two men. A private room on the second floor of the hotel had been secured for them to talk.

"Coffee, Christoph?" Santini asked when they settled in the room. He motioned for Stiller to sit next to him in one of the silk-embroidered chairs. Stiller nodded. He spoke perfect English, so perfect that he seemed overly serious and pedantic. He was anything but. Usually, he would open his conversation with Santini by telling atrocious jokes. Now he sat, staring ahead.

"I'm really sorry about Konrad," Santini said. "About what happened. How are you taking it? When I spoke to you, you seemed stoic. And now?"

"I think I am handling it. I work now, twenty hours a day sometimes. But I am always thinking of him." Stiller's voice caught, the memory of his younger brother too fresh for him to discuss without his chest suddenly growing tight, forcing him to struggle momentarily for air. Konrad was the youngest of five children. And, perhaps because he had been born so late in their marriage, he had been his parents' favorite.

But he was the favorite of his siblings as well, Stiller went on, pouring out memories. Naturally gregarious and self-effacing, Konrad was a star athlete who thrilled his coaches and fans on the soccer field during his secondary and university years. And while he could have completed his mandatory military obligations upon graduation and then turned professional, he would have none of it. Inexplicably, from his childhood days he had been consumed with the desire to fly. And not just any plane. He had to fly high-performance fighter aircraft. The German Air Force was the place for him. He had promised Christoph that he would one day be the best of the best. *He was.* The very fact that Stiller already thought of his brother in the past tense caused his chest to constrict even tighter.

"Do you have any more information about what happened? Who?"

Santini sipped the coffee. It was lukewarm and bitter. Wincing, he shook his head. "No. Nothing further yet. As you know, a militia group in New Mexico—bastards like your skinheads—has been tied to it. Confidentially, I can tell you—and you need to hold this tight for the time being—it's possible that there may be a foreign connection. We don't want it made public yet. You know how the media would jump on it. We need to know what we're up against before the cable news networks turn their hyenas loose."

"I understand," Stiller said. "And it can't help that our countries' relations are so sour. We do not need any more strain just now."

Santini reviewed some of the leads the FBI task force was pursuing. Remnants of al Qaeda. Militia groups. Disgruntled former military types. The Timothy McVeigh votaries who shared his hatred for the U.S. Government and its policies. Other terrorist organizations that were tied into organized crime and drug running.

Stiller had been taking notes in a spiral book. After Santini finished, Stiller said, "Michael, I don't know if it has anything to do with this case, but you mentioned that there's a possible foreign connection to what happened. Here's something we picked up. We had an agent—an amateur, really—working up in Xinjiang Province. His cover was real. He was an archaeologist. I had talked him into it, overseen his training. It was part of a joint operation we had with the CIA. Following up information we had about nuclear activity at Lop Nur. The CIA had to remain in deep shadow because the United States has put the Uighurs on its terrorist list."

"That list is not always up-to-date," Santini said, nodding for Stiller to continue.

"Our man got out a burst message saying that many Uighurs died of radiation poisoning, apparently as a result of radiation of the soil and water. He picked up some soil samples."

"Confirmation of a nuclear test!" Santini exclaimed. "Nice going."

"No. When we found his body, he was naked. No soil samples. But there's more.

"He also met with a Chinese military officer who knew that the disaster at Holloman was no accident."

"What? That does not make any sense. How can there be a Chinese angle to Holloman? Did he have any solid information?"

"The Chinese officer passed our man a typed note with names on it."

"What did the note say?"

"We never found the note. Only his body. The Chinese officer put him on a Lufthansa plane in Beijing. Before the plane took off, he managed to get another message to us about Holloman. The message also said that China was planning 'many deaths in Germany.' He was to meet with me, direct from the airport. He never made it. The driver was killed, too. Shot while he was sitting in the car. Our man was *nailed* to a shed door in Berlin."

"A crucifixion?"

"Actually, he died from two bullet wounds to the back of his skull. Twenty-two-caliber, hollow points. Professional hit. Similar to the way the Mossad takes its enemies out. But that doesn't make any sense. They're on our side. Besides, the crucifixion is not part of their handiwork. It appears to be a message to us. There are German priests in Xinjiang. Been there for many years. The Chinese don't trust them. The BND never goes near the priests there, but we have good connections with the Vatican. Perhaps the crucifixion meant 'Don't send any more missionaries—or spies.' We have advised the Vatican to take the priests out of Xinjiang."

Charles Burkhart's fate in Mexico City flashed through Santini's mind. "Your agent said nothing more in his communications to you?"

"Nothing."

Santini bit into his lower lip, then exhaled slowly. "Not much to go on." He rose up from his chair and shook Stiller's hand. "Christoph, let's stay in close touch on this. I'll give you everything we hear. You do the same."

As the two men started for the door, Stiller stopped and said, "On another matter, some of our security people have been a bit concerned about Wolfgang Wagner's association with Vladimir Berzin. They're both at the conference. Wagner is the Baron's protégé. This Berzin is a pretty rough character, not exactly your investment banker type. He's one of Russia's oligarchs. Not many of them left, thanks to what Gruchkov managed to do before he died. Lots of rumors about Berzin's organization. It's a supergang that traffics in drugs, high-tech weapons systems, nuclear material—and would you believe this? Human organs for the wealthy."

"I've heard of Berzin," Santini said cautiously.

Sensing that Santini was holding out, Stiller laughed. "We are supposed to share, correct? We hear that he's about to run for President. What do your intelligence boys have on that?"

Santini offered no response. He had an uncle who sold aluminum siding. He used to tell Santini about his sales scripts. He was supposed to be standing by the door, hand on the doorknob, when he made his apex pitch. Santini smiled, sensing that another pitch from Stiller was about to come.

"Oh, yes," Stiller said, his hand on the doorknob, "in keeping tabs on Berzin our people have also come across a woman who's been seen in his company."

"I understand your worrying about Berzin," Santini said. "But why the concern about the woman?"

"Wagner is like a son to the Baron. The Baron had asked us to keep an eye on him. That means whoever is seen in his company is of interest to us. That extends to the friends of his friends. . . . You know, with all of the violence going on. People trying to take advantage of the rich and successful. Extortion. That sort of thing."

Stiller grew increasingly uncomfortable with the explanation, and Santini understood why. The BND was not in the babysitting business. And under German law, they sure as hell were not supposed to be conducting surveillance on individuals in the absence of evidence of wrongdoing.

"I still don't understand," Santini said. "What's the problem?"

"The problem is that we can't seem to identify her. She goes by the name Miya Takala. She is managing a small computer software company that is based in Berlin. Her background does not check out. She is supposed to be a native of Finland. She is not Finnish, though she does a good job of speaking German with a Finnish accent. We cannot figure out her nationality. We could bring her in. Pull her passport and squeeze her. But that could get messy. And the Baron wouldn't want that. And judges would get on our ass."

"So you want a little assist in identifying her? That's all?" There was incredulity in Santini's tone.

"No. Our technical people have been picking up her e-mail traffic. Sent to Helsinki, then routed to an accommodation mailbox in Tel Aviv. And it is encrypted. When we are able to break it down, the message is always rather innocuous. Seems to be code language."

"Maybe she's just a businesswoman trying to protect her company's intellectual property."

"Maybe. But it would be helpful if you could have the Agency help us out on this. I did not want to put this request through regular channels for obvious reasons. The Baron would be really upset if we created a problem for him."

And for you, Santini thought.

"Incidentally, the woman's in town now, staying at the new Ritz. Probably to be near Berzin. We have a surveillance photograph of her. I can send it over to you later. Is that okay?"

"Sure, Christoph. No problem. Glad to help." Santini gave him the number for the secure fax located in the communications center next to his hotel room. "Listen. I'm suffering from a bit of jet lag. I need to rest for a couple of hours. Why don't you send the material over in the early evening?"

CHAPTER 29

MUNICH

As the sheet of paper continued to spill out from the fax machine, Santini's stomach started to tighten. He felt that time was slowing down, as if someone were playing his life at the wrong speed, stretching seconds into minutes, moments into hours. He hoped that his eyes were playing tricks.

He saw the strong jawline first. It was sharp, with the skin tight against the kind of bones that cameras love. In the photograph, her hair was wrapped in a turban. But there was no mistaking those full lips, those wide cheekbones that cradled eyes that were as large as grapes. They might have been the color of dark grapes, but color was irrelevant to the woman who owned them. They changed with her mission, with her assumed nationality. This was the face of a beautiful model. But it was one that few had seen, and she was anything but a model.

Even if his imagination was simply raising hell with him, there was no mistaking the long, supple legs that her dress made little effort to conceal. They were the legs of a dancer. Yes, a graceful ballerina . . . and the legs, too, of a . . .

He could feel his emotions start to churn. He had thought that he would never see her again. He still wondered if he had been hallucinating at the National Cathedral, when he thought he had a fleeting image of her in the crowd for Koestler's funeral. It had been how long? Eight years? Ten? God, more than ten years since he first met her at one of those mindless, boring Washington dinner parties that pass as important social events. Her name was not Miya then.

She was in the company of Oscar De Guterez, the Mexican ambassador, who introduced her as Katrina Bissett, an editor of a fashion magazine called *Elite*.

As he sat across from her at the dinner table, Santini was smitten. He had never met a woman so intoxicatingly beautiful. She had raven hair that framed a face that might have graced the cover of *Vogue* or *W.* Her butternut-colored skin was set off by a white designer dress. Santini assumed it was a Halston. His former socialite wife from the Hamptons had a closet full of them.

Katrina had a pleasant but unsettling way of staring across the dinner table at him with emerald-green eyes that danced in the candlelight. She was at once exotic and elegant, clearly a woman of the world, completely at ease whether discussing politics or polo, Flemish art or French wines.

But it was all a lie, he would later learn. One long, elaborate deception.

Her real name was not Katrina but Elena. Elena Solmitz, the daughter of parents who had emigrated from Bialystock, Poland, to Israel in the mid-sixties. Her father, David, arrived in time to fight in the 1967 Six-Day War as a conscript in the Israeli Defense Force.

The Israelis had crushed the Egyptian, Jordanian, and Syrian forces, using superior speed, airpower, and a stunning blitzkreig. But winning the battle did not end the war.

Two months after their defeat, the Arab nations passed a declaration during a summit meeting held in Khartoum. There was to be: no peace, no negotiations, no recognition of Israel. The Israelis would never be allowed to rest. Death was to be their constant companion.

And it became Elena's.

She was only five years old at the time. Her parents had taken her and her brother, Zvi, to visit friends living in a kibbutz in northern Israel, near the Lebanese border. After Elena had spent the day playing with other children and sharing a sumptuous dinner, her father, his arm around her mother,

Sarah, said, "Come, Zvi, Elena. It's time to go. We have a long drive ahead of us and it will be dark soon."

As they entered their car to begin the journey back to Jerusalem, violent explosions erupted all around them. Elena's father tried desperately to start the car. "Come on! Come on!" he shouted, panic in his eyes. He needed to race beyond range of the rockets that were raining down on them in sheets of steel. In his desperation, he jammed his foot over and over against the gas pedal, flooding the engine.

Then his worst fear came flying at them. A Kaytusha rocket scored a direct hit on their stalled vehicle.

Elena, miraculously, was thrown from the car. But she was forced to stand by helplessly as her brother, Zvi, along with both parents, screamed in agony. She raced around frantically, crying for help, looking for water, for anything, to put out the flames. All she found was smoldering ruins, limbs and body parts everywhere.

Within minutes Israeli jet planes flew overhead, launching counterstrikes against those who had attacked the kibbutz. But it was too late. Her family had been incinerated.

Dead. They were all dead.

Dozens of nearby Israeli forces raced to the kibbutz. As one of them gathered her into his arms, young Elena vowed revenge.

A lifetime of it.

Santini did not learn the truth about Katrina for months after their first encounter. Following a very nasty divorce, during the time he was making his way on Wall Street, he was content to play the field as a confirmed bachelor.

But that was before he met Katrina. Everything about her excited him. Her striking beauty, athletic grace. Even her perfume. "What is the fragrance you're wearing?" he had asked her during a dance at the dinner that first night in Washington.

"It's called Enchanting," she said, pulling her head back slightly from his shoulder to see if Santini was making small talk or a more interesting move. "Why do you ask?"

"Oh, just curious. It's very subtle, but . . ." He stumbled, momentarily feeling awkward. "The name seems right. Subtle and enchanting."

He danced with several other women that night, as protocol dictated. But he couldn't keep his eyes off Katrina.

As the guests gathered in the spacious atrium of the National Gallery of Art to await the arrival of their chauffeured limousines, Santini, out of earshot of her escort, said, "I live in New York. We might have dinner sometime at my favorite Italian restaurant?"

Tilting her head in a way that suggested she was both surprised and bemused at his invitation, Katrina asked, "And that might be?"

"Bravo Gianni's. On East Sixty-third. The ambience is good. The food even better. The owner's a friend."

"Why, yes," Katrina replied. "I've heard others speak about it. Yes, I'd enjoy that. I'm very fond of Italian food."

With that she turned to Ambassador De Guterez, who by this time had completed thanking the gallery's director and his wife for their "splendid, customary generosity." As De Guterez walked toward them, he seemed a bit put out by the intensity of Santini's focus on Katrina.

Slipping his arm through Katrina's, De Guterez guided her to the black BMW 750 iL that had pulled swiftly up to the entrance.

"Good evening, Senator," he offered, honoring the once-a-senator-always-a-senator Washington tradition with artificial grace. Just before he slid into the rear seat of the car, he said, "I trust you had an enjoyable time."

"Indeed," Santini rejoined, trying not to glance at Katrina.

A few weeks later, Santini called Katrina. He offered to pick her up at her apartment, but she said that she'd be coming directly from work and suggested they meet at Bravo Gianni's.

The evening had gone well. Gianni had reserved his best table for Santini, the same one that he held for stars such as Bill Cosby and former football great "Broadway Joe" Namath. Santini and Katrina exchanged stories of their backgrounds.

Katrina said her father had been a Swedish diplomat and her mother a journalist for the French newspaper *Le Monde*.

They had met while both were students on vacation in Italy. Katrina had been born in Spain while her father was posted there. Before attending finishing school in Switzerland, she had lived in the ambassadorial residences of five European capitals.

Santini listened attentively, then offered an abbreviated version of his journey from the streets of Boston's "Little Italy" to the United States Senate and on to Wall Street, but somehow he got the impression that Katrina was not learning of it for the first time.

At the end of the dinner, after exchanging fraternal hugs with Gianni and promises to return soon, Santini exited the restaurant and hailed a cab.

"Come on; I'll drop you off."

As they entered the cab, Katrina said to the driver, "The Sherry Netherlands Hotel."

Seeing Santini's look of surprise, she said, "I live there. My magazine owns the apartment. Since I travel so much, it works just fine."

Within minutes they arrived at the hotel. Katrina reached over and kissed Santini lightly on the cheek. "Thank you, Senator," she said as she slid quickly out the door. "I had a wonderful time."

"Me, too," Santini said, "and it's not 'Senator' anymore. It's 'Michael,' if we're to be friends."

"And to be Michael, then from now on, you must call me 'Kat.'"

"Deal," he laughed. "Good night, Kat."

He had planned to have more Italian dinners with her. He was eager to romance her. Sleep no longer came easily to him. At night he would lie awake imagining making passionate, gymnastically impossible love. In his mind, he would see times when they would be slow and exquisitely tender with each other. There were others when they slammed their bodies together recklessly, racing to a climax that would leave them both perspiring, chests heaving, laughing.

For the first time in a long while, the thought of a serious relationship was no longer off-limits for Santini. That is, not until he received a call from Marcus Trelcott. While serving as Chairman of the Senate Intelligence Committee, Santini had known and highly respected Trelcott, the CIA counterintelligence chief.

"I need to talk with you, Senator," Trelcott had intoned. He gave Santini the address of what turned out to be an elegant brownstone on the Upper East Side. They agreed to meet that afternoon.

The gravity of Trelcott's responsibilities was reflected in his lined face. He looked at Santini through dark eyes that were heavily lidded. Eyes that saw everything, eyes of someone who trusted nothing and no one.

Trelcott wasted little time on pleasantries.

"Senator. I spoke with the NDI to get his permission to discuss this with you. This is of a very sensitive nature. Ordinarily, I don't concern myself with the private lives of American citizens. In fact, unless they're working for the CIA, it's off-limits to do so."

Santini sensed that he wasn't going to like where Trelcott was heading. He nodded, but said nothing.

"Yes, sir," Trelcott continued. "But this is personal to you. Personal and dangerous."

"I'm listening," Santini said. He shifted in his chair, his tone telling Trelcott he'd better have a damn good reason to be looking over the shoulders of a private citizen, even one who happened to be a former senator with a headful of secrets.

"It's come to our attention that you've been in the company of a woman who calls herself Katrina Bissett—"

Before Trelcott could finish, Santini was out of his chair, ready to turn physical. "God damn it!" he exploded. "Don't tell me you've been spying on me! A former U.S. senator. That's not only fucking stupid. It's illegal!"

Trelcott remained calm in the face of Santini's outburst. "No, sir. The Agency's not spying on you. NSA passed along an intercept emanating from Tel Aviv—"

"Tel Aviv? You're saying the Israelis are spying on me?"

"No, sir, I'm not saying that. The information that we have

is that one of their top people has established contact with you. It's unclear whether it's at their direction."

"Top people? Katrina? She's no Israeli; she's . . . ," Santini stammered.

"We did a rather thorough background check on her, sir. She's not only Mossad. She's much more. A professional assassin. One of their best."

Trelcott paused. He was an expert at handling agents, telling them exactly enough, giving them the exact amount of motive, the exact degree of warning. "You learned many secrets as the Intelligence Committee Chairman, sir. You have never—*never*—hurt our work. We still consider you an asset. Frankly, we may someday feel obliged to call upon you for assistance. Having said all this, sir, we would like you to read this. It's all here."

Trelcott handed Santini a file folder emblazoned in red letters with the words *TOP SECRET. CODE XENO.*

Santini sat back down in his chair, stunned, his emotions churning. It couldn't be true. Not beautiful Katrina. Not . . . The thought of what this meant for him struck like a bullet. He flipped open the file and began reading.

As Trelcott had said, it was all there. The whole bloody trail. She was a master of disguise, a deadly chameleon who blended in with any environment. Dozens of men killed. Several women. Anyone who presented a threat to Israel. Most of them in the Middle East, but not all. One was hit in Morocco. Another in Algeria. Two died in France. . . .

As Santini finished reading the report, he struggled to remain calm. He could feel a cloud of scandal gathering, coming to embrace him. "Have you shared this with anyone . . . with the FBI?"

"Not yet," Trelcott said, allowing the ambiguity of his answer to hang.

"But you'll have to." By law, the FBI had the authority to monitor and investigate the activities of foreign agents and their contacts with others while in America.

"At some point."

Santini stared hard at Trelcott, trying to determine if Trelcott was toying with him, holding the threat of disclosure over his head to extract something from him. He saw nothing. Perhaps Trelcott was simply expressing the age-old rivalry between the CIA and FBI and their reluctance to share information with each other.

But "perhaps" was just the rub. If he continued seeing Katrina—Elena—he would enter a no-man's-land, subject to public revelation that he was cavorting with a professional spy, an assassin. It didn't matter that Israel was a U.S. ally. As Trelcott said, he once had had access to America's most guarded secrets. War hero or not, he would be open to charges that he had compromised national security. He had paid too high a price defending the honor of his country. He wasn't going to put it all in jeopardy.

Not for love. Not for anyone.

Santini closed the file and handed it back to Trelcott. "Tell the Director that I appreciate his concern."

Trelcott nodded, slipped the file back into a canvas briefcase that was secured by a heavy combination lock, and escorted Santini to the front door.

Santini walked for blocks, thinking, wondering. His dreams had turned into a nightmare. He was angry with Elena. She had put him in an impossible position. "Damn," he cursed. "God damn." Then he reminded himself that he was the one who had pursued her. The finger of blame pointed directly at him.

Clasping his hands together tightly, trying to release the tension that had surged throughout his body, he wondered whether their meeting that first night at the National Art Gallery had been by accident or design, whether Mossad had decided to see if he was vulnerable. Had the dinner's seating arrangement all been by chance?

It made no difference. He had no choice.

He planned not to see Kat—Elena—again. Ever.

Now she was back, this time parading around as Miya Takala. Just another name out of her black bag. But why Germany? And how could she be involved with a Russian Mafiya don?

One who wanted to be President. One who had been on the CIA's payroll.

Stiller had hinted and then dismissed the thought that the assassination of their man had all the markings of a Mossad job. But if Stiller had access to the CIA's files, he would quickly understand why Elena should be put high on the list of suspects who had carried out the hit.

Santini's mind quickly turned to the dossier that the CIA had furnished him on that black day in New York. He remembered the photographs of some of her victims. Almost all of them had died, execution-style, with two hollow-point bullets to their heads.

Santini picked up the phone and dialed Stiller's home. After three rings, he heard Stiller's voice on a recording machine that told him to leave a message. He waited for the long beep to end.

"Christoph," he began, his voice cracking, a mere whisper. "I'll need time to complete the search on the . . . person you've inquired about. It shouldn't take long. As soon as I have something, I'll call."

He slammed down the phone's receiver. "Christ!" he cursed to himself. What was he doing calling Stiller before he knew what in hell was going on? Stiller's counterintelligence operation could be penetrated. He couldn't take that chance.

And he wasn't going to call Jack Pelky to find out what, if anything, the CIA knew about Elena and what she might be up to with Vladimir Berzin. That kind of an inquiry would stir up too much interest by the spooks out at Langley, and his past contact with Elena might surface. And that was not something he needed right now. Not with Joe Praeger sitting in the White House looking for ways to discredit him.

He picked up the phone again and asked his operator for the number of the Ritz Hotel.

CHAPTER 30

MUNICH

It had been a long day, and tonight Miya looked forward to indulging in her daily yoga regime. It allowed her to relax and meditate. After twenty minutes of extending and contracting muscles and tendons from her toes to her neck, she slipped into a warm bath that she had sprinkled with perfumed oil.

She lit several aromatic candles that bordered the sunken marble tub, and prepared to let her mind float amid the bubbles.

The loud ring of the telephone attached to the bathroom wall shattered the tranquility of the moment, causing her to lurch forward reflexively. She cursed, then slipped back into the warm water. Whoever it was could wait.

She tried to regain her calm, but it was no use. Curiosity had entered her thoughts like an uninvited guest and refused to leave. She stepped out of the tub, grabbed a large towel emblazoned with the Ritz's monogram, and wrapped it around her body. Entering the bedroom, she saw the message light flashing on the phone. She pressed the designated button, and listened to the message.

"Kat . . . Elena, this is . . ."

She recognized Santini's voice almost immediately. Reflexively, she slammed down the receiver. It was odd, but the sound of Santini's voice inspired a spark of exhilaration. She had been together with him only twice, but he was still with her after all of these years. She had never met anyone quite like him. If she had ever let herself think of a serious relationship, he would be the one. But it could never be.

It was Israel's fate always to be under attack by her enemies. And it was her fate to help eliminate those enemies wherever they could be found. That meant everywhere, every day. There was no room for love in her world.

She had been but a child when she lost her family, but the memory of their screams never left her.

She devoted years to building athletic skills. Soccer, distance running, archery, marksmanship, martial arts. Her mastery of sports was matched by her skills in the classroom. She was gifted in math and science, like many in her class, but the study of languages was where she really excelled. By the time she completed her two years of service in the Israeli Army, she was fluent in five languages.

But that was not what caught the eye of Israel's famed intelligence service, Mossad. Yes, she had brains, beauty, and athletic talent. All indispensable assets. But most important of all, she was eager to kill. For that she seemed to have a true passion.

Which made her a prime target for "the Messengers," Mossad's elite assassination team. The termination squad was never fully acknowledged by Israeli government officials. Of course, it was known that the Israelis targeted Hamas and Hezbolla leaders for "elimination." They described that as legitimate warfare. Protective preemption. Killing those who were planning to kill them.

The squeamish Europeans howled, but they were powerless bureaucrats who sat on their asses in Brussels and dreamed about lost empires. And what could the Americans say? Wasn't this exactly what they had done in Afghanistan and Iraq and would do wherever they could track terrorist networks?

No. The Messengers would target enemies who thought that geographical distance granted them immunity from harm. With methodical planning, and by exploiting Mossad's vast intelligence network they would trace their enemies' movements, hunt them down, and then strike. Canada, Argentina, Britain, France, Switzerland. Even in America.

A throat slashed here. A skull shattered there. People simply vanishing without a trace. No bodies, no blood. What crime?

Not every mission was a success, of course. One had been badly blown in Switzerland. They had killed the wrong man, and a member of the team had been apprehended and then prosecuted. Israel had been embarrassed. But only for the moment. And they never admitted the existence of any assassination squad. It had all been a terrible mistake by some misguided zealots.

Perfection is never possible in anything. But who could quarrel with 95 percent success? And so the mission continued. And it did not escape the notice of others that Israel never fully denied the existence of their policy of covert assassinations. Let their killer team take on mythic proportions. And let every enemy know that their quiet suburban streets or noisy city cafés would at some designated time contain the agents of death.

Elena became a star assassin, first among equals. She moved easily in any world—art, literature, sports, politics. She was a master of disguise. Blond one day, raven haired the next. She matched eye color to fit the occasion.

Establishing acquaintances and contacts, but not friendships, she would spend only enough time to lure her target into the kill zone. Then she would strike. Never from a distance. It was always up close and very personal.

Now, in her early forties, Elena had tired of her profession. This, she told David Ben-Dar, was going to be her last mission.

She was exhausted. She had lost her edge. And in this business, that loss could prove fatal. It was time for her to come home. Maybe she could train others.

Reluctantly, Ben-Dar had yielded. "Okay, Elena. This will be the last one." He had seemed sincere. But with Ben-Dar you could never be sure.

In a moment her professional mind-set took over. How

could Santini have possibly known she was in Munich? And how did he know where to find her? Either Israeli intelligence had screwed up or Berzin was being watched by the BND. Either way her mission had been compromised.

She picked up the phone again, this time determined to listen to Michael Santini's message.

CHAPTER 31

MUNICH

Santini wanted to meet Elena privately. He took aside the head of his security detail and told him that he was going to meet an old friend and needed some privacy in a public place. The Cave was not his first choice, but it was the only option available. It was located in the basement of the Bayerischahof Hotel. While he was bound to encounter other people there, he knew from experience that sometimes the best way to have a private meeting was to hold it in a public place.

Raul Gomez, his security chief, reluctantly agreed, providing he could do a quick assessment of the Cave. He returned to say, "I'll station myself and two men in the entry of the Cave. We will enter ten minutes after you enter, sir. And we will not go in any farther unless we have to," meaning that Gomez, not Santini, would decide whether to crash the party.

Little had changed there since Santini's last visit. The restaurant and bar had served as a quiet preserve for the younger, upscale Munich professionals who wanted to let off steam after a busy day. On occasion, some might use it for a secret assignation. But this was not without risk. While there existed a code of silence among its habitués, rumors had a way of filtering their way to the local society pages, whose columnists were always hungry for gossip. Santini had found that out the hard way. He had attended a private birthday party there for his friend Detlev Seybold and managed to get caught in the lens of a 35mm Nikon while sitting next to two beautiful blond models who were Detlev's friends.

Two days later, in spite of his having been told that the party was totally private, his picture appeared in *Sueddeutsche Zeitung,* with the caption "U.S. SENATOR PLAYS WITH MUNICH JET SET." No real harm done. Santini was single then and not known to be a playboy. But it was another lesson: Nothing is private when it comes to public men.

He was bound to encounter other people tonight, but he remembered that after eight o'clock the management kept the lights dimmed. There was a fair degree of privacy in some of the booths in the back where he and Elena could talk without being overheard.

Santini arrived first. Tonight was unusually busy, so much so that Santini nearly missed sight of Elena as she made her way past the dark wraparound bar, politely pushing her way past several admiring men. It was the tilt of her head that caught Santini's eye, the way that she might be lining up a victim in the gunsight of a silenced Mossad Special. But maybe that was just his imagination.

Another reason that he had almost missed her. Her glorious dark mane, now bleached nearly white, was pulled straight back and tied into a tight bun. The style gave her a harsh, ice princess look. But of course, she was masquerading as a Finn.

Santini, sitting at a small table at the rear of the bar, signaled her with a wave of his hand. As she approached he stood and extended his hand to greet her, before realizing how awkward it seemed.

Santini embraced her lightly and kissed her cheeks, right, then left, European-style.

"You look—"

"Older," she interrupted, silencing his attempt at chivalry.

"No. More beautiful than I remember," he said, more serious than he wanted to be just then. He was hoping that time would have been less kind, that she would have aged in a way that would have lessened the pain that he felt after so many years of absence, so much time of regret.

"You lie," Elena said.

"No, I mean you look . . ." Santini was starting to feel slightly foolish. Since his divorce, he had had his share of one-night stands, but he did not spend much time in the company of women, especially not a woman like Elena.

Pulling out the table so that she could slip easily into the leather-padded booth, Santini could detect the aroma of Enchanting, the same bouquet that somehow had managed to bury itself into his brain on that night when he first met her. The mind—it always astonished him how it could trap words, musical tunes, floral scents, and then release them years after they had touched the senses. And their release was always unpredictable, triggered by another sound or sight or smell that might be totally unrelated to the original experience. He wondered if Elena had deliberately worn that perfume tonight to torment him. Then again, maybe she was just a creature of habit and stayed with the essence that just seemed to be made for her.

"You don't write. You don't call . . . ," Elena said, making a fainthearted, deliberate attempt to keep the conversation light. But there was an edge to her voice, an anger behind the words.

"I wanted to, but . . ."

"But what? I called you, how many times? And no answer. You dropped me like a virus."

"I had to. I had no choice. Once I found out who you were. Who you worked for."

Elena allowed a long silence to hang over them. Finally, she said, "I see. You thought I was setting you up. To use you as a target of opportunity."

"The thought occurred to me, yes. But it didn't matter if our meeting was intentional or accidental. In my position."

"You were no longer a senator."

"I had certain connections, obligations."

"Guilt by association?"

"Big-time."

"Too bad. I hoped we might have enjoyed a friendship."

Santini locked onto her eyes, eyes that were at once cool and passionate, eyes that drew him into her. "It would have been nice," he said lamely. He silently recounted the nights he had lain awake, thinking about her, his longing only to be overcome by regret and then anger.

A young man with reddish blond, heavily slicked-back hair, wearing a small gold earring in his left ear, appeared at their table. "My name is Rudolph. I'm your waiter this evening. Can I bring you something from the bar?"

Annoyed that he had not seen the man approaching, and wondering if he had been loitering behind them, "Kir Royale, as I recall," Santini said to Elena. She nodded.

Santini ordered a Kir and a glass of Absolut and abruptly dismissed the man. He didn't like waiters hovering around him. They were gossips, sewers who collected information like rainwater.

Rudolph returned in a matter of minutes with their drinks.

Santini touched Elena's raised glass in a silent toast and, in one long draught, polished off his drink.

"Why did you call me? Insist that we meet here?" She scanned the gathering crowd, conveying her displeasure.

"My options to move around are pretty limited. Besides . . ." A loud disco beat momentarily drowned out what Santini had said. Lean bodies dressed in Armani jackets and Calvin Klein jeans started shuffling toward a small dance floor in the center of the restaurant. "No one can hear us talking in here," he practically shouted.

"You're right. Even I can't hear you."

Santini slouched over the table, signaling Elena to do the same. Their heads were nearly touching. "You're traveling in dangerous company."

"Since you know about me, Michael—or should I call you Mr. Secretary—then it should not come as a surprise that I sometimes find myself in dangerous company."

"You've caught the attention of German intelligence."

"So you decide to draw me further into their scrutiny?"

"Elena, no games. I'm trying to warn you." Santini hesitated, unsure of how much to reveal. "A man was found a few days ago. Someone important to the German Government."

"Found?" Elena seemed genuinely intrigued.

"Found with two .22-caliber hollow-point bullets in his head. They think it might be the work of Mossad."

"Michael, please. Don't tell me that you think that I am somehow involved in this . . . murder?" Elena's tone exuded incredulity, but Santini forced himself to remember how skilled an operative she was.

"I've said nothing to them. But they remain suspicious. They know that you are not who you pretend to be, the CEO of some high-tech company. They know nothing of your connection to Mossad. But you are under surveillance."

"Michael. I could say that I am now retired. That Mossad no longer values my services. But you know that would be a lie. The truth is that I am only a field agent."

"And so you just happen to be moving in the company of a man who is involved with organized crime? Just happen to be in the vicinity when a highly placed agent is murdered with all of the hallmarks of a Mossad hit?" Santini searched Elena's face for some hint of acknowledgment. Her eyes, those glorious eyes that took in everything, revealed nothing.

She had to be on a mission with Vladimir Berzin. But why? And why should he believe her story that she was just a mere field agent and no longer in the assassination business?

"Please, Michael, do you really think that Mossad leaves its fingerprints all over the bodies on its hit list?" Her voice was filled with contempt at the absurdity of the notion. "Germany has a large and growing Muslim population. What the Muslims are up to is always of interest to Israel," Elena said, evidently not feeling it necessary to add any further explanation.

But to drive home the point that she thought would be so obvious to Santini, she reminded him of the need for the United States to share a similar concern over what was taking place in Germany.

"You must recall the name of Imam al-Fazazi. He used to preach a special brand of hatred for you and us out of the Al Quds mosque in Hamburg. It has been extensively reported that he called upon Muslims to slit the throats of all Jews and Christians. That was the same mosque that Mohammed Atta attended so frequently before he learned to fly an aircraft into the World Trade Center. We have carefully examined all of the videotapes of al-Fazazi's past sermons. He is still at large, possibly in Morocco, maybe Libya. Eventually we will discover where he is living." She might have added *and where he will die,* but Elena left the clear implication hanging.

"In the meantime, some of his followers have started to surface, and my country thinks it is important to watch them as closely as possible."

This made sense to Santini as far as it went, but there had to be more.

It still didn't answer the question of what she was doing in the company of Berzin. Santini decided not to push Elena on it. She had told him as much of her story as she was going to give him, at least for now.

"Okay, I accept what you say," he said, not sounding convinced. "I just wanted to let you know that you are very much on the radar screen here and that you need to be careful."

Elena reached across the table and touched Santini's arm. "Michael, thank you. I mean that sincerely. You know that in my business—my life—I'm always careful."

Santini nodded and patted her extended hand, wondering if she had been careful with him as well.

Glancing at her watch, Elena grasped at the opportunity to terminate the meeting. "I've got to go. I have some business that I need to finish tonight." She did not offer to explain further. "I think we should leave separately."

Santini agreed.

In one graceful movement, she pulled back her chair, smoothed her dress, and made her way through the crowd that now jammed the bar.

Santini waited a few minutes before calling for the check, trying hard to look indifferent over the departure of his guest. "Beautiful *woman,*" Rudolph said, a bit too bitchily, Santini thought. He wanted to tell Rudolph to fuck off but instead handed him twenty dollars and started for the door.

By now the Cave was probably in violation of the city fire codes. As Santini pushed through a knot of young people who had congregated around the bar, a broad-shouldered, thick-necked man, with dark, thinning hair, used his forearm to temporarily block Santini's momentum. Thinking it an innocent act, Santini tried to push his way gently past the man. He felt the man's arm stiffen. Santini's instincts took over immediately. This was no accident and this man was not about to ask him for an autograph.

"Why are you here?" The words were slightly slurred.

"Just enjoying a little German hospitality," Santini responded, feigning a courtesy he knew was unlikely to be reciprocated.

"Trying to kill more Germans more like it," the man said in a voice loud enough to catch the attention of his friends, who suddenly grew quiet. "You fuckers murdered our boys out . . . where was it? . . . some fucking desert. . . ."

Santini had had more than his share of barroom brawls with drunks who wanted to prove they were alpha males. They usually regretted picking Santini as their target. As an amateur boxer he had a reputation for being able to punish his opponents with either hand. Then, as a Ranger and member of the elite Special Forces, he developed skills that made him a man to avoid making angry.

"Look, let's not—" Before he could finish, the man threw a looping right hand at Santini's head. The move caught Santini by surprise, and only a last-second dip of his head saved him from taking a blow solidly on his jaw. As it was, his attacker's fist glanced off the side of Santini's head, skimming his left ear, turning it beet red, and nearly drawing blood. Santini shoved the man hard, warning him to "back off." One look into the man's glazed eyes told Santini that words were not going to bring about a diplomatic solution to the coming battle.

Santini glanced around to see if his security people were anywhere in the room. His quick survey also yielded some good news. No one else seemed eager to lend the belligerent any assistance. But then again, one look at him told you he didn't appear to need any help. He was built like a Leopard tank. Although his dark head of hair was in the early stages of recession, he was probably only in his mid-thirties. This was not going to be easy.

Fight or flight. Those appeared to be Santini's only choices. He wanted no part of either, but it was clear that he was not going to have the luxury of choosing. The man swung at him again, but this time Santini blocked the punch easily with his left arm. Again, he quickly scanned the room, hoping someone would try to calm his attacker down. The only words he heard were those encouraging their friend Hans to "kick the shit out of the fucker." It had been years since Santini had been involved in any fight, the last one having taken place at the Boom Boom Room in Saigon. Army Rangers were not known for turning the other cheek to avoid a battle. But it was considered bad form for a politician to be seen in bars and really bad form to put a boot up the ass of a mildly intoxicated and boorish patron of a local watering hole, no matter how serious the provocation.

But Santini knew that if this went on any longer, he was going to be up to his ears in elephant shit. There was no way to talk his way out of this. Santini moved in close to Hans to prevent him from gaining any leverage on his looping punches. But Santini was careful not to get so close that Hans could grab him in a bear hug and start crushing his ribs. When the next punch came, he grabbed Hans' outstretched arm, spun his back into Hans' stomach as if he were going to flip him over his back. Instead, in a quick motion, Santini drove the heel of his right foot hard along Hans' right leg, ripping skin off from his mid-calf all the way to his ankle. The blow, delivered with surprising explosive power, stunned Hans momentarily, causing him to drop both arms to his sides. Then the bolt of searing pain raced to his brain, and reflexively he bent over to grasp his traumatized leg, howling in agony.

Hans had been effectively incapacitated. But Santini did not stop. Anger had obliterated reason. His ear was throbbing with pain. The self-control that he had mastered over the years evaporated. While Hans was bent over like a hairpin, Santini took his head in both hands and smashed his knee savagely into Hans' face.

Cartilage and bone shattered with a sickening crack. Hans fell onto his back, holding both hands to his face, trying frantically to stem the flow of blood that now poured from him like an oil gusher.

It had all happened in a matter of a second or two. The crowd of onlookers was as stunned as Santini at his foolish reaction to the provocation. He knew better. There would be hell to pay when this got out. Lawsuits. Tabloids would have a field day. How could he have been so dumb? Was it the pressure of the job that caused him to lose control? Seeing Elena after all of these years? Her cold rejection? . . .

As Hans went down, Raul Gomez and his men shouldered their way through the knot of people. Gomez grabbed Santini by the right arm and hustled him up the stairs and into an elevator. Neither Santini nor Gomez had seen the flash of Rudolph's miniature camera as he snapped away at the prostrate Hans with undisguised glee.

"Thanks, Raul," Santini said as he stepped off the elevator, a hint of mockery in his voice. "You came in the nick of time."

"I'm sure that guy wasn't going to get up for a while, sir," Gomez said.

CHAPTER 32

MUNICH

Entering her suite at the Ritz, Elena tossed her handbag onto a small table in the marble foyer. She moved quickly through the large living room and made her way to a small den area that accommodated a telephone and fax machine. Dropping into an armless chair, she picked up a sheet of lettered writing paper from the desk and began to scribble a quick note to David Ben-Dar. Her nerves were frazzled, and in her business that wasn't supposed to happen. She thought she had been careful with Berzin, avoiding being seen in public with him except at certain business events or on an occasional walk in the park. Not careful enough, evidently.

Now the BND had her on its watch list. Ben-Dar should know about it, and decide whether she was a liability to the mission. She hoped so. She had wanted out of it from the very beginning.

She started to write:

Papa,
   I had an interesting encounter tonight with an old friend from the U.S., the one I had worked briefly with some years ago. He has a new job now, a rather stressful one from all appearances. He said that he had heard from several people that I was making quite an impression in Germany and that several of his friends were following my career in

*business. Very flattering. It's late, but I still have a little
more work to catch up on tonight.*

I'll call from Berlin. I miss you.

*Love,
Miya*

She slipped the letter into the fax machine and dialed a residential number in Finland. A switching station would intercept the fax and reroute it to Ben-Dar's private machine at
Mossad headquarters. It was 2 A.M. in Israel. Ben-Dar would
be there in just a few hours.

After the fax machine signaled that the letter had been transmitted, she took a pack of matches from the ashtray on the
desk, and struck one of the matches against the thin strip of
friction material underneath the book's flap. Instantly, the
match burst into flame. Holding the flame to the letter until it almost singed her fingers, Elena nearly forgot that she might set
off the sprinkler system standing sentry in the hotel's ceiling.
She quickly opened the large window that looked out onto the
street below and allowed the black smoke to curl into the night
air. That lapse was amateurish. A schoolgirl knew better. She
had better calm down and focus on what she had to do next.

She was still upset, but chiding herself didn't seem to help.
She was angry with Santini for calling her. Angry that she
didn't say no. Angry that she was so cold to him. Angry with
who she was, and what she still had to do for her country. She
had paid her dues. Over and over. Her motto had always been
"The best revenge is revenge." But she had had enough of it.

"I swear this is it," she promised herself. "This is it."

As he sat in the soft light of his library, listening to
Beethoven's *Sonata Chiaro di Luna*, op. 27, the wise old mind
of Baron Frederick von Heltsinger was already examining a
new world. Santini had spoken of that world, but he had lifted
only a corner of the curtain that veiled it. He felt betrayed by
Santini, a man he once thought to be honest and principled. It
was clear now that his trust had been misplaced. Santini had

bowed to the pressures and stratagems of those who held little concern for Europe.

The nations of Europe were not equal. Not equal in size, strength, history, or culture. Despite all the proclamations about a united continent, the Baron knew that Europe, left to its own devices, would revert to its old envies and antagonisms. The Brits, French, and Italians would conspire to contain Germany, to tie it up with their legalisms and machinations. Force Germany to sink into a homogenized pool of mediocrity.

The Baron's brooding thoughts were interrupted by his white-gloved butler, Otto, who announced, "Mr. Wagner and his guest are here, sir."

"Show them in, Otto."

The two men entered side by side, as if neither wished to give the other precedence.

"Good evening, Baron von Heltsinger," Berzin said. "Wolfgang has spoken to me often about you. It's an honor."

"As he has about you," von Heltsinger countered, shaking Berzin's hand. He pointed to two deep-tufted chairs and said, "Please make yourselves comfortable." As soon as they had settled, he asked, "May I offer you coffee? Perhaps a brandy?" He raised a crystal glass that he was holding in his hand. "It's quite smooth."

"Brandy for me," Berzin said quickly.

Wagner pondered his choices for a moment, then ordered the same.

Otto bowed, moved deftly to another room, and returned moments later with their drinks on a silver tray.

Von Heltsinger raised his glass and said, "Wolfgang tells me that you have some interesting ideas. The hour is late, but I'm prepared to listen."

Berzin, typically, plunged in without any preliminary pleasantries. "I am convinced that Russia and Germany can combine the best that we have to offer," he said. "A full partnership that marries German efficiencies with Russia's vast natural resources and military power. A German-Russian alliance would make us a true superpower. It could replicate a treaty."

"You speak of Rapallo," von Heltsinger interrupted. "The Treaty of Rapallo." He had not heard the word in a long, long time. The treaty had been named after the Italian town where it was signed. In the secret agreement, made in 1922, Germany recognized the Soviet Union and promised strategic cooperation with the Lenin government. Germany also canceled all prewar debts and renounced all claims stemming from the First World War. The treaty enabled the German Army to produce in the Soviet Union weapons that had been forbidden by the Treaty of Versailles.

"The Treaty of Rapallo. Precisely," Berzin responded. "I know, Herr Baron, that you are a student of history."

The Baron cast a wry smile. "There was a touch of irony to it, was there not? Thanks to Rapallo, the German Army—long before the Hitler regime—was able to manufacture weapons that would be used against the Soviet Union a decade later."

Berzin laughed. "There were, shall we say, unexpected results. But Rapallo did give both nations a strength that each did not have alone. Today there will be only *intended* results."

Berzin went on to describe how he planned to run in and win the Russian special election for the presidency.

Von Heltsinger reflected on what Berzin was proposing. "It's intriguing, Herr Berzin. Not without its challenges. But worth consideration. I need to give it more thought. I'm on travel to Spain for the next few weeks, but perhaps when I return, we can discuss it further."

The conversation was over. After some polite remarks, the Baron summoned Otto, who escorted Berzin and Wagner to the door.

"Good night, gentlemen," the Baron said. He touched Wagner on the shoulder and added, "And thank you, Wolfgang. We'll talk later."

Returning to the library, von Heltsinger reflected on what Berzin had said. Ruefully, he reminded himself of the bon mot "American forces are in Germany to keep the Russians out and the Germans down." Witty. But if the American forces were on their way out, perhaps it made sense to let the Russians in. Not as an invading force, but as a partner in a grand scheme. There was another expression that came to mind. "No permanent friends and no permanent enemies. Only permanent interests."

He had found Berzin to be an imposing figure. Indeed, quite impressive. But von Heltsinger remained concerned about the man. He had promised Wolfgang's father that he would look out for his son. Help him to succeed in business, perhaps even politics. Von Heltsinger's friends at the BND had said that Berzin was ambitious and ruthless. That his wealth was ill-gotten. But had most wealth throughout time been gained honestly? Didn't the strong always take from the weak, the tough from the timid? It was the law of nature. The prize belonged to those who were willing to take chances, to mount and ride history's horse into the future.

Who knows? Von Heltsinger smiled. *If an Austrian-born muscleman could become a famous politician in America, wasn't anything possible?*

He snapped off the library's lights and headed for his bedroom, his mood suddenly lightened. Perhaps it was not so wild a dream to think that Germany could become a political and military force again.

Or that Wolfgang could become Chancellor.

CHAPTER 33

MUNICH

Santini was jet-lagged and totally confused about the time of day or night. He tossed off the down comforter that the German hotels draped over you instead of blankets. *Damn! It's hot!* Perspiration soaked the bedsheets, causing them to bunch up under his back. He felt clammy and unclean even though he had taken a hot shower an hour earlier. The hum of motor traffic wafting through the open window was so distant his ears might have been stuffed with gauze or cotton balls.

Stupid. Stupid . . . He kept cursing himself for what had happened at the Cave. He was losing it. The pressure was getting to him. How could he have let some half-bombed joker provoke him? America had enough problems to deal with. Now he had made it worse. He had just given all the haters an excuse to intensify their attacks. He had made it personal. . . .

Elena. Elena. Her name played over and over in his mind. Her perfume clinging to his brain, suffusing it with a fragrance of such a light and exquisite sensuality that it eluded all description.

He wanted desperately to believe her, even as he knew her words were false. Maybe she was incapable of the truth. Maybe her life depended . . .

Finally, he drifted off, tumbling onto an intangible ledge of miasma, where shapes and forms and sounds were wrapped in memories that had been buried under infinite layers of pain.

"You're a stubborn man, Captain." The voice was calm and

*cruel at once, foreshadowing what was to come. The swish of
the rubber club gave but a second of warning before it struck
him in the kidneys. The pain was so intense that Santini would
have doubled over into a fetal position while he coughed up
blood, had he not been hanging suspended by his arms from
the dank ceiling. Instead, his stomach muscles jerked reflexively, pulling his knees up toward his chest, and then fell down
heavily, the spasmodic motion tearing his shoulders from their
sockets.*

*He stifled a scream, nearly choking on the blood that
sluiced down the back of his throat. He coughed, then spit at
his tormentors.*

*A second blow delivered almost to the same spot caused
him to scream uncontrollably. He clenched his jaws so hard
he thought that his molars were going to disintegrate.*

*"Stubborn and stupid. A very bad combination," came the
cool voice again.*

*Santini knew the torture routine by rote. His squad had
been caught in a savage crossfire of the regular units of the
North Vietnamese Army. He was the only one to survive the
ambush, although severely wounded. He came to regret his
bad luck in living. His captors were convinced that he would
either cooperate with them or pray to join his dead comrades.
In the midst of pain-induced delirium, he had prayed. First
for help and then, when none came, for death. When his
prayers went unanswered, he was convinced that God had
simply abandoned him in that five-by-ten-foot cell that became his home for three years. But why? What sin had he
committed? He had killed, yes. But that was for his country.
For freedom. . . .*

*"Why do you endure so much suffering?" The voice came
again from somewhere just beyond the cone of light cast by
the naked bulb overhead. The same questions always. Spoken
with such mock sincerity. But it was from a different voice this
time, one that had the same singsong quality to it. The cadence was familiar, but not the hint of a French accent that he
had come to associate with two particularly brutal interroga-*

*tors that he and his rail-thin and bloodied comrades had deri-
sively named Prick and Bug.*

*"The American people are calling you Nazis, mass murder-
ers. You have dishonored them."*

Murderers. Dishonored. *The words set his emotions on fire,
hardening him against his tormentors, against the one who
stood back in the shadows, the one with the voice he would
never forget. Never forgive. Never for—*

The blare from the radio alarm clock caused Santini to bolt
upright from the bed. "What the hell?" he cursed, looking
around in the darkness, thinking at first it must be a fire alarm.
Then he focused on the source of the pulsating noise.
"Damn." The hotel service had failed to reset the alarm from
the previous guest, and Santini had never given it a thought. It
was only two o'clock in the morning! His brain had been
summoned to full alert. He would never get back to sleep
now. *Damn.*

He lay back on the bed, pursing his lips in silent protest to
the sheets soaked with his perspiration. In the darkness that
was relieved only by the moon that slipped in and out from
under the line of thin clouds scattered across the night sky,
fragments from his dream began to float past somewhere behind his eyes. That voice. He had heard it recently. But where?
The word *dishonored.* The way it had been said. So long ago.

The brain was a miraculous computer, storing information
in tiny cells more powerful than anything yet invented by
man. Music, songs, words, downloaded and stored on the infinite tablets of the mind. Whom had he talked to recently?
Where in his travels was he most likely to have heard the
word? Could it have been a computer error? Some random,
inexplicable glitch that ejected the word onto the pageantry of
his dream?

Then it came to him. His office at the Pentagon. The Deputy
Minister who had accompanied Xu, the Chinese Minister of
Defense. Li. That was his name. Li. When they were intro-
duced. He had said, "It is an *honor* to meet you, Mr. Secretary."
Those were the only words he spoke in English. They were

spoken haltingly, as if memorized for the occasion by one who was devoid of any language skill. But there was the faint hint of mockery. It was subtle, but it was there. And somehow, Santini had the impression that day that he had met Li before, even though he did not recall ever having seen his face.

Looking at the clock again, Santini calculated that his DIA briefer, Arthur Wu, might still be at work. He swung out of bed, slipped on the robe that hung on the bathroom door. Using the phone on his nightstand, he dialed the room of Alex Dixon, the communications officer who traveled with him.

"Captain," he said, "I need to place a call to Arthur Wu at the DIA in Washington. I'll be down to the secure room in five minutes. Can you get on it?"

"Yes, sir, Mr. Secretary. We're ready."

CHAPTER 34

According to the calendar, it was still winter. But the calendar was no longer a reliable guide. Maybe the environmentalists had it right. We were producing a global warming, a condition that was altering nature itself. The last few weeks were as warm as those spring days that farmers like Josef Kaiser lived for. The sky, a robin's egg blue, was cloudless. Even the earth seemed confused. It was starting to open up.

The few remaining milk cows of Kaiser's thinning herd roamed lazily about the fields that looked as if they might turn green soon. On a day like this, time itself stood still, as if it were Kaiser's grandfather, Rutger, who now gazed out to the horizon and vowed to cut down the forest and till the land for his sons who would follow him.

It was a dream realized and then lost. Farmlands once so plentiful and seemingly endless were now squeezed between the urban sprawl and the ever-expanding military operations of the Americans. How many bases were there? Ramstein, Rhein-Main, Stuttgart, Bamberg, Giebelstadt, Spangdahlem. More than two dozen of them filled with one hundred thousand soldiers and their families. He had nothing against the Americans. They had not misbehaved or acted like conquerors. They did not strut around like some occupying force. Still, they did occupy German territory, forever demanding more land to roll their tanks over, more fertile soil on which to launch missiles against imaginary ground forces who absorbed sulfurous fumes, and metal hotter than a steel mill's buckets.

Grafenwoehr's countryside was no longer the place of Grandpa Rutger's dreams. Once so idyllic it inspired the poetry of German Romantics, today it had become the training ground of NATO countries, with their monstrous tanks, belching forth visions of Armageddon with every percussive cough, the supersonic aircraft screaming overhead while ground troops, looking no more intimidating than toy soldiers, combed hillsides on search and destroy missions.

It all seemed so ridiculous. The Cold War was relegated to the history books. The Soviet empire had dissolved. Russians, no longer in the grip of Stalin and all the heirs to his reign of terror, were trying to find the keys to the kingdom of capitalism. And still they were all out there. The Czechs, the Hungarians, the Poles, the Lithuanians.

Kaiser let escape a sigh of resignation. What would happen to his small farm? Thomas and Stephanie, the last two of his five children, would be moving on to college soon. They had no love for farming, its unrelenting demands for attention, the savage fickleness of the weather, the monopoly power of the large cooperatives. No, they spent their days roaming the vast space of the Internet world, connecting to ethereal voices that extended and echoed into infinite galaxies. He hoped they would find some meaning to it all, that they would make science their servant and not their master, and that they might reach some spiritual place that would bring them comfort and peace in a world that seemed to have lost all sense of moral purpose. Ah, he thought, a smile playing across his face, the meanderings of a man who lamented the passing of his time in a sun that was no longer young for him.

As he shuffled slowly toward the cow barn, Kaiser's gaze drifted. On the horizon were dark objects, initially no bigger than specks of dirt, growing rapidly in size as they approached from the west. He could hear nothing but the sweet chirpings of songbirds flitting about the yard. But he knew that in a matter of seconds the silence would be pierced by the roar of high-performance jet engines and the cows would moan plaintively at the airborne intruders.

How many were there? It was hard to see. Five. No, eight. Another exercise. Another mock battle. He had had to endure so many.

As the combat aircraft roared closer to the boundaries of his property, one plane released a load of small canisters. They burst on impact and emitted a fine mist that shimmered like silver dust in the morning light. He had seen these clouds before. They called it CS, some kind of riot-control gas that they used to simulate a chemical weapons attack. He had gone to the mayor of Grafenwoehr to lodge complaints. The gas was making him and his family sick. Two of his cows suffered lung damage from the gas. One had to be destroyed. How much was he supposed to absorb? This madness had to stop.

His complaints usually were met with benign indifference. *It was a matter of national security. Sorry, nothing can be done. NATO, remember?* Before Kaiser could reach his house to place another call, he noticed something was terribly wrong. Droplets from the fine mist settled on his arms and legs. Vapor entered his nose, burning the lining of his flared nostrils. He took a deep breath, expecting that a rush of fresh air might provide him relief from what felt like gauze being stuffed down his throat. He was choking, suffocating on the mucus clogging the airways to his lungs. Bile was forcing itself up from his bowels.

What was happening to him? His hands began to shake uncontrollably. His legs splayed out from under him. It felt as if a steel spike had been driven into his skull. He had seen his cows slaughtered that way. He tried to call out for help. "Gretchen, Gret—" The words stuck in his burning throat, vowels trapped, struggling to escape. His breathing became shallow, rapid. His eyes felt like raw eggs leaking out of their cracked shells. "I can't mo—"

Within two minutes, Kaiser was dead. Mercifully, he did not live to see how his two children—along with scores of others who were relaxing outside their high school during a morning recess—unknowingly inhaled the poison that came to them in the form of a spring mist.

His wife, Gretchen, did survive. Long enough, at least, to grasp the horror of what had happened to her family before suffering a massive, fatal heart attack.

CHAPTER 35

MUNICH

Santini had just finished eating brunch at the hotel's restaurant on the top floor and was in the process of packing his bags when Admiral O'Neill burst through the door.

"Mr. Secretary!" Admiral O'Neill practically shouted as he rushed into Santini's room. "Turn to CNN. You're not going to believe what has happened. Jesus!"

Santini had never seen Scott so rattled. It obviously wasn't good news. Santini flicked on the small television set with the remote control and felt his stomach churning as the image of Jamie McGregor came onto the screen.

McGregor was CNN's top Pentagon correspondent. Santini always considered him to be a first-rate journalist who played it straight with the news. He had never cut Santini any slack, but unlike some of the others in the "Pack," he never went for the sensational news-breaker story. He had once confided to Santini that one of his superiors at the network in Atlanta had tried to force him to be more aggressive in his reporting. When the executive insisted that CNN had to be first, McGregor had asked, "What happens if the story's not accurate?" The answer was, "To hell with it being right. It's more important that we be first. We can always run a correction later." McGregor refused to cave to the pressure and somehow had managed to keep his job. But now Santini knew that with that same fierce, independent streak McGregor was about to unload a ton of bricks on them.

"This is Jamie McGregor reporting to you live from Munich. CNN has just learned that a NATO training exercise has gone out of control. Hundreds of residents of the town of Grafenwoehr reportedly are dead. Our sources tell us that the cause of death was sarin gas, a toxic poison that affects the respiratory system, causing paralysis and collapse of the esophageal muscles, that in turn leads to cyanosis—a condition that turns the oxygen-deprived body blue and leads to an excruciating death.

"CNN's sources inform us that an American F-16 Falcon released the deadly poison during a joint exercise being conducted by NATO forces. Apparently, the pilot of the F-16, whose identity has yet to be confirmed, thought he was releasing CS, a well-known riot-control substance that was to simulate a chemical weapons environment. We have yet to hear from General John Ellsworth, Supreme Allied Commander Europe, to explain how one of the most deadly chemicals known to man made its way into the arsenal of America's Air Force. This is the same substance that veterans of Vietnam alleged had been once used during a rescue mission . . ."

Santini hit the mute button. His face had gone ashen. He was all too aware of the story McGregor was referring to. It was called Operation Tailwind. Reporters for CNN had alleged that in Vietnam, American helicopter pilots had gassed some of their own people in order to save others. It was a bullshit story. CNN, after having run with it for weeks, finally had to publicly apologize for reporting a story that it couldn't back up. But that was years ago, and McGregor had not been involved. If McGregor was filing this story, then Santini knew it was for real.

He raced down to the control room, startling the communications officer. "Dixon," he barked, "put me through to General John Ellsworth on a secure line directly to SACEUR Headquarters in Brussels. Now."

Within thirty seconds Ellsworth was on the line. Checking the digital screen on the phone identification system, he knew immediately who was on the line and why. "Yes, Mr. Secretary," he answered crisply, trying his best to sound calm when his stomach was swirling in gastric acid. "I just saw the CNN report. We're still trying to sort things out, but it looks like sabotage."

"John, don't give me the fucking 'it looks like' crap. How could anyone penetrate the security of our bases? How could they gain access to our munitions supplies? And what in hell are we doing with sarin gas?"

Before Santini could hammer away any more at Ellsworth, Captain Dixon signaled to him that he had an incoming call from the White House. The National Security Adviser was calling. Praeger. "Shit," Santini said as he put Ellsworth on hold and picked up the line that connected to Praeger's office.

"Santini," Praeger shouted, "have you heard what has happened in Germany?"

"I just heard the report, Joe."

"Tell me one goddamn thing." Praeger began to exhale audibly as if to signify that he was making every effort to control his temper, something he rarely achieved. "Why do I have to learn of a monumental fuckup from CNN? Why didn't you call to give us a heads-up on this?"

Santini started to tell him again that he had just learned what had happened from the very same source that Praeger had. He thought better of it. No sense reinforcing Praeger's jaundiced view of the Pentagon. "I can't tell you what I don't know. This thing just happened. General Ellsworth is holding on the other line, giving me a briefing. There are too many unknowns at this point. As soon as we can sort out what happened, I'll give the President, you, and the National Security Council a full rundown."

"The President wants you back in Washington now. That's *now*. This is a fucking disaster that could ruin us with our allies everywhere! We're trying to rid the world of weapons of mass destruction and we dump sarin gas on an entire community! There's no way we can survive this with some lame-ass excuse of 'oops, sorry.' We've got a little security problem at Ramstein or wherever to hell it is where you loaded that shit up."

"How soon is the meeting?"

"Just as soon as you get back here."

"It's probably a nine-hour flight or more given headwinds. I can be at the White House by late afternoon."

"Hopefully you don't plan to keep the President waiting any longer so you can go brawling in German barrooms! Jesus Christ! On top of everything, you go playing Rambo in Munich. The story's on the wires! Do you have any idea what you've done?"

A loud click ended his conversation with Praeger.

Any remorse that Santini had felt about losing control in the bar quickly evaporated. But there was no way of dismissing it. The tabloids were going to have a field day tying his indiscretions to what had just happened at Grafenwoehr.

Santini had often wondered about "smart bombs," those laser-guided precision missiles that made war look like a video game. Multimillion-dollar weapons, satellites, miniature television cameras. *And we wind up with this: Somebody goofed, switched a label, made a wrong entry into a laptop.*

He got back to Ellsworth. "I have to be in the White House by sixteen hundred Washington time. What can I tell the President?"

"Mr. Secretary, it was no accident. This was an act of war. It had to have been planned and carried out by a sophisticated organization."

"Islamist? Al Qaeda?"

"I'd certainly go with that, Mr. Secretary. It's an operation on the Twin Towers scale."

"Need I remind you, General, that those were *civilian* aircraft? This was gas from a *U.S. Air Force* warplane. I want a report in my hands by the time I arrive in Washington. You can transmit it over a secure fax line directly to me on my airplane. And I want something in that report that I haven't seen on television."

CHAPTER 36

WASHINGTON

"I told you he would be an embarrassment," Joe Praeger said to the President. "I mean what else can Santini do to undermine your leadership? Your chances for re-election?" Praeger said, exhaling loudly, signifying his exasperation. "He beats the hell out of some drunk in a bar who just happens to be a member of the German Bundestag. Then our guys burn the lungs out of hundreds of innocent people with chemical weapons!"

"Don't you think it would be wise to hear what in hell happened before he's convicted? You know, trial before judgment. Isn't that supposed to be the core of our system?" President Jefferson asked. He was a reserved and rather modest man who disliked having to remind his closest advisers—Praeger in particular—not to wear his stars as Commander in Chief. "Or is it his execution you're really after?"

Praeger made it a practice to ostensibly defer to Jefferson during their private meetings. When in the company of members of the President's Cabinet, Praeger acted obscenely solicitous. But privately, he seethed when Jefferson disregarded his advice. In his mind, Bradford Jefferson was a house of cards that would collapse in a strong wind were it not for Joe Praeger.

He considered Jefferson's vaunted success in the business world not so much a reflection of genius as it was lady luck. Jefferson, using his wife's inheritance, had been one of the initial major investors in America On Line (AOL). That was long before AOL merged with Time Warner and took their "synergistic" marriage onto the rocks. He cashed out and made $600 million. Convinced that life anywhere on the East Coast had to be sweeter than in Cleveland, Ohio, he moved his family to Miami. He decided that owning a professional football team would give him instant social and celebrity status. Along with two partners in a venture capital firm, he acquired the Miami Conquistadors, who had been threatening to leave the state. Within two years, the team turned in top-flight seasons and Jefferson's stock began to soar, along with the team's.

But the team's success was for Praeger to claim, not Jefferson. After all, Praeger was the bright young executive in the front office who had found the right managers and coaches. He was the one who had persuaded Jefferson to think on a larger scale, that there was more to life than spending Sunday watching steroid-pumped giants attempt to destroy one another on artificial turf.

Turning tens of thousands of sports fans into political supporters would be a snap. Name recognition, honestly acquired wealth, handsome features, and a wholesome family—all the ingredients necessary for a life in the fast lane of politics.

Of course, Jefferson would need something of a makeover. The four-thousand-dollar Brioni suits would have to go. Too many of the dot-com highflyers had traded them in for orange jumpsuits furnished courtesy of federal penitentiaries.

Even though Jefferson left his association with AOL long before the company had drawn the attention of the Securities and Exchange Commission or stirred the interests of hungry U.S. attorneys, it was better to avoid any subliminal comparisons. Dark blue Canalis would be just fine. And the new Mercedes had to be traded in for American-made cars. A Cadillac or two would be sufficient, along with a more modest home.

Within three years, Praeger had managed to place Jefferson into the race for the governorship of Florida. The odds against him winning a primary race against a popular incumbent, however, were long. That is, until Governor Cal Walker died in a plane crash in what the press described as a "freak accident."

Coasting on an economic boomlet that Walker had generated, Bradford Jefferson became Florida's man of the hour. With twenty-five electoral votes in his hands, he became the clear favorite to deliver the White House to his party, which was precisely what he did. Happy times were here again.

Praeger, who had served as Governor Jefferson's chief of staff and master campaign strategist, was eager for a job promotion. Let his underling Charlie Teeter control the President's schedule and make the trains run on time. Praeger wanted the State Department. That's where he could make the biggest impact. But he knew that would be seen as overreaching. Every wine in its time. National Security Adviser would put him in line to move to Foggy Bottom once Jefferson was re-elected. And nothing was going to stop him from achieving his dream. Not Michael Santini. Not even Jefferson—his creation—the person regarded as the most powerful man on earth.

"Mr. President," Praeger intoned, with a little less of an edge than he had in his voice a moment before. "We managed to allow saboteurs to bomb three German aircraft out of the skies in New Mexico and now our Air Force has just killed hundreds of Germans on their own soil. All on *your* . . . I'm sorry, *our* . . . Defense Secretary's watch."

Praeger still fumed over Jefferson's impetuous decision to appoint Santini after Thomas Koestler's death from anthrax. The fawning press hailed it at the time as a "bold and courageous move." But to Praeger it was absolutely stupid, and it remained buried like a very sharp stone in Praeger's shoe. One that he was determined to pluck out.

"You know how I felt about your selecting him. He thrives on his reputation for being independent. He's way overrated. Frankly, I think the North Vietnamese scrambled a few of his wires. Sometimes he just—"

"Don't pound a nail with a sledgehammer, Joe. Santini was

subjected to torture that few of us could even begin to contemplate, much less endure."

"He's to be admired for that, Mr. President. But heroism doesn't give him license to piss in your punch bowl. Pardon my French. He's a liability to you, to your Administration."

"He's bailed us out on the Hill more than once."

"Everyone tends to forget that the Vietcong cracked him in prison. He signed a confession that he was a war criminal for Christ's sake, but all the butt-kissing reporters that he's conned seem to suffer from a case of accommodating amnesia when it comes to that."

"Come on, Joe, ease up," Jefferson said. "Everyone also knows that he signed it under extreme torture and the way he signed it left no doubt that it was an involuntary act."

"I'm telling you, Mr. President, that they got to him. They fucked him up. Christ, you remember what the FBI found during his security clearance investigation. They said his apartment was furnished with so much Asian art and decor that it looked like a Chinese curio shop."

"So now he's the Manchurian Candidate! Enough, Joe," Jefferson said, his voice turning angry. "Let's find out what happened first, for Christ's sake."

Seeing that he was not going to budge Jefferson, at least for now, Praeger nodded and gathered the copies of wire service stories from the desk. "Yes, sir. But Mr. President, I'm telling you. Santini is a problem and sooner or later he's going to bring *us* down." Praeger knew he was skating on thin ice. He had just insinuated that his fate and Jefferson's were one and the same. He was convinced that Jefferson couldn't succeed without him, but he was usually careful not to be so brazen about it.

President Jefferson's cold stare told him to walk a lot more humbly in the Oval Office.

CHAPTER 37

WASHINGTON

On the long flight back to Washington, Santini's thoughts drifted, as if his momentary sanity depended upon his not keeping the CNN scenes in the front of his mind. The information he received from General Ellsworth was useless. Just a classified list of all the bases in Germany, including Grafenwoehr, where chemical munitions once had been stored. Grafenwoehr was an Army base, and it seemed unlikely that air-delivered canisters containing sarin would have been stored there. The F-16 squadron that participated in the exercise had been stationed in Ramstein. So it seemed probable the sabotage had to start there.

The only thing Santini knew for sure was that wherever the sarin was loaded into the F-16s, it could not have been an "innocent" error. It was deliberate. It was a case of mass murder. But by whom? And why?

As soon as Santini's plane touched down, Curtis pulled up in his limousine. Santini jumped in, clutching the few sheets of paper that General Ellsworth had faxed. He sat scrunched in the backseat of the limousine while Curtis raced back toward the White House, emergency lights flashing and siren blasting on full volume. Luckily, it was Sunday, with little need for Curtis to thread his way through traffic.

Patience with scoundrels or fools had never been high on Santini's list of virtues, and he was not sure that he'd be able to hold his temper if Praeger tried to jump all over him in front of the President and the others who would be present.

Santini had resolved to remain in office not so much out of respect for the President as for the office of the presidency. At least that's how he rationalized his forbearance in the face of Praeger's subtle but persistent efforts to undercut his authority. But there was more to it than this. He stayed because he feared that he was the only one in the Cabinet who could prevent Jefferson from doing something rash. He wasn't going to let the military be used as pawns in the hands of those who were lean and hungry for power. Not if he could help it.

By the time Santini arrived at the White House, the Situation Room was crammed with members of the National Security Council. Attorney General Gregory Fairbanks sat with a tablet of legal-size paper. He was always taking notes. Santini was never quite sure whether he was preparing an indictment or writing a memoir. Beside him was FBI Director Frank McConnell. He was not an official member of the Council, but perhaps he had some information linking the sarin gas attack in Germany to what had happened out at Holloman AFB. Secretary of State Douglas Palmer was engaged in busy conversation with CIA Director Pelky. Director of National Intelligence Ford sat next to what Santini assumed to be Praeger's chair. Along the walls were the usual note takers and NSC staffers. Vice President Dan Moxley looked like the new boy in school. He must have been pulled off the funeral circuit today. He showed up more often at the Washington Opera and on the social circuit than he did at security sessions.

Santini continued to scan the room, as he assumed his seat at the conference table. Air Force general George Whittier, Chairman of the Joint Chiefs, ducked his head under the low transom as he entered the room just ahead of Joe Praeger. Tension hung in the air like a bad odor, but that usually was the effect of Praeger's presence.

"All right," Praeger muttered. "Let's get started. Everyone here knows by now that we have just conducted what's sure to be called an act of terror. More than three hundred Germans are dead." Praeger paused, trying to add drama, but the effort came off as a needless affectation. "Poisoned," he continued, staring accusingly at Santini, "by a United States pilot. This is an international crisis of monumental proportions. This could be the straw that breaks the back of NATO. Turning what remains of our fucking friends against us." His tail was on fire and he wanted everybody there to feel the heat. "It also, of course, sets us back in the war against terrorism."

Santini waited for the fusillade to end. He glanced at General Whittier, who remained impassive. Both men knew that silence was more maddening to Praeger than an effort to rebut him. Finally, Praeger turned to Santini and said, "Secretary Santini, would you care to enlighten us as to exactly how this disaster came about?"

"You know that I don't have the answers yet," Santini answered, his voice ominously calm, warning Praeger not to cross the line with him. "Obviously, there's been a serious security breach at one of our bases in Europe. We're still trying to track down where the munitions aboard the aircraft had been stored and loaded. We should have that information shortly. We have a massive investigation under way to determine how many personnel had access to CS stocks and load-out clearance for our aircraft. As *you* know"—knowing that Praeger didn't know and could have cared less—"these exercises are planned at least a year in advance. So whoever is responsible for this probably had plenty of time to consider how to cover their tracks."

"Just how much time do you think we have?" asked Praeger. "There are riots breaking out all over Germany. Skinheads smashing the windows of American companies, throwing Molotov cocktails at military personnel and their families."

"Joe," General Whittier interceded. "I've ordered all of our troops and their family members to remain on-base. Those who are living off the economy have been instructed to move to our bases immediately, where we can provide accommodations on an emergency basis."

"All well and good, General, but we can't keep them quarantined forever. We need some answers. Fast. The President is going to have to make a statement from the Oval Office tonight. He needs to tell the Germans, and the American people, more than 'we have the matter under investigation.'" Sarcasm dripped from Praeger's voice like battery acid.

Turning to Gregory Fairbanks, Praeger said, "I've asked the Attorney General to research our international agreements and to draft a legislative proposal to submit to Congress for an emergency appropriation. We need to compensate the victims of this terrible fuckup. And fast. We can't wait for the military to conduct an investigation to determine who is at fault and we sure as hell can't insist that our SOFA—"

Fairbanks looked up quizzically.

"Status of Forces Agreement," Praeger said impatiently. "We can't let that be used to limit our financial exposure." Praeger looked defiantly around the table. "Any objections?"

"I've got plenty of objections," Santini shouted. "We need time to find out exactly how this happened. Christ, we don't even know if the Germans somehow were at fault."

"Now I've heard everything! You want to blame the victims? Is that what you're asking the President of the United States to do? Call a press conference and blame the poor bastards whose lungs were burned out?"

"God damn it," Santini shouted. "Don't try to twist what I just said. You know exactly what I meant. We need more time."

"We don't have time."

"So you don't give a damn about the precedent," Santini responded, lowering his voice. "So any time innocent people are killed or injured as the result of a military operation—or, in this case, an act of terrorism—the U.S. Government will roll over and pay. Kiss our sorry ass and every congressional budget good-bye. It's going to be open season on Uncle Sam."

"The President has already decided. We'll deal with tomorrow, tomorrow." Praeger went through the motions of asking everyone for further comment. He got few comments. He then pushed his chair back, his familiar signal that the meeting was over.

Halfway out the door, Praeger turned and, staring at Santini, said, "I forgot to mention that the President and I will be traveling to Germany tomorrow on Air Force One. The memorial service for those who died at Grafenwoehr is going to take place next Friday. The President plans to speak at the ceremony, offering a formal apology on behalf of the American people and telling the Germans of our decision to compensate all of the families. I'll advise the President that he has the full support of his team on this."

"Joe," Santini said, not taking his eyes off the man he detested, "I want to talk to the President."

"Excellent," Praeger said, snapping shut his daybook. "It just so happens that the President wants to talk to you."

Santini moved quickly up the rear stairs of the West Wing, walked through the main reception room and down the narrow corridor that led to the Oval Office. He acknowledged the two guards positioned beside the guest entrance and slipped quickly into the office of Barbara Curran, the President's secretary, who was busily opening up the avalanche of personal correspondence and official gifts that rolled into the White House each day.

"Afternoon, Mr. Secretary," she said pleasantly. "Please have a seat. The President will be with you shortly."

Moments later, while Santini tried to busy himself by skimming through copies of *The New York Times* and *The Wall Street Journal*, she picked up her phone, dialed the intercom, and announced Santini's arrival. Nodding, she motioned for Santini to enter through the rear door to the Oval Office. "The President will see you now."

As Santini entered the room, which always seemed too diminutive, given the power that was exercised there, the first person he saw was Joe Praeger. "Mr. President," Santini said, "if you have no objection, I'd prefer that we have this meeting in private."

Jefferson glanced at Praeger, whose jaw muscle tightened and twitched noticeably: his signal that he objected to the request. Ignoring Praeger's smoldering stare, Jefferson said, "I agree. I think we can handle this alone." Turning to Praeger, he said, "We'll just be a few moments, Joe."

Praeger nodded, picked up his leather-bound notepad, and moved toward the north end of the room. Feigning docility, he said as he departed, "Yes, sir. I'll wait out in Barbara's office."

The door closed, Jefferson signaled Santini to sit on the couch that ran perpendicular to the President's chair in front of the fireplace. It was unseasonably warm for March, but Jefferson enjoyed hearing the maple logs crackling in the fireplace.

"Michael," Jefferson began, somewhat tentatively. The two men had only spent a limited amount of time alone together. Usually the President was surrounded by several key advisers whether in the Oval Office, in his private quarters in the White House, or at Camp David in the Catocin Mountains.

While Jefferson's manner was cordial, there was a certain awkwardness to the moment. Santini was surprised that his tone was apologetic rather than angry.

"I know that the past few weeks have been rough for you and your folks over at the Pentagon. This thing in Germany. My God, I know you had no real control over what happened any more than I did. But I've got to level with you, Michael. I'm starting to hear a lot of chatter. You know, small stuff. Most of it petty."

"Such as, Mr. President?"

"Well, that your management style—how shall I say it?—has become too loose. That you're no longer hands-on enough. That kind of talk's not sticking yet, but you know how this town works."

Indeed. Santini knew how Praeger worked. He had been putting this line out to the White House press corps almost from the day Santini took the oath of office. "You think that the job's too big for me, Mr. President?"

"No, no, Michael. Hell, I'm the one who appointed you because I'm convinced that you're the right man for the job. It's just that . . ."

Santini could fill in the blanks. *It's just that if you're not in control, it means that I'm not in control, and then the background chatter turns into mortar fire aimed at me.*

"Because of what happened at Grafenwoehr?"

"Holloman was a nail," Jefferson said. "Grafenwoehr is turning into a coffin. I need to have some hard facts on what in hell happened yesterday. The Germans have gone ballistic over this, and rightfully so. For them, this accident ranks right up there with September 11—"

"It was no accident, Mr. President," Santini said bluntly. "It was sabotage."

"But Joe said that you didn't know what happened or didn't have an explanation."

"I told Joe that I didn't have any facts yet. I don't know how the sarin was loaded onto our aircraft, by whom, where, or when it was done. But there's no question that this was another act of terrorism. Just like the one out at Holloman."

"Are you saying that the militias are now operating in Germany?" Jefferson was clearly incredulous at the notion.

"No, sir. And I don't think that the militias were really the ones behind Holloman. They were agents, mere strings that were being pulled by someone or something much bigger."

"Meaning?"

"Sir, I need to confide something with you and ask that you not share it with anyone. And that includes Joe Praeger."

"Must be pretty important," Jefferson said, not committing to holding it in confidence.

"I'm working closely with the German intelligence people and we are getting closer to finding the individuals or groups who're behind all of this," Santini said. He wanted to tell Jefferson that there was a possible China connection to it all. But if Praeger got wind of this, it would only feed into his agenda. He was looking for any excuse to turn China into the implacable enemy of the United States. It might very well be the case. But Santini refused to consider blaming China until he had all the facts.

"You sharing anything with the Agency on this?" the President asked, a slight frown appearing on his brow. "The FBI? Homeland Security? DNI Ford? They're the ones who need to be plugged into anything you have, Michael. You can't play Lone Ranger on this."

He had heard that charge before. It was Praeger's pet peeve. *Santini's a loner. Not a team player.* Well, he wasn't on Praeger's team, for shit sure. And he wasn't so sure that he wanted to be on Jefferson's anymore, either. He had voted for the man and had been excited about what he saw in Jefferson from a distance. But the more he saw close-up, the less he liked. Jefferson was becoming more politician than President, just like so many of his predecessors. Santini was disheartened about it. Perhaps he knew all along that he would be.

Every President tries to project an image of strength, moral conviction, and competence. The American people want desperately to believe that their choice will always reflect these characteristics. Too often it is a false hope. Bradford Jefferson was no exception. He looked the part, to be sure. And in the beginning he asserted a brand of leadership that fired the imagination of the people. But over time he became hollowed out by the process of making too many promises to too many groups. Promises that he knew he could not keep. And so, he came under the control of his staff, his top advisers, and the spinmeisters, easily manipulated by those who appealed to his vanity and his desperate desire to avoid rejection by the teeming masses that he had once so dazzled and beguiled.

"No, sir. I am not ready to share. Not yet. I expect that we'll have something solid to report within the next week or so."

"Michael," Jefferson said, shaking his head, rising from his chair, signaling the meeting was over. "I don't have that long. I'm leaving soon for Germany to attend the memorial service for all of the victims. Hopefully, that will buy us a little time by showing America's sympathy for what . . . for what we've done to them. I plan to make the rounds of a half-dozen other European nations to help calm things down. But I have to tell you, you're playing with fire going on this alone. I'll hold off until I get back to Washington. But if you don't have something then . . . Well, you and I will have to have a different conversation."

"Mr. President, on another matter. My understanding is that you're going to offer the Germans compensation. With all due respect, sir, that will—"

"Michael." Jefferson cut him off abruptly. "I can't believe that you're concerned about money over this . . . this disaster. That matter is closed. Done. The conversation I'm talking about involves something quite different."

CHAPTER 38

On this sparkling morning, when the coming of spring was greening the woodlands around the CIA headquarters in Langley, Jack Pelky was in his seventh-floor office, signing off on a report to the DNI for his next appearance before the Senate and House. "The security environment in which we live is dynamic and uncertain, replete with a host of ominous threats and challenges that have the potential to grow more deadly. . . . To meet the challenges of this increasingly dangerous and complex world, our consumers are demanding more timely, accurate, and . . ." And how long DNI Ford would wait until he swung his ax again.

He wondered just how long the Agency could continue to grind out the same pap. Mercifully, Pelky's telephone rang, and, glancing at the console, he saw that it was Santini.

"How are chances for a meet at the tennis court?" Santini asked.

"You're saving me from death by boredom. Give me an hour."

Pelky told his office assistant to alert his security entourage. The security men were used to sudden, unscheduled trips for the DCI; scheduled movements were bait for assassins. So it was not unusual for him to make an unexpected trip, especially to Capitol Hill. And with Congress away during a scheduled recess, the security people knew, he would not be going to the office of a representative or senator but to a place between the Hart and Dirksen Buildings on the Senate side of the Hill. The place was the little-known location of indoor tennis courts with an exclusive clientele: members and former members of the U.S. Senate. The courts were rarely used even when the Senate was in session.

Santini was the first to arrive, his limousine accompanied by the usual black chase van. The two vehicles pulled up in front of the Hart Building. A guard stepped out, recognized Santini, and returned to his post inside. Santini glanced at the centerpiece of the atrium, Alexander Calder's mobile-stabile *Mountains and Clouds,* and shook his head at the sight of it.

Three minutes later, a blue Chrysler slowly cruised down Second Street, checking the scene. Santini's driver, Curtis, waved at the grim-faced men in the Chrysler. They did not wave back. Pelky's limousine and black chase van pulled up on the other side of Second Street. The arrangement called for all the security men to stay outside, and any daily schedule memo that might be produced would not include this meeting.

Santini led Pelky to the tennis courts door, unlocked it, ushered him in, and switched on a battery of overhead lights. Pelky moved two chairs closer together. Santini had often played tennis here, but he had never yet invited Pelky for a game. Pelky, tall and trim, was a better than average player. He was no Arthur Ashe, but he had been captain of the Dartmouth College tennis team.

They did not waste time on pleasantries.

"Praeger was pretty rough yesterday."

"Joe's an asshole. Nothing new," Santini said dismissively. "Jack, I really need your help on this. Turn on all the faucets. Whatever you've got, scrubbed or not."

Pelky nodded. "You got it. The nets are all up. I'll come directly to you. No filters."

"Great. Tell me, on the other thing that I called you about. Did you come up with anything on Li Kangsheng?"

"Well, I thought DIA would have told you all about him," Pelky replied with a quick smile that was not a smile.

"Please, Jack. This is personal," Santini said. He told Pelky about the nightmare. "I did ask Wu—he's my DIA briefer—to see what he could come up with. Nothing. And then he passed it on to your shop. When I heard that, I called you. I didn't want this thing to get out of hand. It might sound loony: 'SecDef has flashback to POW torture.' "

"Our information from back in your Vietnam days is spotty; a lot of it went through the shredders long ago. But I had a damn good analyst go through what we have on Li, asking him if there was any indication he had been in North Vietnam as an adviser. The analyst found out that Li had been a Red Guard and was known as a nasty piece of work, even by *their* standards. He got a kick out of torture. Our analyst believed that the worst of the Red Guards were sent out of China to cool off—North Vietnam was the major venue."

"That narrows things down," Santini said. "But it doesn't prove he was the man I heard. I remember a voice speaking English with a thick accent."

"Right. Well, it turns out that we have a PLA defector—a former colonel—who earns his pay by giving us backgrounds on the PLA players. We asked specifically about Li's linguistic abilities. The colonel says he heard that Li had almost been thrown out of the Red Guards because he had tried to learn English at some self-help night school in Beijing. Not much of a student. Picked up a few words, nothing serviceable. His instructor was a young woman he later denounced. The colonel thinks that he was nastier than the average Red Guard because he felt he had to make up for knowing some English."

"Bingo!" Santini exclaimed.

"There's more," Pelky offered. "First of all, Li Kangsheng, in civvies and under an assumed name, was a member of a Chinese delegation on a goodwill visit to Cuba last year. We know because he went to Lourdes, which used to be the Soviets' largest signal intercept base outside the USSR. We still keep an eye on Lourdes."

"But didn't the Russians agree to shut it down?"

"Well, yes. But you know how these things work. Cuba has been playing footsie with China and hinting that, for a price, China can take over the base. There are still some Russian caretakers there to teach the Chinese all the tricks."

"So it wouldn't be extraordinary for a guy in Li's position to be in an inspection group."

"Right. But what interested us is that Li, accompanied only by an interpreter, left the official guesthouse that the Chinese mission was staying in. 'Slipped out,' our man in Havana said. He was picked up by a car that took him to the Hemingway Marina. He went aboard a Bermuda-registered yacht and had a meeting."

"Met with whom?"

"We don't know."

Santini paused, looked up at the ceiling, then down at his feet. It was his way of handling his smoldering over Pelky's obvious withholding of information. The DIA had become highly competitive under Santini's predecessor, and the CIA still disliked sharing information with the Pentagon, even if there was supposed to be a special relationship between Santini and Pelky.

"I haven't said anything about this to anyone else yet, Jack. But there's some evidence that there could be a Chinese link to everything that's been going down."

"The Chinese?" Pelky asked incredulously.

"Yeah. You know that one of the BND's men was found on the wrong side of two .22-caliber bullets in Berlin. Well, while I was in Munich, I learned that he had just returned from northwest China and claimed that the Chinese knew something about Holloman."

"And?"

"He never got the chance to say who or why."

Pelky's eyes revealed that his mind was already racing ahead, examining every hypothetical connection that Beijing might have to the recent attacks. "Who else knows about this?" he asked.

"No one, to my knowledge," Santini replied. "I told the President that forces outside the militia were likely involved. I hinted that they might be foreign, but nothing more."

"Let me ask you another question. How much do you know about Arthur Wu?" Pelky asked, with no acknowledgment that he had changed the subject.

"Vetted for Top Secret and any compartmentalized material on a need-to-know. He's a little strange, kind of pushy. Why?"

"This is very delicate. NSA doesn't get as much out of China intercepts as we'd like, but it did pick up a message that came from a cell phone in Beijing that had one of those NSA key words that turns on the recorders. The word, in Chinese, means 'top secret.' The Chinese—unlike us—don't throw the word around much. So when NSA picks it up, it records what it can. You don't use 'top secret' on a cell phone unless you're rattled or careless. NSA just picked up a scrap, but your name was in it—loud and clear."

"So? And what does that have to do with Wu? You guys are always trying to kick the DIA around. I can think of a dozen reasons why my name and 'top secret' would be in a Beijing phone call."

"But the other end of this was in the United States, Michael." Pelky pulled his chair closer to Santini's. "NSA tentatively put it in northern Virginia, within a three-mile circle that includes the Pentagon."

"And a magic circle that just happens to *exclude* Langley."

"Sure, Michael. Be skeptical. But I wonder if you shouldn't have the FBI get a secret surveillance order for Wu."

"Let me ask you something, Jack. Did Praeger put you up to this?"

"You know I don't do his—or anyone else's—bidding," Pelky said emphatically, and a bit too defensively to suit Santini.

"Make an official request, in writing, Jack, and I'll be glad to do it."

"I'm not making an official request, Michael. Just a friendly warning."

CHAPTER 39

Santini, sipping coffee at his desk, ran the warning through his mind. First Praeger, now Pelky. Maybe they were right. How many times did the Pentagon have to get burned before it looked in the mirror and saw the enemy? If genius consisted of being able to see the obvious, they qualified as morons. Chinese in their research laboratories. Islamic converts counseling terrorist prisoners at Guantánamo Bay, Cuba. . . . Little wonder they were branded as buffoons.

Still, he cautioned himself, he had to be careful. The FBI success rate wasn't exactly ready for the *Guinness Book of Records*. Labeling someone as a "suspect" or "person of interest" was enough to ruin the poor bastard's reputation forever. The government's subsequent admission of error—even accompanied by a cash settlement—never compensates for the damage done. The shadow of society's suspicion lingers on like a foul odor. It never quite goes away.

He had his own doubts about Arthur Wu from the first day he met him.

But wasn't it ethnic McCarthyism to suspect a Chinese-American of spying? Santini remembered the debacle over suspicions of a Chinese-American physicist working on atomic warhead design. He did not want that to happen in the Pentagon.

He called in O'Neill and told him about the conversations he had had with Christoph Stiller and Jack Pelky. Santini was now convinced that there was a Chinese connection to Hollo-man and Grafenwoehr.

"China?" O'Neill said, shaking his head. "It doesn't make sense. Why would China try to inflame Germany *and* us with a terrorist act? It doesn't fit at all with the way China operates."

"Suppose there is a rogue Chinese group? Suppose this was not official but an off-the-reservation operation? I can't be-lieve that Xu could come to Washington and look me in the eye and have this going on. He represents a country that genuinely wants a solid relationship with the United States. It's got to be a rogue group, probably pissed-off PLA coup planners."

"We have no proof of that—and no way of finding it. That's the CIA's job," O'Neill said.

Santini picked up the carafe and refilled O'Neill's cup. "I'd like us to take a look at China as quietly as we can."

"Us being the DIA?"

"Yes, but before we bring the DIA into this, Scott, I need one more thing. I need you to conduct a little covert operation for me."

"At your majesty's secret service," O'Neill said. "Do I get to go to Beijing with love?"

"Nothing that exciting. But I need you to handle this with some care."

"Shoot."

"Arthur Wu."

"Sir? I don't follow." O'Neill's eyebrows arched.

"Meaning, I've had an uneasy feeling about him. I can't de-scribe what's provoked it. Just that ever since he's showed up, something just doesn't feel right."

Seeing the skeptical look that O'Neill flashed him, Santini said, "Look, I know what you're thinking. It's not a matter of race. You know that. There's a leak somewhere in this place. Someone outside seems to have access to what's going on in this office. I'm convinced that whoever killed Tom Koestler had help from inside."

"And you think it's Arthur, sir?" O'Neill shook his head in disbelief. "He wasn't even here at that time."

"I know. But I need to know more about him. He could have been a sleeper who has been activated. Joe Praeger has been trying to poison the well on Wu. Now Jack Pelky is raising questions about him. I want you to pull his personnel file and review it. Focus on quality-of-life issues. Is he playing around? Buying expensive gifts? Living beyond his paycheck? The whole nine yards."

"And you want me to leave no fingerprints, right?"

"Right."

"Not a problem, Mr. Secretary," O'Neill said as he started for the door. "I do think you're mistaken about him. I reviewed his dossier thoroughly before he was assigned as your briefer. But you're the boss. It shouldn't take too long."

O'Neill was true to his word. He was back in Santini's office within thirty minutes, handing over Wu's personnel file and disclosure papers. Santini scanned the information quickly.

"Father a retired mechanical engineer who did consultant work for the Atlantic Richfeld Company (ARCO) . . . Mother taught Chinese at UCLA in Los Angeles . . . Academic record outstanding . . . Model student from first grade through graduate school . . . Spent six years in the Army and picked up two master's degrees during that time . . . Finances seemed in order. Carried an eighty-thousand-dollar mortgage on a condominium in Arlington . . . Owned a 1987 Cheverolet and a new Cadillac Escalade . . ."

Santini stopped reading. Something was wrong.

"Scott," he said, turning to O'Neill. "Let me ask you something. How much does a fully loaded Escalade go for?"

O'Neill pursed his lips and raised his eyes toward the ceiling. "Fully loaded? Rough guess, fifty-one to fifty-three thousand dollars."

"How can a reserve captain afford such a car? Wu doesn't list any mortgage for it."

Embarrassed that he had missed the significance of what Santini had seen, O'Neill answered weakly, "Good question, sir. Maybe it was an oversight."

"Possible," Santini said, not trying to hide the skepticism in his voice. Wu was too fastidious a man to have overlooked a liability. "Also possible that he paid cash."

O'Neill conceded the point.

"Okay, Scott, this is helpful. Thanks." Santini's dismissive tone conveyed exactly what he felt at that moment. He was disappointed that the omission—a flashing red light—had been either missed or ignored. "I'll take it from here."

Santini's mother, Claire, used to recite the biblical axiom that "the love of money was the root of evil." His father, Salvatore, who labored twelve-hour days in his small restaurant, would rejoin, "It would be nice to have a little more just the same."

Most people wanted more. And some didn't mind selling out their country to get it.

Santini was going to make a personal visit to see if Arthur was one of them.

CHAPTER 40

WASHINGTON

The Capitol Trust Company was housed in a squat, stone bank building, located on Pennsylvania Avenue just three blocks from Santini's apartment complex. It had been in business for well over a hundred years. It was one of those veritable Washington institutions.

Santini had instructed Curtis to drop him at the bank instead of his apartment. He said that he would walk home after his meeting at the bank. Curtis, forever skeptical of allowing Santini to walk anywhere, insisted that he would wait in the armored limousine and drive Santini the three blocks.

It was a persistent point of contention between them. "Look, Curtis," Santini argued, "there's no safe hiding place. Any nut can take me out up close or at long range."

"You're right, Mr. Secretary." Curtis knocked on the tinted, reinforced windows of the limo. "They can't necessarily save your life. What they can do is prevent anyone from kidnapping and torturing you."

Santini knew that Curtis was right. Still, he was determined not to live in a total cocoon. He was going to walk, terrorists be damned.

Curtis yielded. After all, Santini was his boss. Besides, he knew that Santini would be shadowed, and not so discreetly, by his security detail.

Santini entered the bank and was immediately greeted by Robert Fitzgerald, Capitol Trust's senior vice president. Santini had phoned Fitzgerald earlier and indicated that he had to speak with him about a very sensitive matter.

Fitzgerald had served as an Army officer in Vietnam, and when Santini had returned to Washington to open a brokerage account with the bank the two men struck up a friendship.

"Mr. Secretary," Fitzgerald said, as he escorted Santini into his paneled office. "Good to see you again."

After shaking hands, Fitzgerald motioned for Santini to sit on the leather sofa. "Over here. It's more comfortable."

Sitting down, and declining an offer of coffee, Santini wasted no time in telling Fitzgerald what he wanted.

The bank officer rolled his tongue across his lower lip and shook his head. "I'm sorry. I'd like to help, but I can't do that. As a fiduciary, the law requires us to maintain the confidentiality of these records. We'd have to have a court order or something equivalent."

"Bob, the law no longer requires a court order."

"You're right. But under the Patriot Act, the Attorney General or someone in the Justice Department has to authorize it."

"True," Santini said. "I could call Gregory Fairbanks and get a couple of FBI agents over here in ten minutes. But then Justice would have to open a file on Mr. Wu. Things, as you know, have a way of leaking in this town. Wu could end up getting burned—and just because I have a suspicion, nothing more."

Fitzgerald said nothing for the moment. Clearly, friendship and duty were in deep conflict.

Santini knew that trying to bully Fitzgerald wouldn't work. An appeal to a code of honor shared by old warriors just might: "Bob, we both fought in a war because we believed in the same cause. I just need you to tell me whether Wu has made any large deposits during the past six months or written any unusually big checks. If the answer is 'yes,' I'll have the FBI initiate an investigation. If it's 'no,' everything stops there."

"I could lose my job over this."

"If Wu is dirty, Bob, the country has a hell of a lot more to lose." Santini could feel a flash of anger in his voice and forced himself to regain control. "I wouldn't ask you for this if it wasn't important."

More silence.

Fitzgerald, his jaw muscles tightening, finally nodded. "Okay. If it's as serious as you say." Rising from the couch, he moved toward his desk. "I'll need to get a few pass codes and dig back into the records to scan copies of the checks he drew on his account. Is tomorrow soon enough?"

"That's fine, Bob. I don't want any paper trail on this." Handing Bob his business card, which contained a gold embossed eagle on it, he said, "Here's my direct number at the Pentagon. My secretary's name is Margie. She'll put you through directly to me."

Santini shook hands with Fitzgerald, looking directly into his eyes. "I really appreciate this. I know it's not an easy call."

"It's okay," Fitzgerald said softly.

"No one will ever know. You have my word."

As Fitzgerald watched Santini pass through the bank's heavy glass doors and stride out onto Pennsylvania Avenue, he swiveled in his executive chair to face the large computer screen that sat on his credenza. He began the search.

"Word of honor," he kept repeating to himself as he typed away. He hoped he could put Santini's word in the bank.

The call from Fitzgerald came early the next morning. Santini had just finished his staff meeting when his phone began to ring. He waited until the room cleared before hitting the answer button.

"I have the information you asked for," Fitzgerald said in a half whisper. "Is this a good time to talk?"

"Yes, Bob," Santini said. "It's fine. Thanks for getting back to me so soon."

"According to our records, Mr. Wu made a deposit of two hundred and eighty thousand dollars on January 16th of this year. Again, according to what we have, he drafted a check for fifty-three thousand, eight hundred, and seven dollars a week later—"

Santini could feel his neck start to flush. His instincts had been right. Wu was on the take. He interrupted Fitzgerald's bland recitation. "The check was payable to?"

"Tyson Cadillac," Fitzgerald answered.

Santini had found the mole. A dagger pointed right at his heart. The man who gave him the intelligence brief each morning and then told his spy masters everything that Santini was up to. Was it his fate to always be the target of opportunity? First when he was Chairman of the Senate Intelligence Committee and now . . .

"By the way, Secretary Santini," Fitzgerald added, "that big deposit that he made in January?"

"Yes?" Santini answered, expecting even more confirmation of Wu's treachery.

"The check came from the law firm of DLA Piper Rudnick, one of the biggest firms in Washington. From what I can determine from the photocopy of the check, it appears to be from his parents' estate."

Whatever air that was in Santini's balloon suddenly evaporated. "Damn," he almost muttered. Now what? Wu had lost his father or mother. Maybe both. He was no traitor.

"Thanks, Bob. This clears up a major problem for me."

Clears it up for Arthur Wu, he thought, but it didn't solve his problem. Information was somehow getting out of the Pentagon, and he still didn't have a clue as to how.

Or through who.

Two days later, O'Neill was in the limousine when Santini came out of his apartment house. "Sir, Wu found something that was right under our noses." When Santini informed O'Neill what he had learned about Wu's finances, O'Neill was relieved. Now, revealing what Wu had learned, he did not exhibit any display of vindication in citing Wu's discovery. "Damn," he said. "Maybe the CIA is right about the DIA."

"Let's hear. And don't forget, Wu is DIA."

"Right. Well, here it is. Two months ago, the Chinese sent an advance team to the States to check out Xu's tour of DOD sites. The idea was that when you made a visit to China they would produce a mirror image of Xu's visit. The advance team was handed off to State's attaché office, which is one of those fish-or-fowl places where State and DOD are supposed to liaison—God, I hate that as a verb." O'Neill grunted, and Santini knew that what was coming next was not going to be joyous news.

"I can't believe what I am about to report. But Wu, bless him, saw the paperwork and has squirreled away copies if you or the FBI wants it."

"Wants *what*? I know you've got something hot. Spit it out."

"Among the places that the Chinese delegation cased was Holloman Air Force Base."

"What! And the FBI hasn't turned this up?"

"Who knows? We're in one of those situations where one part of the so-called Intelligence Community puts out a net for information but doesn't query the other IC guys. Wu, being a computer whiz, works all night running a Holloman search, data mining, as they call it. And he finds the Chinese at Holloman. It turns out that the delegation, which had been quartered in a Holloman motel, had been under loose DIA surveillance. But no one bothered to fold that surveillance report into the FBI's Holloman investigation. Sound familiar?"

O'Neill shuffled through his inevitable stack of three-by-five cards and began speaking rapidly, infusing urgency into his voice. "Wu checks the surveillance records and finds that a member of the delegation had evaded surveillance for two brief periods." He looked up from the cards and shook his head. "I can't believe this stayed in some damn DIA database." He sighed and went on. "The Chinese guy made phone calls from the motel to a pay phone. Then, when Wu searched another intelligence data bank, he found that the FBI had been tapping that pay phone because it had been used by a militia group. And—"

"Don't tell me," Santini said. "The militia group was run by that guy named Prentice. The guy who was supposed to have died because he accidentally set off some homemade explosives."

Santini had been taking notes on a yellow legal pad. His mind was racing. "Do we know who the Chinese guy was?"

O'Neill looked down at his three-by-five cards and said, "Captain Chang K. Y. Yew. There's a thin DIA file on him. He's an officer in the Ministry of State Security, *not* the PLA."

"Thanks, Scott. Please give my regards to Wu. And tell him to keep his head down. He still has some enemies out there." Santini recalled a famous spy case. A Marine named Lonetree had fallen into a KGB trap while on embassy duty in Moscow. When he went to a CIA officer to confess the spying, the CIA played with the idea of running Lonetree as a double agent—without telling anyone. Eventually, Lonetree's espionage was handled not by the FBI or the CIA but by the Naval Investigative Service, which came close to bungling the case.

Santini scribbled a few words on his legal pad, tore off the page, pulled an envelope out of his desk drawer, put the page into the envelope, and sealed it.

"Call Curtis and tell him to take you to Langley. I'll call ahead. I want you to give this to Pelky, stand there while he reads it, and watch him shred it. Then wait until he gives you a note in one of his envelopes."

O'Neill never asked questions in a situation like this one. "I'm on my way," he said.

Santini's note read:

What do you know about a Chinese named Chang K. Y. Yew? Is he operating independent of Chinese government? All I need is a yes or no. I'll explain next time we play tennis.

> *Best, Michael*

Ninety minutes later, O'Neill was back. He handed an envelope to Santini, who ripped it open, took out the sheet inside, and read:

Don't know. And please stay out of our business.

> *Jack*

"Son of a bitch. Pelky is holding back, Scott. He's holding it tight until his analysts figure a good way to give it to Praeger."

"Sir, I feel compelled to say something that may sound out of line."

"Please, Scott. I respect you for whatever you want to say. I don't need a warning."

"Very well, sir. I feel that you're getting into Pelky's lane. And if he believes that you are off on your own intelligence operation, he'll raise hell and give Praeger a bigger knife to cut your balls off."

"I've got to risk that, Scott. I don't want to sound paranoid, but it feels like it's all being aimed at us." He swung his right arm out, as if to encompass the Pentagon. "We're the Department of Defense. We have to do the defending."

CHAPTER 41

WASHINGTON

On weekends, the pace at the Pentagon drops off to low voltage. Most of the high-strung workaholics try to devote a few hours to their families and churches during that time. They tend to pray a lot in their business. It helps them get through long separations and the constant fear that they or their friends will meet with tragedy.

Of course, those who served on watch duty, the security people, and the intelligence analysts all had to remain at the ready. The fear of more homeland attacks was not just a matter of paranoia. America had real enemies and they were waiting to strike at the least sign of inattention or weakness.

The physical fitness buffs who were addicted to the weight rooms and basketball and racquetball courts always managed to hang around the POAC, the Pentagon Officers Athletic Club, the underground facility that was buried less than a hundred yards from the River Entrance Portico of the Pentagon itself. Occasionally, Santini would join O'Neill and some of the young bulls in his front office for a game of what could only be described as Extreme Basketball. He had never been spotted as NBA talent, but Santini could more than hold his own with those who would try to teach "Mr. Secretary" some of the rougher aspects of the game. No holds were barred or mercy shown to anyone who stepped out of his uniform onto the court. Out there, they were all equal in rank. It was good for morale, and word of Santini's "man of he people" attitude, along with his "six-pack" abs, spread like wildfire throughout the building. The SecDef was one of *them*!

But not today. Santini needed time to dig through the intelligence reports. To try to find some pattern of activity, starting with what had happened at Holloman. Stiller had to be right. Those two corpses in Berlin certainly made him almost surely right. The Chinese were somehow involved.

Accidents always happened. Military operations, including training exercises, were inherently dangerous. America was likely to lose at least one hundred or more of its young people every year in fixed- and rotary-wing aircraft crashes. And that didn't count how many would die in continuing operations in Afghanistan, Iraq, and elsewhere. A C-130 Combat Talon Special Operations transportation plane goes down in Honduras. Or a Black Hawk chopper clips a radio tower in Macedonia. Lucky if they got more than a three- or four-line blurb in *The New York Times*. But everyone understood the ground rules. American troops were the best of the best because they trained hard. Took risks. Stretched the envelope. That was all a part of belonging to the best military on the planet. No whining.

But more than bad luck or defective equipment was at work here. Assuming that there was a rogue group of Chinese, what was their agenda? *Are they trying to destroy our relationship with Germany? Why?* Santini tried to link the facts: find motive, opportunity, means.

They had opportunity at Holloman. And, given the help of the militia, they had means. But motive? Santini rubbed his eyes in frustration, stepping away from the conference table now littered with the avalanche of classified documents and cable traffic he had requested.

"Scott, I still can't figure out what in hell is going down. The sabotage out at Holloman. Why would the Chinese be involved with those militia wackos?" Santini had asked O'Neill to spend the weekend with him to try to connect the dots.

O'Neill, rarely out of uniform, today was dressed in jeans, sweatshirt, and Puma tennis shoes. And while casual in appearance, he was always regimented in his analytical process.

"I think," he began, mindful that he should challenge Santini obliquely, "that we need to consider several alternatives. First, even though we think the militia is a collection of meatballs, they still could have been behind Holloman without the Chinese. They're not Georgetown social material, but they are clever. Remember, Timothy McVeigh was no genius, but he managed to take down a federal building in Oklahoma City."

Santini smiled inwardly at O'Neill's attempt to assume collective ownership of his bias toward the True Americans crowd.

"Secondly," O'Neill continued, "I think you're right that the militia types could not have been involved in the Grafenwoehr disaster. There is some loose international affiliation amongst the right wing, anti-government zealots, but it's a real stretch to think that they could have planned and organized the gas attack without coming up on the FBI or BND nets. Anything on that scale has to be a terrorist group, probably state-sponsored terrorism. But the Islamists don't seem to be involved. Not a peep out of them. So we come back to the Chinese and that cryptic warning from Stiller's spy, at least for Grafenwoehr. But I can't get the connection between Grafenwoehr and Holloman."

"You know what you're grappling with, Scott? You're looking for motive. Prosecutors always want that. We can show the White House all we have now—and even what may still come up in the way of evidence. But we can't give them motive. That's the hang-up."

"Yes, sir." O'Neill laughed. "So I'll just have to go back to square one and think our way through the possibilities."

"At that rate, I'll be in a nursing home before you're finished," Santini jibed. He had done the very same thing himself. Gone back to square one, methodically reviewing every piece of the puzzle.

"Al Qaeda has the capability. There are hundreds of them still on the loose."

"Yeah, but hard to believe that the Chinese would link up with Muslim extremists. Or the militia, for that matter. The militia may hate the Germans, but they're white, and pigment to those losers defines the human race. They're pure racists. To them, Arabs are no more than sand—" Santini cut himself short. He was not known for being "politically correct," but he had watched too many of his black friends die on the battlefield defending the values of this country. Values to this day that too often excluded them. He could never use the word. It was demeaning, dehumanizing. Yet that's how racists still considered black Americans. Less than human. Un-American.

"And," he continued, "there's little reason for al Qaeda to kill Germans. It's not as if the German government has been on the front lines with us in the war against terrorism."

"No," O'Neill said, "but if they start killing enough Europeans, the Euros may think twice about not getting involved in what they believe is America's jihad with the Islamic world."

"I don't think so, Scott. I don't think Holloman and Grafenwoehr have anything to do with conventional terrorism. The Chinese or some rogue group has focused on Germany. They want to break us off from Germany. But they're leaving no fingerprints. No return address."

"What about the stuff that Hartley is working on?" O'Neill asked. "More pieces of the puzzle. That guy Charles Burkhart, found with his tongue cut out. He sounds like the Holloman bad guy—but who was he working for? Where's the Chinese connection? And what the hell is that word on the paper in his belt?"

"One of these days," Santini said, "we're going to see all the answers on the *Post* page one, courtesy of our friend Hartley." He paused, suddenly scanning his mind. "*Tago,*" he said. "The word was *Tago.* Some kind of contact name or a code word or— Wait a minute! Tago. *I've heard that goddamn name before.*"

Instinctively, he reached for the console on his desk and punched the button that would summon Margie. But this was Sunday, and she was not there.

"Scott! Where the hell would Margie have put that FBI briefing on the Orchard?"

"She files in a couple of ways, sir. Thematically, chronologically—"

"I don't give a damn how she files. Tear her files apart and get me that briefing paper," Santini shouted. Then, calming down, he added, "It's got *Tago* in it. I swear it."

O'Neill strode into Margie Reynolds' office, whirled the combination lock on one of the file drawers, pawed through the files, and pulled out a blue folder emblazoned with the FBI seal, rushed back into Santini's office, and triumphantly handed it to Santini.

Santini pulled the briefing book out of the folder, thumbed through it, and held it up with his own show of triumph. "Here it is! Tago. The FBI identifies him as the, quote, visible head, or street boss, unquote, of the Orchard. He's a Chechen who is Berzin's right-hand man. There's the connection!"

"Wonderful, sir. But . . . well, it's a *Russian* connection. Where is the Chinese connection?"

"It's both, Scott. The criminal underbelly in Russia, a rogue group in China. I'm convinced. And you?"

O'Neill paused to pour more coffee into his mug. "A possibility, sir. A good possibility, but built on hunches. You'll need more than hunches." He held the glass coffeepot over Santini's mug. "Another shot?"

Santini nodded. It was his sixth cup of the morning, and it was only ten o'clock. Santini took a gulp and nearly spit the coffee all over O'Neill. "Jesus, Scott," he said. "This tastes like yesterday's dishwater. Tell the guys in the mess to brew a fresh pot."

"Only one in the mess, today, is me, sir. It's Sunday, and I didn't think you wanted me to bring in the crew. I'll give it another try." He disappeared into the adjoining conference room, which led to a small kitchen area.

Santini got up and stretched his arms, fighting off the fatigue from another sleepless night. *Amazing,* he mused. *Agent Leslie Knowles gives a briefing at the White House about money laundering and the Russian Mafiya and identifies Tago as a major operative. Then some field agent working the Holloman investigation—who's got to be one of Randall Hartley's sources—finds a scrap of paper with Tago's name on it and the information never gets up the food chain to Knowles or to the FBI Director. Just goddamn amazing!*

Staring out through the tall windows past the parade ground that served as an overpass to Route 110, he focused on the marina, where dozens of boats were anchored. Those boats had always bothered him. They were in direct line of sight of his office. From any one of them someone could put a rocket up his ass with very little trouble . . . and it then dawned on him: If they could fire a rocket-propelled grenade, why not an electronic beam? Why couldn't they put a laser on those windows to pick up conversations? Or maybe just have a receiver to pick up a transmitter buried somewhere inside the office? One that would escape the weekly security sweeps if it was activated only when someone on one of those boats decided it was safe to do so?

He remembered that was precisely what had happened at the State Department some years ago. The transmitter in the State conference room lay dormant until it was turned on by some Russian guy sitting outside the building in his automobile.

When O'Neill entered the room carrying the fresh pot of coffee, Santini touched his lips with the forefinger of his right hand, signaling O'Neill not to talk. Santini motioned for him to follow Santini out of the room. Once outside, he said, "Scott, maybe I'm crazy, but I think that room is hot. Wired. Everything we've been saying could be picked up by someone sitting on a boat down in that marina. I don't fucking understand it. This place is buttoned up tighter than Fort Knox. But we let those goddamn boats park right off my front porch! Have we got the Three Stooges doing our security around here?"

"I think all of those boats belong to retired military, but I'll jump on it right now, sir."

"No. First thing tomorrow, go to the sweepers' office. Do not talk in their office. Slip them a note and have them come to the Big Four meeting at seven o'clock. While the meeting is going on, we'll discuss some unclassified bullshit and they can use their brooms, or—"

"EEDs."

"What?"

"Electronic Emission Detectors." O'Neill had been a Navy

fighter pilot, or aviator, as he preferred to be called. He was deep into technology and even deeper into acronyms. It drove Santini mad at times.

"I don't care if they use vacuum cleaners. I'm convinced that room has bugs. If I have to, I'll call the boys in from the Agency or the Bureau to get the job done. Even the Orkin man if I have to."

"Sometimes we use people from the Defense Protective Service. Other times from NSA. And I believe they've taken countermeasures to prevent anyone from penetrating the interior office space, but I'll get on it first thing tomorrow."

"And, Scott, one more thing. *Quis Custodiet Ipsos Custodes?* I want you to rerun a security check on the sweepers. Just to be sure they're not on someone's else's payroll."

The man, rubbing his hands to stimulate some warmth, dipped below the deck of his thirty-foot sailboat. He was wearing jeans, a heavy blue sweater, and brown Top-Siders. It was a little cool to be out on the Potomac, but when you owned a boat like his, there were no holidays on repairs and maintenance. To most of the people at the marina, he was a familiar figure. With his tanned skin and white, neatly trimmed beard, he looked as if he spent a good deal of time in the sun. A devoted sailor, to be sure. He was known simply as "Chas" to Stan Anderson, the manager of the partnership that held the concession to the marina. The marina actually belonged to the U.S. Government, in the form of the National Park Service.

Once belowdecks, Chas turned quickly to his task. Extracting a new Iridium phone from the small desk next to the leather couch, he climbed back onto the starboard side of the boat. He needed a clear, unobstructed line of sight to the set of Iridium satellites that circled the globe. Ironic that the Pentagon had to intervene to keep those birds flying. Good for the Defense Department. If DOD had allowed those satellites to burn up in the atmosphere, the Pentagon would have lost access to the 10 percent of the telecommunication traffic that did not belong to commercial telephone companies. Even better for Chas. He chuckled as he dialed a coded number that was as familiar to him as the one on his phony Social Security card. Making a connection today was not going to be a problem. The sky was cloudless and the air crisp. Perfect for an encrypted call to his friend in Beijing.

His friend needed to know that the Secretary of Defense and Randall Hartley had become too curious for comfort.

CHAPTER 42

BERLIN

They were walking once again in Vladimir Berzin's favorite part of Berlin, the Kudamm, a dazzling cluster of smart shops and cafés. Next, Elena thought, would come dinner and then what Berzin had said would be a night of love. *No,* she had told David Ben-Dar. She had demanded a risky face-to-face meeting in a Berlin safe house. And she had told Ben-Dar that she would kill Berzin before she would sleep with him.

Tonight she would tell Berzin that she had to attend to a sick mother in Helsinki. Not much of a story, but it would get her out of Berlin. Out of this charade. She was burned in Germany anyway. The BND was unmasking her. That was her reason. But Ben-Dar had blamed her decision on the sudden reappearance of Santini in her life. Perhaps Ben-Dar was right. Perhaps.

"And do you agree?" Berzin asked.

"I'm sorry, I was far away—"

"And thinking of us? Well, I can forgive. What I said was this: Now that I am involved in politics, perhaps you might consider moving to Moscow."

"Tell me something, Vladimir. How is it possible for you to visit Berlin with the election coming in another month?"

Berzin laughed. "To see you, my dear Miya. For that, I'm never too busy. Besides, most of my campaigning I do on television. And the polls show me an easy winner."

"Still . . . ?" she began.

Berzin's cell phone rang. He took three steps, as if he were planning to walk and talk. But he stopped suddenly. She could see his face tighten. He nodded, then shook his head, as if the party on the other end of the phone could see him. She had never seen him so disturbed. Intuitively she knew it was important. She clutched Berzin's left arm, put her head close to his chest, and made her best attempt to pout. She strained to hear the voice that had stopped Berzin in his tracks.

"Sorry, Miya. Sorry. Business," he said, flustered, the phone still to his right ear, his right hand gripping the phone as if it were a lifeline. The few words she could detect were in Russian, but the voice, light and staccato, was almost singsong. She could detect that the speaker was of Asian origin. Berzin was responding in Russian.

She forced her mind to switch from speaking and listening German. She knew enough Russian to rate a 5.3 on the Mossad linguistic scorecard (fair conversational ability). She produced a facial expression that showed boredom and no comprehension of what she was hearing.

"Impossible!" Berzin said in Russian. "Impossible! There's no way Santini could know."

Elena momentarily wondered if Berzin could feel the rapid beating of her heart.

"I will see that he no longer presents us with a problem," she heard him say. "I will take care of the situation. You have my word. I'll have Tago on a flight by tonight. And he'll deal with that reporter, too."

Berzin returned the cell phone to his pocket and put his right arm around Elena. "Urgent business," he said. "I am afraid that I must return immediately to Moscow."

"I'm so sorry," she said, pouting again. "Business, for both of us, is entirely too important."

He hailed her a cab. As it pulled up to the curb he kissed her on the forehead. "Soon, Miya, this particular business will be over. I will see you soon. Very soon." He beckoned the driver of his trailing Mercedes limousine, slid into the backseat, and rolled down the window.

As the car started to pull away, Elena lifted her right hand to her lips. "*Auf Wiedersehen,*" she said.

He looked puzzled. "Now that's rather formal. You usually say, '*Ciao.*'"

"Perhaps I am becoming too much of a Berliner," she said, trying to smile.

Maybe it was just because she had at that moment decided that she would use her German passport instead of her Finnish one. She, too, was planning a flight.

CHAPTER 43

WASHINGTON

In a motel in Bethesda, Maryland, a few miles north of the Washington line, Tago knocked on the door of Room 212. A burly, bushy-haired man opened the door a crack, then threw it open and greeted Tago with a bear hug, a Russian bear hug.

"A thousand welcomes, Tago!" he bellowed in Russian. He wore a black T-shirt, jeans, and a pair of black rubber-soled shoes.

"The name is Basil," Tago said, pushing out of the hug. His Russian passport and visitor's visa bore the name Basil Kasyan.

The big man nodded and laughed a big, openmouthed laugh that exposed three gold teeth and a strong whiff of whiskey breath.

"So, Mikhail," Tago said, pointing to the half-filled bottle of Virginia Gentleman on a table near the door, "vodka is no longer your favorite drink?"

"I am an American now . . . Basil," Mikhail said, motioning Tago to a chair. "I love America! Good women. Good whiskey."

A man lying on one of the double beds stood, nodded silently toward Tago, and sat down on the edge of the bed.

"As full of speech as usual, Aslan," Tago said, nodding back to the man on the bed. Aslan, who wore only a pair of white undershorts, had the body of a weight lifter. On the bicep of his right arm was a tattoo of a gray wolf, a symbol of Chechnya. Under the wolf was *Aslan,* written in the peculiar Arabic script of old Chechnya. Tago, a fellow Chechen, had a similar tattoo on his right arm. Mikhail, a Russian, had no tattoo.

Aslan picked up the *Time* magazine he had been reading and began thumbing through the pages. Then he looked up and said, "We change countries. You change your name."

"What does that mean?" Tago snapped.

"You know very well what it means, my friend."

Mikhail stepped in front of the bed, preparing to referee another argument between Tago and Aslan. Mikhail, ever the peacemaker, took a step toward the bed and sat down next to Aslan. "We said we would obey orders, Aslan. Remember that."

Aslan threw the magazine to the floor. He had looked in vain for any news about Chechnya, a country forgotten by a Western press focused on the Middle East. Aslan and Tago had fled Chechnya in 1999 after blowing up a Russian Army barracks. They eventually found themselves in Moscow, where Mikhail befriended them as outlaws and later saw that they were inducted into the Orchard. Aslan and Mikhail worked as general musclemen, with an occasional wet job, as hits were called.

Tago had made his way into Berzin's inner circle while making sure that Aslan and Mikhail were well treated. At Berzin's orders, Aslan and Mikhail, bearing impeccable credentials showing themselves to be naturalized Americans, were sent to America, Aslan to represent Berzin in the U.S. version of the Mafiya, with Mikhail as Aslan's personal muscleman.

"After this job, you will get a chance to return to Russia, Aslan. I promise," Tago said. "And you, Mikhail, you may have your choice—vodka or whiskey." He tossed the keys of his rental car to Mikhail. "Get your bags into the car. You are checked out." He looked at his watch. "We leave in fifteen minutes."

Tago ordered Mikhail to drive down Wisconsin Avenue, across Military Road, to Connecticut Avenue to the National Zoo. Mikhail parked the black BMW in a half-empty lot near

the Elephant House. Tago led them to a bench and sat between
Mikhail and Aslan.

"You have studied and destroyed the maps and photos?"
he asked. They both nodded. "We have two subjects, one
somewhat more difficult than the other. We will do both today. We cannot afford to waste time. Let us go over the
plan."

Randall Hartley's favorite Georgetown building was a few
blocks from his house. It was called Dumbarton Oaks, a
nineteenth-century mansion built on what was once the crown
of a wooded valley. As he walked down Thirty-second Street
toward the entrance, he thought that there still was a
nineteenth-century air about the stately building, an oasis in
the social bustle of Georgetown. In the Music Room here in
1944 the Dumbarton Oaks Conference laid down the principles
that evolved into the charter of the United Nations. Now behind the redbrick walls was a museum that housed a priceless
collection of pre-Columbian art. Hartley, an amateur collec-
tor, was to speak at a symposium about the epidemic of art
theft in Latin America. The speech had been well publicized
in the *Post,* of course, and would be recycled as an article in
next Sunday's "Outlook" section.

Hartley was about fifteen feet from the concrete stairs leading to the door of the museum when a boy in a red sweatshirt
came hurtling along the sidewalk on a skateboard. Hartley
stepped aside, shoulder against an iron lamppost. Around the
corner came a black BMW sedan. In what seemed one long
moment, Hartley saw the boy fall, saw bits of brick fly, heard
a ping on the lamppost, and fell to the sidewalk when the
boy's careening skateboard ran into him and tripped him. As
the sedan passed, he thought he heard a shout in a language
that was not English or Spanish. Russian? Maybe.

Still prone, he saw the museum door open and quickly shut.
He reached into his pocket, pulled out his cell phone, dialed
911, and said, "Shooting. Drive-by, Thirty-second Street at the
Dumbarton Oaks entrance. Car heading south." In a crouch he
ran to the boy. Red was staining red. The boy's eyes were open,

but he was no longer seeing. Hartley hit a button on the cell phone and said, "Hartley. Give me the metro desk. . . . Yeah, I just saw a drive-by shooting. Right in Georgetown for God's sake!"

The day had been another one of exile for Santini. President Jefferson and Joe Praeger had still not returned from their extended trip to Europe, and the memorial service in Berlin for the victims of what the White House delicately called "the unfortunate gas incident." *That's a new kind of gas. Unfortunate gas,* Santini thought.

Santini had offered to go, but Jefferson had told him that he would be a liability—as a potential target, that is. "And security is already a nightmare. You would only make it worse."

Security. One word to cover so much of life today.

They'd be back soon. Jefferson would expect Santini to have resolved what in hell was going on. But Santini would have little to offer him except his resignation.

Santini stepped out onto the terrace of his apartment overlooking the Navy Memorial. Below was the statue of a lone sailor staring across a map of the world that was cut into the polished stone surface of the memorial.

Nemir Haddad, a private equity fund manager in London, had sent Santini a box of his favorite cigars. The package had been whisked off to the inspection facilities at the Pentagon to be sure no explosives or biological agents were inside and then returned to the apartment. Every piece of mail was treated the same way. Irradiated just to be sure anthrax spores were not lurking inside. Santini wanted to light one up tonight just to check whether the X-rays and radiation had killed the taste of the cigars. He hoped not. Castro would take offense.

The security people were getting out of hand, he mused, moistening the Davidoff with his lips before striking a long-stemmed match. They had a right to be worried after Tom Koestler had been taken out by his cats, but they left Santini almost no zone of privacy. *Almost.* Inside his apartment there were no cameras to record his movements. Presumably, no taps on his telephone, at least no U.S. Government taps. But he always assumed that the Russians and the Chinese had managed to lock onto his non-secure conversations. And to make the intelligence round-robin game complete, NSA probably picked up whatever the Russians and Chinese were transmitting back to their home bases. So, as a general rule, he said nothing on his private line that could possibly be of interest to anyone. His friends understood both his brevity and his banalities. Others just assumed he was arrogant, self-important, or simply boring.

There was one other area denied to his security detail: his massive wraparound terrace, which was large enough to accommodate 150 people. "And open and unprotected enough to allow any assassin with a small-caliber rifle to pop you from the twin building right next to us," Raul Gomez, the head of the security detail, had frequently reminded him.

The luxury apartment building was Gomez's worst nightmare. There was the threat posed by the underground public parking that permitted hundreds of cars to enter and exit the building structure without any inspection for explosives. He would usually find the concierge at the front desk asleep in the early morning hours. Strangers would walk in with the residents and never be asked for identification. Once in, they could either roam the corridors or gain entry into a vacant apartment. Once in an apartment, they had total access to the wraparound terraces that graced each tier.

Gomez had no way to conduct twenty-four-hour surveillance on the four floors of apartments above Santini's. The best Gomez could do was maintain a three-man detail in a nearby apartment and set up a surveillance camera to monitor everyone who approached Santini's front door. During one of the high-threat alerts, Gomez had urged Santini to move into officers' quarters at Fort McNair, which was not far from the Pentagon. Santini would have none of it. This was his residence, and no one was going to drive him out of it.

He drew deeply on the tightly packed tobacco. It yielded a thin stream of smoke that he was almost tempted to inhale. Santini shifted his gaze from the Justice Department and National Archives buildings to the sight of the U.S. Capitol dome, gleaming with breath-halting beauty, conferred by hidden floodlights. This panoramic view, resplendent in its sweep of Greek and Roman architecture, transported Santini to an era of history that he was convinced had to have been simpler. No less violent, perhaps, but surely an era of greater clarity and simplicity.

As Santini settled back into his lounge chair, puffing serenely on his treasured Davidoff, three men, all dressed in black, their heads covered in ski masks, slipped over the decorative molded plastic barriers that separated the condo units. Their rubber-soled sneakers emitted no sound to alert Santini, who was now lost in reverie, exhausted from the day's schedule.

Wielding a spring-handled club containing a leather-wrapped lead weight, the first assailant struck Santini savagely behind his right ear, rendering him semiconscious. As he fought back the cloud that had enveloped his brain, and struggled to get to his feet, the other two men pinned his arms behind his back and roughly snatched him out of the lounge chair. He spread his legs wide, desperately trying to gain his balance. Weakened from the blow to his head, Santini felt his legs buckle. He dropped to his knees. Again, the three men pulled him to his feet, dragging him to the edge of the terrace. *Jesus Christ! They're going to throw me off the terrace!* He could see tomorrow's front-page stories.

> *Michael Santini, Secretary of Defense, became the second Defense Chief to die during the Jefferson Administration. He is the second one in American history to jump to his death, James Forrestal having been the first. Friends say Santini was in a state of severe depression over the tragic gassing of innocent German civilians last*

*week during a NATO exercise. It was also well
known in White House circles that President Jefferson had lost confidence in Santini's leadership
at the Pentagon and was planning to fire him
upon his return from his trip to Europe.*

"Who are you?" Santini yelled. "Why are you doing this?"

"You've been fucking with the wrong people," came a muffled, thickly accented response. "Now we're going to splatter
your ass on that sailor down there."

This time Santini went down on his knees deliberately, trying to slow their momentum. His resistance was rewarded
with a fist pounded into his face. Blood poured from his nose
and into his mouth as he gasped for air. He was not going out
with a whimper. Breaking his right arm free, he swung his elbow and caught one of his assassins in his throat, shattering
his larynx.

"*Agghh.*" The man clutched his throat and collapsed.

Just when Santini thought he might escape, the bigger of
the two remaining assailants struck him on the back of his
neck with the lead club. Santini crumpled to the floor of the
terrace.

Moving quickly now, the two men struggled to lift 190
pounds of deadweight up over the three-foot-high security
railing on the edge of the terrace. They were so preoccupied
with their task that they failed to see another figure slide
gracefully over the molded partitions and center the infrared
beam of a large-caliber assault pistol first on one ski mask and
then on the other.

Pfft. Pfft, like two muffled coughs. Two men down with
large holes in their heads. A third *pfft.* His shattered larynx
was no longer a problem for the last man down.

Elena moved quickly to Santini, who was regaining con-
sciousness and groaning in pain. Two other men joined Elena
on the balcony and helped to carry Santini back into his apartment. Once he was settled there, they gathered the bodies of
the three assassins and carried them off to a unit they occupied on the same floor.

Santini was sitting upright on the floor as Elena pressed a cold washcloth on his forehead. "You're lucky, Michael, but you're a mess. Though you're better off than your ski bum friends. Looked like they wanted you to take a bungee jump without the bungee."

An acrid smell filled Santini's senses. His mouth tasted like a sewer. He looked down and saw that he had vomited on his shirt. Rubbing the back of his neck, embarrassed that he had been so easily overwhelmed, Santini struggled to make light of what had happened.

"This is an awfully hard way to arrange a date," Elena quipped, as she helped him to his feet.

"How did you . . . ? You must have known what they were going to do? How—"

"I could tell you, but I'd—"

"I know. You'd have to kill me." Santini coughed, causing his raw throat to burn with pain. "Old joke. Bad one, too."

"Let's just say I have my sources."

"Okay. Fair enough. But can you tell me who they were? Who they worked for? Why they tried to kill me?"

"Two of them were émigrés, one Russian, the other Chechen. They lived in and operated out of Brighton Beach in New York. They're in the Orchard, Vladimir Berzin's Mafiya. Goons who kidnap and kill people who don't pay their gambling debts or protection money."

"And the third?"

"His name was Tago. A psychopath who was . . . Berzin's pit bull." She saw no sense in holding back now. She knew about Tago because she was not just watching Muslims in Germany. She was there to track Berzin's activities with Wagner. The two of them were up to something. She had been sent to find out what it was.

"Was he behind the disaster at Holloman? The gas attack in Germany?"

"Yes." Elena hesitated momentarily, searching for just the right qualification. She didn't want to overstate her conclusions. At this point they were still assumptions.

"And?"

"And no. He was basically the contract killer. We know he was carrying out orders from someone else."

"Someone else? It sounds as if you aren't sure."

"I don't have a name yet. Michael, you've got to protect me on this. I know it's a high-ranking Chinese general. I don't know who he is. I do know that he's not operating with the sanction of the leadership. I have to be careful."

Indeed, thought Santini. For years, Israel had been building a very quiet but very profitable relationship with China. Selling them high-tech military equipment, covertly co-venturing on a number of secret deals. And all the while turning their heads as China continued to send technology and technicians to help Iran build conventional nuclear power. Power that would one day enable the Iranians to develop nuclear weapons. Weapons that could then be turned against Israel. Santini never understood how the Israelis could sell out their long-term future for such short-term gains. Maybe they thought that they could persuade China to discontinue dealing with Iran. More likely, they thought the United States would take down Iran. Maybe . . .

Elena returned to the refrigerator to get more ice, wrapped it in a dish towel, and then pressed it on the back of Santini's neck. "Are you okay, Michael? Do you need any pain medication?"

"No, no, I'll be fine," he said, showing a bravado he did not feel. "The medicine cabinet has more painkillers than a pharmacy." Moving out into the large living room, he motioned for her to sit down.

"No, Michael. I can't. We've got a lot of work to do. We have to get rid of the bodies. Hopefully, no one saw what happened out on the balcony. The last thing we need is for the police to show up."

Santini was quick to agree. There was no way he could explain away three dead men. Especially *these* dead men. It looked as if some drug deal had gone bad and he was mixed up with it. The DEA and D.C. narcotic squads would be all over him like buzzards on roadkill. Joe Praeger would have a field day.

"We won't have much time before Berzin calls to check

with Tago to see how the mission went. When he hears nothing he—or whoever wants you dead—will be sending others."

Santini simply nodded. She was right. He knew that if Berzin was not going to come after him again, then his Chinese puppet master would.

"Elena, I really need you to help me find out the names of the people behind all of this."

Elena stared hard into Santini's eyes. Finally, she said, "I'll see what I can do."

Meaning, Santini understood, that she would have to think about it.

CHAPTER 45

WASHINGTON

Elena was torn over what to do. Santini had asked her to dig deep into Israeli intelligence files. This was not what she was trained to do. Assuming she could even find the entrance key to the House of Mossad, she would confront hall after hall of mirrors, where the sheer multiplication of reflections would induce dizziness and near delirium. Code names, aliases, cover stories, cryptic deceptions—all designed to protect Israel's national security. Not exactly its crown jewels, but who could say what else might be compromised in the process?

And wouldn't her efforts be nothing short of treason? Sure, America was Israel's ally, but she would be operating without official authority. And who knew what deals David Ben-Dar might have cut with the Chinese? She had come to Washington without permission. She had already compromised her mission. There was no way that Berzin wouldn't realize that she was the only person who could have known about his plan to kill Santini.

Santini was asking her to put a lot more than just her career on the line. Initially, she thought it would be best to go to the Israeli Embassy and make contact with David Ben-Dar to let him know what had happened. Without revealing exactly what information Santini had asked for, she might be able to detect whether Ben-Dar would be open to such a request. But she knew the answer to that. Ben-Dar would insist that he discuss the matter through official channels with Jack Pelky. Presum-

ably that was precisely why Santini had asked her for help and
equally why he was unwilling to go to the CIA directly.

"Give me the names of the Chinese," Santini had implored.
It sounded so simple. But Israel's relationship with China was
anything but simple.

Selling weapons to China made little sense to Elena. She
had challenged Ben-Dar over the wisdom of transferring technology to this growing Asian power. "Isn't it possible that
China will just re-engineer the designs and end up shipping
their version of our systems to others to be used against us?"

Ben-Dar had labored over this very question himself and
had argued the case with Israel's Defense Ministry. "Elena,"
he said, having lost the debate, "whenever we do business
with anyone, more than business is involved. We gain access
to markets, but to something far more important—to information. If the Chinese see us as a good supplier, perhaps they
won't run the risk of biting the hand that's feeding them."

"And if they do?"

"Two things are possible," Ben-Dar had said in a tone that
was that of a rabbi, a teacher. "One, we can always sell our advance technology to India, China's historic adversary. That
should help to keep them honest."

"Or?"

"Failing that, we can hear and see things in China before
it's too late for us to do anything."

What Ben-Dar said had proved right. Israeli intelligence
agents had picked up information through Chinese sources
that Russian nuclear materials might be on their way to
Hamas and Hezbolla. That would mean that Israel could be
held hostage to extortion: Get out of the West Bank, Gaza,
Jerusalem—or die!

"Never again," she muttered to herself, the motto of every
Israeli. No walking submissively into gas chambers. No more
crematoriums. No weakness.

Long ago she had vowed to kill those who had killed her
family, those who were determined to exterminate every Jew.

Vladimir Berzin, she knew, had murdered one United
States Secretary of Defense and had just tried to assassinate

another. Hundreds of innocent Germans had been gassed, and now he and his Chinese friend were undoubtedly planning something even more horrific.

By the time Elena arrived at the Israeli Embassy in Northwest Washington, she had changed her mind.

As she approached the gate to the embassy on International Drive, she slammed the car into reverse, confusing the guard who was moving toward her. The trunk of the Cadillac just missed planting itself into the nose of a Hertz rental truck. Jamming the accelerator down hard, Elena gripped the steering wheel tightly in her hands as the car lurched forward, fishtailing into traffic. Motorists' horns blared in protest; the cars' tires screamed as they bit into the pavement.

Against every voice that cajoled and warned her to forget about Santini, to let him turn to the CIA for help, Elena fought back. Yes, she had done enough tonight by saving his life. But this was not about him. A madman was playing with fire, a fire that could go nuclear. And if America found itself in such a war, who could predict where it would stop? Israel would find no safe haven from the fires of hell.

There was no time to go through official channels, and even if it were possible, there was no guarantee that Ben-Dar or anyone else would listen. She would have to explain to them later what she was about to do. She had no choice. She had to help Santini. He only wanted a few names.

There was one person who could help her. As she sped back toward Georgetown, she hoped he was home.

Saul Teischer was not pleased to hear his phone ring at 11:30 P.M. Calls that late always meant trouble. Someone in the family had died. Or some terrible tragedy was unfolding. Or the Chairman of the Senate Intelligence Committee was calling, demanding that Teischer prepare some report on some rebellion that was taking place in some obscure town in Papua New Guinea. It wasn't as though he was in a deep sleep at that hour. Rather, that was the hour he reserved for *The Sopranos,* which he had taped earlier in the evening while he was still working in the office: sixteen hours reading intelligence reports, talking to Agency operatives, preparing the Committee for congressional hearings.

Teischer had been born in Israel forty-four years ago. He had immigrated to the United States during the early Reagan years and had become a naturalized U.S. citizen. He was one of the few people on Capitol Hill who retained the status of dual citizenship. Rarer still was the waiver granted to Teischer through his boss, Senator David Steadman, that allowed him access to information classified as *Top Secret.* Steadman had friends in very high places at the National Security Council. Jack Pelky had protested, but Praeger had overruled the DCI. "Give the clearance," Praeger had instructed Pelky. "The President wants Steadman to have his man on the committee staff. Besides, he might just give us some insight into what the Israelis are up to from time to time. After all, they've had better luck in dealing with terrorism than we have."

Fat chance of that. Pelky had asked Teischer to give up his Israeli passport until he left the Intelligence Committee. He refused to do so.

Maybe he should just let the damn thing ring. The caller ID function on his phone said only: *Private Caller.* Hell, that could mean anything. Obnoxious telemarketers. Phone sex solicitors. Wrong number . . . *Whoever is calling will give up after six rings when the answering machine kicks in.* Wishful thinking. Whoever was on the line wouldn't leave a message and wouldn't stop calling! Exasperated, Teischer finally picked up the receiver. He was prepared to unleash a torrent of expletives to this intruder. "Who the hell is calling me at—"

"Saul, it is me: Elena. I need your—"

"Elena, my God, it's been so long. Where are you? Are you in town?"

Questions tumbled out of Teischer with genuine warmth. He had not heard from Elena in more than a year. He missed seeing and talking to his cousin. He loved her deeply. So many times he had cursed the heavens that they were blood relatives, because she was the woman of his dreams. He controlled himself by rationalizing that but for their blood relationship he probably never would have met her in the first place. He was lucky to have had the chance to know her at all. Still . . .

"How can I help you?"

If Saul Teischer thought that Elena might be in need of light conversation around midnight, he was quickly shaken from such wishful thinking. He couldn't tell whether it was anxiety or exhaustion written on her face, but she clearly was out of sorts. Devoid of any makeup, wearing black slacks, a loose-fitting sweater, and Nike aerobic athletic shoes, Elena clearly had not come from a formal dinner at the White House. He had never seen her dressed so casually or looking so intense.

She may have been dressed for a visit to the gym, but she was all business. Names. She needed the names of Vladimir Berzin's Chinese connections. Who were they? When did they meet? Where?

But why did she need them? And why not go to Mossad? Or to the CIA? Why him? Why now, at this hour?

She gave him no answers. "Trust me," she said simply. "It's important. I need your help. Tonight."

And help she would get. While not knowing of her specialty in assassinations, Teischer knew that she was a favorite of David Ben-Dar. That was good enough for him.

After all, it was not as if he had to move mountains. No, it was a walk in the park. Or, more accurately, a jaunt through the jungles out at Langley.

"Make yourself at home," Teischer said. "I don't think this will take long." He went into his bedroom office and closed the door.

It never failed to amaze Teischer how jealousy and infighting were like oxygen to bureaucracies. September 11 be damned! Turf protection remained the order of the day.

Allen Dunhill, the Secretary of the Department of Homeland Security, knew that the CIA dutifully presented him with intelligence information that gave the appearance of full cooperation but was carefully screened to keep him in his place, which was outside the *real* intelligence loop. What he got was always a week late and ten dollars short.

Dunhill had complained to President Jefferson, but the President did not frequently bestow Oval Office visits on Dunhill, who was smart enough not to make all those visits occasions for complaints. He picked his time to do his grumbling. The President always said he would plead with Director Pelky to work with Dunhill as a full partner in the war against terror, and the President kept his word. Pelky would click his heels and salute. He would cooperate for a few weeks. Then the flow of information would slow to a trickle, forcing Dunhill to decide whether to use up his complaint quota. He realized that Pelky also knew about complaint quotas and he played the heels-click-and-salute like the longtime insider that he was (and Dunhill was not).

Dunhill tired of the charade. He instructed his technical team to burrow covertly into the Agency's most coveted secrets. It was a major challenge, but not an impossible one. When he took his complaint to one of his deputies who handled computers, the deputy sent him a technician named Brian Goren. Dunhill was astonished how quickly Goren, a twenty-four-year-old computer genius, was able to walk electronically into Pelky's office, open files marked *Top Secret, Amber Light,* and *Transom,* and leave no fingerprints. Incredible!

What Dunhill failed to realize, however, was that his own security was just as easily penetrated. The Department of Homeland Security was still in its supposedly temporary headquarters, the former Navy communications security site in Northwest Washington. The installation was old and lacked the elaborate computer network that Homeland Security needed. So technicians like Goren jury-rigged connections. At the same time, Homeland Security was plugged into the Intelligence Community's Intelink, which hackers see as nearly impenetrable. Some of the jury-rigged connections stayed that way, even after the installation of more secure, more sophisticated networks.

Teischer had suspected that Homeland Security would be the weak link in Intelink. He had confirmed his guess long before Elena made her request. And it would not be the first time he had looked in CIA files for data about the Agency's activities. But no need to tell her how easy it was going to be. It only took him a few keystrokes to get into Pelky's front office through Dunhill's back door.

As soon as Teischer got what Elena wanted, he loaded it from his desktop computer onto a three-inch disk, which he inserted into an ordinary-looking laptop. He brought the information up on the screen, pressed the *Print Scrn* button, then brought a second screen up on Word, copied the first screen's image onto it, and hit the *File, Print* button. A printer hummed and produced a single sheet of paper. Teischer repeated the process three more times, each time answering *No* when asked whether he wanted to save what was on-screen. There would be no record of any of these images because they did not exist as files. The three-inch disk and those four pieces of paper, which he would give to Elena, would be the only record of his work. He placed the three-inch disk in a microwave-size device that demagnetized it and then melted it into a shapeless lump.

Elena was pacing the room when he emerged and closed the door behind him. "I think this is what you want," he said. "Pelky will blow his top when he discovers that his superduper Intelink was entered."

"And it's untraceable?"

"Oh, it's traceable, all right. I decided to close the account tonight. They'll be putting in a new system, and this old dog will have to learn some new tricks," Teischer said.

"But if your entry is traceable—"

"Don't worry. I booby-trapped Homeland's top-dog database. A double click on any Homeland computer mouse will send a command to delete Homeland intelligence data at the rate of thirty megabytes per second. When the CIA and Homeland tiger teams try to find out what happened, they'll find a clue showing that the CIA entry and data destruction was the work of a Homeland tech guy. His name is Brian

Goren. I met him when I was posing as a hacker at one of their get-togethers about ten years ago. He was barely in his teens.

"Funny thing, I never liked him. I decided at the last minute to hang it on him. I had thought I would make it the National Security Council. Somebody from there has been hitting Pelky's files pretty hard. Maybe I'll try to find out who. We might be able to make use of that someday. Like the taps on Watergate when Monica lived there."

Elena listened patiently, then asked for one more favor. Teischer sighed when he heard Elena say the words "before six A.M."

CHAPTER 46

The pulsing music pounded softly in the background, to General Li's obvious annoyance. Three times the sound technicians had installed soundproofing panels from Taiwan and three times they had failed. *But no matter,* Li said to himself. *Soon I will not need this hideaway. And soon places like this will be no more.*

"Events are moving swiftly," he said as soon as the others were seated before him. "We have started the ticking clock. A North Korean general—Kim Dae Park, some of you have met him—has just entered the Swedish Embassy in Beijing, claiming he is defecting. He will be believed because we have seen to it that the Swedes and Americans have obtained knowledge of his cell phone conversations with real dissidents in North Korea. His false story will also be believed. He will assure the Swedes that North Korea is planning to use the normal spring exercise as a cover for a preemptive strike against South Korea.

"The Swedes, so-called neutrals who may just as well belong to NATO, will immediately alert the CIA station chief at the American Embassy. He will send a flash report to CIA headquarters and that will touch off a panic response in Washington. National Security Council analysts, giving their chief Praeger what he wants, have been predicting that exact scenario. America will begin to divert most of its resources toward South Korea.

"There will also be a second false story. It has been presented to an agent who writes for *Mainichi Shimbun,* Japan's most influential newspaper. He will write—and show well-counterfeited proof—that for many years the United States has stored tactical nuclear weapons at several bases in Japan, for use against the North Koreans or to protect Taiwan against us.

"Most Japanese will believe this story because of a *true* story that was revealed some time ago. You may remember that thousands of special munitions made of depleted uranium were fired at a firing range in Okinawa. We, too, have examined depleted uranium projectiles as armor-piercing anti-tank weapons. They are effective, but the dust of the exploded weapon is feared to be dangerous. Examination of the dust has shown that it contained small traces of plutonium and other radioactive particles, spiking fears of leukemia and cancer. Scientists dispute this, of course, but few believe them. All of this will be dragged up again when the false story appears today. The story will cause a political furor in the Japanese Diet. There will be calls for the United States to pull its forces out of Japan.

"We will then launch a lightning strike against Taiwan, using our new submarine force, ballistic missiles, and amphibious assets that we have hidden from satellite observation. Using electromagnetic pulses, we will destroy Taiwan's command and control systems. When the strike is launched, we will temporarily blind United States satellites. Taiwan will fall quickly. The United States will be taken completely by surprise and will have no choice but to concede defeat or wage war against China. Before they make such a choice, we will disclose that China has more than fifty ICBMs, not the paltry twenty that appears so often in CIA reports."

"And *The New York Times.*" Colonel Zho Zhenzen laughed. Li had told him confidentially that he was on his way toward getting his first general's star. The news had emboldened him to speak up.

"They will not dare to attack us," Li continued. "No one else gives a shit about Taiwan. No one will support America's zeal for Taiwan's little experiment with democracy." Li spat the words.

"Isn't there a risk?" Wang Gui asked timidly.

"Yes. But there is greater risk in doing nothing. In waiting for America and its puppets to surround us, stuffing dollar bills down the throats of Chinese businessmen, corrupting us with their capitalist greed. No, we must act now while our leverage is greatest and they remain bogged down in Iraq, Afghanistan, and, soon, Korea."

"What do you think President Chi will do when he learns of our attack?" Zho asked.

Li looked at him as if he was an imbecile. "It will be too late for him to do or say anything. Do you think he could admit that the military acted without his authority? That the Great Captain was asleep at the helm while a mutiny was underway? What message would that be to the world? Are you suggesting that he would hold a press conference and say it was all a terrible mistake, that he'll give Taiwan back? He will react just as he did after the Lop Nur test—by doing nothing." Li could barely contain his contempt for the very thought.

"No. He will claim full credit, saying that it was his idea. That his patience with Taiwan's open defiance had been exhausted. That the United States was playing a devious game by slowly walking us into accepting Taiwan independence— what the diplomats call a fait accompli.

"Don't worry. Chi will be hailed as a bold—and victorious— leader. We shall make the Americans choke on one of Mr. Praeger's favorite Latin quotes: *'Oderint dum metuant.'*"

Li could not suppress the cleverness of his remark, one that Major General Zhou Xi had once relayed to him. Zhou had taught Li how to pronounce the words so that Li could give the impression that he was far more educated than his subordinates. That was before he had Zhou hanged from the lamppost in Tiananmen Square for his treachery and betrayal.

Li felt obliged now to translate the Latin for those in the room: " 'Let them hate as long as they fear.' "

CHAPTER 47

Santini had finally fallen asleep. But his sleep was so light and fitful that the humming of his fax machine awakened him. *Who the hell is sending me a fax? I never get faxes here, except for those goddamn offers for Caribbean cruises.* He turned on the bedroom light and went into the nook that served as his office.

At the top of the fax was a *Washington Post* clipping:

Tragedy Strikes Son of
Agriculture Secretary

Robert Orly, the 17-year-old son of Agriculture Secretary Thomas Orly, was shot and killed while skateboarding along a Georgetown street. According to an eyewitness, Randall Hartley, a Pulitzer Prize–winning *Post* journalist, a black BMW sedan pulled alongside Orly as he traveled down 32nd Street, past Dumbarton Oaks, one of Georgetown's most exclusive residential streets.

Hartley, who lives in the neighborhood, said three men were in the car. One pointed a small automatic weapon equipped with a silencer and shot Orly several times in the chest and head. The youth's skateboard tripped Hartley, who fell behind a parked car and escaped harm.

According to police, Orly was a troubled youth

with a history of drug abuse. Investigators believe
this may have been a drug-related killing. If so, it
would mark the first time that drug violence has
extended its deadly reach beyond the killing
zones of Northeast Washington.

Written in script below the clipping were these words:

Starbucks is a sure cure for your headache.

The message was signed: E.

At three minutes before six, Santini stepped out of his
apartment and headed toward his car. "Wait a minute, Curtis,"
he said. "I've got to pick up some coffee."

"Yes, sir. I'll swing around the block and pick you up."

Santini jogged to the end of the block, crossed the street,
and entered Starbucks. Six coffee drinkers were lined up on
stools at one of the windows. A couple more of them were
awaiting their orders. He tried not to look as if he was looking
around. He recognized no one, but he thought that one of the
coffee drinkers, a man in a rumpled old green raincoat, had
stared at him for an instant. That happened often enough not
to make all the starers Mossad agents. But the man got up and
stood behind Santini, who was stepping to the counter. "That
Jamaica Mountain blend is my favorite," the man said. "Believe it or not, it's good for headaches."

When Santini ordered Jamaica Mountain, the clerk looked
over his shoulder and smiled at the man behind him. Santini
paid for the coffee and watched as the clerk took a one-pound
bag nearer his reach than hers. She gave Santini his change,
and smiled again. Santini assumed that she thought the man
who had paid her to do this was passing dope.

Curtis was parked at the curb. "Thanks, Curtis," Santini
said, climbing into the back. He opened the bag, and the
aroma of coffee wafted through the car.

"Can't wait, sir? Are you going to *chew* it?"

"It's a new blend, Curtis. I think I'll try for a minute of
shut-eye."

Santini pressed the button that raised an opaque pane of bulletproof glass behind Curtis' head, surprising the driver. He couldn't remember the last time the Secretary had raised that glass.

Santini reached into the bag and found four tightly folded papers.

The Chairman of the Joint Chiefs, Air Force General George Whittier, and his Vice Chairman, General Hector Ramirez, were not prepared for what was unfolding at the Big Four meeting today. Neither was Walt Slater, Santini's number two, who functioned as the Department of Defense's chief operating officer, running the world's largest corporation. In fact, the Big Four were totally confused. The Secretary had never allowed anyone else in the room during their daily meetings. It was not only a breach of protocol but also a breach of security. And yet today there were three total strangers moving noiselessly about the room, holding what appeared to be sophisticated electronic devices and sending one another hand signals.

Santini had opened the meeting by recounting some of the more gruesome aspects about the latest sniper attack in Michigan. Five Muslim women had been shot in as many days. After a statewide manhunt, the local police, working with the assistance of an FBI profiler and a psychic, were able to apprehend the sniper. He turned out to be a "she"—Sara Dresner, a prominent civil rights attorney whose only daughter had been blown up by a suicide bomber while she had been on her honeymoon in Bali, Indonesia. A psychiatric examination had been ordered by the court to determine Sara's mental status. A radio talk show host conducted an informal poll. More than 85 percent of the callers supported Dresner. She may have been temporarily crazed, but she was not crazy. So what if it was an act of pure vengeance? Tough luck. Let them go hump camels in Kuwait.

After no more than five minutes, the anonymous technicians slipped out of the room. Moments later, Scott O'Neill entered and slipped Santini a note. Santini nodded to O'Neill, who then departed without breaking the silence. General

Whittier looked quizzically at Ramirez, knotting his brow in a way that gave his face a slight grimace.

"Gentlemen," Santini intoned, conveying a gravity that replaced the wistful regret that was there a moment ago. "I want you to keep this in the strictest of confidence." All three nodded in unison, thinking the request unnecessary. "What I'm about to tell you cannot, at least for the moment, go beyond these four walls."

Again came the assent, but this time with a trace of resentment on the faces of the three most trusted members of his power circle. Santini then proceeded to tell them what he had uncovered, laying out in detail the information Elena had given him earlier that morning, including the identification of Li as the leader of a rogue group planning a coup.

General Whittier's eyes shifted around the table first to General Ramirez and then on to Walt Slater. What in the world was Santini talking about? An agency mole in Russia had killed the President of Russia? A Chinese rogue general was leading a coup? The very same man who had overseen Santini's torture in Vietnam? All at the meeting wondered whether their boss had taken leave of his senses. Was this some kind of delayed post-traumatic stress syndrome playing itself out at the expense of national security? Wasn't this a matter for the CIA? Why in hell was Santini telling all of them this if they were not supposed to share it with anyone? And why did he have a bandage on his head? It was all too bizarre.

Chas liked working for the rogues. He was a rogue himself. He had joined the CIA right out of college and volunteered for the paramilitary group that slipped into Iraq in 1990. But the brass had deemed him psychologically unstable and kicked him out after a hushed-up investigation into a bungled plot to kill the husband of a woman he was sleeping with. He had drifted into the netherworld of the mercenary—South Africa, Paraguay, Tajikistan, where the rogues found him. They fixed him up with a new identity, gave him some training, and here he was, earning plenty of money and not taking many chances. . . .

He sat belowdecks at a console that folded out from the bar. The conversation in Santini's office had ended and needed to get to Beijing immediately. Chas slipped off his earphones and switched the digitalized audio stream to the burst transmitter. Aimed automatically at the Chinese satellite, the transmitter transformed the interception into a message compressed into seconds. He detached the laser-beam receiver from its bracket and was about to stow it when a red light began flashing. Someone had flooded the target with a powerful detection device. He had been found.

Calmly, he followed the procedure. He hit the panic button that added: *Detected. Emergency shutdown* to the burst transmission. Then he threw the thirty-second time switch to ignite a thermite charge that would destroy his audio files and equipment. He ran up on deck and sprinted down the dock to a boathouse. He stabbed at the remote in his hand, raising the boathouse door.

He knew the usual courses of the helicopters buzzing in and out of the Pentagon heliport, only a few hundred yards away across the marina lagoon. Now one was coming from the other side of the river, from Bolling Air Force Base, and he could see the rappelling ropes hanging from it as it lowered and aimed at his sailboat.

He ran into the boathouse, leaped into his cigarette boat, a shallow-hulled vessel with a sharp prow. He roared out, his V-hull planing the boat, letting it ride on top of the water. As it gathered speed, choppy waves surged across the marina, rattling the docks and flooding the sailboats.

He veered onto the Potomac, heading southward to Woodrow Wilson Bridge. The University of Virginia's women crews had three racing hulls in the water, practicing for the annual George Washington Invitational Crew Classic. Each hull had eight rowers and a coxswain. One of the hulls was passing across his bow. He cut it in two, impaling one of the eight young women on his hull. Another girl, mortally injured, disappeared in a swirl of shattered hull and oars. In the wake of Chas' boat, the other hulls swamped.

He could hear the helicopter behind him. He was outracing it. If he could reach the bridge, the helicopter would have trouble getting over him. He knew the river well. He could never make it out to Chesapeake Bay. But he could run aground downriver, hijack a car, take the driver as hostage, and make it up from there.

Something made a splash fifty feet ahead of him. As he passed through the spray, he saw a U.S. Coast Guard boat dead ahead on a collision course. He turned sharp to starboard. Another splash. Rocket fire from the Coast Guard. He turned again, and a rocket slammed into his hull. The boat shook, shot forward, and plunged into the river like a submarine. Hurled into the water, Chas smashed down on a piece of wreckage, breaking his right shoulder. As he sank beneath the surface, the helicopter thundered overhead. A paramedic leaped into the river, dived, and brought up Chas. The Coast Guard boat came alongside. The executive officer put down her M-16 and helped him and the paramedic into the boat.

"I don't know why the SWAT boys were after you," she said. "But we've got you for killing two innocent rowers, you sorry-looking bastard. I wish to hell we could throw you back in."

An hour after the meeting broke up, O'Neill motioned Santini out into the hallway of the E-Ring. "You were right about the room being bugged. We must have IQs lower than a snake's ass. I mean how could we have been so dumb as to—"

Santini had little interest in self-flagellation. "What did the sweepers find in the room?"

"Wasn't *in* the room. It *was* the room."

"Meaning?"

"Basically, a laser audio attack involves a laser source outside the target facility, a target within the facility, or a target attached to the facility and a laser receiver-demodulator—"

"Scott, you sound like an Air Force officer. For Christ's sake don't give me a physics lecture. Just explain it in simple English."

"Sorry, sir," O'Neill said sheepishly. "Basically, what the boys found was someone was bouncing a laser beam at your windows. Objects such as white or light-colored drywall—especially glossy painted ones like yours—framed artwork, or something as innocuous as a brown paper lunch bag, they all convey open audio frequencies. The guy operating the laser uses a powerful telescope to retrieve the scattered light. Once the laser source is correlated to the light returning from the telescope, the audio can be retrieved through interferometric analysis. The same system will pick up computer keyboard signals. Each key sends its own signal. Any messages you typed on your computer can be reconstructed."

"Okay, Scott. Enough. I got it," Santini said, holding up his hands, momentarily staring at the large portrait of Joshua Lawrence Chamberlain, the Civil War hero whose courage and battlefield leadership were legendary in the halls of the Pentagon. Could the image of this magnificent man have played a role in the compromise of national security? Santini was outraged at the thought of it.

"We gave the son of a bitch enough time to transmit the conversation he was picking up. Our ninja boys went after him at the marina, but it was a Coast Guard boat on routine anti-terrorist patrol that nailed him. The son of a bitch killed two young women rowing on the river. I just hope the Attorney General will demand the death penalty. But the DIA says he's singing like a bird, and debriefing him may keep him alive for a long time."

CHAPTER 48

When he began planning his coup, General Li worked from the seedy disco owned by the PLA. Now, three days after revealing his plans to his inner circle of conspirators, he had set up his rogue command center in the Beijing headquarters of the PLA.

On paper, the Party Central Committee controlled the PLA through the party's Central Military Commission. But party members sympathetic to Li had helped him pack the commission with his handpicked regional commanders and pro-Li assistant service chiefs. The civilians of the Party Central Committee were focusing on economic matters and leaving day-to-day military issues to the Central Military Commission. Taking advantage of this lack of civilian control, Li had essentially assumed control of the commission and secretly transformed it into a general staff answerable to him.

"Chinese boxes," his staff called it: Li's command was nested, officially unseen, inside the commission. The practical effect of this arrangement was that Li now had access to PLA communications and to the intelligence data from the Ministry of State Security.

Captain Chang K. Y. Yew, the officer who acted as Li's English interpreter, had set up Chinese boxes in the Ministry of State Security. Chang, despite his low rank, had a great deal of power because of his connection to Li. It had been Chang who had set up the rogue faction functioning within State Security, gaining access to unlimited funds. Chang had set up a Li intelligence network in the United States, beginning with An Sing Li, a beautiful Chinese student he had personally recruited before she left Beijing to attend George Washington University.

Even while An was in her senior year at George Washington she had gotten a part-time job as an intern at the National Defense University, not far from her apartment in Southeast Washington. Then she was given secret clearance to work on Chinese-language material turned in by the U.S. intelligence agency for analysis by specialists at the university's Near East–South Asia Center for Strategic Studies. After she graduated, she was hired by the Center.

She managed to secure a position working for the National Security Council, as a translator of Chinese documents. Ironically, due to the initial low-level position she occupied, she never came to Joseph Praeger's attention. Her security clearance was raised to Sensitive Compartmented Information. The promotion and clearance upgrade were the results of luck rather than any machinations by Chang or An Sing Li. But Chang had taken credit for An's placement and basked in the recognition that she was providing intelligence whose principal value was in building up Li's reputation as a man with a window into the secret activities of President Jefferson's National Security Council.

Li's day began with an urgent call from Chang, who asked for an immediate meeting. He entered Li's spacious office, dreading his audience. Bad news enraged Li, and Chang was bringing bad news. Li did not motion Chang to sit. The captain stood stiffly at attention before his frowning general.

"The assassination attempt on Santini failed," Chang said.

"I can see from your face that there is more," Li responded coldly.

"Yes, General. There is more," Chang said, handing Li a folder.

Li dropped the folder on his desk and said, "Tell me. Your reports have too many words."

"The agent known as Chas has sent his last message. It is an interesting message."

"*Last?* Why last?"

"He has been captured."

"Betrayed! He had to have been betrayed!"

"I do not believe so, General. His last signal—we had a code word for 'I am discovered'—came near the end of his report. It appears that he was surprised. I do not believe there was betrayal. Technically, his communications were vulnerable. It was only a matter of time. General, I beg of you: Think of what he sent before capture. *That* is what is important."

"You exceed your rank, Chang. Junior officers do not give suggestions to generals," Li said, smiling at Chang's anxiety. "That is not how to walk the path to higher rank. But very well. The message, please."

Chang, occasionally reading from a transcript, relayed what Chas had heard from his interception of Santini's words. Chang began by quoting Santini's description of the Rapallo plan developed by Berzin and Wagner. He also passed on the report that Berzin had probably ordered the killing of Gruchkov. With great foreboding, Chang revealed that he recently learned that Berzin had once been a CIA spy.

Li exploded into one of his patented tirades. "He was spying for the CIA? Do you know what that means, you fool? Berzin probably sold us weapons that have been corrupted by the Americans! Either that or he gave them internal drawings and documents that will allow them to render the systems useless or even program them so that they turn against us in the course of battle!

"And you dare say that your Mr. Chas was not betrayed?" he shouted. "And what of that little beauty you were screwing? Where is she? Do we have anyone we can trust in America?" Li went on with a familiar litany of betrayal, beginning with "the traitor Major General Zhou Xi," and, drawing on his imagination, he continued to recite the names of others, many of whom were no longer alive.

As soon as the catalogue ended, Chang took a breath and said, "Because of the capture of Agent Chas, I have not attempted to contact Agent An. I believe that she will not be named by Agent Chas."

"Not be named? Do you really think that he won't give the Americans everything? I am afraid, Captain Chang, that your little American intelligence system is no more."

"I greatly regret the capture of Agent Chas, General Li. But there are other assets that can be reached and directed by Agent An."

"Assets like those mindless thugs who bungled the attack on Santini?"

"General, those men were . . . donated by Berzin."

"Berzin! Berzin the great traitor! You tell me that he is plotting with that . . . that German. I want him dead! I want him dead!"

"That can be done, General Li. State Security has dependable assets in Russia."

"Russia! I never want to hear that word again!" He picked up the folder, took out the report, read for a few moments, and then tossed it back onto his desk. He looked up at Chang and said, as if his words were an afterthought, "See to it that he dies. That will be all."

Chang congratulated himself for deciding not to tell Li that Santini obviously knew some details of Li's coup plans. Chang did not want to decorate a lamppost. "Thank you, General. You have the situation in the palm of your mighty hand."

Flattery never bothered Li; it was, he told himself, a price of leadership.

An hour later, he called in his principal advisers, among them Wang Gui and Zho Zhenzen. They possessed enough confidence to speak often at such meetings. Li accepted this because he recognized them as his brightest subordinates. He saw them as soldiers, warriors. In his military mind, Captain Chang was an intelligence officer, not a soldier.

Orderlies filed into the room, bringing trays of tea. Li motioned for the men to sit in the armchairs arranged in an arc before his desk. As usual, he began the meeting without prelude.

"We have had betrayers, men who thought they could outwit us. Men like—"

"The Russian?" Zho Zhenzen asked.

Li nodded, a slight frown passing swiftly across his brow. *How,* he wondered, *did Zho guess that? Well, he is bright.*

"Yes," Li replied. "Berzin. A spy! He has been plotting with a German, uniting Russia and Germany." He closed his hands, palm to palm, as if he were crushing something. "There will be no Berzin."

CHAPTER 49

At 3:30 P.M., Santini got a call from the White House: an emergency meeting in twenty minutes. President Jefferson and Praeger had returned from Europe late last night and were not wasting any time, Santini thought. He suspected that Jefferson had bowed to pressure from Praeger and was going to demand his resignation. He was prepared to pack it in.

Praeger had undercut him every step along the way. He had stayed this long because he had always been a good soldier, prepared to follow the orders from the Commander in Chief. The President had to be something more than a puppet on the end of a string. Jefferson was bright and capable enough for the job. But he had been hollowed out by the process, reduced to little more than a mannequin spouting the words of his speechwriters. No, Santini was prepared to abandon the job, whether or not Jefferson asked him to go. But he knew, of course, Jefferson wouldn't confront him directly. Santini still had too many friends up on Capitol Hill and in the press corps. They would criticize Jefferson for making Santini a scapegoat. His chances for re-election would be put at risk. And re-election had become Jefferson's only guiding star. It would have to be Santini's decision, one that he would offer up patriotically "for the good of the nation."

When Santini entered the Oval Office through the private entrance, he saw immediately that this meeting had an agenda different from the one he expected. Secretary of State Douglas Palmer was there, along with DNI Ford, Director Pelky, and, of course, Praeger. All three were sitting on the couch that ran perpendicular to Bradford Jefferson's high-back chair. They all looked at Santini as if he did not have a bandage on his head. The logs in the fireplace crackled and snapped behind the President's chair, giving warmth to an otherwise austere setting.

Arriving a second behind Santini was Whittier, the Chairman of the Joint Chiefs. He was carrying a thick notebook and what appeared to be large maps that were rolled and bound up with rubber bands. As soon as General Whittier was seated next to Santini, Jefferson was sipping coffee that had just been served by a white-jacketed Filipino man who moved sylphlike throughout the room. Jefferson cleared his throat in a practiced gesture, attempting to signify the gravity of the moment.

"Gentlemen," he intoned, "thank you for joining me. Director Ford has brought to my attention a very serious matter. Jack Pelky's team out at the Agency has reliable information indicating that the North Koreans may be planning to launch a surprise attack against our ally the South Koreans. Apparently, they intend to use their normal spring exercise as a cover for the operation. If they proceed with their plans, several million people are likely to die.

"As we all know, they have developed chemical and biological weapons, and we think they now have at least seven or eight nuclear bombs that they could unleash if they see us trying to respond with reinforcements or retaliate. This, gentlemen, could lead to World War III, if we simply sit back and do nothing.

"I've asked General Whittier to prepare a plan that would allow us to launch a tightly drawn preemptive strike to decapitate the North Korean leadership and selected units of its Army."

Santini was stunned. He could not remain silent any longer. "Excuse me, Mr. President, but General Whittier has not spoken to me about any war plans."

"I shouldn't have to remind you, Mr. Secretary," Preager injected quickly, "that the Chairman serves as the *principal military adviser to the President.*"

"And to me as well. You know—or at least you *should* know—that the Chairman is not in the chain of command. I am," Santini shot back. "And I shouldn't have to add that you are not in that chain, either!"

"Gentlemen, enough. Michael, this is an advisory meeting only," Jefferson said soothingly, trying his father-knows-best routine to calm Santini down. "I asked you to be here so you can hear exactly what contingencies are available to me as Commander in Chief to respond to an emergency situation that poses a grave threat to our national security. After General Whittier briefs us on the military options open to us, I expect to hear your recommendations for or against taking any action."

Santini leaped into the opening. "Mr. President," he said, "I think we need to hear from Director Pelky about the nature of the intelligence he's acquired and just how reliable he thinks it is before we ponder whether to go off to war with North Korea."

"That's a good point, Michael," Jefferson said. Casting a wary glance over at Praeger, he nodded for Pelky to proceed.

"The information came in over the weekend, Mr. President," Pelky said. "A high-ranking North Korean general defected and sought refuge in the Swedish Embassy in Beijing. Somehow they were able to overcome objections from the Chinese government and take him in. The Swedes called our guys at the American Embassy and gave us the full dump on what Kim Song Jo is up to. The Swedes think this guy's legit, and we're inclined to accept him as a credible source."

"Jack," Santini said, his tone conveying total exasperation. "You're telling us that you've got one uncorroborated source and you're buying it without more?"

"No, Michael, that's not all we're going on. You know we follow the North Koreans *very* closely. If they put an extra gallon of gas in one of their tanks or armored personnel carriers we know whether it's regular or high-test. There has been some movement of their heavy artillery even closer to the DMZ than normal. And they've hauled more of their Nodong missiles out of storage than we've seen in past exercises. Right now, all of this is still ambiguous. But if you couple it with the defector's story, we've got to assume the worst."

"But if we start to take any action that looks like a prelude to a preemptive strike, we could produce a self-fulfilling prophecy," Santini countered. "We need to think this through, Mr. President. I remember reading that after the bullshit the United States and the British swallowed on Iraq from Mr. 'Curveball,' the Intelligence Community vowed never to accept single-source reporting again."

Praeger couldn't resist jumping into the fray. "The Intelligence Community didn't see those planes coming into the Twin Towers or the Pentagon, Secretary Santini," Praeger said, allowing his voice to turn shrill. "Do we have to wait until the North Koreans devastate downtown Seoul before we do anything? How many times do we have to get screwed over by those bastards before we take them down?"

"You want to take down a few million South Koreans with them, Joe?" Santini asked.

"There you go again, wimping out by holding up women and children as a shield. For Christ's sake!" Praeger exploded. "We should have called their bluff a long time ago. The Chinese have been dicking us around, claiming we have no influence with the 'Great Leader.' That's pure bullshit and you know it. They could have shut him down in a matter of a few days. No, they have a hand in this and it's time we called it."

"I'm afraid Joe's right on this, Michael," Jefferson offered, nodding his head in affirmation. "If we show any sign of weakness, any hesitation to take action, they'll move. And our South Korean friends—not to mention our own forces—will meet the very fate you're concerned about.

"Okay. Let's move on and hear from the Chairman. I want his best advice as to what we can do to deter the North Koreans from doing something so thoroughly stupid."

"Yes, Mr. President," Praeger said, but he didn't stop talking. "I just think that the time has come to stop acting like a bunch of wimps letting the schoolyard bullies intimidate us."

"Joe, I said 'enough,'" Jefferson said, allowing a rare scowl. "General Whittier, please proceed."

Praeger reshuffled the papers he held in his lap, satisfied that he had gotten in the last word.

"As you know, Mr. President, we've got approximately thirty-seven thousand U.S. troops stationed in South Korea. Combined with the ROK forces, totaling about half a million men, they constitute a pretty formidable fighting team. But the North Koreans have as many as eight hundred thousand men poised just north of the DMZ with about eleven thousand artillery pieces forward deployed with them. We have to assume that they've loaded chemical and biological agents into a lot of those artillery shells. That can make life real uncomfortable for us."

Santini looked at Whittier and winced inwardly. The Chairman had fought in Vietnam and almost every battle since then and had the scars and bone replacements to prove it. Like most men who had seen war up close, he was reluctant to put people into battle unless there was a damn good reason for it. But like most professional soldiers of his generation, he tended to underplay the description of the horrors you have to deal with when bullets and bombs start to fly.

"If, Mr. President, you wanted to deter them," Whittier continued, "you might consider sending another aircraft carrier to the region. I spoke with Admiral Stockdale last night, and he said he could probably get us a carrier battle group up there in the next several days."

"But we may not have enough time, General," Jefferson said. "If they decide to move in the next twenty-four to thirty-six hours, that carrier won't do a damn bit of good." Jefferson clearly had been primed by Praeger to assume the North was definitely going to attack and soon.

"Yes, sir. But if you publicly announce your decision, and then send a MAU—a Marine Amphibious Unit, that is—from Okinawa, along with a dozen squadrons of F-16s to Misawa, that could put an ice cube or two into their shorts. And, Mr.

President, there happen to be a couple of Los Angeles Class submarines on an exercise in the area. They're loaded with some Tomahawk land-attack cruise missiles. If they surfaced in Kim's backyard, he'd probably understand that he'd be in very serious trouble if he makes any move against the South."

"Isn't it also the case, General," Santini intervened, "that if we have to go to war, the President will have to announce a call-up of the reserves, and that it's far better to do that long before we get into a firefight with the North Koreans, rather than after?"

"Absolutely, Mr. Secretary. Our people are already way overstretched right now, and we're going to need some time to get them trained and ready for battle. We wouldn't want to repeat what we did during the first days of the Korean War back in the early fifties."

"But isn't it also true," Praeger rejoined, "that we could put Kim out of play with a few nuclear weapons that we could fire off one of our Trident submarines?"

"We could, sir, but we'd be crossing a threshold that would invite international condemnation."

"What would invite condemnation, General, is defeat," Praeger shot back. "That's not an option for us."

"Agreed, sir," Whittier said, looking for someone to pull Praeger off his back.

"Mr. President," Doug Palmer finally said in his practiced, professorial tone, "I think it would be wise to contact President Chi on the hot line before you make your decision—"

Before Palmer could continue, Praeger raised his hand, his index finger pointing straight up. "Mr. President, that would be a mistake. Chi will deny that the North Koreans are up to anything. Either that or he'll slow roll us until it's too late for us to do anything to stop Kim. No, wait until our forces are in place; then make the call."

Santini didn't wait for recognition to respond. "There's no way that Kim won't learn that our forces are underway. He'll be convinced that we've made the decision to take him and his regime out and that he's got nothing to lose."

Jefferson turned to his CIA Director. "What do you think, Jack?"

Pelky, who usually projected a calm and all-knowing demeanor, looked startled. "As you know, Mr. President, I'm not in the policy-making business—"

"No, I understand that," Jefferson said impatiently. "That's not what I'm asking you. What I want to know is, how do you think Kim Song Jo will respond when he sees our forces knocking on his door?"

Pelky paused, his furrowed brow turning pensive, and said, "It's too close to call, Mr. President. It's fifty-fifty as to what he'll do—"

"Come on, Jack," Santini erupted. "For Christ's sake. This is no fifty-fifty call. I've read the profiles on Kim. Xenophobic, impetuous, self-delusional. We send our warships off his coast and we expect him to be struck with a sudden case of rationality?"

Praeger saw that Pelky was about to concede to Santini's point and pulled out his rhetorical trump card. "The only thing that Kim understands is power. We can't afford to look weak or vacillating in dealing with him. If we do, our allies won't trust us and our enemies won't fear us. Mr. President, this is a defining moment for America."

Jefferson nodded gravely, visibly moved by Praeger's final point. "Thank you, gentlemen," he said, as he pushed back his chair and stood up. "I appreciate having the benefit of your thoughts. I need to ponder this more, but I expect to make a decision shortly."

As the members of Jefferson's national security team began to file slowly out of the Oval Office, Jefferson turned to General Whittier and said, "Mr. Chairman, I'll contact you directly once I decide on the best course of action."

Jefferson's last comment hit Santini in the chest with the subtlety of a jackhammer. The decision to challenge Kim Song Jo had already been made. The meeting in the Oval Office had been a sham. Pure window dressing so that the word could get out to the press that everyone had had the opportunity to be heard. President Jefferson had to make a tough call. That's why he was elected, and that's what the American people expected him to do. Santini could see the White House spin machine in operation already.

And Jefferson had made it crystal clear that he, as Commander in Chief, was going to bypass Santini and deal directly with the Chairman of the Joint Chiefs of Staff. Santini was being cut out of the chain of command!

As Santini made his way out of the Oval Office, everyone managed to avert their eyes from him. They understood exactly what had just taken place.

As soon as he was outside the White House, Santini jumped into the backseat of his limousine, hitting the button that sent the interior glass privacy partition sliding up. His emotions were on fire and he didn't want to see or talk to anyone right then. Curtis got the message and kicked the Cadillac's engine into high gear.

Santini could not believe what he had just witnessed in the Oval Office. "Defining moment, my ass," he muttered to himself. *Hundreds of thousands of lives are at stake and we're about to roll the dice.* It was a reckless, riverboat gamble!

Why, he wondered, *didn't Douglas Palmer raise hell about what Jefferson was about to do? He even caved on his pathetic hot line request!*

And Pelky ducking on what Kim Song Jo was likely to do when he saw an armada coming at him. Jesus!

None of this made any sense.

The President was about to make a very big mistake. Santini had to stop him.

And he knew that he didn't have much time.

Standing with his hands tucked into the trouser pockets of his suit, President Jefferson stared out the bulletproof windows of the Oval Office that looked out onto the neatly manicured lawn. "Santini was pretty upset when he left," he said in a voice that was noticeably apprehensive. "What do you think he'll do, Joe?"

"He serves you, Mr. President. He'll either get with the program or get off the team."

"You think he'll resign?"

"He wouldn't dare quit at a time like this. He'll get all moody and pout for a while," Praeger said reassuringly. "But in the end, he really has no choice but to support you. Heroes don't go weak in the knees in a time of crisis. At least, not real heroes."

"I hope you're right, Joe," Jefferson said, not sounding convinced. "I hope you're right."

As soon as Santini entered his office at the Pentagon, he pulled out the Palm Pilot wireless phone that he kept in the inside pocket of his suit jacket. The private hot line feature he had hoped to use failed. Somehow the signal had been blocked. He quickly concluded that trying to call Minister Xu through the Ministry of Defense would be useless. Chinese bureaucracy rivaled a Rubik's Cube in complexity. Even if he could get through on the phone, Li's men were likely to intercept it.

Then he remembered that Xu had given him a private number to call. He retrieved the card that Xu had given him that night at the reception at the State Department. Turning to his desktop phone, he punched in the numbers that had been handwritten on the card, and waited. The first attempt produced only a busy signal. The second, a recording, asking him to leave a message.

He turned again to his Palm Pilot. Using a stylus pen, he tapped in the letters *Xu*. His e-mail address appeared immediately on the small backlit screen.

Xu. S.O.S. Urgent. Respond immediately.

Santini

He waited. Minutes passed. Nothing. He hit the re-send button. Again, no response.

Frustrated, he next tapped out the letters *H-a-r*. Instantly, the name *Hartley, Randall* emerged on the screen, along with Hartley's private telephone number.

* * *

"I see by the paper that you had a close call, Randall."

"Skinned knee and a ripped-up pair of slacks," Hartley said. "Thanks for your concern."

"I need to talk to you, Randall. Something has come up and I need your . . . insight." Santini was talking on an open line and knew that someone was always monitoring his conversations.

"Well, you know I'm always eager to be of help. Must be *real* serious." It was Hartley's way of trying to tease out as much information as possible from the very beginning of the conversation. The two men had not talked since the trip to Munich.

"It is, Randall. Do you have time to visit?"

"For you? Absolutely. Where?"

"I can be at your place in fifteen minutes."

"You're on. I'll brew some coffee."

General Whittier was not a happy man.

He hadn't been back in his office more than thirty minutes before President Jefferson called, telling him to move forward with the deterrent plan they had discussed.

Leaning back in the leather chair his wife, Pamela, had given him when he completed his tenure at the Special Operations Command, he felt anything but pride at the moment.

He was surprised when Jefferson called him earlier that morning, requesting him to dust off and bring to the White House all Oplans and ConPlans for action against North Korea. It struck him as unusual because the North Korean leadership hadn't been acting up recently and he hadn't seen any intel reports to the contrary.

But with the North Koreans you could never tell. One day they threatened to turn South Korea into "a sea of fire"; the next, they offered to open up direct trade with their misguided but loving brethren. Like it or not, they managed to stay with you like a bad virus.

Until this morning it had never occurred to Whittier that Santini had been cut out of the loop. Worse, Jefferson made it clear that he had lost confidence in his Secretary of Defense.

Santini had too much pride to stay on. It had been a real screw job. And there was no doubt that Joe Praeger had his hands all over it.

Whittier cussed at himself for being an unwitting participant in the scheme. He should have known something was up, checked with Santini to coordinate what they would say at the meeting. Too late now.

Jefferson, the Commander in Chief, was his boss. The man who appointed him Chairman. But Santini—a fellow warrior—was the one Whittier counted on to keep the White House from running off on some wild-ass mission impossible.

Reluctantly, Whittier swiveled around to the console behind his desk and picked up the receiver on his secure MLP. He punched the button that connected him directly to Admiral Jesse Stockdale, Commander of Pacific Command.

Stockdale answered on the second ring. The caller identification on the phone showed him that Whittier was calling. "Stockdale here, sir."

Conveying a matter-of-fact calmness that he did not feel, Whittier indulged in a few customary pleasantries. Then he said, "Jesse. I need you to contact the two 688s out on Operation Bonanza. Direct them to proceed at flank speed to the coast of Krypton. Radio silence until further instructions."

Stockdale hesitated a moment, as if waiting for further elaboration. Hearing none, he said, "Got it."

Whittier then placed a second call, this one to General Pete Perkins, the commanding officer of the Marines based in Okinawa.

"Pete," Whittier said without prelude, "need a MAU to head out to Krypton. Call it Exercise Gold Band."

"Showtime?"

"Not sure. Stay tuned," Whittier said.

When he hung up, Whittier stared at the book he kept on his desk, right next to the Bible he had inherited from his father. The title of the book was *Dereliction of Duty*. It chronicled how America's military leaders had permitted their judgment to be twisted and manipulated by politicians. Truth had become the first casualty in Washington's corridors of power. More than fifty-eight thousand men had to be buried in the fighting that followed.

History, as Mark Twain observed, didn't always repeat itself, but it did tend to rhyme.

If the defector's story is real, then taking action now just might discourage Kim Song Jo from doing anything foolish. If it is phony, then we could damn well start a war that would kill God knows how many thousands.

The dogs of war are barking—at us or with us, that is the question.

In less than twenty-four hours, he'd know the answer.

Curtis managed to get Santini over the Key Bridge and through Georgetown traffic in less than twelve minutes. Santini always worried that Curtis would one day plow that two-ton tank into a sidewalk café, killing dozens of people. But Curtis knew every inch of that limousine and every foot of pavement in Washington, D.C. He could have entered the vehicle in a NASCAR race and emerged without a scratch. During the time he had been at the Pentagon, Santini had been late only once, and that was when Joe Praeger held him up at the White House, preventing him from greeting Xu on his arrival at the State Department.

Hartley greeted Santini at the front door. He was dressed casually in baggy cord pants, a burgundy crewneck sweater, and a pair of tennis sneakers. He smiled broadly as he shook Santini's hand.

Seeing the bandage on Santini's head, he asked, "You all right?"

"Yeah, I'm fine. But how about you? You came close to some bullets."

"They all missed. Missed me, that is. What's the reason for the visit?"

"I need to talk with you privately."

"Always look forward to a *private* chat with you," Hartley said, a touch of irony in his voice. The number of private conversations he had had with Santini over the years were fewer than his fingers. "Why don't we go upstairs?"

Santini and Hartley exchanged small talk until they had climbed three flights of stairs and reached Hartley's home office. Santini suspected that the stairs provided Hartley with his only form of exercise.

Santini had been to Hartley's office only once before. He had been surprised to find that Hartley had at least two or three assistants working full-time, taking calls, typing away at large HP computers, and stuffing voluminous sheets of paper into dozens of filing cabinets that lined the walls.

But this afternoon, the two men were alone, except for Hartley's Maltese dog, Hoover. Santini was not sure whether it was a play on the name of J. Edgar Hoover (as the FBI had been a frequent target of Hartley's investigations) or the dog simply ate every scrap of food he could find and inhaled it like a vacuum cleaner.

Hartley handed Santini a *Washington Post* mug steaming with hot coffee as they settled onto a plush leather couch. "Tell me how I can help, Mr. Secretary."

"Randall, what I'm about to say is still highly classified. You and I have had discussions before about how I feel about sharing any information with you, classified or unclassified."

Hartley dipped his head in acknowledgment but said nothing.

"Something has come up that I need to run by you, but I need you to promise me that you won't share it with the *Post* or anyone else."

Hartley put his coffee on the table in front of the couch. "You're right; we *have* had this conversation before. And you may remember that I can't make such a promise. All I can do is promise you that I will take into account any national security concerns you have. If I think it could jeopardize lives or in any way harm the country, then it goes no further. But that is the best I can do."

Santini hesitated, troubled that he would have to reveal this information to Hartley without a pledge that it would be held totally confidential. "Okay," he said finally. "The Agency has picked up information through the Swedes that a North Korean defector insists that Kim Song Jo is about to launch a surprise attack against the South. Jefferson is thinking about sending the Marines and a couple of 688s to the region. This could suck in China, maybe Russia."

"What do you think about the defector's story?" Hartley asked noncommittally.

"I don't know. Frankly, it came totally out of the blue. What I don't understand is why Pelky is buying it without more. And I can't figure out why Ford is just sitting back on this, keeping mum, acting as if Pelky is the DNI."

"Everybody is on edge, ready to pull the hair trigger," Hartley said. "No one wants to be accused of waiting until we get hit and failing to connect all the dots. Ford is getting famous for doing and saying absolutely nothing. And Pelky probably thinks he'd be hauled up before the Congress and crucified if he failed to accept the report. That's one of the biggest tragedies of the consequences of the September 11 attack. Ready, fire, aim. You don't have to be right today, just first."

"But we could start a world war on totally false information."

"Precisely. Which is one reason why the *Post* is about to do an exposé on this very subject."

"But I thought you said—," Santini said, shaken by Hartley's quick dismissal of his concerns.

"Relax, Mr. Secretary. One of my sources out at the Agency gave this story to one of my former fellow working stiffs at the *Post* a few days ago. I've been running all the traps on it long before you arrived. You haven't given me anything they don't already have."

"What do you think?"

"I think it's a phony story," Hartley replied. "Maybe Kim Song Jo thinks he can rattle the U.S. Maybe he is trying to frighten Japan or is trying to gain leverage in the upcoming negotiations. But it makes absolutely no sense for the 'Great Leader' to launch a military attack."

"Well, sure. The guy would have to be wacko to do it," Santini said. "But maybe he thinks he could claim he was provoked by rumors that Jefferson was planning a 'preemptive decapitation.' Or he thinks he could launch a quick strike and then count on his friends at the UN to rush in and save his ass before we wiped him off the face of the earth."

"No. He has too much to lose. And right now things are going in the right direction for him. I'm convinced it's disinformation, and so are the people I talked to, people in the Agency. It looks like Pelky is getting bulldozed by Praeger. There is a mystery, though: Who's putting it out and why? I haven't quite figured out exactly who's manipulating this behind the scenes, but I hope to find out soon."

"How soon," Santini asked, "before the *Post* runs with the defector story?"

"My guess is within a couple of days. I'm not in the reporting business any longer, as you know, but I'm confident that Don Graham will want to move with some caution on this one. There's a lot at stake if the *Post* is wrong."

"Yes, and just as much if you're right about this being a case of disinformation that we responded to." Santini drained his coffee mug, thanked Hartley for meeting with him, and moved quickly toward the stairs.

Hartley stopped him, placing his hand on Santini's shoulder. "One other thing, Mr. Secretary. A *Post* reporter on assignment to Tokyo picked up something else which might be of interest to you." Pausing to lend a touch of drama to what he was about to say, Hartley continued. "He heard that the Japanese press is pursuing a story that the U.S. has been secretly storing tactical nuclear weapons on one of our bases there to be used against North Korea or the Chinese if they ever attacked Taiwan. Now that would create quite a firestorm for Prime Minister Yakashita, wouldn't it? You might want to check it out."

Santini just shook his head. Part denial, part disgust. *Jesus, if this phony story made it into print, the Yakashita Government could fall. Either that, or he would demand that we shut down all of our operations in Japan.*

"There's something more, Mr. Secretary," Hartley said, after another pause. "My friends at the Bureau tell me that three freshly shot bodies were found at Hains Point this morning."

"Not that unusual for D.C. these days," Santini cautiously responded.

"Well, two of them were Chechens and had tattoos—wolf symbols and their names. One of the names was Tago."

"Tago," Santini said, placing a hand on Hartley's shoulder. "You had a closer call than you think, Randall."

Randall nodded. "I know, Mr. Secretary. Have a nice day," he said, closing the door behind Santini.

PART 3

Can you come to the square?
Dare you come to the square
When that hour strikes?

—FROM THE SONG OF THE
DECEMBRIST REBELS DURING
THE REIGN OF NICHOLAS I
(QUOTED IN DAVID REMNICK'S
LENIN'S TOMB)

Racing up the Pentagon's front steps, Santini swept past the guards on duty. He raced up the stairs that took him to the Eisenhower Corridor and slipped into the rear door to his office. Once again, he tried to reach Xu. Once again, the phone proved fruitless. This time he typed out an encrypted message on his Palm Pilot:

> *White House is mistaken about North Korean intentions to attack South. Threat of war imminent. Contact me ASAP!*

Again, no response.

"Scott, I need to get to Beijing," Santini said.

"Not a problem, sir. I'll get one of the Boeing 757s gassed up and ready to go. I'll notify Protocol, call Policy, and gin up the usual gaggle of press people."

"No, I need to go alone. No press. No anybody. And I've got to get there in less than twelve hours."

O'Neill snapped his head back, expressing astonishment, signaling the impossibility of delivering what Santini wanted. "Mr. Secretary, we like to say that the difficult is easy and the impossible will take a bit longer. But this is over the top. No way can we get you there in less than sixteen to eighteen hours. And DARPA [Defense Advance Research Projects Agency] hasn't figured out a way to beam you up." Pursing his lips and exhaling as if he were trying to blow up a balloon,

O'Neill continued. "Sir, can I ask who you plan to meet and why the rush?"

"Scott, the President is about to send a MAU and a couple of 688 subs off the coast of North Korea."

"What?"

"The Agency claims a defector from North Korea maintains that Kim Song Jo is about to launch a preemptive strike against the South at any moment, and he wants to send Kim a message."

"Jesus! How solid is the defector? Have any of our guys had a chance to debrief him and check him out?"

"No. They're relying on the Swedes. I don't understand what in hell is happening. Pelky is under constant pressure from Praeger. But this is irresponsible. No job is worth having for something this fucking crazy. China could ratchet this thing up in a nanosecond. And the Russians have a security deal with Kim. This could turn into a very big bonfire if we don't stop it."

"Let me play the devil's advocate for a moment, sir. What if Pelky is right? Our guys could turn into chop suey if they're hit without warning."

"It's not going to happen, Scott. It's disinformation. A ploy. General Li, the same PLA fanatic who has been behind Holloman and the gas attack, is setting us up with a scam. I'm convinced that they are going to hit Taiwan while our attention and forces have been diverted to defending South Korea."

O'Neill's face revealed deep skepticism. "We've seen no intelligence that shows any preparatory moves by China to attack Taiwan—"

"Precisely, Scott. That's because they've moved all of their short-range ballistic missiles within striking range during the past several years. They completed some combined arms exercises in the straits back in January. You know that they can go anytime. And the Taiwanese have not done a goddamn thing to prepare for war. Christ, they've even refused to harden crucial command centers. If they get hit, they'll fold like a cheap tent in a stiff wind. Twenty-four, forty-eight hours at best and it's over."

"Then why are their political leaders still throwing hints about voting for independence from the mainland?" O'Neill asked. "I thought they knocked that off a couple of years ago."

"Because they think that the Chinese wouldn't dare strike them. China is going to host the Olympics in 2008 and President Chi wouldn't risk international reaction to any military aggression. Besides, they're convinced that Uncle Sam will always come to their rescue. I'm telling you, Scott, we're being set up. It's the oldest martial trick in the book. Feint left, go right. It was my best move in the boxing ring. Left jab, right cross."

"May I suggest, sir, if that is the case, that you place a call to the Chinese MOD. Talking to Xu by phone, sir, if I may say, is a hell of a lot faster than trying to fly there to talk to him in person."

"No, Scott. I've tried to call him. No answer. Besides, the information I have is explosive. I'll need to meet directly with the Chinese President. We need to keep calling Xu to see if he can set up a meeting for me, but I've got to do this in person. There's no way a phone call can stop what in essence amounts to a military coup. They'll never believe me unless I can lay it out for them directly."

"Well, I hate to be negative, but, Mr. Secretary, we are shit out of luck. There's just no way I can get you there in time."

Santini paced back and forth before the large bay windows of his office. "What about the Blackbird?"

"The SR-71 Blackbird? Didn't Congress cancel that program back in the late eighties?"

"They—we—did. A big mistake. In 1995, we were able to put three hundred million dollars back in the budget to reactivate three of them. I think NASA has been experimenting with them down at their Dryden Flight Research Center. They're looking at the impact of sonic booms, the use of ultraviolet video cameras, and laser air data collection systems."

"You know, I had completely forgotten all about that plane. The Air Force owned it and they weren't about to share it with us lesser mortals."

"It could get me there, couldn't it, Scott?"

"Yes, sir. It'll go coast to coast in an hour. Course, it may take a few hours to move NASA off its ass and have it flown to Andrews. But once there, yes, sir, it will put you in downtown Beijing in just a few hours. There is the problem of refueling, and I'll have to work out the kinks on that, but I'll get on it right now."

O'Neill, suddenly energized, moved quickly to the office door. "Let's hope those babies are still running. I'll call Frank Gunter over at NASA and get his top-level buy-in. He won't know all the details, but he surely can get Edwards motivated and focused on what is doable on a tight time line.

"And I know a former U-2 pilot, Chuck Smith, who works in the Joint Staff J-38 ROD." Seeing Santini's eyebrows furrow, O'Neill added, "Sorry, sir, that's Recon Operation Division. He should be able to help me sort out what we can do for you by tomorrow morning. They're always doing special sensitive missions without any notice."

As soon as O'Neill hung up on Chuck Smith, he began making ask-me-no-questions calls, laying on tanker requirement to the Tanker Wings at Travis Air Force Base in California and Fairchild Air Force Base in Washington.

O'Neill's calls to Gunter and Smith worked because O'Neill had a way of conveying urgency and need without going into detail. People trusted him and accepted his requests without a reason why. It did not happen every time. But it happened often enough for O'Neill to become a legend in the Pentagon.

His next call was to another flier friend, Buz Murphy, a retired Air Force lieutenant colonel who had been an SR-71 pilot and later an instructor. He went to work for NASA when the Air Force stopped flying SR-71s in the late nineties. He lived near Edwards Air Force Base.

"Here's the deal," O'Neill told Murphy. "I want you to fly the SecDef nonstop to China on a mission unapproved by anybody but the SecDef. The code name for the mission is . . . Dragon Fire." O'Neill tried to avoid conveying the fact that he had just pulled the name out of his ass.

"Okay," Murphy said. "That'll be our call sign. Give me the details."

A little more than an hour after Santini told O'Neill to set up the flight, O'Neill was standing in front of Santini's desk. "At twenty-one hundred, sir, we'll get started with a briefing on what has been set up for tomorrow. Meanwhile, we can get Xu to back-channel President Chi Zhiqiang to set up your meeting with him the next morning. I suggest that you find out where he would prefer for you to land to maintain secrecy."

At 9:00 that night, O'Neill briefed Santini: "Mr. Secretary, as we speak, a SR-71 Blackbird is lifting off from Edwards Air Force Base in California. It is being flown by one of our most experienced pilots, Buz Murphy. He'll be your pilot tomorrow for your flight to China. As luck would have it, NASA had this aircraft ready for a functional check flight tomorrow. The checking will be done tonight en route to Andrews. A KC-10 tanker full of special JP-7 fuel and all the required servicing items and support personnel will depart in about two hours, arriving at Andrews around oh five hundred tomorrow.

"You will be departing Andrews with the aircraft call sign Dragon Fire, and this will cue all the FAA support centers that you are an SR-71 requiring prioritized handling. Refuelings have been set up for you south of Seattle with two KC-135Q tankers, which routinely refuel the SR-71s for NASA. A KC-10 tanker is en route to Fairchild Air Force Base, Washington, right now to pick up the JP-7 fuel. It will take off in time to fly south of Attu Island in the Aleutians to give you your second refueling at about three and a half hours into your flight.

"There will be a third refueling in the Sea of Japan from a pair of old Q-model tankers from Kadena Air Force Base on Okinawa. There will also be support for you operating out of Misawa Air Base. There is still JP-7 fuel stored at Kadena for national emergency use such as this. You will cross South Korea supersonically and turn north over the Yellow Sea to approach Beijing from the south. This route avoids any Russian or North Korean overflight problems. Your en route time will be about six hours and your approximate arrival time at Beijing will be oh five hundred local time.

"I've passed your suit and shoe size and weight to Edwards. Two space suits will be on the support tanker due into Andrews around oh five hundred.

"At the High Altitude Chamber at Andrews you'll be fitted for your space suit. Then there'll be a quick altitude chamber session to check the suit for fit and leaks and to train you to use this protective suit during your flight. You'll get a quick lesson on how to be a Blackbird passenger before you suit up."

When the briefing ended, Santini tapped out another message to Xu:

> *Vitally important this meeting with you and President Chi take place. Everything at stake. Will arrive Beijing Fri-0500 on SR-71. Clear airspace. Santini.*

He hoped that this time, the message would get through.

Santini and O'Neill spent the night in the Pentagon. O'Neill slept fitfully on a crash pad he had brought, while Santini snoozed on a Murphy bed he had had installed in a small study area of his office. Santini left a note for Margie, telling her to cover for him as long as she could.

> *Can't say where I'm going. Use the "undisclosed destination" line if you have to.*

O'Neill alerted Curtis, telling him to pick up Santini at 0445 at the Pentagon. "We'll be going to Andrews, Curtis," O'Neill told him. "But you will not need a chase car to follow you, and you will not know the Secretary's destination. It's one of those things, Curtis. We all have to keep our mouths shut."

"Not a word, Admiral. Not a word," Curtis said.

CHAPTER 51

ANDREWS AIR FORCE BASE

The support tanker from Edwards arrived on schedule. A team from Physiological Support moved the G-suits to the altitude chamber. An officer from Reconnaissance System Testing was laying out a short course in what a non-flier had to know about the backseat equipment of an SR-71. The aircraft itself had taxied into a huge hangar and the doors had been shut. Few people at Andrews even knew it had flown in. In the hangar, the aircraft was being yo-yoed to fill its fuel tanks with JP-7 and make sure that no air was left in any tank. Planners were starting to align the astro-inertial navigation system for the flight plan to China. The system would keep the aircraft within three hundred feet of its course without the need of any navigational aids.

When Santini's car reached the Andrews main gate, Curtis slowed down for a check-in but was immediately waved on in. To keep the SecDef visit low-key, there was no security escort, no paperwork. The officer in charge of the High Altitude Pressure Chamber met Santini at the door and hurried him into the training room.

"The SR-71 has never had a fatality, Mr. Secretary," the officer said. "And we sure don't want to break that record."

"I'm with you on that, Major," Santini said.

Two sergeants appeared and helped Santini into his space suit and helmet. The fits were perfect. They then took him into the chamber. As soon as he was settled in a seat like the real one he would soon be in, the chamber operator raised him to a simulated twenty-nine thousand feet.

"This is what the cabin will be like on the mission, Mr. Secretary," the operator told him through the intercom in his helmet. It sounded to Santini as if the operator were in the helmet with him.

Fifteen minutes later the voice came on again: "Mr. Secretary, stand by for an emergency simulation. There is nothing to be alarmed about. You are about to feel how it would be if the cabin suddenly lost pressure."

With a whoosh that sounded like a hurricane, the air rushed out of the chamber, which now simulated sixty-five thousand feet. Santini's G-suit fully inflated. He panicked for an instant because his arms and legs felt as if they did not belong to him. The panic vanished when he realized he could move, but only with comic awkwardness. "I feel like the Pillsbury Dough-boy," he said.

"You're doing okay, Mr. Secretary. We'll be bringing you back down to twenty-nine K. You'll be here for a little less than an hour."

When his acclimation was over, Santini, still in his space suit and carrying his helmet, was taken to a small cafeteria, where he met Buz Murphy. They were served steak and eggs.

"Mr. Secretary," Murphy said, "we'll be in Beijing in about eight hours. Your mission name will be Boss, and I'm going to be calling you that, if you don't mind. My mission name will be Irish. So you call me that. I want you to know that this is the best mission I've had in years. And I've had a few like this one, the kind I'll never be able to talk about." Murphy slipped a piece of toast around his plate to mop up the last of his eggs. "I'll see you in the aircraft . . . Boss," he said, and gave a thumbs-up.

Santini was not a pilot. He had no training in dealing with G-forces or with ejection techniques. While he was wondering about this, a master sergeant with hash marks up to his elbow approached. He escorted Santini to a small bare room, where, in a Texas drawl, he gave the SR-71 passenger lesson O'Neill had promised.

"You will be in the rear seat, sir," he said. "That's where the RSO—the Rear Seat Observer—sits. The RSO usually has a lot of things to do. All you've got to do, sir, is sit there. In front of you, when you get in, will be a special RSO card made up for you. You'll see, sir, what the emergency procedures are, and what you might have to do if the pilot tells you to do it. With all respect, sir, the pilot, he's in charge."

The sergeant slipped a small bag around Santini's waist. "Survival kit, sir. It ejects with you." Then he strapped a shoulder holster on Santini and handed him a 9mm Beretta. "Also survival, sir. You're authorized to carry this. I checked your personnel record, sir. It's a standard routine, sir. I saw you were rated high-proficient in this."

Santini slipped the Beretta into the holster and said, "Admiral O'Neill makes sure I go to the target range religiously, if that's the word."

Air Force medics appeared next and made Santini, fully suited, breathe in pure oxygen until they were satisfied that he was thoroughly oxygenized. Finally, all other gases had to be filtered out of his body and he was taken to a van. O'Neill was waiting for him inside. Santini waddled into the van with a helmet under his arm. The suit and helmet, he had been told, were the same kind that crew members wore on the Space Shuttle.

The van had reached the SR-71, which stood outside the hangar. The Blackbird was a needle-shaped aircraft about the size of a Boeing 727. Old as it was, it remained the fastest and highest-flying production aircraft in the world, reaching speeds over Mach 3, nearly 2,000 miles per hour, while flying at altitudes of eighty-five thousand feet or higher.

"This bird passes everything on the highway but a gas station," O'Neill said, gazing on the aircraft. "Look at those J-58 engines. Each one of them has thirty-two thousand pounds of thrust. Big enough to drive the *QE II*. They have to take off with a very light fuel load and then marry up with a KC-135Q tanker that's a flying gas station. You're going to see a couple of those mobile stations up there before you arrive in Big China Town. The good news is that the SR-71 can travel up to twenty-five hundred miles without refueling. The bad news is, it burns up twelve thousand gallons every ninety minutes."

"Guess we'd better keep that Saudi pipeline flowing," Santini quipped, remembering now why the critics of the aircraft had once consigned it to the boneyard.

An Air Force blue sedan pulled up and a lieutenant colonel got out, carrying a clipboard. "Excuse me, Mr. Secretary. Both the pilot and the RSO must have thorough medical exams before taking off. I have prepared waivers." He handed the clipboard to Santini, who grasped it clumsily in his thick gloves.

"They need to be signed by a responsible officer," the lieutenant colonel told him, stammering in embarrassment.

"Very well, Colonel," Santini said. He signed as the Secretary of Defense and handed the clipboard back. "I hope this ends the paperwork."

Santini climbed into the rear seat of the plane and waited patiently as the ground crew started the engines and then went through about twenty-five minutes of preflight checks.

A green light, okaying the Blackbird to taxi, came from the car that had already been out to check the taxiway and runway for any metal objects that could harm the aircraft's tires or engines. The sleek long black aircraft moved quickly with powerful grace. Just short of the runway "Dragon Fire" halted for the green light from the tower that meant "take the runway."

"Two minutes to takeoff . . . Let's get on with it, tower!" Buz muttered.

As Murphy gave the traditional thumbs-up sign, Santini felt a familiar surge of adrenaline flow through his veins. This was battle time. Once again he was a warrior. He flashed a thumbs-up to O'Neill.

A green light from the tower. A quick last systems check. Santini turned the upper-right knob on the IFF squawk to normal. Brake release.

The twin afterburners ignited, slamming Santini against the back of his seat. Time seemed to compress as the aircraft accelerated to over 250 miles per hour in twenty seconds. Santini had the sensation that he was riding a runaway freight train that was never going to make it to safety. Then, at what seemed to be the last moment, the plane lifted off, elevating gracefully. They were airborne. Washington FAA Center made radar contact and transmitted, "Dragon Fire cleared as filed." No response was given or expected.

He prayed that he would make it in time. He had never known many atheists in foxholes back in Vietnam. As they rocketed up into the blue eye of God, he didn't think he'd find many up there, either.

CHAPTER 52

It was only six in the morning, but Joseph Praeger was already at work in his office. When he heard a loud sonic boom to the northwest, he dismissed it as just another damn military exercise.

His office in the West Wing of the White House belied its power. It was a corner office to be sure, but large enough to accommodate only a small conference table, a desk, a chair, and a couch that could accept the mass of two people. The walls were adorned with original abstract art oils, a gift from Prime Minister Herzog during Jefferson's first trip to Israel. Praeger was chagrined to learn from White House general counsel that unless he was willing to pay the full market price for the art, it would remain the property of the U.S. Government upon his departure from office. Maybe, he thought, Jefferson would purchase it for him. And why not? Jefferson owed him everything. Big-time.

But modest as the office was in size, virtually all of the country's political energy flowed directly through its walls into it. Here was the nerve center of the White House, not the Oval Office. He was the man in charge.

Feeling satisfied that he had persuaded Jefferson to send two carrier battle groups and a Marine Amphibious Unit to tell Kim Song Jo that he was fucking with the wrong people, Praeger settled down for a scheduled meeting with Director Pelky, who was waiting outside in the anteroom of his office.

Pelky had come through for him in front of the President yesterday. He wouldn't forget that when it came time for the new round of appointments in Jefferson's second term. Maybe Pelky should be the next Secretary of Defense. The annoying buzz of his intercom interrupted his momentary reverie. "Charlotte, I thought I told you to hold the calls for the time being."

"Yes, Mr. Praeger, but it's General Tom Milstar on the line. He said it was very important that he speak to you, that he really—"

Praeger cut her off. "Okay, Charlotte, okay. Put him through. And tell Director Pelky that I'll be with him in a few minutes. Ask him if he wants coffee or a cold drink."

"Yes, sir," she said, relieved that Praeger's vaunted quick temper seemed to have cooled off.

Praeger picked up the phone reserved for secure communications. Tom Milstar, a four-star Air Force general, was in charge of NSA, once so secret an arm of the government that the standing joke was that its acronym stood for "No Such Agency." This agency was Uncle Sam's giant ear. Its gargantuan radars and satellites could and did suck up virtually every communication in the atmosphere like a vacuum cleaner. Parallel processing computers could download the information at the speed of light, cracking open encryption codes that were naively thought to be indecipherable.

While General Milstar was obligated to report directly through the chain of command to Santini, he had opened a secret line of communication with Praeger. Milstar, it seemed, had been promised a promotion to become Deputy Director of Central Intelligence. And from there, maybe he even had a shot at one day sitting in the Director's chair. Might have to retire from the Air Force first, but hell, anything was possible. At least that's what Praeger had intimated.

"Sorry to interrupt you, sir, but we picked up something hot late last night and thought you should know about it."

"No problem, General," Praeger said, with just a slight hint of annoyance in his voice that said that this better be important.

"Secretary Santini sent an encrypted message on a wireless

computer—one of those handhelds—to the Chinese Minister of Defense, Xu."

"Saying what?" Praeger asked, his curiosity now fully up and running.

"Saying that he needed to speak directly with the Chinese President. Something to the effect that the White House had misunderstood what the North Koreans were doing. It was not entirely clear."

Praeger could barely contain his anger. *America's Secretary of Defense telling a fucking communist that our President had his head up his ass, and didn't understand what China's toadies were up to! God damn! If that wasn't insubordination. If that wasn't giving comfort to the enemy.*

"Sir, There's more. The Secretary has requisitioned an SR-71 Blackbird from NASA and is—"

"Blackbird? What in hell is that, General?"

"It's the next best thing to a rocket, sir. Faster than a bullet. And he's well on his way to Beijing riding in it." Milstar did not explain how NSA managed to record domestic voice transmissions, as opposed to international ones, which it was authorized to do. But he knew that for Praeger this was a nicety that needed no explanation.

"Jesus Christ!" Praeger exploded. "Where is he now? How close to Beijing? How long before he arrives?"

"Can't tell you that right now. We probably won't be able to know his whereabouts until his pilot makes his next air refueling and communicates with the tanker. But you might call NORAD. They can probably get a quick fix on the Blackbird's location."

"Thank you, General. This is very important information. Thanks for keeping me in the loop. Call me back immediately if you can get exactly what Santini said to the Chinese."

"Roger that, Mr. Praeger. Out here."

Why do these guys have to play these silly toy soldier games? "Roger" this. "Roger" that. "Out here." Why don't they just say "okay" and hang up?

Roughly punching the intercom button on his phone, he barked to Charlotte, "Tell Director Pelky that something has just come up and that I have to cancel. Then call the President's secretary and tell her I'm on my way down. I need to see him. Now!"

Moments later, Praeger stormed past the Secret Service guards posted outside the Oval Office. President Jefferson had arrived in the Oval Office an hour earlier than usual. He needed to be briefed on the breakfast meeting he had this morning with a delegation from the Council on Foreign Relations. They were going to present him with the Pete Peterson Award for Leadership.

It was clear that Praeger was in a rage, but that in itself was not unusual.

"Mr. President," Praeger fumed as Jefferson settled into the tall leather chair behind his desk and began to sort through a pile of mail that he was to sign. "We've got a problem. *Your* Lone Ranger friend over at the Pentagon is on his way to Beijing to meet with *your* counterpart, Mr. President. This is a fucking outrage. Defense Secretaries don't meet with heads of state—not without your permission. He is assuming *your* powers. He's going to tell the Chinese President that you don't know what you're doing. That you're in over your head."

President Jefferson exploded. "What? He . . . what?" This was not going to be easy. Santini, in spite of all that had happened at the Pentagon during his watch, continued to be lionized by the press corps. Santini's appointment was the one time Jefferson had overruled Praeger, and now he had to swallow charbroiled crow.

"Okay, Joe, okay. I agree. He's gone too far. You're right. This is the last straw. I want you to put a stop to that meeting. And as soon as you can, get Santini on the phone so I can fire him."

"With pleasure, Mr. President," Preager said triumphantly. "I know this is not an easy decision for you, but it will be seen as an act of real leadership, I promise you. Real leadership."

Praeger moved quickly to the phone sitting on the credenza behind Jefferson's desk. The white phone console had more than a dozen quick-dial buttons on its surface. Praeger

punched the one that connected the President to General
George Whittier. Once Whittier was on the line, Praeger hit
the intercom button so that Whittier would understand that the
President was about to give him a direct order.

"Mr. Chairman," Jefferson began, dropping his voice two
notches, "I understand that Secretary Santini is on his way to
Beijing and is flying in something called a Blackbird." Jefferson waited to hear some confirmation from Whittier but was
greeted only with silence.

"General, did you hear what I just said?" Jefferson asked,
clearly annoyed.

"Yes sir, Mr. President; it's just that I was not aware of any
such trip planned by the Secretary. He's never mentioned it to
me. And frankly, I'd be awfully surprised if he was traveling
in an SR-71. That would require—"

"General," Jefferson snapped, "he's in the goddamn plane
right now. What I need you to do is to call whomever you call
in this situation and tell me exactly where Santini is right now
in that plane. My understanding is that you have the ability to
do this. Am I right?"

"Yes, sir. Will do."

"And one more thing, General. I don't care what you have
to do to stop it, but that plane is not to reach Beijing. Do I
make myself clear? This is a matter of national security. Santini has engaged in a major breach of his duty." Jefferson, energized by the tone of command in his voice, then added, "It
may very well be that Santini has been serving the interests of
the Chinese rather than ours."

Praeger looked at Jefferson, pleased with Jefferson's display of anger and resolve.

"General Whittier, I repeat, I don't care what you do or how
you do it, but neither Santini nor that plane can be allowed to
land in China."

"Mr. President, as you know, I'm your principal military
adviser. I'm not in the chain of command. I suggest that you
speak directly with . . ."

"General, don't play any goddamn games with me on this. I
know what the law says about who is and who isn't in the

chain of command. The Secretary of Defense has decided to make himself unavailable," Jefferson said, letting the acid drip from his tone of voice. "Now, are you suggesting to me that I, as Commander in Chief, cannot designate you to communicate my directive to our combatant commanders?"

"No, sir. I've always played by the book and . . ."

"The book, General, is a specific order for you to see to it that an unauthorized flight taken by my Secretary of Defense is grounded. This is not a decision made by you, but one conveyed by you on my behalf. If you won't do it or can't do it, then I'll put somebody over in your office on it who can." Before Whittier could respond, Jefferson clicked off the connection.

"Well done, Mr. President," Praeger said as he rushed out the door.

CHAPTER 53

MADRID, SPAIN

Baron Frederick von Heltsinger loved his ranch, the thoroughbred horses that romped around the four hundred acres of rolling hills and ponds that were filled with natural spring water.

Here, just a few miles from King Juan Carlos' royal country estate outside Madrid, the Baron could relax in total privacy and replenish the spirit that had sustained him during his seventy-six years. There were no intrusions here, no constant nagging of phones and must-have meetings with those beseeching favors from him. Here he could gain perspective, sniffing the bouquet of a Chateau Margaux as the sun slipped below the horizon, turning the sky into blended layers of spectacular red and gold.

It was the handiwork of God, to be sure. No cosmic accident, no random collection of atomic particles, could account for a vision of such glory.

After spending a week in Morocco on business, the Baron had come here. After two days of grouse hunting, his thoughts turned to the meeting he had with Wolfgang and Vladimir Berzin that evening in Munich.

The Baron had remained intrigued with the notion of a new Rapallo. The United States was turning its back on Germany. Russia was emerging as a powerful new source of energy. A prosperous middle class was growing there. Intellectual capital was plentiful. And, of course, Russia had nuclear weapons.

Corruption was rife there, too, and there still was a whiff of the Wild West outlaw activity. But that would pass. The rule of law was bound to take root, and when it did, other nations would rush to invest their capital. It was just a question of time.

But the thought of Berzin still troubled von Heltsinger. He worried about the scope of the man's ambition. Russia had been making good progress in developing democratic institutions. But with President Gruchkov's untimely death came a leadership vacuum. Berzin had in mind a radical departure from Gruchkov's vision for the future. Maybe it was right to change course, to form a strong alliance with Germany. But was Berzin as corrupt as the BND had informed him?

"Shall I place the call through now, sir?" Otto asked, his tone that of the humble servant.

"Yes," the Baron said. He had decided to call his old friend Vasily Yurchenko, a recently retired Russian Defense Minister who had attended his conference last year.

Moments later, as von Heltsinger sat out on the terrace gazing at the sunset, Otto handed him a portable phone.

After they exchanged a few words of greetings and small talk, von Heltsinger said, "Tell me about Vladimir Berzin. I need to know everything you know."

When Yurchenko finished, von Heltsinger was in shock. "You're sure? Murder? Gruchkov? . . ."

He hung up the phone, unsure of what to do. Yurchenko had no proof, but he was convinced that Berzin had arranged for Gruchkov's helicopter to be shot down. It was retribution for Gruchkov's crackdown on the oligarchs. Yurchenko was serving as Defense Minister at the time and had to take responsibility for what had happened.

If Berzin would kill a President, then Wolfgang was in danger linking up with such a man.

He had to warn him.

CHAPTER 54

MOSCOW

The chartered Dornier 328 carrying Wolfgang Wagner to Moscow was beginning its approach to the same desolate airport where he had seen the Money Plane and the murder of the passenger it carried. He felt a chill ripple down his back. It seemed far less than two months ago since all this began. He looked out the window at a brilliant blue April sky. He leaned back in his chair, pleased with the thought that the plan was coming to an end.

Berzin and a chisel-faced man were standing at the bottom of the stairs. Wagner recognized the man as Anatole Churkin, the young general who had retired so he could work on Berzin's campaign. Churkin had achieved almost a rock-star status in Russia after he had saved a company of soldiers from a vicious ambush while they were on a peacekeeping mission in Afghanistan.

Berzin greeted Wagner as he walked down the bottom step.

"Welcome to Moscow," he said heartily, wrapping his arms around Wagner. He nodded to Churkin, who stepped forward. "Allow me to introduce General Churkin," Berzin said. "He is going on ahead. I wanted him to meet you because he will be your guide during those times when I must meet my people."

"And you, General?" Wagner asked politely. "You will not be campaigning?"

Before Churkin could answer, Berzin said, "My people want to see me, not some substitute."

"I am afraid that Mr. Berzin is right," Churkin said with a tight smile. "I am a campaigner, a battle campaigner. I will see you at the dacha." He bowed slightly and walked toward the black Mercedes that pulled out as soon as he entered it. Next to the Mercedes was a longer black car that Wagner did not recognize.

"There is little need for campaigning," Berzin said, draping an arm over Wagner's shoulder. "Believe me when I tell you that I will surely win."

Berzin had invited Wagner to spend some of the last days of the election campaign with him and join with him in the election night extravaganza, which Berzin had described in great detail. It was as if the celebration were somehow more important than the predicted victory. Here was the real Berzin, the man of power, the man who controlled everything, the man who made up the rules. Now the game was an election, and the game already had been deadly.

"What was the reaction in Germany to my speech?" Berzin asked as they walked toward the waiting car.

"Outstanding."

"And did your leak work well? About Rapallo?"

"Of course."

"Perfect!" Berzin exclaimed. "*My* media spreads the news today in Russia. It's all working exactly as I wanted. Russia gets a future and a past simultaneously. Wolfgang, I am a genius!"

Berzin was laughing, perhaps in self-mockery, Wagner thought. Or perhaps because he really did believe that he was a genius. It was as if he was growing before Wagner's eyes.

"Like my new car?" Berzin said. The driver opened the left passenger door. Wagner entered. A burly man had got out of the right front seat and opened the rear right door for Berzin. Wolfgang had expected to see the man named Tago. But he did not ask about this. Berzin discarded people—in various ways—and it was wise not to ask questions.

There were two backseats, covered in maroon leather. Each was about the size of a seat in an airliner's first-class section. Between them was a wide compartment. Berzin settled into his seat, swung out a tray, and reached into a refrigerated section to pull out a bottle of champagne and two glasses, which he placed on Wagner's tray. He pressed a button, and a slim laptop computer unfolded from the back of the seat in front of him. The press of another button raised the one-way glass partition between the front and backseats. The car headed toward the gate.

Berzin uncorked the champagne and filled the two glasses. "Fit for a President," he said with a sweeping gesture. "A replica of the stretch Cadillac, armored to the design used by the U.S. Secret Service." He leaned forward to peer at the computer monitor, then slammed it shut and pressed a button. The computer disappeared. The road turned off the narrow airport road and swung onto the highway to central Moscow.

"I am afraid that I must go on to meet some important people—some very *rich* people—and meet you later," Berzin said. "I will drop you at the dacha. Churkin will take care of you."

"You treat him like a servant," Wagner said.

"He *is* a servant, a servant of the revolution."

"You're posturing, Vlad. You act more like a dictator than a President. You should be reading Ignazio Silone."

Berzin laughed. "Another one of your boring literary allusions. Wolfgang the intellectual, the man who read every word Lenin ever wrote. And believed it."

"Whatever wisdom that may have found its way into your brain is wisdom that came from me," Wagner said. "Even a genius needs to look at a book instead of a mirror. Silone was an Italian writer—his real name was Secondo Tranquilli—who was prosecuted by the Mussolini fascists. He wrote about Italian peasants. He was a good man, Vlad. A very good man."

"And why are you talking about him here and now?"

"Silone once said that fascism is a counterrevolution against a revolution that never happened. You are telling me that Russia is some kind of victim, a country that would be strong if only . . . if only. You are telling me that we are creating a German-Russian alliance because the world has somehow interrupted Russia's history and denied her destiny. You want a counterrevolution against a revolution that never happened."

Berzin poured himself another glass of champagne, slapped Wagner on the shoulder, and said, "I want power, Wolf. And I have power. As for your wisdom—"

In one of the armrests of Berzin's chair was a telephone. It rang. He picked it up and said, "Berzin." He looked annoyed. He had asked his assistant to hold off phone calls in the car.

"Die, Russian pig," said a hoarse voice.

"Who the hell—"

The undercarriage and the body of the vehicle were heavily armored. The roof's armor was thinner. Flying over the car, too small to be picked up by radar, was a reconnaissance drone four feet long. The drone had been built in Israel, given to China as a sales model, and cast aside when China began building bigger and better unmanned aircraft. Captain Chang had traced down the drone after a hurried talk with Ministry of Security assets in Chechnya. He had the drone flown to Moscow in a Chinese military aircraft that was carrying supplies for the Chinese Embassy. It was then delivered by truck to a warehouse near the grand nineteenth-century building that housed the Sandunovskiye Baths in northern Moscow. There a Chechen engineer fitted it with a high-explosive bomb and launched it from the warehouse roof. Now he sat on a crate in a dark loft on the top floor and watched a dot moving on a computer screen. The dot vanished as the drone, homing in on the phone, hit the car's roof.

A massive explosion ended the lives and plans of Vladimir Berzin and Wolfgang Wagner.

A muted CNN was always flickering on the television screen behind Scott O'Neill's desk. With the peripheral vision that had made him a formidable basketball player and fighter pilot, O'Neill could tell, without actually looking at the screen, when *Breaking News* appeared. He would swivel his gaze and decide whether the breaking news required any reaction from him. If it did not, he continued working on whatever was before him. Today *Breaking News* made him look up and listen—and held his attention.

"We're bringing you live footage of a bombing that just

took place in Moscow!" an excited Wolf Blitzer announced. "First reports indicate that Russian presidential candidate Vladimir Berzin and an as-yet-unidentified passenger were killed when the car they were riding in was destroyed by some kind of explosion. There is some confusion about exactly what happened. One eyewitness claims that the car was hit by a rocket-propelled grenade. Another, that it was a low-flying missile. No one has yet to claim credit for the act—"

O'Neill almost reached for the phone and punched the button on his direct line to Santini. But there was no way he could reach his boss this morning.

He looked at his watch. Santini must be close to Seattle by now. Radio silence was crucial to the mission's success. *Breaking News* would just have to wait.

CHAPTER 55

EN ROUTE TO BEIJING

Dragon Fire was four hundred nautical miles east of its West Coast refueling area.

"Attention, Boss," Murphy said. His voice, coming through the helmet's intercom, seemed to bounce off Santini's brain. "I am going to call off five numbers. Please double-check the numbers as they appear on the UHF radio layout in front of you. Seven . . . eight . . . eight . . . two . . . zero."

"Check," Santini said. His quick-learn instruction card explained that the numbers were for securing ranging to determine the tankers' distance and bearing from the SR-71's rapidly closing position. The mission had been flawless so far. Now Santini felt a slight shift as the aircraft began its descent and deceleration.

The sun had just now risen on the West Coast. Santini saw the two tankers ahead at twenty-five thousand feet, wings gleaming against the lightening sky. As the SR-71 hooked up under the tanker, Santini could see the first tanker's wings slightly in front and above him. He had a sensation of absolute motionlessness.

"I'll be talking to the tanker on a boom interphone," Murphy told Santini as the refueling began. "Nothing can be heard outside this connection."

"Good morning, Irish," the tanker aircraft commander said, beginning a rapid conversation about details of the refueling. Then he added, "It's great being in a genuine operation again." Nothing more was said about the mission. Neither the commander nor his crew would ever ask a question about a special operation. As the first tanker retracted its boom and veered away, the second approached and began an identical procedure. Santini knew about in-air refueling's need for clockwork efficiency. But, as a close-up spectator, he was nonetheless amazed.

After an exchange of farewells, the second tanker followed the routine of the first and rapidly disappeared from sight as the SR-71 accelerated and sped east, heading for a spot south of Attu Island. Now the speed was faster than the sun, and darkness engulfed them.

CHAPTER 56

WASHINGTON

Ever since Air Force General George Whittier became Chairman of the Joint Chiefs he had prided himself on keeping out of politics. His predecessor had warned him that politics came with the job. But Whittier had insisted that he could advise the President professionally and not compromise his sense of military honor. Now, on this day, he began to wonder. He had cleared his agenda indefinitely, told no one on his staff what was happening, and concentrated every brain cell on a matter of absolute politics: The President was accusing the Secretary of Defense of . . . of what? Bad judgment? Treachery? Treason?

Whittier was fuming. He hurled his favorite Mont Blanc pen across the room, knocking over a small crystal eagle awarded to him years earlier by the Air Force Officers Association.

Whittier was on a secure phone, listening to General Frank G. Holtzer, commander of NORAD, the North American Aerospace Defense Command. Whittier had once served at NORAD alongside Holtzer. They had sat at consoles in a combat operations center carved deep within Cheyenne Mountain, near Colorado Springs. Two young captains watching for the first warning that the world was about to be blown up. Those had been the Cold War days, when defense of America meant keeping an eye out for the Russkies. Now it could be anybody. Whittier could picture the endless stream of data—99 percent probably useless—pouring into NO-

RAD's Combined Intelligence and Fusion Center, which analyzed terrorist intelligence from more than fifty government agencies.

Whittier had cautiously told Holtzer only that he had to get a location on an SR-71 carrying the Secretary of Defense. Holtzer knew there was far more to tell, but he also knew that there are times when you didn't ask questions and this was one of those times.

"Here's the dump, George," Holtzer said. "There is a KC-10 currently orbiting south of Attu Island awaiting Dragon Fire's next refueling, which will take place in just about an hour. And tankers have taken off from Misawa AB, Japan, for a third refueling in the Sea of Japan. I can e-mail you copies of the authorization orders for all this. It looks kind of off—"

"Negative on that, Frank," Whittier said. "I don't want any paperwork. I just wanted to see the scene. Now, here's what I want. In my name, order the KC-10 at Attu to duck-butt the SR-71 to Elmendorf AFB in Anchorage. Then patch through to Misawa and recall those tankers. I'll call Dragon Fire on HF radio and tell them their mission is scrubbed."

"Roger, George. But if Dragon Fire doesn't acknowledge, it could end up in the Pacific."

"I am well aware of that, Frank. Out here."

Whittier hit another button on his console and ordered the duty officer at the National Military Command Center to connect him via HF radio to the SR-71.

CHAPTER 57

OVER THE NORTH PACIFIC

Buz Murphy's HF crackled. He heard the Dragon Fire call sign, then "Denim Midnight," the code words that meant he should break radio silence for an important message.

In the backseat, Santini heard the intercom voice of Murphy: "There's a high-priority message inbound. Make sure your communication set, which is located on your left-side panel, has the HF button pulled up so that you can hear this message."

Murphy hit his transmit button. "Roger, Big Voice. Go ahead with your message for Dragon Fire. I'm ready to copy."

"Secretary Santini. This is General Whittier. The President is aware of your mission. He has directed me to end your mission. I am terminating all your tanker support. Pilot, duck-butt your tanker back to Elmendorf AFB in Anchorage. If you do not comply with this command you will run out of fuel, most likely over the North Pacific, before you can reach any alternative airfields."

Murphy cut off the radio and spoke over the intercom. "Sir, any instructions?"

"What the hell is a duck-butt?"

Santini sensed Murphy's smile when he replied, "It means I slow down this aircraft, aim at the tanker's butt, and follow him. We call that a duck-butt order. Well, sir, what do we do?"

"What are our options?"

"Sir, we're dead in the water where we are. I might be able

to stretch to an alternative field in the Aleutians or the Navy airfield on Adak Island. And there's one more option—but it's tricky."

"Tell me."

"We may be able to con them. These KC-10 crews don't re-fuel Blackbirds that often. Maybe we can fool them into what our real fuel need is. We can tell them we are so low that we need fuel to duck-butt to Elmendorf. If I can get enough fuel we can get to the Sea of Japan and see if you can work something on the radio to get us a replacement tanker. With the current DEFCON alert status in the Far East there should be a tanker on strip alert at Misawa or orbiting over the Sea of Japan to provide continuous fighter support. If I can find a tanker, we can proceed to Beijing but at a slower speed—if you consider 1.5 Mach slow—because these tankers will probably not have the JP-7 for us to burn. With no tanker, we may get as far as Misawa AB in the northern part of Honshu Island, Japan. I don't know what your options will be from there."

Santini silently gave thanks to whomever it was who had given Buz Murphy his wings, then said, "Irish, call the NMCC back and say we'll comply. Then let's see if we can con that tanker."

"Yes, sir. While I'm doing that—and figuring out our low-fuel story—hit the continuous button on the UHF radio. That will initiate tanker ranging again and let us see if there really is a tanker waiting for us in the Aleutians."

A stream of numbers flowed into Santini's mind. The contact range and bearing numbers were still being transmitted. "It looks like they're still out there waiting for us. So we don't go in the drink," Santini reported over the intercom.

"Not quite out of it yet, sir. Whittier says he has already given the orders to the Elmendorf tanker. They'll know something is up. And we've got to think fast. Here it is, right dead on track."

In front of them in the darkness was what looked like a flying city of lights, a tanker so much larger than the KC-135s that it dwarfed the SR-71. Santini suddenly remembered a sign that hung over O'Neill's desk. He said it was an Irish Fisherman's Prayer: *Dear Lord, be good to me. The sea is so wide and my boat is so small.*

"We'll hook up here in a second and let's see what the tanker crew instructs us to do," Murphy said.

The KC-10's boom made contact and a green light flashed on Murphy's control panel.

"Irish," said a grimly controlled voice over the boom phone, "this is Lieutenant Colonel Cantrel, the tanker aircraft commander. I have been instructed to refuel you only if you agree to accept the duck-butt to Elmendorf. I have already begun a northeast course. I will not refuel if you do not accept these conditions as directed by the Chairman of the Joint Chiefs of Staff. Do you understand these conditions?"

"Roger, Colonel," Murphy replied. "We are not going to argue with you. Because my special passenger is not trained to help me, I must depend on your navigation to lead us to Elmendorf, because I can't change my mission computer plan from the front cockpit."

"I've never refueled one of you guys before," Cantrel said. "Do you have any special procedures?"

Murphy's right arm shot up, thumb extended. Over the intercom he told Santini, "Looks good. They don't have many clues." Then, speaking on the boom phone link, he said, plaintively, "Can you guys start the refueling right now? I'm very low on fuel."

"How much do you need for the duck-butt to Elmendorf?" Cantrel asked.

"I'll give you a number in a minute. Meanwhile, please get started. I'm not that fuel-efficient at these speeds."

Before beginning the refueling, the tanker copilot had told the NMCC that Dragon Fire had agreed to divert and estimated an arrival at Elmendorf Air Force Base in three hours.

Murphy, back on the boom phone, said, "I figure I'll need seventy thousand pounds of fuel. That includes enough for a weather-divert capability. How about commencing the fuel transfer? Then I'll join you on your right wing for the rest of our divert."

"If you try anything funny during refueling, Irish, I'll disconnect you immediately. Is that clear?"

"Roger that, Colonel."

Cantrel kept the boom phone line open so that Murphy could hear him tell Boom, the chief of the refueling operation, "Do not—repeat, do not—give him a pound more than he is required. And, Boom, keep a close watch on everything that is going on. Irish, we're now steady on our northeast heading, so you'll not have any more turns to contend with during the refueling."

"Roger that, Colonel," Murphy replied; then, on the intercom he said to Santini, "This will work. I'll get the fuel and we'll do a disconnect. And then we'll leave them to pick up our route to the west. Boy! Are they going to be pissed! Think about the options you might be able to exercise to get us a tanker. With a tanker I can get us to China."

"What a gorgeous aircraft!" Boom exclaimed as the refueling began. "You are a steady Eddy."

In a few minutes, Murphy went on the boom phone and said, "Fuel required has been transferred and standing by for aircraft disconnect."

"Disconnect completed," Boom replied.

A moment after disconnect, the copilot said on his intercom, "Co to Boom. I don't see them coming up on the right wing."

"Co, I'm looking for them," Boom said, speaking swiftly. "I've lost them in the dark. . . . Wait! Jesus! He kicked in the burners. He's heading west like a bat out of hell."

"Oh, shit!" Cantrel said. "We've been screwed. The bastards have dropped away. I can see their afterburners flaming to the west in their climb." He switched a dial and shouted into his headset, "Dragon Fire! Dragon Fire!" There was no response.

Cantrel switched to the NMCC channel.

CHAPTER 58

"We have the pilot from the tanker saying something about the divert, General," the duty officer at NMCC said.

Whittier nodded and gestured that he wanted to take over the situation. He put on a headset and held a phone with an open line to Praeger. Whittier put his right hand over the mouthpiece and said, "Colonel Cantrel. General Whittier here. What happened?"

"Sir, he broke his word. He . . . the son of a bitch, sir, he got fuel. Then he disconnected and roared off. He's out of sight already, heading west."

"Okay, Colonel. You did your best. Return to Elmendorf and secure. This whole operation is highly secret. No paperwork on it, no discussion. Tell your crew it didn't happen. Clear?"

"Yes, sir."

"Roger. Out here."

Whittier took his hand off the phone mouthpiece and heard a sputtering sound. "What the hell is happening, Whittier? I know something's fucked up. Nobody leaves me hanging on a phone, Whittier. What the hell happened? Another DOD fuckup?"

"I have unfortunate news to report, Mr. Praeger," Whittier said, using his Pentagon briefing voice, a slight smile appearing through a theatrical frown. "Secretary Santini has a very resourceful pilot. He has tricked our diversion tanker into refueling them and then departed to the west. We have no contact with them at this time."

"What the hell do you mean, no contact? How can the Pentagon not be in contact with one of its aircraft?"

"Communications of this type, Mr. Praeger, are extremely difficult, especially if the pilot hits the 'off' switch. If you wish to know the details, I can send a qualified communications officer to your—"

"Don't give me any more of your crap, General. I don't want one of your stooges explaining fuckups to me. I just want you to do what I—what the Commander in Chief ordered you to do. Get Santini on the ground—or in the drink. He cannot continue to China."

"We are tracking him, Mr. Praeger, and I am being fed the tracking information from NORAD. He is heading for the Sea of Japan as per what appears to be his original plan. There is no tanker for them there and they will have to land in Japan or eject over the water."

Praeger could hardly control his rage. "Why, you—I give you one small task to complete and you fuck it up. You had better figure out some way to bring that aircraft down or I'll walk into the President's office and demand he immediately remove you for your incredible ineptness. Do you hear what I'm telling you? You have one last chance or you are truly dead meat!" Praeger slammed the phone down.

Whittier firmly supported the supremacy of civilian leadership over the military. But he also believed that the principle of civilian leadership had to be based on selecting people whose central interest was that of their country and not some personal agenda to secure power.

Whittier turned to the ashen-faced communications duty officer, who had never had a shift like this one. "Get me General Holtzer. I'll take it in the Tank," he said, referring to the Joint Chiefs of Staff Conference Room. Whittier stood, looking weary. He picked up a yellow legal pad he had been doodling on. He wrote a few words on it and handed it to the duty officer. "I just made everything about this code-word compartmented," he said. "The code word is Friction. You are never to discuss Friction and you are not to log a word of what happened here in the last couple of hours. Is that clear?"

"Yes, sir."

"I am putting this Friction document in the JCS secure safe. If anyone over you ever asks you anything about what happened here, say it is code-word compartmented and refer him directly to me. Or . . ." Whittier hesitated. "Or to my successor, whom I will brief."

"Yes, sir," the officer said as Whittier strode off to the Tank.

Behind the guarded doors of the Tank, Whittier picked up a phone. "Frank. Glad you're still there."

Holtzer laughed. "Till the end, George."

"Well, you might be saying something prophetic, Frank. I need to know where that Blackbird is."

"Affirmative. I figured you'd want to know. We've been tracking it. It's about one thousand klicks from China and closing fast."

"Well, Frank, we have to talk. And talk fast."

CHAPTER 59

OVER THE NORTH PACIFIC

Murphy checked his climb profile and nodded to himself. The colder air had reduced their fuel consumption. There was a long-shot chance that the Blackbird could make it to China if he changed the route—and risked his life and that of his passenger. He felt he could not do that without a chat. He pressed the intercom button.

"Boss, let me tell you the situation. Our planned route took us around Russia and North Korea. But there's a narrow area along the North Korean–Russian border where the risk of being shot at by advanced surface-to-air missiles is less. A quick passage and you're into China before either country can react. Even so, this makes for an extremely tight fuel profile. But if we have to eject, at least we'll be over China instead of over the big blue sea."

"If you think we can do it, Irish, let's go for it," Santini said.

"But you could also get us an insurance policy. If they ordered the Elmendorf divert, you can be damn sure that they're cutting off the last refuel and pulling the tankers back to Misawa. And they know that we're not listening to any divert orders."

"Right. What can I do?"

"A call to George Whittier. I've got to warn you, though. If we break radio silence, a lot of hostile listening posts are going to wake up. Russian, Chinese, North Korean air defenses will be on to us even more than they are now."

Santini realized that Murphy referred to the Chairman by name because he wanted to have Santini play it man-to-man. "He's under terrific pressure," Santini said. "It's his job, his whole career. The White House. Well, no need to go into detail. Still, it's worth a try. Use my regular code name. Road Runner."

As they leveled off at cruise, doing Mach 3.2, Murphy switched to the encrypted Big Voice global network on the HF radio and said, "Big Voice, this is Dragon Fire with Road Runner, needing contact with Chairman Whittier at the NMCC. Connect us through."

Static jangled the voice that responded, "This is Big Voice. Please say your call sign and request again."

Murphy repeated the call and, through the intercom, told Santini to switch on his HF. Another voice came through the static, loud and very clear: "Dragon Fire, this is Brigadier General Ralph Ebbits, Blue shift commander, NMCC. Confirm Road Runner needs to speak with the Chairman."

"That is an affirmative, General," Santini said. "This is Road Runner."

"Stand by for General Whittier, Road Runner."

"Greetings, Road Runner. I have a message for you. Here it is: 'I always knew that if ever I were in trouble, you would always come for me, if alive.' Or, to put it another way, 'Fuck Praeger.' "

"Got that, Sherman!" Santini said.

"Road Runner, I want to get you those Misawa tankers," Whittier continued. "I've ordered them back. But I don't know if it's too late."

"Talk to Irish," Santini said.

Murphy cut in: "If you can give me the tanker call sign and location, sir, I think I can find them. And, if it's an old Q tanker, you can have them set their COMNAV-50 UHF radio rendezvous code six-four-one-seven-two. That will make this relatively easy."

"Affirmative, Irish. I've slurped from a Q myself a while back in my career. Have code numbers. Will go to work on that. Out here."

Murphy switched from radio to intercom and said to Santini, "That's looking good, Mr. Secretary. But what was that Sherman code, if I may ask?"

"When I became Secretary of Defense, General Whittier wanted to tell me I could count on him. He's somewhat of a shy man, not much for speeches. So he gave me a small brass plaque with a quotation from General William Tecumseh Sherman to General Grant. That was the quotation he just repeated."

Whittier, still in the Tank, put in a direct priority call to Admiral Jesse Stockdale, Commander of the Pacific Command.

"Jesse. This is George. No time for small talk. I have an emergency need for a refueling in the Sea of Japan. What is the current status of our tankers during this DEFCON? Do we have any orbiting in this area? I need to know if any of these tankers are the old Q models. Also, a set of Qs was recalled an hour or so ago. You were not in the loop of that one—and be glad of that. I need those tankers back in position, ASAP."

"Sounds like a great flap, George. Okay. Hold for an update. I've got the duty controller checking. But I thought admirals and generals didn't have to work the details."

"The devil's in them details, Jesse. Believe me. Let's get cracking."

CHAPTER 60

NEARING BEIJING

Murphy had figured he had nineteen minutes of flight left when he saw the Q tanker's wing lights.

"We're going to get you to Big Town, Boss," he said. "All our worries are over."

Not quite, Santini thought. *But most of the job is just being there.*

He watched as Murphy skillfully linked with one Q tanker, then another, using his calm and convincing voice as a tool to guide the tanker crew. None of them had ever refueled an SR-71 before. But they responded perfectly to Murphy's directions.

"Good going, Boom," Murphy said as the second tanker was about to disconnect. "Your guys are real pros."

"The pro is you, Irish. Take her with our blessing."

The black of an ocean night gave way to dots of light as the aircraft passed over the Korean coast. Murphy pulled out every bit of speed as they passed over Korean and Russian airspace. "I know in my gut that they can't touch us," he said over the intercom. "But they sure as hell know something's zooming past. There'll be a lot of air controllers scratching their heads."

"When do we give Beijing the news that we're dropping in?" Santini asked.

"Got it figured, Boss. We're going in on a commercial protocol. English is the universal air-control language. So I didn't have to learn Chinese. We'll be within Beijing International Airport control in about fifteen minutes. I'm open on their frequency. All we have to do is hope your host has lined up a welcoming committee and not SAMs. Switch on your HF to hear it all."

The next voice Santini heard belonged to a Beijing air controller. Then came Murphy's cool voice, and a technical dialogue began. Santini saw long lines of lights stab the predawn darkness and felt the deceleration as Murphy swung around for his approach. He landed as smoothly as he had taken off eight hours before.

As soon as the canopy slid open, Santini slipped out of the seat harness, doffed his helmet and gloves, awkwardly scrambled his way onto a wing, and then jumped to the tarmac. His legs dipped under him momentarily. Steadying himself, he turned to see Murphy making a smooth exit.

"Thanks, Buz—I can call you that now. Thanks much. Someday you'll get a medal for this."

A long black Mercedes sedan—a custom-made Mayback—pulled up alongside the aircraft. They had landed far from the terminal, in what Santini assumed to be a VIP area.

The driver opened a passenger door. Defense Minister Xu stepped out, waved his right hand, and said, "Greetings—"

Xu's voice was swallowed up by the sound of gunfire that ripped across the length of the Mercedes, puncturing holes in the heavily armored doors. The bullets flattened into slugs the size of silver dollars. The last round in the burst entered Buz Murphy's right eye, blowing out the back of his skull and scattering chunks of bone and brain along the Blackbird's fuselage. Shards of concrete from the tarmac sliced through Santini's G-suit, one sliver nearly embedding itself in his forehead.

The bullet that hit Xu's extended arm spun him around as if he were a rag doll. He clutched at what remained of his nearly severed arm, desperately trying to stop the blood that was gushing out of a ruptured artery. The bodyguards in his chase car had been completely taken by surprise. Unable to locate the source of the gunfire, they panicked. Two of the men were cut down, the .50-caliber bullets ripping open their intestines. Three others fired wildly in an arc with automatic weapons, hoping to hit their invisible assailants. Santini narrowly missed becoming one of their victims.

He shoved Xu into the backseat of the limousine and yelled for the driver to go, waving his arm. It was a motion that needed no translation. Jumping in next to Xu, Santini used his scarf as a tourniquet, wrapping it around the Defense Minister's shoulder. Another Mercedes raced across the tarmac and cut in front of the car carrying Santini and Xu. Santini yanked the Beretta from his holster. But in an instant he realized this was a security car, arriving fast but too late to offer much security.

Dawn was breaking over the horizon. He could barely see the vast stand of trees that edged both sides of the boulevard leading to the highway into Beijing. The speedometer hit 150 kph. At this speed, Santini judged that they could reach Tiananmen Square in less than thirty minutes. President Chi Zhiqiang was waiting for them in the Great Hall. With luck, he would be able to save his friend.

A thin layer of fog had started to settle on the highway, almost completely shrouding the car ahead. Suddenly, a blinding flash tore through the fog and for a split second Santini could see the security car rise off the road, explode, and roll over.

Xu's driver stopped the car. Santini rapped him on the shoulder and shouted, "Go! Go!" Santini's old bush fighter's instincts had never left him. He knew an ambush when he saw one. This car was a sitting duck for the ambushers, who had blown up the wrong car.

Or had they? The driver spun around, a pistol in his hand. Santini grabbed the driver's arm. The pistol fired a shot into the padded pearl-gray roof, shattering a light. Santini, his left hand gripping the driver's wrist, raised his Beretta and fired one shot into the man's face. He climbed into the front of the car, opened the driver's door, shoved out the body, slipped behind the wheel, and floored the accelerator. Someone fired from the woods to the right. Bullets thudded against the armor. Through the rearview mirror Santini could see the smoke arc of a rifle-launched grenade, which exploded about ten yards behind him.

In previous trips down this highway, as an official visitor, he had noticed that all intersections had been blocked off for VIP motorcades. The Mayback was moving like a black bullet, and at this speed there was no margin for error.

Every few minutes, Santini shouted to Xu, who had struggled to sit upright in the rear seat, his neck arched against the padded headrest. "We're almost there. Hang on! Just a few more minutes!" *Almost where?* his inner voice shouted back. How in hell did he get himself into this mess? How was he going to get out of it?

As he reached the outskirts of Beijing, traffic slowed him down. He was coming in from the northeast and knew that the highway led to Tiananmen Square. As he entered the business section of the city, he recognized some landmarks. Just off to the right he spotted the Holiday Inn Crowne Plaza. A few more blocks and he would see the International Hotel. There he would swing right onto Jianguo Lu, one of Beijing's main thoroughfares.

Now, along the boulevard he saw scores of elderly Chinese performing their morning ritual of tai chi in graceful, martial arts movements, keeping their muscles flexible.

He hit the accelerator again when he saw the expanse of the square, the place that had once transfixed the world during a brief uprising by human rights activists. Startling a police officer in his white traffic circle tub, Santini screeched into a skidding turn, jumped a curb, careened off a low concrete barrier, and sped into the square. Ahead was the long, low silhouette of the Great Hall of the People, a gigantic columned structure that made no pretense to beauty. Only power. *In one minute—*

The helicopter angled in from the left, at the edge of his vision. In a moment, he recognized it. His mind absurdly brought up a page from a briefing book, but his subconscious was trying to save his life. He saw in his mind's eye the diagram of the Wuzhuang Zhisheng-9. The WZ-9 was China's first indigenous anti-tank attack helicopter. Mean killing machines: 23mm cannons, unguided rocket launchers, machine guns, wire-guided anti-tank missiles.

Santini veered toward the helicopter, knowing that the turn would be a surprise. If there was any good news about the WZ-9, it was the fact that it had a flight crew of only one, and he might be rattled by orders to shoot up the Minister of Defense in Tiananmen Square.

What was he thinking? *Only one!* One was enough to chew up a small convoy of tanks. And maybe the coup had already started and this guy *liked* the idea of killing the Minister of Defense. But if he could just keep the pilot distracted with something, he might be able to make it to the Great Hall.

The WZ-9 fired its cannon and its machine guns. Because the car and helicopter were closing fast, the cannon overshot, gouging a small crater about thirty feet behind the car, and the machine guns' slugs blasted a garland of holes in the Mao Zedong Mausoleum and seriously wounded several pilgrims lined up to visit the tomb. Santini sped and turned, skidding directly toward the steep, broad steps of the Great Hall.

He stopped at the bottom of the steps, jumped out, and gently lifted Xu onto the pavement. The young guards at the front entrance to the Great Hall looked confused. Xu was seriously wounded. He was being half-carried by a stranger—a European or possibly an American. Where was the Minister's security detail? Who was this man? *Should we shoot him or rush to his assistance?*

Santini immediately realized he and Xu were both doomed. Idly, he wondered which weapon the WZ-9 pilot would choose.

The WZ-9 made a wide turn, banked at a forty-five-degree angle, leveled off, and lined up on Santini and the Mercedes Maybach. The helicopter stood off, fired a torrent of machine-gun fire that missed him by inches, and then hovered for the kill.

A rocket hit the car, lifted it into the air, and turned it into an inferno. The percussive blast hit Santini like a sledgehammer, sending him and Xu hurtling onto the sharp-edged stairs.

Instinctively, Santini twisted his body so that Xu landed on top of him, cushioning the blow to his ravaged arm.

Panic was starting to replace the pain that was coursing through Santini's body. He and Xu were completely exposed. There was no place to run to. No place to hide. They were turkeys in a turkey shoot. *No. This is not it.*

Santini couldn't understand it. The pilot hesitated for several seconds, just hanging in the air. It was almost as if he was toying with them, extracting every last moment of sadistic pleasure at the thought of shredding Santini and Xu into little pieces.

But the hesitation was enough to allow Santini to collect himself.

There was one chance.

The handgun tucked under his left arm.

The Beretta, he reminded himself, was a side arm, a personal defense weapon. It's good for up-close and real personal kind of combat. Maybe you could hit the side of a barn at fifty meters. But that's just what that WZ-9 looked like right now. It was so close that Santini could almost touch it.

Santini ripped the gun out of the shoulder holster and in one motion rammed the slide back, jacking the first shell from the magazine into the chamber, automatically cocking the hammer.

Gripping the pistol with both hands, Santini took aim and squeezed off every round left in the magazine. He didn't count. He just kept squeezing, trying to keep the shots in a tight circle. If he did it right, if he got lucky, he could punch a hole in the fuel tanks and turn that sucker into a giant firefly. *Bam. Bam. Bam. Bam. Bam. Bam.* Bingo!

The aft section of the helicopter burst into flame. Seconds later, a secondary explosion sent the chopper pirouetting wildly. It hit the ground hard and then tipped over on its side, the rotor blades shattering as they dug into the pavement.

The pilot struggled frantically against the restraining harness that had him trapped in the burning wreckage. His screams were quickly consumed by the smoke and flames.

Then, just behind the cockpit, a door swung open as a uniformed officer scrambled out to safety. Blood was streaming from a deep cut just above the bridge of his nose. His left arm dangled at his side.

Santini stood in disbelief. The passenger was Li! And he was running toward Santini, brandishing an Uzi.

Santini aimed first and fired. *Click. Click.* He was out of bullets and out of luck.

Li brought up the Uzi with his good arm and fired as Santini lunged toward him. Santini snatched the gun out of Li's hand.

Frantically, Li looked about for assistance, shouting to the guards who were still standing at the front doors of the Great Hall. They were nearly paralyzed by the scene that had unfolded in front of them. They recognized Li easily. He was one of the most powerful figures in the military. But they also saw that he had tried to kill Xu, their Minister of Defense.

They shouted something unintelligible at Li but made no move to assist him. Santini tossed the Uzi aside and put Li on his back with a single blow that shattered his nose.

Santini leaned down to pull Li to his feet. Li twisted and pulled a long blade from a sheath clipped to his belt. The finely honed steel glinted in the morning sun.

Santini grabbed Li's wrist and turned his hand toward his throat. When the tip drew blood, Li let go and the knife fell. Santini felt adrenaline pumping through his entire body. Looking at Li, he remembered the rat of a man who had supervised his torture. That man had watched the Vietcong break Santini's bones, watched how they had brought him to the edge of madness, watched how some of his fellow war prisoners had died like dogs.

Fury erupted inside him like a volcano. He delivered a kick directly into Li's groin, sending him howling to the ground, his right hand clutching testicles that Santini hoped were buried now in his tonsils. Li was finished. Santini was not. He crouched and seized Li by his hair, pulling his jaw up so that their eyes met.

"You rotten motherfucker," Santini shouted over and over, as he landed blow after blow, shattering Li's jaw, pounding him mercilessly into an unconsciousness from which he would never return.

As Chi's motorcade turned into the massive square, his small security team saw the burning carcass of General Li's helicopter. Instinctively, they barked orders to Chi's driver. "Divert! Divert!"

The violent turn of the car surprised Chi, tossing him to the vehicle's floor. Gathering himself into an upright position, Chi was able to see the wreckage through his car's rear window. "Stop! Stop!" he shouted. "We will go to the Great Hall as planned." His voice crackled fire and brooked no dissent. His four escort vehicles reversed course and encased their President in an armored cocoon.

Sirens now blaring, they raced to the foot of the Great Hall. Arriving there in seconds, ten men spilled out onto the plaza, pirouetting around rapidly, their automatic weapons sweeping in a wide arc.

President Chi jumped out of his vehicle and rushed toward Santini, who was releasing the pressure of the tourniquet he had applied to Xu's arm. While Chi's security force was small—there had been little threat of terrorism in Beijing—there was always a personal physician who traveled with the team to deal with any medical emergency. The physician, Cao Gangshou, followed Chi to tend to Minister Xu. He made a quick examination, testing Xu's blood pressure.

"It's serious, President Chi," Cao Gangshou said, "not fatal. He's lost a lot of blood and is in shock. We need to get him to a hospital immediately. The General Hospital is closer than PLA 48."

Nodding, Chi signaled his approval. Two of the security men lifted Xu into one of the SUVs and roared off to Beijing's General Hospital. Chi then wrapped his arm inside of Santini's, a gesture of friendship that Chi did not easily bestow toward others, and escorted him up into the Great Hall.

* * *

As the two men walked down the massive hallway, both seemed little more than diminutive, almost doll-like, figures. The Great Hall, constructed in just thirteen months back in 1958 and 1959 to celebrate the communists' victory in the Chinese civil war, contained a central room that could accommodate thousands of people, along with a number of smaller, but still substantial, meeting rooms that were named after each of its provinces.

President Chi escorted Santini into the Fujian room. Fujian was the province located directly across from Taiwan. If there was any symbolism involved in the selection of the room, Santini failed to notice it at the moment.

Chi settled into one of the low-backed chairs that was dwarfed by the sheer size of the room with its thirty-foot-high ceilings. He offered a cigarette to Santini, who politely declined the offer. Chi lit one for himself, drew deeply on the tobacco, and then exhaled a thin stream of smoke. Next, he motioned for a servant to pour tea.

Santini observed the leader closely. Chi had an expressive face dominated by eyes that were at once intense and yet, somehow, calm. Serene and self-confident as he appeared, there was a coiled, catlike quality about him.

Speaking through his interpreter, Chi said, "Secretary Santini, I must say that what has happened here is a great mystery to me." He paused, allowing his interpreter to repeat his words in English.

Santini kept his eyes focused on the President while listening carefully to every word.

"Last night," Chi continued, "Minister Xu contacted me and advised me of your plans to travel to Beijing and of your insistence that we meet."

Again, a pause for the interpreter.

"Then I received an emergency call from President Jefferson, who urged me not to meet with the man who has betrayed his country."

Santini made no attempt to interrupt or explain.

"Both requests were quite extraordinary. I had no idea that your arrival would be quite so . . . traumatic."

"Nor did I, President Chi," Santini quickly added.

Chi drew again on his cigarette that was now reduced to a stub. "Tell me, please, why you have come. What exactly is happening? Your message spoke of the imminence of war. What war?"

Santini's emotions were now under control. The adrenaline that had coursed through him like a flash flood had subsided.

For the next ten minutes, he gave a description of General Li's relationship with Vladimir Berzin; how he was behind the killing of Secretary Tom Koestler, the Germans at Holloman and Grafenwoehr; how he planned to attack Taiwan after diverting American forces to the Korean Peninsula . . .

Chi sat motionless throughout, and when Santini finished he nodded, making it clear that he understood the gravity of what had happened.

"You have my word, Secretary Santini. I will take immediate action to deal with all who have been involved with this treachery."

Santini had no doubt that China's leader was a man of his word.

CHAPTER 61

MOSCOW

The people of Russia were in shock, their political system shaken to its foundations. First, President Yuri Gruchkov had died when his helicopter was shot down. Now, Vladimir Berzin had been burned beyond recognition by what Russian investigators determined was a thermobaric mini-rocket, a high explosive round launched from an unmanned aerial vehicle.

What was happening to them?

Dizzying accounts came pouring out of the media. Rumors were rife that the assassination of Berzin was blood revenge by those who believed his hand had been involved in Gruchkov's violent end.

But Russian intelligence officers—all ex-KGB with ties to the Orchard—quickly floated stories that both Berzin and Gruchkov were victims of Chechen terrorists.

Michail Zirinsky, the right-wing nationalist politician known for his virulent anti-Semitism, claimed that the aircraft that fired the missile had been made in Israel and that Mossad had targeted Berzin for elimination because of his business dealings with a German industrialist who had ties to neo-Nazis in Germany.

The Russian people didn't know who or what to believe. They were confused and scared.

Most political pundits were convinced that Dimitri Solokov, the Russian Prime Minister who had been serving as interim President, would win the presidency by default. But following Berzin's death, Solokov announced that unspecified health factors precluded him from seeking his nation's highest office. After consulting with political leaders in the Duma (Russia's parliament), Solokov ordered that the special election be delayed for sixty days.

Several new faces surfaced suddenly on the political scene, one of them belonging to Anatole Churkin, the recently retired general. He filed papers qualifying him as the candidate of the PDP, the People's Democratic Party. He promised to root out bureaucratic incompetence, end special treatment for the rich, fight organized crime, and return power to the Russian people.

His brief association with Vladimir Berzin, one of the very rich oligarchs whom he now promised to eliminate, seemed of little relevance to the adoring public. After all, he was a genuine war hero. That he was also married to one of the most beautiful and talented ballerinas in all of Russia only inspired the press to compare the couple to America's Kennedys.

The Russian people, it seemed, were ready for their Camelot.

Chinese justice was said to be swift. And in this case it was sure.

President Chi rounded up all of Li's rogue officers, and after a quick hearing, held in secret, they were convicted of subversion and summarily executed.

Chi canceled the activation of Chinese missiles that were to target Taiwan, then called on North Korean President Kim Song Jo to cancel his military's spring exercise. It took little effort. Kim's secret police rounded up all known associates of the false defector, General Kim Dae Park, and had them hanged. The general eventually made his way to Vancouver, Canada, where he served as a consultant to an obscure think tank.

President Jefferson ordered an immediate reduction in the alert status of American forces and stood down the Marine Amphibious Force and two Los Angeles Class submarines that he had ordered sent toward North Korean waters.

A war that could have killed hundreds of thousands had narrowly been averted. Armageddon would have to await a future arrival.

An article appeared in *The New York Times,* leaked by an unnamed high-level official, stating that a Chechen-based terror group had been responsible for the disaster at Grafenwoehr, Germany. A small amount of chemical munitions left over from the Cold War era, believed to have been removed and destroyed years ago, had fallen into the control of the terrorists who had managed to infiltrate the base and switch aircraft munitions. The group wanted to punish the German people for Germany's support of Russia in what they described as a "vicious and unconscionable war against the legitimate struggle of the Chechen people."

According to the story, what appeared to be a gross violation of proper security measures by military officials at the base was now under intense investigation. The White House official added that "the tragedy was just one more brutal example of the need for all nations to redouble their efforts to rid the world of weapons of mass destruction and to join the United States in the fight against terrorism."

Hardly full disclosure, but give the White House credit for creativity.

The entire affair, however, was too big to cover up completely. For example, a civilian who happened to be a former SR-71 pilot had been shot and killed by members of the PLA.

According to a statement the White House released to the press, it was all a case of monumental misunderstanding that could be reasonably explained.

Secretary Santini, known for his determination to master every detail involved in controversial decisions, had secured a test ride on the last remaining operational SR-71. He wanted to satisfy himself and die-hard congressional critics that the plane's technology was truly a legacy system that had no possible utility in the transformational goals of the Pentagon.

Flying near the Chinese border, the aircraft developed mechanical and fuel difficulties and had to make an emergency landing at the Beijing International Airport. Although Capt. Buz Murphy believed he had secured proper clearance to land the aircraft on Chinese soil, that message had not been made clear to the PLA, which had been providing security against possible terrorist threats at the airport. Young conscripts had used deadly force without authority.

President Chi offered a public apology to the American people, thereby diffusing a serious backlash. In a televised address, he explained that another terrible accident occurred that same morning in Tiananmen Square when a Chinese helicopter, during a routine overflight, crashed and burned, injuring several persons queued up outside Mao's tomb, along with the pilot and one of China's most distinguished military officers, Deputy Minister of Defense Li Kangsheng. Fortunately, the square itself was empty at such an early hour, and so there were no further casualties. *And few witnesses,* Santini thought. *A pretty thin cover.*

But it would buy everyone some time. Eventually, a leak would spring from somewhere in the Pentagon or White House. Too many people knew small pieces of information. Someone would put them all together. Someone like Randall Hartley.

But who could say? Maybe it would all be overtaken by events. A smallpox outbreak here or abroad. India and Pakistan reversing course in improving relations, inching toward war, once again, over Kashmir. Iran declaring that it had gained membership in the nuclear club. Martial law declared in Venezuela. More slaughter in the Middle East. Or maybe the Israelis and Palestinians would finally stop digging fresh graves and agree to heal ancient wounds. After all, some things had a way of working out. President Jefferson fired Joe Praeger for nearly starting a major war. It was too little and too late to satisfy Santini.

Although Jefferson had pleaded with him to stay on, Santini made it clear that he could no longer serve him. Santini resigned from office, issuing a short news release that said that he wanted to return to Wall Street. It was too abrupt a decision to be credible, but Santini didn't give much of a damn.

At his flag-fluttering, marching-band, pass-in-review retirement ceremony at Fort Myer, Santini stood in a receiving line and greeted them all: Xu Ling, with his right arm in a sling . . . Christoph Stiller, newly promoted to director of the BND . . . Arthur Wu, looking harried because he had just come from a U.S. Courthouse, where he had testified before a grand jury that had indicted one of NSC's Chinese translators, An Sing Li (formerly of the Chinese Ministry of State Security) . . . General George Whittier, still wearing his Chairman's emblem, untouched by the court-martial he had risked . . . And, last of all, Santini's successor, Jack Pelky, who was gracious enough to say, "I'll be happy if I do half as well as Michael Santini." Jefferson's appointment of Pelky was not all bad. Overall, he had done a decent job out at the Agency. A little too eager to please the President to suit Santini, but maybe it just went with the territory.

One person who was not there was Santini's old friend Baron Frederick von Heltsinger. The Baron, upon learning of Wolfgang Warner's violent death in Moscow, suffered a fatal heart attack while vacationing at his country estate in Spain. Chancellor Klaus Kiepler announced that a special memorial service would be held soon in Berlin to pay tribute to von Heltsinger's memory and many contributions.

Santini had nearly considered breaking his silence, shortly after his retirement ceremony, when rumors started to appear in *The Washington Times* that Jefferson had forced him out, thinking he was just too much of a liability; that his cowboy antics had almost caused irreparable harm to America's relationship with China, not to mention the damage that had been inflicted by the Pentagon under his watch to U.S. relations with Germany.

Praeger might be gone, but the White House press office was still in the business of throwing everyone overboard to protect the President. White House fingerprints were all over the ass-covering, phony story. Maybe one day, Santini would tell the world what had really happened.

Inauguration Day. Television had been promoting it for weeks. NBC, after what critics described as having paid more than a king's ransom, had won the world rights for televising the event of the year, the swearing in of the new President of Russia.

Now the big day was here. NBC had convinced the Russian presidential press office to schedule the inauguration for 4 P.M. so that the U.S. East Coast could see it for breakfast.

Santini and Elena sat before the large television screen in what Santini called his flop room, cups of coffee and bagels on the table before them. Nothing was more important to Santini right now than the woman who sat curled up beside him.

Elena had served notice to David Ben-Dar that she was finally through with her professional career. She had seen too much death, had done too much killing. She wanted to lead a different life, have the opportunity to start over. Maybe that wasn't possible. Maybe Ben-Dar would find a way to bring her back. There were no guarantees.

The television pundits were using up time before the inauguration to analyze the surprise election of Anatole Churkin, the late Vladimir Berzin's top adviser, a hero to millions of Russians for his bravery on the battlefield. Churkin had captured the imagination of the Russian people with his promise of a clean government and a commitment to rebuild Russia's military power and prestige. He would end the special privileges enjoyed by the scandalously wealthy. The Russian people would continue to enjoy the fruits and freedoms of democracy. But they were entitled to regain a sense of the greatness of their past as well.

As soon as Churkin was sworn in, NBC spent a few moments televising the cheering throng filling Red Square. Then, just before Churkin began speaking, NBC switched to the splendor of St. Basil's Cathedral, where the world's political and entertainment stars were gathering for the huge celebration.

"Michael, what do you think about Churkin?" Elena asked, her hand massaging the back of Santini's neck.

Santini paused, sipping his coffee. "Don't know much about him. I hope he's as good as the Russian press has painted him. Young, dynamic, with a bold vision for the Russian people. God knows they need it."

Like most Americans, Santini and Elena spent the next couple of hours watching the pageantry.

An Army chorus, accompanied by the Moscow Symphony Orchestra, sang a modified version of the old Russian national anthem:

"God Save the President!
Powerful and Sovereign,
Reign for Glory, for Glory to us.
Reign for Terror to the Enemies,
Young President, God Save our President!"

The presidential band played Russia's modern national anthem, and Russia's newly elected President and his ballerina star wife waved joyously to the crowd, which roared its approval.

"God Bless the President!" they chanted. "God Bless the President!"

"It looks like happy times are here again," Santini said to Elena. "For the sake of the Russian people, I hope so. They're entitled to look forward to a better future than the ones they got under the old Czars, communists, and autocrats."

But the dark side of the moon kept appearing in Santini's thoughts. It was something that Pelky had said at the reception that followed the retirement ceremony. He had shaken Santini's hand again and whispered, "Anatole Churkin is going to be good for Russia. And good for us."

It seemed odd and inappropriate to Santini at the time. What did he mean, *"good for us"*? And why did he choose that moment to say it? Was he praising the vision that Churkin offered to the Russian people or was he slyly implying that Churkin, like his mentor, also had been on the CIA's payroll? And had the Agency gained an asset in the President? Was this really a new beginning they were watching unfold in Red Square or simply a rerun of all the schemes and deceits of the past?

Santini looked over at Elena and dismissed the thoughts that had been nibbling away at him. Let someone else worry about tomorrow. He held in his arms the woman he loved. Whatever else might happen, this was a new beginning for him.

As he reached over to kiss Elena, the phone next to the couch rang harshly, angering him. "Damn," he muttered. Reaching over to disconnect the phone line, he glanced at the caller ID box in the center of the phone.

It read: *Randall Hartley.*